Francis Tiffany

This Goodly Frame the Earth

Stray Impressions of Scenes, Incidents and Persons in a Journey Touching Japan,

China, Egypt, Palestine and Greece

Francis Tiffany

This Goodly Frame the Earth
*Stray Impressions of Scenes, Incidents and Persons in a Journey Touching Japan, China, Egypt,
Palestine and Greece*

ISBN/EAN: 9783337127718

Printed in Europe, USA, Canada, Australia, Japan

Cover: Foto ©Andreas Hilbeck / pixelio.de

More available books at **www.hansebooks.com**

THIS GOODLY FRAME
THE EARTH

*STRAY IMPRESSIONS OF SCENES, INCIDENTS
AND PERSONS IN A JOURNEY TOUCHING
JAPAN, CHINA, EGYPT, PALESTINE
AND GREECE*

BY

FRANCIS TIFFANY

BOSTON AND NEW YORK
HOUGHTON, MIFFLIN AND COMPANY
The Riverside Press, Cambridge
1895

To

EDWIN B. HASKELL

To you, dear Friend, I gratefully dedicate these few out of the countless happy experiences we shared on our trip round the world.

FRANCIS TIFFANY

CONTENTS

GETTING UNDER WEIGH

		PAGE
I.	Providing Funds for Travel	1
II.	Across the American Continent	2
III.	The Action of Wheat on Imagination	3
IV.	The Rockies	4
V.	The Pacific Ocean	6
VI.	Linguistic Privileges	8
VII.	Arriving out	9

JAPAN

I.

I.	First Impressions	13
II.	The Promotion of Domestic Happiness	14
III.	Yokohama	15
IV.	Japanese Women	18
V.	The Japanese Smile	20
VI.	The Curio Fever	23
VII.	Straws	25

II.

I.	The Rice Lands	27
II.	Kamakura	28
III.	The Buddha	30
IV.	Back to the Finite	34
V.	The Philosopher's Perch	36

III.

I.	Miyanoshita and the Hakone District	42
II.	Rice as Motive Power	42

III. Bamboo Grass 43
IV. The Fujiya Hotel 44
V. Volcanoes and Personal Cleanliness 45
VI. The Ten Province Pass 46

IV.

I. An Historical Glimpse 48
II. The Nikko Groves 51
III. The Nikko Temples 53
IV. Popular Use of the Temples 56
V. Simplicity of Japanese Civilization . . . 58
VI. Japanese Bells 60

V.

I. Japanese Manners 63
II. Japanese Heroic Moral Standards 68

VI.

I. Source in Nature of Japanese Art 72
II. Variety in Unity 74
III. Broad Influence of Japanese Art 78
IV. Physical Conditions affecting Art 79

VII.

I. The Question of Missions 82
II. The Buddhist Reaction 86

VIII.

I. The Scientific Broomstick-Drudge 89
II. The Crusading Spirit 92
III. The Day of the Pacific Ocean 94
IV. Good-By to Japan 95

CHINA

I.

I. At Sea again 97
II. Consistent Conservatism 97
III. World Building 101

CONTENTS

vii

IV. So near, and yet so far!	101
V. Inside the Walls	104
VI. Out into the Country	105
VII. The Handwriting on the Wall	108

II.

I. Hong Kong	110
II. Canton River	113
III. Canton's River Population	115
IV. Business and Religion	116
V. The Shamien	117
VI. Inside Canton	119
VII. Canton's Examination Halls	122
VIII. A Government of Philosophers	126

THE TROPICS

I. Away from Hong Kong	135
II. Tropical Yearnings	136
III. Singapore	137
IV. A School for Sculptors	139
V. A Ravishing Drive	141
VI. The Botanical Garden	143
VII. A Borneo Philosopher	144

CEYLON

I. The Culmination of the Tropics	149
II. Blood thicker than Water	151
III. Kandy	152
IV. Christmas in Kandy	154
V. The Peradeniya Botanical Gardens	158
VI. An International Ecclesiastical Interview	159

INDIA

I.

I. Pondicherry	163
II. The Hoogly	165
III. Darjeeling	166
IV. Again Mongolians!	169

viii

CONTENTS

    V. The Apotheosis of Machinery 170
   VI. At Last the Himalayas! 174
  VII. Tiger Hill 176
 VIII. The Alps and the Himalayas 178

II.

    I. Calcutta 180
   II. How Empires fall 182
  III. Hindu Traits 183

III.

    I. Benares 186
   II. Street Scenes 187
  III. The Ghats 189
  IV. Burning the Dead 190
   V. Sati, or Widow-Burning 192

IV.

    I. Lucknow 195
   II. The Siege of Lucknow 197
  III. Cawnpore 199

V.

    I. Oriental Savings-Banks 204
   II. Happy or Miserable? 206
  III. Reaction from Bad Example 209
  IV. Gaudium Certaminis 212

VI.

    I. A Glance at History 215
   II. Eliminating the Tartar 217
  III. India's Alhambra at Agra 220
  IV. Woman in the Evolution of Architecture . . 223
   V. The Oasis 225
  VI. The Taj Mahal 227

VII.

    I. Delhi 232

VIII.

I. Jeypore 238
II. An Elephant Ride to Amber 241
III. Mt. Abu 245
IV. Ahmedabad 251

EGYPT

I.

I. Prelude to Egypt 255
II. Semitic Prophets 257
III. The Desert 260
IV. Ismailia 262
V. The Land of the Rod 264

II.

I. A Study in Egyptian Babies 267
II. Nile Hints 269
III. The Gizeh Pyramids 272
IV. Memphis and the Sakkarah Pyramids . . . 277
V. Knight-Errants of the Shovel 281
VI. The Tomb of Thi 284

III.

I. Characteristics of Nile Scenery 288
II. Pantheistic Animism 290
III. The Later Tombs of Egypt 294
IV. The Temples of Egypt 302

PALESTINE

I. De Lesseps building better than he knew . . 311
II. Jaffa 312
III. Jaffa to Jerusalem 313
IV. Sacred Cities 317
V. In what Frame of Mind ? 318
VI. A Stroll to Bethlehem 322
VII. The Church of the Nativity 324
VIII. The Spirit and the Flesh 325
IX. The Jews' Wailing-Place 327
X. The Dead Sea and the Jordan 329

BAALBEC AND DAMASCUS

I. Beyrout and the Lebanon Ranges . . . 335
II. Baalbec 338
III. Damascus 339

ASIA MINOR AND GREECE

I. The Sail to Smyrna 347
II. Smyrna 348
III. Constantinople 351
IV. First Introduction to Attica 351
V. The Parthenon 353
VI. Eleusis 357
VII. Marathon 359
VIII. Athens' Parting Benediction 360

THIS GOODLY FRAME
THE EARTH

GETTING UNDER WEIGH

I. Parsons or otherwise, large numbers of the impecunious stoutly aver that they, too, would be glad of a trip round the world, were it not for the cost of the thing. This is no valid excuse. It need not cost one a penny, nay, on the contrary, prove the happiest means of escape from the outlay one is subjected to by staying prosaically at home. "What is the paradoxical fellow driving at?" will be the natural outcry. Well, at a statement of the plainest matter of fact. Nothing further is requisite than to drop in unexpectedly of an evening at the house of a generous-hearted friend, — one of the kind who, having freely received, loves freely to give, — and then and there to have your breath taken away by his sudden exclamation, "I want to go round the world, and I want you to go with me! Say yes, and it shall not cost you a yen, a rupee, or a piastre."

In a flash start up before the mind's eye snow-crowned Fujisan in Japan, with all the Himalayan giants from Mt. Everest to Kunchinjinga, thundering with the voices of their united avalanches, "Take up with him on the spot!" In gentler notes, the same is caressingly murmured by the waves of the Indian Ocean, lapsing on the roseate, palm-encircled beaches of Ceylon. Finally, from out the mysterious depths of the halls of mighty Karnak breathes an echo as from the remotest ages, " Ephemeral child of the brand-new Columbia of to-day! not a mummy in Egypt but would leap to burst his cerements of cloth and bitumen, and cry ' Amen ! ' at such an offer."

It is, then, a distinct pleasure, before proceeding, to record the impressions of travel that ensued; thus, by so simple a suggestion, to smooth the elsewise rugged way for others, — impecunious perhaps in purse, but millionaires on scenery, architecture, and the metaphysical abysses of Oriental Theosophy.

II. Before visiting foreign lands, it is said to be a good thing to know a little of one's own, so as not to mistake a chance wheelbarrow one may light on in Timbuctoo for an entirely novel invention, and so write home in too naïve a strain of enthusiasm. Certainly, in crossing the American Continent to embark for Japan, one has a chance to see a good deal of his own native land, as well as — if he mean to sail from Vancouver — of the Canadian Dominion.

It is, perhaps, well enough to pass over the scenes of absorbing interest that lie on the route between Boston and St. Paul. The perils and fatigues of the same journey have been undergone by previous explorers, — notably by Lewis and Clark, and later by General Frémont, — who have recorded their topographical impressions inch by inch. So to plunge at once into unknown realms!

III. Getting away at nightfall from St. Paul, Minnesota, one awakens the next morning to find himself afloat on a boundless ocean of wheat lands. The assertion of men of science that if, undistracted by sharks and horse-mackerel, the codfish had a free chance to rear to a marriageable age all the sprightly young fry they spawn, they would in ten years pack the Atlantic solid with cod, has here become outright demonstration in wheat. As one rolls along through South Dakota, North Dakota, Manitoba, and beyond, a horrible nightmare of wheat is begotten in the imagination. All the dread monotony is experienced of a system of "solitary confinement" in wheat. Now, the word of Sacred Writ demonstrates its awful truth, "Man shall not live by bread alone," as, physically and mentally congested with wheat, one feels his gorge fairly rising at the thought of swallowing a crumb of a roll or a cracker. As well offer a man dying of thirst in the Sahara desert a tumblerful of sand instead of water!

Nor is this all. With equal oppression is imagination drowned, as in an elevator bin, in its every struggle to picture the lives of the inhabitants of such a farinaceous region. Of course they marry and are given in marriage. Lovely young maidens

are led to the altar; but between the mind and every
image of the charming scene is interposed a thick
mist of "Bridal Veil" flour. No! it is vain to
struggle further with the wheat hallucination.
Just as dolls are stuffed with bran, so the baffled
traveler finally succumbs to the delusion that,
should he tap a vein in the arm of one of the
natives, there would flow forth, not a stream of
ruddy human blood, but a stream of A No. 1 Pills-
bury's best.

IV. "It is wisely ordained," says Goethe, "that
the trees shall not grow up into the skies."
Only roll along far enough over the dead-level prairies, and at last is vouchsafed to weary man a rainbow of promise that not even the waters of wheat
shall continuously prevail over the face of the earth.
Faint indications begin to attest that, in the
geological "struggle for life," a perpendicular as
well as a horizontal, a jackscrew as well as a flat-
iron principle is at work in nature. Hurrah! a
hill as high as a woodchuck's burrow. It is big
with prophecy of the Rocky Mountains. Vaster
throes of an earth in labor succeed, and bring
forth, — is it a huge barn? No; a veritable Alp
as big as a barn. One is startled at the subterranean energies iuvolved. But, so far, all is
but prelude. Tired of dead level, Nature finally
rises a sleep-refreshed giant, heaving up, first on
knotty knees and then on his mighty shoulders,
the cumbering bedclothes of the prairies, with an
air of "It's time to get up!" What a Titan of a

fellow is stirring at last, becomes in a few hours revealed.

Before I actually saw them, I never could get a vivid conception of the essential genius of the Rocky Mountains, — at any rate as displayed along the line of the Canadian Pacific Railroad. People are forever darkening counsel by comparisons that serve merely to show what a thing is not. Switzerland has towering mountains; therefore as the Rocky Mountains tower, they are the American Switzerland. In point of fact, they are the precise counterpart of Switzerland. The Rocky Mountains are, as their name implies, the *Rockies*, just as the Alps are what their name — the *Alpen*, the high pasture slopes — implies. In Switzerland the snow-line descends four or five thousand feet lower than here, and so secures superb expanses of snowclad flanks and peaks. Then, below the line of softest ermine, succeed enormous stretches of emerald green grass-lands, dotted with herds of cattle. Demand this of the Rockies, and they will flatly answer: " Under such a dazzling sun we cannot keep on our snowcaps ; and, as for your deep-uddered Swiss kine, their milk would dry up here in a day. But take us as we are, and we defy Switzerland to parallel us."

The Rockies are right. Such Titanic sublimity of rock formations, such wrestlings and writhings of uptilted and contorted strata, such spectacle of a vast rock creation groaning and travailing in pain until now, where else is it witnessed on so stupendous a scale ? Now, in the Alps, all this elemental convulsion of nature, this Titan reign of chaos, is largely veiled from sight. It is covered with perpetual snow; it is hidden under regal mantles of green. Here the Titan is naked, — "naked and not ashamed." His gigantic osseous structure, his thews and sinews, all that constitute him Briareus, are seen in violent action. These are his boast, his glory. "What went ye out into the wilderness for to see? A man clothed in soft raiment?" Such is the burden of this John the Baptist mountain dispensation.

People may quarrel, if they will, that Michael Angelo is not Raphael, or Dante, Petrarch. For one, I find it much wiser to enjoy both types of men and mountains. So, thank God for the Rockies!

V. It is a great experience to set sail, or, more literally, to begin to twirl propeller from Vancouver. Before reaching the open ocean, one carries with him for twenty-four hours superb mountain ranges; on the right gradually trending northward to Alaska, and on the left southward toward the State of Washington, Mt. Baker looming up in the far distance 15,000 feet in height. Then, too, how soothing to qualmy stomachs the thought that the vast ocean on which one is embarking has earned for itself so mild and pacific a name. "What's in a name?" A vast deal, provided its bearer lives up to it. On the other hand, how small mitigation is it of a sentence to rack and thumb-screws, that it emanates from a raging tyrant habitually addressed as His Serene Highness! Equally true does all this hold of oceans.

To be perfectly candid, the Pacific is as fully entitled to the benefit of an alias as any poor inconsistent human creature whom dire necessity compels to alternate between rôles as divergent as those of exemplary deacon of the church in one place and disreputable gambler or horse thief in another. It got its Serene Highness title from the early voyagers, who, after a six weeks struggle to round Cape Horn, amid a whirl of gales, sleet, hail, fog, and distracted albatrosses, at last made northing enough to reach the beatific realm of the trade winds, and then, — sky-scrapers, studding-sails, everything set, — to be wafted day after day over a summer sea that by contrast seemed heaven. Rejoicingly as Dante, when escaped from the terrors of Inferno, could they now sing, " To run over better waters the little vessel of my genius now hoists its sails, and leaves behind itself a sea so cruel. . . . A soft color of oriental sapphire which was gathered in the serene aspect of the air, pure even to the horizon, renewed delight to my eyes soon as I issued from the dead air that had afflicted my eyes and my breast. The fair planet which incites to love was making all the Orient to smile."

" O widowed northern region, since thou art deprived of beholding these ! " is the continuation of Dante's strain more befitting those who sail from the high latitude of Vancouver, — at least as a general rule. The voyage is run on the short circle, close enough to the Aleutian Islands to let one see now and then what a heaven on earth they must provide for gulls, seals, and walruses. None the less, so far as we were concerned, all the way across to Yokohama the Pacific lived up to its inviting name. People there are, of course, in whom the subjective element so preponderates over the objective, that they will get seasick under any conditions. But there was really no external justification of their conduct. With such a superb steamship as the "Empress of China," with such an unspeakable green and gold dragon breathing defiance from her bow, with the privilege of two smoke-stacks, two propellors, two hulls, admirable fare, and almond-eyed Chinese waiters in long blue robes and pigtails, it was nothing short of deep-dyed ingratitude to turn up the nose in nauseated disgust.

VI.   Bound, as we were, for the Orient, there was in these Chinese servants, — gliding to and fro in their felt slippers like silent ghosts, their flowing robes gently undulating and their pigtails swaying in harmonious concert, — an element of Arabian Night enchantment hard to describe. We felt in it our first gentle plucking back, our initial weaning from the brimming breasts of the Occident at which hitherto we had drawn our sole ethnological nutrition ; an initial weaning very grateful, it must be admitted, from the long-wonted realm of split trousers, creaking boots, bleached-out skins, and eyes devoid of that furtive side-glance that seems to look all round and behind an object.

Besides, from a purely linguistic point of view, these Orientals furnished a university-extension course in philology that was a liberal education in itself. On first going abroad, my friend and I were guiltless of a Chinese word. Yet scarcely had we been a day at sea before we could ask for oxtail soup, curried rice, fillet of beef, or pistachio-nut ice-cream; yes, and what was more to the purpose, without fail get them.

Spite of all that may be urged by pedants, bent on glorifying their own attainments, Chinese is not a difficult tongue to master,—at any rate under the Meisterschaft system practiced on board the Vancouver steamships. The scheme is beautiful in its simplicity. For example, ox-tail soup is merely No. 1, curried rice No. 2, fillet of beef No. 3, and so on and on to the end of the bill of fare. All that is needful is to call out the requisite number, and presto! the dish smokes on the table. Thus, as by a wave of an enchanter's wand, is dissipated in an instant the whole baleful fog of linguistic confusion precipitated on the world by the defiant impiety of the projectors of the Babylonian Tower. American, Frenchman, Chinese, Hindoo, every man hears his fellow speaking in his own tongue in which he was born.

VII. We were thirteen days on the passage, and yet on going down into the engine-room, the night before our arrival out, it was a startling surprise to find that the ship's screws had not yet made a million revolutions. Night and day, without an instant's intermission, had the mighty hearts of the engines been throbbing, and not yet a million pulsations recorded. No finite mind can frame a conception of what a million means, say the greatest mathematicians. Now I felt it. Jay Gould, with his seventy millions, dilated in my mind to truly astronomic and cosmic immensity.

The day before our arrival, it rained. Should we, then, have rain and mist to blot out the glorious spectacle of the sail into Yokohama bay? Only this once on our whole voyage had our steam siren been kept sounding for fog, making us then perfectly comprehend why Ulysses plugged with wax the ears of his crew when the other siren lifted her sweet voice from the rocks. No! It could not be that we were doomed to chilly drizzle and to a blotting-paper atmosphere soaking up all the delicate outlines of the coast. Nor was it so. A glorious sunrise transfigured sky, sea, and land; and, lo! in ideal beauty of proportion, from cone to base, stood out snow-crowned Fujisan, lording it all over Japan. Oh, the beatitude of volcanic forces, when they eventuate in such a miracle of beauty! Tamer and more prosaic than the man who knows no fiery passions is the land that knows no earthquakes. Who, with a soul of poetry in him, would not gladly see some adjacent county of Worcester torn from its rooted foundations and lifted 12,000 feet nearer heaven than it ever stood before, to secure from his own windows the daily vision of such a joy forever?

By nine A. M. we were at our moorings, and soon

surrounded by scores of *sampans* eager to take passengers ashore. As the radiant September morning was warm, and the competitive sculling with huge sweeps, of the most vigorous kind, clothes soon came to be felt unbearable. Not that, to begin with, the boatmen had much on. But now in a trice that little came off, to a mere loin-cloth. What an intoxicating feast of backs and chests, and loins and legs, developed by a lifetime of stand-up rowing! Æsthetically exhilarating was the sight, as though all the statues in the Vatican — Apollo, Hermes, Antinous, Ganymede — had suddenly leaped down from their pedestals and taken to sculling *sampans*. Only, instead of white marble, their bodies were of gold bronze.

Satan's malign work in the Garden of Eden it was that first suggested clothes. Not yet have Japanese boatmen given in to the shamefaced, guilty dogma. So, devoutly be it hoped that no misguided missionaries will feel bound in conscience to make a poiut of the obnoxious tenet, — at least for sculler-converts.

JAPAN

I.

I.
No traveller ever knows so much about a new country, — its race characteristics, its institutions, its art, literature, and religion, — as during his first three days stay there, or before he has had time to pick up enough of the language to say good morning. It is a pity, then, to let the world lose the benefit of his first intuitive divinations.

Perhaps there is a certain occult irony in the fact that one's earliest innocent impressions of Japan are gathered from his perch on the seat of a two-wheeled adult baby carriage called a jinrikisha, in which a male Japanese drags him round, instead of, as in his previous infancy, a Hibernian lassie, and that, too, at a pace befitting the greater hardihood of his time of life. If of a philosophic cast of mind, one's first speculations naturally turn on the comparative advantages, as an instrument of propulsion, of a man or a horse. The conclusion is entirely in favor of the man. The horse is a brute; the man is a rational being. The horse shies or runs away; the man does neither. The horse is incapable of conversation; the man is at once guide, philosopher, and friend. Serene contemplation and active driving are incompatible, as is witnessed in the biographies of so many philosophers who have run over countless children, smashed the vehicles of other people, and ended off with breaking their own necks. To see a country to profit, one needs to give the rein to his own free fancy and not to the jaws of a brute beast.

II. From his first day even in a foreign land the humane and enlightened traveler is eagerly on the lookout for fruitful ideas to carry back with him. He yearns that those who have to stay at home shall reap some benefit from his being happy enough to get away. Loud, then, was my Eureka of joy to find, in less than half an hour, that Japan had startled me with a suggestion which opened up visions of enhanced domestic bliss to millions in my native land. It took this shape. Bicycles are essentially anti-social and selfish institutions. The only valid plea for them is that they develop the calves of the legs. But calf for calf, these Japanese runners would bear away the prize at every cattle-show in the country. What, then, if in America, tender, but straitened husbands, incapable of a horse and wagon, would but consent to abandon their selfish wheels and to brace their thews and sinews to the chivalrous work of treating their delicate wives to frequent jinrikisha spins on the Brighton road! Contrast with this the murderous adage about a chance to kill two birds with one stone! Here, at a stroke, is power to impart fresh health and joy to two loving mates, along with delightful associations of scenery and companionship that would perpetually endear them to one another.

Let the next convention in the higher interests of woman take up seriously this weighty matter. Depend upon it, man will never be taught his rightful place in creation till put into the shafts and spurred on by duty and love to make his six miles an hour for the health and delectation of his better half. As to the future erection, in some great public park, of a statue smiling benignantly down on a thousand flying jinrikishas, and to which, as they speed by, happy wives and proud husbands look up with eyes brimful of gratitude, — be all that as it may!

III. Like all seaport towns, Yokohama presents an odd intermixture of native and foreign characteristics. Old and new Japan here jostle one another in the queerest fashion. At anchor in the harbor lie huge modern steamships and iron-clads, along with clumsy junks, — while, ashore, Chinese lanterns and electric lights, bare legs and stove-pipe hats, straw sandals and india-rubber boots, mingle in the most incongruous way. Here comes along a man in a rice-straw thatch of a cloak, suggestive of a porcupine in a partially quiescent state, — his quills prone instead of erect with anger. As a device for shedding rain it is peculiarly effective, each separate straw serving as a distinct conductor. But the next man wears a cheap mackintosh. Incongruities like these might be multiplied to any extent.

There is a foreign resident as well as a purely Japanese quarter of the town. The first is built up with high, solid hotels, dwellings, and warehouses, as a special invitation to earthquakes. Along its water line runs a broad boulevard called "The Bund," planted with trees, and commanding an entrancing view over the bay. The second, or Japanese quarter covers ten times the space with its low, story-and-a-half wood structures, chimney-less, cellar-less, and with the rounded corner posts set into grooved stone sockets, to admit, under earthquake shocks, of a "bye-baby-bunting" oscillation that must be soothing to the feelings. The streets are entirely unpaved, so that in times of rain every man, — and the same law applies to women, — has to become a "pavement unto himself" by wearing pattens, with cross pieces set underneath, that raise him two and three inches from the ground. For so short a people as the Japanese, this proves an immense enhancement in dignity of appearance, and in rainy weather they wear a truly imposing look.

Certainly, to one accustomed to the brick and stone built cities of America and Europe, there is something in the first sight of a great, swarming beehive of a city made out of nothing but frail wood structures huddled close together, that is calculated to make him shudder at the thought of kerosene, and question how great the blessing our own country has conferred on Japan by sending out this especial form of missionary enlightenment. Earthquakes were bad enough, but earthquakes and kerosene, hand and glove with one another! For miles on miles stretch these low, wood structures with no distinctive architectural feature but aboriginal Tartar roof, — a plain outgrowth of the primitive Tartar tent, — together with a capacity of lying all open to the public gaze unexampled elsewhere.

Indeed, in Japan, the sliding-door principle reaches its acme. We at home know it merely as a means of practically throwing two rooms into one, while here the entire interior partitions of the house are all sliding doors, in the shape of screens covered with glazed paper. Add to this that the whole street front is daily taken off the house, and it will be clear at a glance that no other country in the world incites laudable curiosity to so rewarding a study of all that is going on in its shops, parlors, sleeping rooms, nurseries, and kitchens. So accustomed, indeed, are the mass of Japanese to living in public, as no longer to be conscious of the fact that they are in public. Having no contrast in their minds of the feeling of privacy, they are as perfectly at their ease under the eye of man as under the eye of the sun. Each man is thus shut up to establishing his own castle inside his own skin. It were a curious subject of investigation how much this perpetual living in public has had to do with the formation of a marvelously perfected external ceremonial type of manner, — very charming, very seductive, no doubt — but which reveals no more of what is actually going on inside the man than the shell of a turtle reveals the emotions really agitating his troubled or peaceful spirit. Nature, after all, has a way of " getting even " with all kinds of circumstances.

None the less, Japan is the country of countries for watching the perpetual going on of the external comedy of human life. The curtain is always up and the play in lively progress. This is the first spell of fascination exercised on the spectator. In Europe and America, on the contrary, the reflective traveler is perpetually annoyed at being shut out by doors and blinds from any free study of the domestic life of the inmates. Should he steal up to a window and flatten his nose against the pane of glass, his conduct is deemed intrusive. But how else can he hope to gain adequate comprehension of the sacred seclusion of the English or German home ? Here, thank Heaven, one can quietly loaf, and, without discomposing husband, wife, or child, watch everything going on within, — yes, and very likely know just as much about it as he did before !

IV. As for human beings, no sight at first makes so fascinating an impression on the new-comer in Japan as that of the young women. They are such dainty, miniature creatures, and wear such a guise of having just flitted down from the pretty pattern on a paper umbrella, that it is impossible to take them seriously as responsible beings. If a bevy of them laughingly sprang back on top of such an umbrella and re-grouped themselves into the original design, it would not surprise one a bit. A halo of perpetual child grace surrounds them.

The pretty patterns of their robes, with wide-opening sleeves and gayly-flowered belts; their shining black hair done up to last a week without re-dressing, and stuck through with gilt and enamel pins enough to hold it safe in a gale of wind; their golden yellow complexions shot through with a rosy blush; their dainty figures and ever smiling eyes, all combine in a charming Pinafore picture that calls out the oddest kind of a half tender-father, half fond-lover feeling in the breast. Easily in prettily modified shape, revives the essence of the old Greek fable, — how some exquisitely artistic Pygmalion of a toy-maker, infatuated over the charm of one of his own daintiest productions, should have wrung from the gods the boon of power to make it actually breathe and live.

Often at home we hear an infatuated parent say of his charming little girl of ten, " Oh that I could keep her as she is, and never have her grow a bit older or bigger ! " Well, here is the very thing before one's eyes, — the artless grace of childhood lingering on, spite of calendar, marriage, and motherhood. Yes; but they are only playing at motherhood, as little girls play with dolls; they surely cannot mean that you shall take the baby in earnest !

Such, — open to future correction — is one's first inevitable impression of these dainty creatures. Culture, as the word is understood in New England, has made no inroads on their complexions or eyesight. They have never read Emerson, never dipped into Kant. Their sole " categorical imperative " is to charm by amiability. Their faces shine as with the reflected light of an insensible perspiration of amiability. Amiability transpires from every pore, and forms a visible nimbus around their whole personality to an extent of at least eighteen inches.

It would be half invidious, however, to characterize this child charm of the young women of Japan under the aspect of arrest of development. The phrase implies something abnormal and stunted. On the contrary, they seem to have reached their full stage of child maturity, and never to have been meant to go any farther, — never to have been fashioned to reach self-consciousness. As one grows familiar with Japanese gardens, planted with miniature beeches, pines, and oaks, adorned with miniature rivers, bridges, and lakes, and set off with a miniature volcano and with a miniature gorge suggestive of Fujisan and the abysses on its flanks — the whole pretty scene from Lilliput seems lacking in flavor of natural human interest till one sees in his mind's eye these dainty little beings turned loose to play there.

Indeed, as a preacher, one would hardly know how to adapt a serious sermon to their spiritual estate, but would feel the duties of his responsible calling graciously fulfilled in taking his little flock to picnics and watching them *smile*.

V. Some one has written a book on the Japanese Smile. I have never read it, but here is my spontaneous impression. For a thousand or more years now the smile has been the most vital tenet of Japanese social religion. Unintermitting as has been their devotion to the cultivation of chrysanthemums and wistarias, still more unintermitting has been their devotion to the cultivation of the smile. "The road to happiness and the road to fortune lie in the smile," is a familiar proverb. Even if one is to communicate the news of the death of his nearest and dearest, or of the burning down of his house, or of the total wreck of his property, he is to do it with a smile. Let no one trouble another with a sign of grief or pain! Most especially is this the law for women, the end and aim of whose existence is to charm her superior, man, — the being for whom she was created. Now, nothing short of a thousand years of'inherited practice could have achieved the result witnessed on every hand. What wry faces we make when trying, in company, to smile cheerfully over an ulcerated tooth! but the Japanese woman can do it as naturally and sweetly as though the malign molar were a piece of French confectionery.

For example, only a couple of days after arriving, I went with my travelling companion into the country to visit a man who had, for a number of years, been a servant in his household in Massachusetts, but had now returned to Japan and taken unto himself a young wife. The two were living in a very humble way, raising silk-worms.

Duly taking off our shoes, we politely entered in our stocking feet, and before long were presented to Mrs. Tokyo, as, by way of disguise, I will call her. Oh, the inimitable grace with which she glided down on hands and knees before us, and touched the ground three times with her forehead! In my whole life I never felt so queer a sense of somehow or other being the blessed babe, subjected to the adoration of the shepherds. No doubt the mental confusion was pardonable in the case of one, for the first time in life, an object of female worship. My friend and I, of course, did our best to return the salutation; but we must have appeared sheer barbarians. Veiled in her flowing robes and girt with her broad, rich belt, Mrs. Tokyo's every movement was grace itself; while our stiff joints enacted the angularity of a pair of skeletons at a court presentation.

The more formal part of the ceremonial over, we now sat down together on the floor matting, Mrs. Tokyo with her feet and limbs tucked under her as daintily as a bird tucks her head under her wing, and we with ours sprawled out. Now came the chance to study, at close quarters, the mystery of the Japanese smile. At every pleasant word addressed her through the wretched medium of her husband's interpretation, the smile beamed forth afresh, with a sort of afterglow lingering on till another sunrise broke in rose and gold. And yet all this while the poor, dear creature must have been suffering torture. To her we were as envoys extraordinary and ministers plenipotentiary from Teheran, infinitely her superiors in education, social position, knowledge of the world, — in everything but grace. But all inward torment was hidden behind the girlish glee and sweetness of the smile.

"What force of will, what power of self-control!" the New England mind would argue. No, there was no will in it. The Japanese smile is a national institution, and not an individual act. It is the distilled essence of a thousand years of transmitted practice. Though at the farthest remove in beauty from the abstract grin which was all that remained of the vanishing cat in "Alice in Wonderland," it none the less represents just such an abstraction. No need is there of anything behind it. In the majority of cases there is nothing behind it. It now floats disengaged on the air, without conscious motive, *pure smile per se.* Involuntarily, I recalled the words of Napoleon to the French troops in Egypt, — "Forty centuries look down upon your deeds!" Only the words took on the slightly modified shape, "Forty centuries smile on you through the lips and eyes of Mrs. Tokyo!"

VI. Of course, to one habituated to the streets of an American or a European city, with their massive buildings and plate-glass windows for the display of goods, the uniform monotony of the long rows of plain, low, frontless structures of wood imparts, in Japan, a decidedly shanty-like look to a city. Perforce, one thinks of an immensely magnified Leadville, or like mining towns in Colorado, struck with a stupendous "boom" of prosperity, while still in the board and shingle stage of architectural evolution. Once, however, begin to inspect the treasures exposed in the shops, and forthwith Aladdin's battered old lamp is at its magic work. What a wealth of bronzes, vases, exquisite designs in porcelain, lacquer, inlaid work, ivory carving! The shop seems but a cheap wood-box to pack all these costly articles into. One cannot escape a half-humorous sense of how thoroughly Wordsworth would have enjoyed such an exhibition of "plain living and high shop-keeping."

Now sets in, with all who have money to spend, the mania of curio-buying, — as distinct a form of malarial fever as attacks those first reaching the Congo, or the Niger, in Africa. The blood-temperature mounts to 105°, the eyes glare wild, the cheeks burn with a hectic flush. Only to think of it! — the century-old Feudal State of forty million people suddenly broken up, and such a wealth of Daimio and Samurai armor, pikes, swords, trinkets, carvings, bronzes, precipitated in an avalanche on the market, — not to speak of the shoals of infinitely clever artisans ever in the background to supply new antiques as fast as the old ones are exhausted.

Personally protected myself from any attack of the curio-fever by the quinine tonic of lack of funds, it was still vastly interesting to study the violent symptoms in others. However stoutly cynical moralists like La Rochefoucauld may deny it, there is, after all, such a thing as disinterested shopping, — shopping through pure unadulterated sympathy with a friend who is able to indulge in lavish expenditures you yourself cannot afford. For the exercise of this virtue, I was most felicitously blest, as in the instance of my opulent traveling companion, the fever broke out in the most virulent shape from the day of our arrival in Yokohama, — to the degree even of causing him, in the delirium of the first night, to rave about cabling for an additional letter of credit so immense in sum total, that hardly could the Bank of England have cashed it. In three days he had accumulated Samurai swords enough to equip a regiment of cavalry; screens enough to fence in Boston Common; exquisitely embroidered silk bedspreads enough to cover all the beds in all the wards of the Massachusetts General Hospital; ivory carvings enough to create a panic among the yet remaining elephants in Africa. Vastly instructive was it to go round with him and see him purchase experience. It was a liberal education in shopping.

VII. In recording one's impressions of a new and strange land, it is perhaps only just to set down first those that seem lighter and more trivial. Light and trivial, however, they are not to one who looks at them with a deeper eye. Straws show which way the winds blow and the currents set. So, if only one learns these grave facts, what matter that it was a dancing straw that taught him. Moreover, in venturing on a little unobtrusive book, it will never do for the writer too suddenly to throw open the flood-gates to the mighty tide of statesmanlike views, philosophic speculation, æsthetic range and rapture, he feels himself capable of pouring forth. This might frighten off modest readers, humbly distrustful of their power to cope with such a mind.

II.

I. AMONG the first excursions from Yokohama the visitor to Japan is eager to make, is the one to Kamakura, to see the colossal bronze image of the Buddha.   How often had I read and dreamed of this, and now it was realized romance that it was so close at hand.   One leaves by rail, and, after a ride of twenty miles, takes to the omnipresent jinrikisha for a few miles more.   The rice-land country, through which the train runs, is beautiful beyond praise.

Not personally addicted to rice as an article of diet, — unless, perhaps, as a mere vehicle for the piquant stimulus of curry, — I was soon forced to admit that the cultivation of this cereal for purely æsthetic ends would prove an enhancement of the charms of the Garden of Eden.   At this late September season of the year, the rice-lands stretch out in the sunshine a sea of gold.   Since rice declines to grow except in water, and water declines to stand still except on a perfect level, the immense area of alluvial deposit in which the plant roots wears the look of a lake of luxuriant, sunlit vegetation.   Encircling in graceful curves this vast burnished expanse — now jutting out into it in promontories and now retreating to leave space for lovely bays — are hills densely wooded, completing the picture with ravishing contrasts of form and color.

Curiously enough, each charming little valley, with its brook winding down between the densely wooded hills to the shining level of the plain, now delights the eye with the exact transcript of a series of beautiful cascades of golden rice. As in the gardens of Versailles, streams of water are made to run down great flights of broad stone steps, breaking into a gentle fall at each successive step, so here the same effect is wrought by utilizing the water of the descending brooks for successive terraces of rice. So vivid the impression of life and motion, that literally it seems as though the beautiful plant itself had taken to the mobile ways of the element in which it grows. When one pictures the scene of an infinite variety of these lovely little valleys, pouring their brooks of gold through luxuriantly wooded defiles into a sea of gold below, he will have presented to the mind the sight that makes one of Japan's most characteristic beauties.

II. Though once a capital of Japan, with 1,000,000 inhabitants, all that remains of Kamakura to-day is a struggling village on beautiful Sagami bay, the next bay southward of that of Yokohama. Besides a temple to Hachiman, the God of War, and another to Quannon, the Goddess of Tenderness and Love, and the great image of the Buddha, here called the Daibutsu, no traces remain of what, in 1400, was an immense city. All has lapsed back to primitive hills, valleys and trees.

At first one is tempted to smile derisively at the statement that a million people once joyed, suffered and died here in a crowded capital, and to say, "Oriental figures must be taken with oriental statistical imagination!" But this were a mistake. Japanese cities leave no ruins. With the removal of Mikado, or Shogun, to another spot, — and sixty times has this occurred in the course of Japanese history, — the card-board city is abandoned to rot away or be burned for fire-wood, — just as with the North American Indians: when the chief shifts his camping ground, the whole wigwam village must follow in his train. It is the same experience, only on a vaster scale. Perhaps, as a symbol of the transitoriness and evanescence of all finite things, of the vanity of the griefs and passions barricadoed in the wriggling ant-hills of human life, no spectacle could be presented more fitted to attune the mind to the contemplation of the serene, Nirvana-wrapped Buddha. As one walks meditatively nearly a mile back from the sea shore, along an avenue shaded with century-old cryptomerias, to the elevation on which are seated the temples of Hachiman and Quannon, it is the counterpart, in this temple of Nature, of traversing the main aisle of a Gothic cathedral to approach the Holy of Holies of the altar.

III. All this delay is not keeping the colossal Buddha too long waiting. He recks not of time or space. He dwells in a realm in which the finite is swallowed up in the infinite. He has entered on Nirvana. While he is seated there, century after century lapses unheeded by. The magnificent feudalism of the past is broken in pieces; the noisy Occident clamors at the gates of the Orient; the thunder of Commodore Perry's guns reverberates in Yokohama Bay; the fierce, discordant shriek of the locomotive, symbol of the insane restlessness and fever of the finite, tears the quiet air into shreds. But he broods on, forever lifted out of and above the whole mad "causal nexus" of desire, pursuit, possession, leading inevitably on to satiety, heart-break, greed, crime, dust and ashes.

Overwhelmingly one feels all this, as through an avenue of giant trees he approaches the colossal image of the Buddha. It is vast enough in its proportions to seem a part of surrounding nature, to awaken the vague sense of sharing the purely elemental life. The prosaic mathematics of size simply belittles and vulgarizes the weight of the impression. In a sitting posture fifty feet high, forty feet broad, eyes three feet, mouth seven feet long, — these are statistics for the empty, gaping crowd. One hastens to fling the figures off his mind, and, instead, to revert to Keats' awe-inspiring parallel of Saturn in the gloomy grove; so like and yet unlike.

> "Deep in the shady sadness of a vale
> Far sunken from the healthy breath of morn,

> Far from the fiery noon, and eve's one star,
> Sat gray-haired Saturn, quiet as a stone,
> Still as the silence round about his lair;
> Forest on forest hung about his head
> Like cloud on cloud."

Colossal embodiment of a great world-religion that has brought rest to millions of the weary and heavy-laden, the tranquil, breathless essence of that rest revealed in its now super-sensuous founder, — such is the significance of the vast presence before one! The mighty head bowed in serene tranquillity, the breathless calm, the peace too massive, too diffused, too elemental, to suggest any finite form of thought, of desire, of emotion, — yes, the peace *passing understanding*, which could not be what it is if the understanding could grasp and measure it, — this, the ineffable, interior heaven of the supreme mystics of all ages, of Plotinus, Boehme, Saint Teresa of Avila, is what the great image makes palpable to soul and sense.

Still, it naturally may be asked, is it not to its colossal magnitude that the Kamakura Buddha owes the main reason of the overwhelming impression it exerts? Of course, it is to this, if only we add colossal magnitude suffused through its every dreaming atom with indwelling soul. Magnitude means magnitude. The little may suggest, but cannot body forth, the vast and circumscribing.

All the sublime creations of the ages are colossal in mass. The wrestle of Job with the Almighty, the Prometheus of Æschylus, the Lear of Shakespeare, the Satan of Milton, the Fifth Symphony

of Beethoven, each and all are and must be colossal
to produce the effect they work on the mind. Desolation, defiance, revolt at injustice, heaven-storm-
ing aspiration, each and every passion of the breast
of man is in these vast creations raised to super-
human proportions. On any other terms, as well
expect miniature raised-map reductions of the Alps
and Himalayas to do the work for the imagination
of their rock-bastioned, cloud-girt, snow-and-ice-
crowned originals.

Here then, first, gets its overwhelming expression the root-thought of Buddhism, — the soul uplifted like a sunlit peak above the clouds of this
storm-troubled sphere. Out of the cloud-realm
pour down on all who dwell below the dank, driz-
zling rains, or dart the lightning forks that shatter
earthly good in ruin. Above them lies the un-
troubled ether. And toward the supreme embodiment of this thought in the Kamakura Buddha it
would seem as though the very elements of earth-
bred havoc had conspired. Once the statue was
covered in by a temple, where, penned in such a
petty, finite enclosure, its majestic effect must have
been wholly lost. In rolled from the ocean a great
earthquake wave, sweeping away every vestige of
the temple, but leaving the mighty, dreaming
Buddha unstirred from his base. He heard it not,
felt it not, but brooded on in impassive calm. And
so, century on century, he sits under the open sky,
wrapt in his infinite peace. The rains descend,
the lightnings flash, the woods rock in the roaring
gale, dynasties rise and fall, Lilliputian tourists

from the far West peer and peep, and air the last fashions of a trivial world around his mountain base. But he is oblivious of it all. It cannot penetrate Nirvana, where he dwells in unbroken rest.

It is a great privilege to pass even a brief hour before this stupendous symbol of the faith of millions of one's fellow creatures, and to be led by it into nearer communion with one of the vast world-interpretations of the problem of human destiny. Indeed, it leaves behind in the heart a yearning to spend, in a kind of spiritual retreat, the mornings of a whole month, meditating in such a presence. For who can fail to recognize how immense a rôle the essential principle of Buddhism has played in the spiritual history of reflective and sensitive minds in all ages and in all lands.

Heart-sick weariness over the dust-whirl of the finite, — its petty cares, its mosquito stings, its commonplace vacuity, its fitful fever of hectic excitement, — surely one does not need to cross wide seas to encounter minds fretted as with sharp acids that have eaten in the pattern of all this dreary scheme of human life. Those there are, of course, to whom nothing is tragic, men, and women too, incapable alike of the rapture of joy or the agony of grief that are the vital substance of the heavens and the hells of deeper natures, — men and women who could sleep heavily through Gethsemane, or, should they chance to awaken for a moment and catch a glimpse of the Son of Man in his agony, would, at their deepest, but utter their sympathy in an "Ah! really! I suppose it all must have been quite a disappointment!" and then resign themselves to sleep again. And, as the world goes, they are good, average people.

Historically, however, and with all deeper and higher minds, this shallow or stolid complacency in the presence of the suffering of human life has never held its own. At the root of Christian monasticism, of the theology of the mediæval Catholic church, and of the wide-spread shapes of Calvinism and Jansenism, lies an element always kindred to the Buddhistic despair of the world, — the deep-down sense that the world, as it is, exists but to be denied and ultimately delivered from; while in how much of modern philosophy is the whole strain pitched in the same minor key ! Hegel but repeats the Buddha. Nor is this mere theme for regret. Better any religion or philosophy, however dark the colors in which it paints the actual, than shallow acquiescence in the world as it is, with no suffering consciousness of its evil, nor yearning for redemption from its appalling mystery.

IV. Spite of all that lies latent behind it, or breaks through in deeper intuitions, this world is, after all, a very finite, bustling, kaleidoscopic world. Pure, abstract being is too metaphysical, at any rate for tourists, and anon must be broken up by the prism of the five senses into trees, flowers, society, laughter, lunch, eager curiosity, and keen-eyed perception. Emphatically did we feel this when we left the mighty, brooding presence and took once more to our jinrikishas.

We were a party of nine, each one of whom had three coolies, two to run tandem in front and one to push behind. Thus, in single file, we stretched out in double-quick procession several hundred feet; and, as the coolies evidently "felt their oats," from the bowls of rice they had eaten, we were soon speeding along at a rattling pace.

What exquisite garden culture in the fields on either hand! Every inch of soil how made to tell, and to tell in two to three crops in rotation! The blooming buckwheat, the polished lanceolate leaves of the Japanese potato, the feathery-topped carrots, — never a weed there put in trace of competition in any struggle for the survival of the fittest for the pot of the Japanese peasant. And yet how tiny each separate little patch of beans, or rice, or what not! Doll vegetable gardens they looked. Yes, everything in miniature again! Again, infinite concentration on the minutest details, — the irresistible shaping force that necessitates the form everything takes in Japan, agriculture, service, manners, ornamentation, lacquer or cloisonné, carving, painting. On pain of death, with starvation as herald of the doom, no one may dare to slight a feature of his work. Yet all is "unresting, unhasting," to a degree that, spite of his motto, Goethe himself could never reach over the most elaborate finish of a poem.

We were bound for Enoshima, a beautiful promontory jutting out into the Pacific, its forest-crowned top the seat of a famous temple, and, at its base and climbing its slope, a fishing village, where all kinds of beautiful objects arc made of the shells, seaweeds, sea-urchins, sponges, and corals gathered from the deep. Breaking journey only for lunch at a charming half tea-house, half hotel sanatorium, where, in the shelter of pine groves sifting out any chill from the winds, delicate Japanese and Europeans seek relief from the more exposed situation of Yokohama bay, we started out again under a weight of obeisances from the bevy of girls in attendance that made each one of us the equal in consciousness with the sultan of the Sublime Porte. Whereas, at home, we Americans are but ordinary " sovereigns," and no one of the seventy million sovereigns shows a jot of respect for the royal insignia of the others. Of course, as became good republicans, we now felt correspondingly exalted.

V. Of all the " coigns of vantage " for a philosopher, — better far than any basket suspended between heaven and earth, — commend me to the seat of a jinrikisha. No other such throne of contemplation does the world afford. One is utterly alone. No care for himself demands attention. No voice of another disturbs the silence of his meditation. Fresh material of observation is opened up to him at every turn. Far from having to spin spider-film theories out of the bowels of his own consciousness, like the student in his closet, eye and ear are on the alert to furnish data that can be relied on to confirm or to rebut his shaping generalizations.

What might not Immanuel Kant have become under these conditions! At first, perhaps, the jinrikisha philosopher is all eye, all rapture. " Oh, the ravishing beauty of this land!" he constantly exclaims, as he is smoothly whirled high above the sea along a road from which he looks down to the beach below fringed with creamy foam, or off over the dreamy surface of the water to bays and promontories and mountain-crowned islands, steeped in so poetic an atmosphere. Next, to turn a defile, the road curves inland a mile or so, where orange-trees hang thick with fruit, and the persimmons show red and gold among the foliage, and the steep slopes of the defiles are waving with the feathery plumes of the bamboo, till again, the cry, " The sea! the sea!"

But your philosopher on his perch is no fool of sense and time and space. He will both eat his cake and have it. By degrees his outer eye begins to close and his inner eye to waken. Then inevitably looms up again before him the Nirvana-lapsed Buddha of the morning, and he begins to ruminate on the nature of the century - long influence the mighty dreamer has exerted on the children of this mobile race about one on every hand. So, here for his speculations!

From the very superficial view I have been enabled to take of the Japanese people of to-day, it seems to me that the Kamakura Buddha over-expresses the character of the influence Buddhism has exerted on them. The great image dates back to the thirteenth century, to the times in which the original Buddhistic missionary spirit had not yet lost its first vitality. Far more of India, and of its deep pessimistic despair, and of its deep-down yearning for deliverance through simple escape from all that makes up to it the weary summary of finite existence, is manifest in the statue than holds actually true of the Japanese people as one sees them now. They are not an Oriental race, in the sense of a race dwelling under the overpowering heat and among the jungles infested with the tigers, cobras, scorpions, and malarias of Hindostan. Quite as much are they a northern as an Oriental race, and latitude plays a far more significant part in the development of a people than longitude.

In reality, the Japanese are more nearly allied in temperament to the French than to the inhabitants of India. They may derive their main religious conceptions from India, just as the French derive theirs from Judæa; but they have modified them profoundly. After all, this term " Eastern " is a misleading term. It implies simply east from some conventional point, say Greenwich. Every place on the globe is east from some other place. But this fact is nothing in comparison with such a question as that of north or south, that of a temperate or of a tropical climate. Japan is breaking away from the East in the conventional sense, and is coming to the consciousness that her future means alliance with America and Europe, with their science, politics, philosophy, and ultimately with their more hopeful religion.

All this signifies that the Japanese are not overpoweringly a brooding, dreamy people, but an alert, mobile, impressionable, at once artistic and practical people. They dwell in one of the loveliest and most diversified countries in the world, with coast lines as changeful as those of Greece and its archipelagoes, with a flora of the most marvelous variety, with mountains, lakes, forests, and meadow lands of extraordinary beauty. All this they enjoy to the full with a naïve, childlike, unreflecting delight. They do not seek the forest as the Buddha did, to get out of the glare and heat of every-day reality, to be free to brood undisturbed, to have all the distracting multiplicity of light and color and form quenched in twilight obscurity, that the inward alone may possess the mind. Rather is their delight sought in the fascinating diversity of the outward and the finite. The tint of a cherry blossom, the delicacy of a bit of moss, the graceful curve of a spray of woodbine, the dart of a bird at a butterfly, or the motion of a fish in a pool, — these they prize above all the abstractions in the world or beyond the world. To catch, as it were, on the wing the living spirit of all these, to reproduce them at once with fidelity and freedom in metal, wood, ivory, embroidery, dress-pattern, sketch in color, — to make the most ordinary household utensils reminders of them, and fragrant with their beauty and perfume, — just here lies the attitude of the Japanese mind toward nature.

Be it confessed, the profounder questions of human life and destiny have in no age taken a strong speculative hold on this people; while the more practical and superficial ones have been marvelously resolved. It is in vain that one will seek among them for any deep original thinkers on social, philosophical, ethical, or religious subjects. From China, with India behind it, they have imported their theology, moral and social systems, manners, and art in its myriad forms. These they have modified in accordance with their own social needs, exquisite taste, and placidity of temperament. With them, the awful Buddhistic temple of India becomes a miracle of fanciful and intricate lacquer work; while the superb groves of cryptomerias, pines, and camphor-trees surrounding those temples are the happy play-grounds of thousands of children and of throngs of merry-making pilgrims.

None the less, in just the same sense that Europe is Aryanized Christian, so is Japan still thoroughly Buddhistic in attitude, the present rage for Herbert Spencer notwithstanding. Like all Oriental peoples, the Japanese are penetrated with the sense of the evanescence of life, that it is a vapor which vanishes away, a bubble that bursts and is gone. Still, it is a beautiful bubble, iridescent with rainbow colors and bright with a thousand charming reflections. Even if not that, at least it can be borne with quiet patience or ignored with quiet indifference. Anyhow, it is a small matter, not worth breaking the heart over, if there is such a thing as the heart. Beyond the bourne, the ancestors live on in some vague, impersonal way. Burn incense to them and plant flowers on their graves, to keep alive the dreamy sentiment. Soon will the like be done for us. Meanwhile, there are careless, pretty children to play with, cherry blossoms, wistarias, lotus flowers wherewith mildly to intoxicate the senses, crowds of neighbors to chat and gossip with, charming designs to work out in wood, ivory, and metal, " unresting, unhasting " work to keep the mind diverted from worry, with, crown of all, retirement from the cares of life at fifty, when the children will look out for us !

Such is the creed, even though, as with all creeds, sharp and stern inroads are made on it by the tougher experiences of life. But the mistake of mistakes is it to think that creeds effect nothing because they are unavailing to effect everything. They are an atmosphere, tonic or depressing, unconsciously breathed in at every inhalation. To " break up the tables with a laugh " because, forsooth, the Roman Stoic sometimes cut a wry face over an agonizing toothache is a very shallow way of dismissing to limbo the value of a shape of faith that put iron into the blood of millions. All great world-ideals, Christian, Buddhist, Stoic, Epicurean, Mohammedan, are working forces of incalculable range and power.

I. FOR lack of space I must pass very rapidly over the impressions left by an excursion of some days to Miyanoshita, Hakone lake, and over the Ten Province Pass to Atami on the seashore, at which last point even Sir Edwin Arnold's multitudinous command of gushing vocables gave out, and he was forced to lie down and pant in breathless incapacity of further expression. The excursion was poetry from beginning to end. As nobody ever looks out the position of any region on the map, it is perhaps superfluous to add that the peninsula of Idzu, on which Atami lies, is south and west of Yohohama bay, and that the Hakone region back of it is mountainous. Natures there are, however, that must get vent topographically or die.

II. To mount from Yumoto to Miyanoshita, an ascent of 1400 feet, our jinrikisha runners did the five miles of steep uphill work inside of fifty minutes, including a momentary stop for a sip of tea, generally their only stimulant. We had three coolies each, and all through the awful pull they smiled like cherubs. "Let the galled jade wince, our withers are unwrung," was snapped out from every elastic muscle. And yet we Americans insist that a vegetable diet is unequal to imparting strength. These fellows, moreover, have intellect enough left to refresh themselves after their tough work by playing chess, that most strenuous of relaxations for all but Napoleon Bonaparte.

III. As the road wound along a picturesque mountain gorge, far below at the bottom of which was a leaping river, broken by frequent waterfalls whose white foam shone out in relief against the dense foliage, gradually there opened upon us the higher slopes of the mountains, as they rose clear from the forest, clad in a pure naked beauty of olive-green that was a fresh revelation in Japanese scenery. These slopes stretched as wide-ranging and unbroken as the pasture lands of the Alps, and yet in color offered such a contrast. "Symphonies in olive-green, with infinite variations in light and shade, on the same theme," painter Wynants would have called them. Yet as we feasted in delight on their poetic beauty, we could make out no herds of grazing cattle or flocks of nibbling sheep. None the less, as Wordsworth puts it, these seeming pastures were an " appetite," awakening in us vague but delicious reminiscences of happy grazing days in bygone stages of being. Why should not living sentient cows and sheep of to-day enjoy the feast along with us ; they chewing the cud of the juicy grass and we the cud of its æsthetic charm?

It seemed a wrong. It was a wrong. The " symphony in olive-green " was of bamboo grass, whose flinty silicious sheathing cuts the coats of the stomachs of the countless herds it might otherwise nourish. Yet Japan is three fourths mountains, and, in certain immense regions, the bamboo grass is everywhere. But for it, the hills might be as white with flocks and as rich in the browns and reds of dappled cattle as Wales or Scotland. A high price this to pay for simple beauty, but oh, how beautiful it is! What a light, too, it cast on an enforced vegetable diet. Free will is not so absolute a thing as we are apt to take it for.

IV. Should I attempt to describe the Fujiya hotel in Miyanoshita, it would only be to swoon like Sir Edwin Arnold before Atami. Once in a while, even in this imperfect sphere, is the ideal reached, and the ideal is the ideal, the standard of perfection, alike whether in hotel, poem, or strain of music. Not only have the Japanese sent abroad their brightest young intellects to study medicine and philosophy in Germany, military and naval science in America and England, engineering in Switzerland, but wherever a culinary mind of the highest order has emerged above the average level, they have dispatched it swift to Paris, to master the subtlest secrets of the white-aproned, paper-capped artists presiding over the kitchens of that famed metropolis. Again a straw, but a straw that shows which way the wind blows. Let no one hope to understand the Japanese apart from a study of the instinctive imitativeness, the infinite pliability, with which they adopt all varieties of new ideas and lift them to perfection.

Beautiful, however, in all its appointments as was the Fujiya hotel, it was in its service that lay its crowning charm. This service was wholly in the hands of the daintiest of miniature girls, every flowered pattern of whose crêpe dresses and every hue of whose silk belts seemed to have been selected by a presiding artist. Early each morning came a tap on the door, iu would glide a little fairy with a tray of coffee and toast in one hand, and over the arm a long, loose bathing-gown. The tray she would deposit on a little table by the bedside, and then with a sunny smile lift a lump of sugar for the cup. Another lump? The smile beamed more luminously. Still another? It was diffused over the whole face. The temptation was almost irresistible to exhaust the whole sugar bowl, to see how far human ecstasy could go. Then would she withdraw and wait outside till, arrayed in the loose flowered kimono, you were ready to have her pilot the way for you to the bath.

V. Just as the Japanese are vegetarians and owe it to the bamboo grass, so are they the cleanest people in the world, and owe it to volcanoes. How would Buckle, the original inventor of the relations between human history and physical environment, have leaped with joy to find himself stared in the face in Japan by such confirmations of his theory. Until the advent in Europe and America of that last infliction of human woes, the plumber, — with his elaborate system of overhead cistern, water-back, boiler, and circulating

pipes, — nobody ever thought of bathing; while in
Japan, on the other hand, Nature had for thousands of years been carrying on the whole elaborate process of supplying her children with boiling
water without a word of advice, or a bill, from so
unnecessary a functionary as the man of lead.　The
rain-clouds were the overhead cisterns, the volcano
was the furnace, the subterranean springs were the
boiler, the running streams were the circulating
pipes.　Not that every portion equally of Japan
had a volcano at command to heat its water and
fill its bathtubs.　Still, they were plentiful enough
to introduce on the widest scale the luxury, and
to make it the custom, till now every peasant in the
land has his tub, with natural or artifical volcano-
attachment, in which he boils himself daily till
fatigue or rheumatism are dissolved away.　Who
after this will say that foreign travel is not immensely improving in the vast generalizations it
opens up before the reflective mind?

VI.　It is a day's journey from Miyanoshita to
Atami over the Ten Province Pass.　Too
steep, the climb and descent, for the jinrikisha,
one now betakes himself to the kago, a palanquin
with long bamboo poles borne on the shoulders of
four coolies.　It is useless to attempt long descriptions of scenery.　Enough that the way leads over
the backbone of the Idzu promontory, waving
with vast stretches of plumy bamboo grass, and
looking down on either side to the sea breaking in
curves of foam on the beaches.　Ten Provinces

are commanded by the eye, while over them all Fujisan rears its superb snow-crowned cone. Wise is the mountain whose " soul is as a star and dwells apart." One Dante, one Milton, one Fujisan! Atami I will not venture to picture. The fear of Sir Edwin Arnold is before my eyes.

IV.

I.   Fifty miles or more north of Tokyo, in a mountain region of peaks six to eight thousand feet in height, lie the famous memorial temples of Nikko, perhaps the most sumptuously adorned of any in Japan. Before undertaking to say a word about them, let me make a brief allusion to the past religious history of Japan.

The day was when the Buddhist church played the same great rôle in Japan that the Roman Catholic played in mediæval Europe. Just as Italy, Spain, France, Germany, and England were covered with monasteries, abbeys, and countless ecclesiastical foundations by the one, so was it here in Japan by the other. The same principles of human nature were at work in either case. Thousands and tens of thousands were driven by the turbulence and misery of ages of domestic warfare to seek refuge in the church. Mikados, set aside by more powerful rivals or voluntarily abdicating in sheer world-weariness, shaved their heads and assumed the garb of the monk. Powerful barons, heart-sick at last over their lives of violence and cruelty, hid themselves in penitence in the cloister. Broken traders, peasants brought to ruin, women blighted in their affections, refined and tender natures of all kinds that could not bear the stress of the outside world, betook themselves to this one haven of rest. Riches poured in. Enormous grants of land were made by princes and feudal lords. Temples were built by them in atonement for their sins. Theological schools were founded in countless numbers; while the Peter's pence of the poor amounted, in the aggregate, to enormous sums of steady revenue. Then followed the same results that were witnessed in Europe. Abbots and bishops became powerful forces in politics and in actual warfare. Ignorant and ferocious swarms of monks made themselves the terror of whole counties. Rival theological schools rent the land into discordant sects in the advocacy of hair-splitting metaphysical distinctions. Veritable sages and saints appeared. But the fatality of the Japanese mind, with its imitative rather than original characteristics, manifested itself through all. No new contributions of any spiritual depth were added to the imported creed. No monumental works of theology like the " Summa " of Saint Thomas Aquinas, no rich hymnology, no treasuries of devout thought like the " Imitation " of Thomas à Kempis, no noble manuals of worship to compare with the Roman Catholic Missal or the English Prayer-Book, were the return to the world for such lavish outpourings of the common means.

On every hand to-day stand these truly colossal ecclesiastical foundations. They cover the mountain-sides with their square miles of temples, dormitories, groves, and gardens. They have their great ranges of state apartments for abbots, bishops, princes, and feudal lords. They bear witness to an age when they must have yielded substantial satisfaction to the millions who otherwise would not have maintained them. Not alone did they allay superstitious fears and furnish retreats to men weary of the world. They inaugurated systems of festivals and pilgrimages which were the happy holiday experiences of the masses of the people, in whose minds were at the same time sown the seeds of instruction in the knowledge of good and evil. Moreover, the fundamental theological view impressed was at the last remove from the agnosticism of the original Indian Buddhism. Amida, the supreme, self-conscious Deity, had become incarnate in the Buddha to redeem mankind from suffering. It was not the lone, isolated Buddha, it was Amida Buddha, the divine-human, that had conquered and triumphed over the realms of misery, and who, in infinite compassion, showed the way of blessedness. Nor was this all. To the popular imagination, at least, were opened up visions of a heaven bright with hierarchies of angels, and of a hell terrible with the torments of the wicked, as many a picture in the temples reveals, even though these supernatural visions never took such hold on the vaguely dreaming minds of the Japanese as on the minds of more highly vitalized and passionate races.

Many and beautiful, too, were the parables and legends thus spread abroad through the hearts of the peasantry. Let me give one of them, — the Japanese version of the poor widow in the Gospels, whose copper mite cast into the treasury out-weighed, in the sight of God, the gold of the rich man. Be it premised, for the full understanding of the story, that the avenues leading to the temples in Japan are lined with high, monumental stone or bronze lanterns, many of them of great cost. The touching parable runs thus: A certain rich man presented a temple with a hundred fine lanterns, while a poor woman, who had no money to give, cut off her hair, and, selling it, bought a cheap and humble one. After they had all been set in place, they were one night lighted up at a festival. Then the god sent a powerful wind; and, lo! all the hundred lanterns of the rich man were blown out, while the poor widow's burned bright and clear through the whole night. Thus did the god bear witness that the liberality of the heart was the one thing precious in his sight.

II. I have already alluded to the enormous spaces and superb groves surrounding great numbers of the temples. It would be an ample return for circumnavigating the globe to find one's self wandering for a single day under the awful shade and overpowering height and spread of the giant cryptomerias, pines, firs, and cypresses that cover the whole sacred mountain on which lie the Nikko temples. Where the great avenues are cut through them, with their frequent rises of stately flights of stone steps, the century-old trunks, lifting in enormous girth to a towering height, present a scene of monumental grandeur that Karnak in

Egypt cannot surpass. It is arboreal architecture on so stupendous a scale that the aisles of a Cologne cathedral dwindle into insignificance in comparison. All the ancient Druid in one's blood comes out; and his life, long centuries back, when the groves were the only temples, revives and swallows up the present and the intervening past. Half haunted did I feel with a strange fancy that here was the actual heaven to which the devout, nature-loving spirit of Asa Gray, our own peerless botanist, had been sent after its beautiful life on earth. How would he worship in such a presence!

Far more in these groves than in any of the temples does the inmost spirit of the Buddhistic Nirvana seem to express itself. " Come unto me, all ye that are weary and heavy-laden, that are lonely, world-weary, sin-sick, and I will give you rest!" is the voiceless invitation breathed abroad. Quietly a strain comes stealing into the mind like that of Wordsworth's lines : " Thought was not: in enjoyment it expired. Wrapped in that still communion that transcends the imperfect offices of prayer and praise, his soul was a thanksgiving to the power that made it: it was blessedness and love." Ah! could one but spend a long, full summer among the groves of Nikko, he would " come " to his own deep, inward self, healed of his wounds, life's fitful fever quenched, the power of the world over him dissolved away forever.

III. Far less is it beauty or dignity of form than magnificence of ornamentation that impresses one in a Japanese temple. Given a column, a frieze, an open-work cloister, the beam of an overhanging gable, and the Japanese artist has merely something to start with. We are accustomed at home to go wild over a piece of their exquisite lacquer-work. But here, in many a temple, the whole interior — columns, ceiling, altar, floor, images, shrines, candelabra — is one regal jewel-box of lacquer and gold, the entire splendor above reflected, as in a limpid pool, in the mirror of the lacquered floor beneath. In many an instance the effect of the whole is one of such gorgeous yet harmonious glory that the mind is absorbed in the spectacle as a beautiful unity; but this is not the abiding feeling, as in the grander orders of architecture, where the structural character is such that the whole is greater than the parts. In the vast majority of these temples the case is reversed, and the parts are greater than the whole. Soon you find yourself kneeling down to admire the delicate work on a bronze, or marveling at the exquisite designs in red and gold on a lacquered shrine, or lost in delight over the flowers and arabesque work in panel after panel of the ceiling. Neither would it be fair to the genius of a people who express themselves in detail rather than in mass to do otherwise. Not so much one commanding mind as myriads of exquisitely delicate craftsmen, you feel, have wrought this beautiful result. For years on years, in such structures as the mortuary temples of Ieyasu and Iemitsu in Nikko, thousands of the most artistic, æsthetic-fibred, patient, consummately skilled workmen the world ever saw were kept unintermittingly at their task. Thus, inevitably, the mind becomes overpowered by the simple historical fact, and says : " Well, if I cannot see the woods for the trees, then I will see the trees by themselves. There is a whole world of cunning beauty in their bark, their clinging vines, their lichens, their buds, leaves, and flowers ! "

It is the work, then, of a rarely endowed people, instead of the work of a few exceptional men of genius, that one admires in these temples. The impression they leave on the mind is far more artistic than religious. The Japanese mind, be it repeated, is the perfection of the finite. It has no brooding, infinite element in it, and expresses little of this in its architecture. Now and then an image of the Buddha is so beautiful in its serene peace, is so lost in supersensuous contemplation, that you feel yourself in a Catholic church in Italy, with an image of the redeeming Saviour before you. But this was a type already fixed in India ages before it reached Japan. No, the distinctly Japanese contribution to their temples is that of the grace, variety, charm, joy, of the world of birds, vines, flowers. Is not a peacock or a pheasant a glory of iris-hued color ? Is not a spray of cherry blossoms a ravishment to the eye ? Is not a school of fishes, as they swirl in graceful curves through the water, something to arrest and fascinate and make one gaze forever ? To work out these ideas, with naïve delight, in the most exquisitely wrought, colored, and gilded wood-carving; in the chasing of every brass jointure of a beam; in the superb gilded candelabra of lotus leaves and flowers; in gold-based screens covered with chrysanthemums, wistaria vines, wrens, herons — here lies the work in which the Japanese are as happy and at home as children reveling in the meadows and woods of springtime.

If, then, I were called upon to express my own personal feeling as to the impression wrought by the actual temples of Japan in comparison with that of the groves, avenues, and quiet, secluded gardens environing them, it would be in somewhat the following fashion that I should have to set to work. I enjoy immensely visiting many a temple; but I enjoy it very much as I should visiting a transfigured and sublimated curio shop, exquisitely harmonized in its details. I dote on lacquer. I am as crazy as any woman over embroideries. My finger-tips itch with kleptomania at the sight of choice bronzes. Screens painted with herons, wild geese, cherry blossoms, and wistaria vines, delight me with their life and grace; and as for a polished floor, — a limpid pool for the exquisite reflection of ceiling, gilded pillars, magnificent altar, — I could drown myself like Narcissus in it. Over the gilded and painted open-work, wood-carvings of flowers, peacocks, cranes, doves, monkeys, dragons, and griffins, I could delight to linger, in such places as Nikko, Tokyo, or Kyoto, a couple of hours every morning for a month, examining them bit by bit. But the interiors are, as a rule, too small to produce any overpowering effect;

and no great central religious idea dominates the infinite variety and contrariety of the details. Indeed, very often I feel a half-humorous smile playing over my face when, after a season of real communion with a serenely beautiful Buddha seated on the lotus leaves above the altar, his eyes closed, his face suffused with a sense of ineffable peace in interior withdrawal from the world of sense, I suddenly become aware of all the splendid elaboration of minute and varied detail around me. Has the inwardly Illuminated One, after all, closed his eyes a-purpose, that he may shut out the bewildering distraction of the finite multiplicity of his own temple, to lose himself in the oneness of the immutable and unchanging?

IV. In accordance with this spirit in which they are conceived and adorned, the temples in Japan are something widely different in use and purpose from the churches in Europe and America. Set, as they are, in the midst of immense spaces and superb groves, they furnish the parks, the playgrounds, the places for picnics and pilgrimages for the people. Temple and tea-house meet and kiss one another. The ceremonial worship is conducted by the priest, while the men and women who, as devotees, come up to say their prayers are, as a general rule, quickly through with it. They clap their hands to notify the god they are there, mumble a few unintelligible repetitions of words the original meaning of which is now lost, then clap their hands again to notify the god that they have done and he may go, and themselves adjourn for rice, tea, and chat. Indeed, immense numbers of the prayers are simply written out for the worshipers on slips of paper, and then hung on the gratings of shrines. So far does this go that in many of the Shinto temples the awful-looking war-gods and gods of thunder and hurricane who guard the entrance are seen literally covered with innumerable spit-balls thrown by devotees who have first chewed up their paper prayers and then discharged them with force enough to make them stick to nose, chest, or leg. Thus have the worshipers attested that they "mean business," and that the god shall have no excuse for pleading he did not know they had been there. The earnestness is certainly praiseworthy, only, one would think, a little at the cost of devout reverence.

Very much of the same piece with the externality, rather than spiritual inwardness, of all this, is the impression made by certain immense octagonal structures, filled with all the writings of Buddhist literature and made to revolve on a kind of capstan fitted with handspikes, one sees in many a temple. The most ignorant peasant who turns this once round is entitled to the same "merit" as though he had read every one of the sacred writings stored within. One cannot but feel what a labor-saving device for professors it would be if at least one of these could be imported and set up in each theological school in America. A single turn of the capstan, and, lo! the stupidest fellow at Princeton or Andover has got all the good out of

" Edwards on the Will," Hegel's " Philosophy of Religion," or Lotze's " Microcosmos " ! The whole cruel innuendo would at once be taken out of the old Greek saw, " There is no royal road to knowledge." Still, historically, one cannot but be touched at the loving and pitiful spirit for the ignorant and disinherited manifest in so many of these mechanical devices for bridging the painful abyss between the learned and the simple, the recluse student and the treadmill toiler. And, after all, how many an arid pedant, who passes muster for the " merits " of whole libraries devoured by him, has all his life only been working the capstan of just such a machine.

V. The more one journeys about Japan, the more is he impressed with the unique simplicity of the type of civilization it presents. Let him once grasp a few of the fundamental ideas that underlie it, and he has the key that interprets nearly everything before his eyes. Of the bewildering complexity of European civilization there is little to perplex the mind. Leaving out the changes wrought in the last thirty years, the same plough that turned up the soil one thousand years ago turns it up to-day, the same junk that furrowed the waters a thousand years ago furrows them to-day, the same order of architecture that reigned a thousand years ago reigns to-day.

Go to Venice, for example, and at a glance of the eye see how one grand dynasty of architecture has succeeded another, the Byzantine giving place to the Lombard, the Lombard to the Gothic, the Gothic to the Saracenic, the Saracenic to the Renaissance. Here, on the contrary, one single order has maintained its own for ten or twelve centuries, — originally an importation from China through Corea. It is the Tartar order, derived, no doubt, in the beginning from the old Tartar tent, with the immense curving and overhanging roof, and often series of roofs, with which every child is familiar from geography pictures of Chinese pagodas. On large buildings this roof is very effective, its great height, great sweep, and the facility it, offers for the ornamentation of its ridge, eaves, and beams, giving it the elements of a distinct and noble form of construction. But what, by degrees, oppresses the mind is the monotony of its repetition, making one often close his eyes to relieve the weary sense with changeful memories of Greek porticos, Roman arches and domes, Gothic aisles and spires. Not only is this Tartar order the one unfailing feature of the temples, but it is equally that of all the feudal castles and keeps remaining for inspection to-day. Mounted on the angles of the immense cyclopean walls that formed the fortifications, the castles are all simple modifications of the Chinese pagoda. Evidently, in this so artistic people there was no spirit of initiative to conceive a new architectural idea; or rather, perhaps, this perpetual repetition is an instructive bit of history, proving the inevitable result of being for ages cut off from contact with any but a stereotyped nation like the Chinese, instead of lying open, as Europe did, to the manifold influences of Egypt, Persia, Phœnicia, Greece, and Rome.

I dwell at some length on this illustration from the architecture of Japan for the sole purpose of emphasizing the simplicity and lack of complexity characteristic of this people. The same principle runs through everything. The traveler's duty is neither to praise nor to blame, but simply to try to comprehend. If a nation has been cut off from the advantage of a liberal education in the humanities at the great world-university, why, then, it has been cut off from such advantage; and all is said. The only fair thing is to weigh and appreciate and be grateful for what they have done with their own opportunities. But this is not the spirit in which so much has been written about Japan. Rousseau's outcry of joy over his discovery of the archetypal, altogether adorable savage who was to regenerate sophisticated Europe by his artless ways, was only a forerunner in effusiveness of the outcry raised over the discovery of Japan. Japan was the original Eden before the Fall, — the Fall in Architecture, Painting, Poetry, Refinement, Instinctive Touch with Nature. *O sancta simplicitas!*

VI. I cannot quit the solemn groves of the Nikko, or, indeed, of any of the great Japanese temples, without a word about their bells, with all the deep, mysterious, mighty murmur of the ocean in them. Wherever one may wander under the giant cryptomerias and among the moss-grown tombs of abbots and monks, the low, rich, powerful undulations of these bells come rolling in on the ear like the sound of harmonizing billows on the shore. Enormous in size and weight, hung in low pagodas but a few feet above the ground, and struck only by ponderous beams of wood swung outside, they are always free of access to any passer-by.

To stand beneath, and in part within, the dome of one of these great bells is an experience for a lifetime. The lightest stroke of a knuckle, and like a vast beehive the ponderous mass is in instant billion-fold molecular vibration. How it hums and hums and hums! How massive, how deep, how sweet, how prolonged, the tone! The ear lingers and lingers on it, and it will not die away. One feels at the soul centre of a vibratory world, from which stream out undulations that set pulsing and throbbing the whole surrounding grove, and whose tremulous wave motions float on and out through a responsive universe. Matter, in every material sense, is dissolved away. With the mind's eye one sees, clearly as did Sir Isaac Newton, that all the atoms of matter that go to make up the solar system might be "shut up in a snuff-box," — so free, so elastic, and such planetary spaces apart do they swing.

Ah, the symbol of our human life heard pulsing here in this great bell! The natures we have revered and loved, because capable of rich, deep, prolonged reverberation, how in the spirit are they drawn about us now! — the souls in whom, gratitude once kindled, sympathy touched, devoutness moved, these divine emotions vibrate on through life. In contrast with this, beings there are whose whole response to the impact of love or sorrow seems but as the petty click of a spoon on the rim of a teacup. Lingering resonance is there none. The momentary click, and all is by; while these deep ones, like the great bells, at each touch of renewing memory hum and reverberate in every spiritual molecule. Devout idolater does one become, as he breathes the prayer, "Oh! for the capacity of long, rich reverberation like thine! Without it, how shallow, how fleeting all human experience." So at least is it murmured in the ear by the deep-hearted bells of Japan.

V.

I. A SINGLE Boston truckman has a vocabulary of vituperation that would more than suffice for the whole city of Tokyo, with its million and a half of inhabitants. As for jinrikisha men here, if they chance to collide abradingly to scalp or skin, they graciously smile on one another as though it were but one more of the amenities of the profession. The most ordinary meetings and partings on the street are accompanied by profound obeisances enough for a court presentation. Externally, then, there are few visible signs of friction. Of the swarms of children, no one evinces the slightest addiction to pulling the hair of another, at any rate in public, and where there is any sanctuary of retirement for doing it in private is more than eye can make out. Amiably the smallest tot of a six-year old girl carries her twenty-pound little brother tied to her back, as though he were born there, so careful of her burden, as she plays ball with her mates, that rarely a collision of shaven heads occurs. To crown all, it has roundly been asserted that even Japanese babies are never guilty of the impropriety of crying. But this is untrue. They do cry, and that lustily. But then, they are so very young! Perfect manners at six months would be an unreasonable expectation even in Japan.

What is the meaning of all this? one begins to ask. Are these people so much kindlier, more considerate, more sympathetic, than we are? For the first week in Japan the new-comer is actually under strong enough illusion to be capable of believing this; so fascinating, so charmingly acted, is the comedy of manners played before his eyes. He recalls our own brusque ways at home, and thinks, "Oh! that we might ever hope to be as innately courteous as these people." The fact is, he has simply knocked the brains out of his judgment on the near bottom through an attempt to dive to profound depths in a pool not over two inches deep. It is the mistake one is forever making in Japan through taking outside for inside, expression for impression.

Americans are too direct, even blunt, in their ways, to know much about the philosophy of acting, especially where the acting is so perfect as to have become a kind of substituted second nature, entirely able to dispense with any original first nature. "If you want to make me weep, you must first weep yourself," said Horace. "Not a bit of it," replies Delsarte, the great authority with modern French actors; "on the contrary, if you want to make me weep, be sure to keep your own eyes dry. Your weeping would spoil all. Train your artistic perceptions, and then attend strictly to the outside presentation. If you can work to such imitative perfection facial muscles, gasping respiration, convulsive action of voice, as to look as though you were suffering, then will you have me, my tender wife, and my ingenuous children, dissolved in floods of tears, even though all the while you are impassive as an oyster, or as cool as a cucumber. Once absolutely master the external signs, and they need no more vital connection with the state of mind within than the false face with which a child convulses with laughter or frightens into hysterics his little mates."

For a thousand years Japan has been under tutelage to an omnipresent Delsarte, working from outside to inside, — or little matter about inside. From Mikado at the top to coolie at the bottom of the social scale, one undeviating standard of manners has been held before the eyes of the most instinctively imitative people on the face of the earth. Originally an importation from China, this standard has been elaborated through centuries of study into ceremonial etiquette which, through constant repetition, has ended by becoming automatic. No one ever saw anything else, no one ever dreamed of anything else. There was one way of saluting a superior, one of saluting an equal, one of saluting an inferior; and anybody's head would have been cut off who should have ventured to depart from it.

From his earliest impressionable years, then, the Japanese child saw nothing but prostrate artisans saluting Samurai, Samurai saluting Daimios, Daimios saluting Shoguns, till the whole ceremonial became organized into him as thoroughly as are their now instinctive habits into our setters and pointers, — perhaps the best-mannered of our own population.

Little girls of ten will one see in good families, whose finish of breeding would have awakened the envy of a duchess at the court of Louis XIV. Female servants will one be lost in marvel over, at a dinner in the house of a Japanese gentleman, whose grace and quiet dignity are the quintessence of lady-like refinement. " Trifles make perfection, but perfection is no trifle," is the motto.

Now if it meant all it says, the angels in heaven could not live up internally to what this code of manners expresses externally. Happily, no one is expected to live up to it internally. It is a purely artistic production, made to gratify the instincts of an artistic people, ceremonially evolved to smooth life of its asperities, to render the comedy agreeable, and to flatter by the perpetual interchange of surface courtesies. The knave goes through its motions quite as creditably as the saint; the liar, thief, or ruffian quite as effectively as the gentle or sincere. Nor is it to be denied that it renders things vastly attractive on the outside, and even exercises a strong inhibiting power over outbreaks of petulance and rude passion. But the moment the mind goes deeper, it is felt at what a frightful cost all this is purchased. It falsifies the nation to the very core. It kills the sense of the relation that should subsist between genuine impression and corresponding expression, and perpetually suggests the idea, "All that is requisite is as good a heart as can be made of a head." Thus, after a while, every man of frank, unconventional nature begins to hate this manner for its false, its shallow, its monotonous excess, and in his wrath to say, " Till the Japanese have worse manners, they will never learn genuine courtesy! Till they get rid of their masks, they will never understand the social charm of the free play of joy, love, sorrow ! "

For all its ceremonial elaboration, the gamut of expression in Japanese manners is a very restricted one, comparing in range and variety with the best European about as a child's one-octave toy piano, with tinkling glass keys, as over against the compass of a Steinway Grand, with its sounding-board and resonant bass and treble. It makes more show at first, while in reality the range of shifting light and shade that lights up with genuine love, humor, intelligence, sympathy, reverence, a fine face with us is in comparison as an orchestra to a tinkling guitar.

This must be so. There is nothing behind the Japanese face — politically, morally, intellectually, reverentially — that can hold a moment's comparison with that which is behind the faces of those who are free-born heirs of our complex, magnificent historical past. Strange ignorance of this is it which has led so many travelers to attribute to the Japanese a depth of quality that in the nature of things, the order of evolution, can in no way belong to them; and until one sees into the simplicity and even monotony — albeit a " monotony of endless variety " — that is characteristic alike of their literature, their poetry, their architecture, their music, their politics, and even of their art, he will never read them with discrimination. They evolved a wonderful miniature civilization, but a miniature one it ever remained till they were brought into contact with races of a higher strain and a grander inheritance, — with what ultimate result, it remains yet to be seen.

II.　Would one form a vivid conception of the ideals with which the aspiring youth of any country fires its heart, there is no better way than to visit the tombs of those canonized as the foremost heroes, sages, or saints of the land. Is one in Italy? Then to the tombs of Dante, St. Francis, Mazzini, let him go. In England? Then to those of Shakespeare, Cromwell, Nelson. In America? Then to those of Washington and Lincoln. For like insight, whither shall one betake himself in Japan? Without question to the graves of the Forty-Seven Ronins, who so loyally and ferociously avenged their Feudal Master. There will he find young men burning incense on a scale as nowhere else. And why? Because the heroic moral standards of Japan are as much bound up with purely feudal ideals as were once those of the Scotch Highlanders, and because of the popular response to the idea that the supreme end of fidelity to the chief sanctifies any means in the way of the most savage cruelty, of wholesale suicide, of the sacrifice even of wifely chastity. Read, in Mitford's Tales of Old Japan, the story of the " Forty-Seven Ronins," as inspiring and as revolting a commingling as the annals of any people can show of magnificent self-abnegation, with tiger cruelty; of the stoical endurance of year-long hunger and outlawry, with capacity to keep at a white heat the fixed fanatical idea of avenging a wrong done a master; yes, and of absolute consecration of wifely love to a husband's honor, along with glorying in the degradation of her womanly purity as a means to subserve his ends. The man who can read this story without high-wrought admiration for such qualities of loyalty, courage, and fathomless contempt of self, has no sense in him of the heroic; as equally the man belongs back in the realm of savagery who does not shudder at such Moloch sacrifice, on a blood-reeking feudal altar, of all other graces and sanctities of life.

Here again we have Japan through and through, the paucity of her ideas, the limitation of her range of emotional response, her incapacity, so far, for the complex and synthetic, as clearly revealed in the narrowness of her heroic moral standard as in the lack of harmonic depth in her tinkling music. The wife of the Scotch Highlander outlawed in the service of his chief would unshrinkingly have faced with her husband starvation on the wintry hills; but once had it come to the issued of degrading her person, to supply him with means to carry out his fell purpose, heroically would she have cried, " Nay! I will stab myself to the heart for you, but pollute myself, even for you, never!" Other test is there none of the scope and elevation of a nation's moral standards than the range and character of the acts that — alike by its wives, its citizens, its soldiers, its tradesmen, its statesmen, even to save home or country — would be spurned in abhorrence.

It was a lovely October afternoon on which my friend and I visited the graves of the Forty-Seven Ronins, the focal heart of the Japan of the near past, as also of its burning present. Overhead arched the great trees, and quietly near by brimmed the clear pool in which, as triumphant avengers, they washed the bloody head of their master's insulter before depositing it on the master's tomb, and then themselves inaugurating a holocaust of harakiri. " After life's fitful fever, they sleep well," while all about stand the great stone lanterns, heaped in their interiors with the ashes of incense-sticks burned as tributes of reverence. Yet in those ashes, I felt, still glowed a devouring fire, with which Japan will have to account. These worshipers, — they are the sons and grandsons of the old Samurai, the former feudal retainers. They are the educated classes of to-day, the leaders in faction politics, the civil and military officers, outwardly changed through a thin veneer of Occidental culture, inwardly the same at heart. Rely on them for splendid courage and self-sacrifice, and you will get it. Rely on them for savage partisanship carried over into the new relations, for a spirit that will stick at nothing, — not at the last extreme of calumny, deceit, brutal violence, assassination, in behalf of their party chiefs, — and equally will you get it;

nay, are already getting it. Not in vain do they burn incense at the graves of the Forty-Seven Ronins. The Forty-Seven Ronins are their national moral ideal, as much as Garibaldi is the Italian's; Nelson, the Englishman's; Lincoln, the American's. Not that there are not noble exceptions, and many of them. I speak of the rank and file.

VI.

I. No form of art has ever become popular, that is, a source of genuine pleasure to large numbers, unless through ideally interpreting to them ideas and sentiments deep-rooted in their own experience. Back of the epoch of the great Greek sculpture were the happy Olympian games, through which thousands were educated to appreciation of all the fine points of a developed human body, and to keen delight in them. Thence the cordial welcome, hailing a beautiful statue. Back of the epoch in Italy of the painting of Perugino and Raphael lay the life and preaching of St. Francis of Assisi, dowering all the hillsides of Umbria with human countenances lit with the same mystic love and rapture which these great masters later transferred to the canvas. Thence the devout greeting of their works. Even where the artist himself did not feel it, the people felt it.

Equally, would the mind surrender itself to the peculiar charm of the painting of Japan, must one first seek to get into living touch with what lies behind it in the common heart, that is, into living touch with a popular naïve enjoyment of nature, as instinctive as the delight of the bird in singing, of the butterfly in palpitating in the sunshine. With us at home there is so much affectation about nature on the part of many who hardly, without yawning, can linger for ten minutes over the loveliest view, as to make it at times a positive relief to come across a man or woman bluntly audacious enough to say, " I hate nature ! " It is not so in Japan. Literally are the Saints' Festival Days the days of the flowering of St. Cherry Blossom, St. Wistaria, St. Lotus, St. Chrysanthemum, the holidays in the Church Year of Nature, when thousands of devotees flock out to worship at these incense-breathing shrines.

On St. Maple Day, when the gold and crimson aureoles of all the saints of this communion are transfiguring with the reflexes of their sheen hill and mountain side, what a spectacle to wander out into the country! Thousands on thousands of people, men, women, and children, are abroad. Forth and back they trudge, perhaps twenty miles, and all to see the tints and dyes of the maples, and to bring home red and gold branches of them. In America, we would think there must be something going on as well worth attention as a fire or a strike. No, it is nothing but the maples, and they furnish æsthetic stimulus enough. How all day long do the people enjoy themselves! Is it any wonder, then, they love an art that renders back to them these happy sensations, and that revives in their breasts such charming memories! Of this art, they ask for no hidden symbolism, no inner mystic interpretation, — ask merely that it shall renew for them their own delight in its original. In their own minds, while in the presence of

nature, all is undefined, floating, sensuous charm.
Let the artist feel this, and give it delicate expression.

II.　　A few themes, with endless variations per-
formed on them, — here lies the essential
characteristic of Japanese art.　But how charming
these variations are!　Many the novelty-hunting
English and American tourist who is heard exclaiming that he is sick to death of cranes, and
would like to take a gun and blaze away at a thousand or more superfluous screens decorated with
them.　This a Japanese could never understand.
To him the crane is the same yesterday, to-day, and
forever.　He enjoys him wading, patting the mud
with his feet, preening his feathers, alighting, rising from the shore, capturing a frog, whirling in
mid-air, and has continued thus to enjoy him for
no end of centuries.　He wants him on his teapot,
his cup, his screen, his match-box, his wall picture,
his wife's dress, his bronze charcoal-burner, his
lacquered box or cloisonné vase.　Too much crane
he cannot have.　And exactly the same is his feeling about lotus flowers, cherry blossoms, chrysanthemums.

Such for ages was the one art demand of the
Buddhist prelates, the Daimios, Shoguns, and Mikados; while the artisan artists, their absolute de-
pendent subjects, lived on the merest pittance, and
devoted whole lives of patience, skill, and naïve delight in natural objects to gratifying the taste of
the only classes who commanded wealth.　With no

hope to rise out of their narrow lot, no stimulus to worldly ambition or covetousness, no distractions to turn them aside to other interests and pleasures, they found their sole enjoyment in art for art's sake, and a little rice or millet to keep alive on. Time was a matter of no importance; for to them there was no meaning in our American phrase, "Time is money." No; time is the leisure spirit, to absorb and brood over impressions, to work them out quietly to perfect expression, to achieve at last something that would please the Daimio. Of high-wrought passion there is in Japanese art no trace: of childlike delight in living close to nature through art, no' end. Dante declared that his verses made him lean. No Japanese could ever say this, or even comprehend its meaning. A sublime poet like Dante, agonizing over such a theme as Hell, Purgatory, and Heaven, might well cry out that it was drinking up his blood and making his flesh to waste away; but the artist, the beginning and end of whose work is to invite one to mere delight with him over the motion of a fish in the water, needs to be but a genial, impressionable child of nature, face to face with brook, tree, and sunshine.

To take in all this, let one visit, for example, the famous Nijo Palace in Kyoto, the palace of the last of the Shoguns of the Tokugawa dynasty. What an historical commentary, the building itself, on the simplicity, the infinite variations on a few themes, of all things Japanese! One story high, and differing no whit in architectural structure from the

plainest artisan's house on the street except in the
immensity of its ranges of apartments, to its rich
and splendid decoration it owes all its distinction.
The same style of framework, only constructed of
rarer woods; the same sliding divisions between
the rooms, only painted by the greatest artists;
the same open-work in the ramma, or ventilation
screens, only here translated into the most fascinating carvings of birds and flowers! Very magnificent is the effect; for the paintings on all four
sides of the rooms, from floor to ceiling, are on a
ground of gold, and the splendor of the lacquer-
work on the beams, together with the marvelous
beauty of their gilded jointures of chased metal,
awakens the sense of a universally diffused glory
of sunshine. And yet in everything is revealed the
Japanese simplicity of sensation. One thing at a
time, and without excitement or hurry.

Wander in imagination, on the other hand,
through the apartments of a European palace, and
recall how in each room attention is distracted by
an endless multiplicity of objects. The paintings
are here a landscape, here a cattle piece, here a
group of figures, here a portrait; and the mind is
exercised with the distressing psychological problem of seeing how many things it can take in at the
same moment without missing any or enjoying any.
How different in the apartments of the Shogun's
palace! Enter one of them, and you find its
pictured walls entirely given up to a single subject,
say, to marvelous delineations of wild geese, —
wild geese swooping down in a flock on a pond, wild

geese startled with fright and beating the water with their wings in their frantic attempt to rise, wild geese floating gracefully on the limpid mirror of the surface, in the double beauty of reflection. Evidently, the subject of interest is wild geese themselves, and not a competition of attraction between them and Cupids, elephants, the battle of Waterloo, and Hamlet improving the occasion of Yorick's skull for moral reflection. Now, the result of all this is a calm, contemplative, wild-goose frame of mind. You become absolutely fascinated over this one realm of nature ; and, if you have a side thought, it is only to wonder why Titian and Raphael should ever have wasted their powers on madonnas, saints, and Venuses, when they might have consecrated them to wild geese.

Again, you enter another room. The artist who here has the whole field to himself is evidently a devout, mystical worshiper of bamboo. " There is but one glory of the vegetable creation, — bamboo ; and I am its prophet," is the substance of his creed ; and in ten minutes he has converted you to the only sound and orthodox faith. Why care any more for riches, honors, luxuries, so long as bamboo exists, " so exquisite in its grace," as the French artist said, " that we can even forgive it for being useful " ? To live, move, and have your being in the mind of such an interpreter of bamboo, — this seems the one unspeakable privilege of life, immediate revelation to you that the sole end of art is to create a soul into you which henceforth shall be one with the lilt of stem and dip and rise of ostrich-plume foliage of such a plant as this.

Here are but a couple of illustrations of hundreds that might be given from this same Nijo Palace. And yet, delightedly as I felt their beauty, had I had along with me a bright, enthusiastic little girl of seven, she would have felt it just as keenly. While, in a Dresden or Florence gallery, she would soon have yawned with weariness over so much beyond her reach of thought and feeling, here she would have taken in everything as naturally as though herself in the woods or on the shore of a lake. Thus becomes clear the reason for the universal popularity of Japanese art, — the reason why, sweeping all before it, it has informed and illumined with its spirit every branch even of the humblest manufacture.

III. Out of all this simplicity and lack of complexity on which I dwell, there grew one admirable result. Poor and rich, ignorant and cultivated, could alike appreciate the kind of art the land brought forth. With people in Europe and America, it would be the sheerest absurdity to say that anything like this is possible. The story runs that Dante once burst into a blacksmith's shop and pounded the blacksmith for presuming to sing one of his own recondite sonnets. Wordsworth, Tennyson, and Browning have their select circle of readers, Raphael and Angelo their esoteric worshipers, the Greek statues their limited groups of sincere appreciators. But outside of such select circles the works of these mighty spirits are severely let alone. No farmer craves the Transfiguration on the side of his teapot, the Laocoön on his cart-harness, or the Prophets and Sibyls of the Sistine Chapel on his wall paper. In Japan, however, the exact reverse holds true. The deepest and most beautiful thing any Japanese artist has produced lies level in its essential spirit with the genuine appreciation of every man, woman, or child who has any fineness of sense-perception, any first-hand joy in nature. Here, I repeat it, is an art that has made itself a universal national possession. The young girl wants its graceful forms and harmonious colors on her skirt and belt; the housewife wants them on her cups, saucers, and tea-caddy. The boy wants them on his kite; the brazier wants them for his pots, the joiner for his open-work carvings. In fine, everbody wants them for everything; and everybody gets them. Go into the cheapest bazaar of three to five cent articles, and they are all stamped with the same sign manual of beauty. The very cakes and confectionery are such exquisite renderings of scarlet maple leaves, or chrysanthemums, that you would vow they had just been picked up in the autumn woods or cut fresh from the plant.

IV. Japan, in its whole extent and with all its countless little islands included, is about as large as North and South Dakota combined. Only one twelfth of its soil is arable, and even that, in large part, solely through the immense artificial system of irrigation, on which depends its rice crop. And yet its population is over forty millions. Divide the possible product of the soil of one twelfth

of North and South Dakota among forty millions
of people, and it is plain what a mouthful it would
give to each.   And yet the country was for centuries hermetically sealed against imports from foreign
countries.   Patient, untiring industry in cultivation
was then the only safeguard against starvation.
So poorly fed a race could not work at a high speed.
It was unfitted for spurts.   It must economize its
forces, and expend them at low pressure only.
Given centuries on centuries of this, and one order
of nervous fibre is determined, as much as, given
fifty years of working high-speed reapers, threshers,
winnowers, and elevators, another sort of fibre has
been developed among us.

With the artisan-artist class the same simplicity
of environment prevailed.   They, too, were poorly
and monotonously fed.   The demand made on them
for the products of their skill had little variety in
it.   From father to son descended the same crafts
and technique, the same simple pleasure in exercis-
ing them.   The patrons, moreover, for whom they
worked were the cultured classes of a race exquisitely endowed with æsthetic judgment.   For century on century every rich temple eagerly added to
its wealth of essentially similar bronzes, lacquer-
work, vestments of brocade, embroideries, screens,
carvings, images, and had its great fire-proof storehouses in which the larger part of its treasures
was laid away.   With the feudal lords the like
passion prevailed.   Every castle boasted its immense ancestral collection of rare and beautiful
objects, from which could be drawn at any time

for inspection vases, porcelains, superb dresses, arms decorated with every delicate fancy of carving or inlaid work. As there were no innovations of new ideas, invention was stimulated simply in the direction of imparting fresh grace and charm to the old.

VII.

I. As a general rule, it will be found that the more dissolute and shameless the life an American, Englishman, or German is leading in Japan, the more conscientiously is he opposed to missions, and the lower in the scale does he rate the motives and character of missionaries. Really pathetic, for example, is it to hear him enlarge on the cruelty of introducing the standards of our severe and ascetic American sisters among these unconscious children of nature, their eyes not yet open to the fatal knowledge of good and evil.

Along with these stanch champions of the primitive Eden before the Fall into the lost innocency of moral distinctions, one encounters another class equally severe on missionaries. It consists of hypersensitive, æsthetic natures, so ethereally organized as to live in perpetual danger of "dying of a rose in aromatic pain." They tremble lest under the hot sirocco breath of the missionary, the aroma will be dispelled from the flower, the dew exhaled from the grass.

As, after the most exhaustive investigation, I could never discover that any representative of either of these classes had ever been near a mission, I was forced to the conclusion that their judgments were either too dissolutely or too æsthetically *a priori* to be entitled to great weight.

There is, of course, a sense in which it is perfectly legitimate for the modern man to hate missions. The old idea of a mission was that of a war of extermination on the part of the votaries of a foreign religion, refusing to recognize anything divine or eternally human in the creeds it had come to supplant. The new idea — the one that is just beginning to dawn on the world — is that of a courteous, loving compassion between two peoples of the faiths and practices that seem to each most sacred. It is founded on sympathy, founded on the recognition of the great historico-divine influences which, through race, situation, institutions, have shaped each nation. It is a simple libel to say that this idea is not largely recognized by the missionaries of to-day to Japan. They were the first to introduce well-ordered schools, broader female education, instruction in medicine, hospitals presided over by men of real science, with a hundred other good things. I say this all the more willingly because, from my tenderest years, I was brought up with a rabid hydrophobia against missionaries that would have staggered the resources of Pasteur. Is there not, then, such a thing as taking a broad, historical view of missions, — as well of their past as their future?

Like every other nation, Japan in the past was indebted to missions for its highest religious and material development. East Indian Buddhism, Chinese Confucianism, these were the great theological and ethical influences that shaped its faiths and codes of conduct. Emphatically as the landing of Gregory IV.'s missionaries in England meant to the then barbaric island contact with Roman civilization and law, contact with Christianity's splendid inheritance through Judæa, Persia, Greece, so, in the far-away past of Japan, the landing of Buddhist monks and Confucian teachers meant contact with the profounder religious conceptions and higher ethical codes of great races, with thousands of years of thought and experience behind them. So has it always been, and so must it continue to be. The race or nation which idly and vainly boasts that it is sole creator of the best it has is only a magnified and monstrous image of the individual man, who, arrogantly calling himself self-made, falls down on his knees and worships his silly little creative self.

Japan has already given an enthusiastic welcome to one class of missionaries — not very disinterested ones, it is true — from the West; that is, to ship-building, railroad-contracting, factory-establishing missionaries. She has ardently received the science, the mechanic arts, the materialistic philosophy of the West; and no wonder it has seemed to her an "Arabian Nights" revelation. But, to confine ourselves simply to the English-speaking nationalities, is this all America and England have to offer, — America and England, who have in their spiritual blood Isaiah, Jesus and Paul, Plato and Aristotle, Marcus Aurelius, Epictetus and Seneca, Newton and Leibnitz, Shakespeare, Phidias, Raphael and Angelo, Kant and Hegel, heroes, divines, sages, and saints innumerable? No man who feels anything of devout gratitude for what all these magnificent influences have been to him can have a moment's hesitation in saying, it would prove an unspeakable boon to any people, never yet in living contact with so grand a hierarchy of powers, to be brought into vital relations with them.

Japan, alas! has cause enough to say, on the score of the brutal international treatment she has received from England — though in a far less degree from America, — "If all your splendid inheritance from the past has made you capable of no nobler spirit than you have showed to us, we want none of it!" In one sense there is no answer to make to such an arraignment. But, in another sense, there is. Nationalities are as yet but big, bullying brutes in their dealings with weaker powers. The higher influences pleaded for have so far lifted individuals rather than corporate masses. But individuals they have lifted by millions. Why, then, should not the most advanced minds among the nations exchange their highest ideals, profoundest thoughts, deepest sentiments, aspirations, and hopes, and so work on sympathetically for a better future?

No historical student who should attempt to compare Japan's inheritance from the past with that of Europe and America could for a moment hesitate as to the enormously richer, higher, and more complex character of the latter. Now, at last, this new-found race of the East aspires to take a place among the active, powerful, progressive

nations of the world.   The day was in the far past
when Germany and England were stirred with the
like impulse; and their end was effected only by
becoming heirs of the culture, order, and religion
of the christianized Roman Empire, with Greece,
Asia Minor, and Egypt behind them.   Why must
not Japan go through some similar leavening process, if she is to take coequal intellectual and spiritual rank?   A grand historical ancestry in the
spirit she must have; and, just as into this ancestry nation after nation in Europe was adopted,
till it became freeborn child by assimilating all that
was best in its culture, so must it be with this new
aspirant among the nations.   The world's highest
achievement is no monopoly, but the common
property of the world.   Did Greece possess it once?
did Judæa possess it once? did Rome possess it
once?   It was but held in trust for Germany,
France, England, against the day when their majority should have come.   Equally is it held in
trust for Japan.

II.   Entirely apart, however, from every question of proselytism, or of the extent of the
conversions to Christianity made by Protestants or
Catholics, — and they are increasingly large, —
no thoughtful observer can fail to recognize the
strength of the reaction that has set in within the
bosom of the Buddhist church itself.   It is a false
idea that Buddhism is dying out in Japan, that is,
among the masses of the people.   On the contrary,
under the stress of Christian competition, it has been
incited to a strong and salutary revival, born of the

stimulus of contact with a more vivid religious faith and with broader humanitarian ideas. As to the government attempt to regalvanize Shintoism, and to enact it into a national cult, it proved an abortive failure. There was nothing vital in Shintoism to regalvanize, unless a low form of hypnotic spiritism rife among the most ignorant. The whole idea of its revival was a sheer antiquarian fad, a politico-religious masquerade in a frippery of worn-out old semi-ecclesiastical clothes.

With Buddhism, however, it was otherwise. It had a deep hold on the popular heart, alike through superstition and through elements in itself of depth and spirituality. Among its monks and abbots are numbered to-day men of the highest birth, the noblest character, and the richest philosophical culture in Japan. There is now building in the city of Tokyo a Hongwangi temple, which in splendor will rival any that Japan ever saw ; and it is a curious fact that, in the work of hauling the beams and other heavy material for its construction, six great sets of cables, — woven entirely of the hair of women who had shorn their locks to dedicate them to this sacred service — have already been worn out, while the seventh set of like cables is in daily use. Certainly this attests in Buddhism the survival at least of a force of capillary attraction that would excite amazement even in a treatise on physics, and which surely were hard to surpass in the annals of any other form of religion.

Yet it is these very women that have thus sacrificed to the temple service their crown of glory, who are to be most deeply benefited by the revival, which European Christianity, with its ineffably higher ideal of woman, is setting on in Buddhism. Dear, gentle, patient beings, they need it, and, by all that is ennobling and enriching, they ought to have it. So ingrained is their sense of the inherent inferiority of their sex, so much is there latent in their sweet, self-sacrificing natures that has had no chance of sympathetic development, so little do they dream of what is hidden in the chivalrous, romantic love of man to woman, that a marvelous revelation is in store for them; yes, and is already breaking, through contact with the womanhood of the Occident.

Here, in truth, in the work of noble Western women yearning and toiling for the intellectual and moral education of young girls, is a leaven that is destined to permeate and uplift the family life of Japan. The best thing now in this family life, the most spontaneous and beautiful, is the love of the little children. Japan is the paradise of childhood. But the paradise of the wife it is not. Not for an hour would a high-souled American woman endure the indignity of the relation as on the average it is found. No wonder then, that, with sensibilities stung to the quick, such women feel it a sacred obligation to strive to lift their sisterhood in the East into the higher realm of dignity and honor in which they themselves live. Truly, in contrast, it is a bit exasperating to read so much that has been written on Japan by Americans, — scientifically keen-eyed, perhaps, but with about the religious endowment of monkeys — on the absurdity and futility of every kind of mission.

VIII.

I.   JAPAN has just now reached her ebullient Sophomore year in the world-university curriculum. No doubt the Sophomore year is a stage of inflation necessary to pass through before arriving at the chastened dignity of the Senior. But it has its temporary perils. Small wonder, then, that at present the Japanese are topheavily overladen with conceit. Only to think of it! How comparatively few the years since the Imperial University of Tokyo was founded under the actual title, "An Institution for Examining into the Writings of the Barbarians," — Newton, La Place, Watt, Lyell, and Darwin, all summed up under that engaging category! Yet already, having squeezed whatever they knew out of German, French, American, English professors, have the Japanese quickly sent home the majority of them, and themselves taken their places; as equally they have done with European railway contractors, civil engineers, ship-builders, and-locomotive builders, and are beginning to do even with Teutonic brewers of lager beer. Did the world ever see the like! Very natural the feeling that they have sucked the whole contents of the Occidental scientific orange and thrown away the skin.

Now, it would be entirely feasible to ship on

board a New England coaster any bright young fellow from Cape Cod, and, putting into his hands a sextant and giving him a short run through Bowditch's Navigator, in a few days, to enable him to take to a hair the schooner's exact position at noon. Quite pardonable in him, moreover, would it be, should he at first see himself in the light of a full-fledged peer of Joshua, who commanded the sun and moon to stand still, and they obeyed him. None the less might not his mind be set down as reverentially incomplete should he fail, on maturer reflection, to admit that the Jacob's wrestle of Copernicus, Newton, and La Place to wrest from the heavens their secret was entitled to a modest share of credit in the success of the observation. Any skilled mechanic can make a sextant, any average intelligent youth use it, but behind it lies a race of intellectual giants and the sublime mathematics of infinite space.

The art of war, the art of naval construction, the art of engineering, the art of organizing common schools, universities, upper and lower houses of legislation, all these have the Japanese borrowed as achieved results from more advanced nations. It has been the most stupendous piece of ab-extra imitation the world ever saw. But have they borrowed at the same time the great germinal minds, the inventive genius, the depth of character, the centuries of political experience, out of which these things have come, and which remain to-day in Europe and America the potency and promise of a vast succession to follow? The golden eggs Japan no doubt has, but has she the prolific intellectual goose to go on laying new ones?

Very superficially as yet does Japan take in this weighty previous question. Dazzled with excess of light reflected from the material triumphs of modern European science, she mistakes this for the whole core of Western greatness and force of character. As she thinks with superior amusement of her old theory of earthquakes, how they were caused by an enormous catfish nine hundred miles long that underlay their main island and every once in a while grew so mortally tired as to have to flop over for relief on to his other side; and as she contrasts this now discarded theory with the complete seismometrical apparatus at the Imperial University for measuring the strength and duration of every shake; very properly is she as proud as the Cape Cod youth handling his new sextant. But what is going to be the outcome of such a sudden revolution from top to bottom of all old ideas and methods, the Japanese will never know until experience shall have made it clear. Europe quietly grew into these ideas, Japan jumped heels over head into them. It is the surface questions they have so far attacked. The scientific broomstick drudge, after the analogy of the old fairy tale, they have set to drawing water, and he is deluging the house with it by the bucketful; but the formula for laying him, before he drowns out the whole family, is another matter.

II. No one can watch the brilliancy and perfection of the evolutions of the Japanese troops, can note her huge ironclads and the steady growth of her commercial marine, can read her newspapers, or catch the spirit of her young men, without feeling, as it were, on the eve of a new crusade. I use the word crusade deliberately. Japan is on fire with the sense of a great historical mission. She is the ordained champion of the new ideas of the West in their advance on the immobility of the East. Not the French, when, after their own revolution, their armies swept irresistibly over the rest of Europe, to destroy the last remnants of Feudalism and to inaugurate the new era of the Rights of Man, were inflamed with a more passionate faith in a special rôle of destiny.

The mercurial temperament has ever proved a factor to be reckoned with in human history — quite as much so as quicksilver in the thermometers and barometers that measure temperature and atmospheric pressure. Again and again, in the story of France, from the days of the Crusades to the days of the French Revolution, has this temperament changed the whole current of European history. Quick to adopt new ideas, and chivalrous in championing them, France has always been the brilliant, even though quicksilver, Abélard of Europe, the intellectual Hotspur. Without the leaven of her ever-fermenting spirit, how much more slowly would have risen the heavier dough of Germany and England! True, she has always had the " faults of her qualities," and bitterly has she suffered from them.

Now very keenly do the Japanese enjoy being called the French of Asia, and not unnaturally, so strikingly similar are their virtues and vices. Not that the Japanese are in any way the national equals of the French. Little do they take it in, what a wealth of historic experience and of the deepest and gravest thought in literature, morals, and religion furnishes the make-weight to Gallic lightness, mockery, and impetuosity. Still, much is there in the old Samurai spirit of Japan — the valor, the patriotism, the artistic courtesy, the loyalty, the contempt of gain — that could easily take the place of the chivalry of France, as equally there is in this same spirit much that would readily lend itself to political experiments of fatal rashness and to factional embroilments of internecine ferocity.

At the same time, along with this quicksilver of the French temperament, the Japanese enjoy the privilege of an insular position that gives them substantially the same advantage in respect to Asia that England has always held in respect to Europe, and which will render them the great naval power of the East. Centuries ago they beheaded the ambassador and destroyed the Invincible Armada of the else irresistible conqueror Genghis Khan; and that, too, at a time when all China and much of India submitted to his power and to that of his successors. Thus, in the Japan of to-day do we see a thoroughly warlike people at a crisis of their history in which they have been fused into a unit in flaming patriotism and in the intoxication of new ideas. In all this lies, I am sure, the prophecy of the coming national Peter the Hermit, who is to launch the new crusade of the long-gathering hosts of Western thought and civilization on the immobility of the East.[1]

III. The Mediterranean has had its great day, and still has it. The Atlantic has had its great day, and still has it. Now is dawning the great day of the Pacific. Face to face with one another, on the opposite sides of this mighty expanse, Japan and the United States, along with Siberian Russia, are destined to play an imperial rôle on the stage of the coming future of Asia. It is only the beginning of things that is witnessed to-day ; but out of the shadowy future already loom vague but overwhelming shapes of movements involving a new destiny for hundreds of millions of people. The United States opened this fifth act

[1] This was written before the outbreak of the Japanese-Chinese war. Nothing in the results that have followed can surprise any one who has studied the situation in the two countries. A fight between Japan and China is like a race between two steamboats, the one with a paddle wheel on either side, the other with a paddle wheel on one side and a clumsy oar on the other. In China everything is mongrel. She has adopted just so much of Western science and civilization as has been temporarily pounded into her by England and France, and despised the rest of it. Japan, on the other hand, has adopted everything to the last military shoestring. Moreover, in China, there is no patriotism and little or no trust between men. The government is rotten to the core. The officer has no faith in his soldier, nor the soldier in his officer, nor has either faith that the report of the numbers, the ammunition, the provisions on hand, are not totally false. This is one of the drawbacks of a system of universal cheating and lying, at any rate when applied to the art of war.

in the great drama of historic humanity when she sent out Commodore Perry with his fleet, to force Japan into the alliance of the nations. Little did she dream what she was doing. Now, however, that it is done, let the two powers cultivate the friendliest of relations, and feel themselves natural and inseparable allies. Above all, outright must it be recognized that the day is past for any longer regarding Japan from the mere sentimental point of view of a land of artistic impressionists. Her artisan class, the most deftly-trained and the most cheaply fed in the world, is soon to render her a truly formidable competitor in the industrial struggle of the nations.

IV. Fascinating has been the experience of a two months' stay in Japan, storing the mind with delightful memories it will always be a happiness to revive. The natural beauties of the land no words can duly praise, — its chains of picturesque mountains everywhere ; its seacoast lines, varied in outline and steeped in as poetic an atmosphere as those of southern Italy ; its luxuriant and profusely varied flora ; its innumerable and commanding temple sites at Tokyo, Kyoto, Navas, everywhere, with their solemn Druid groves. Add to all this ever present beauty of nature, the perpetual open-air comedy going on in the street life of the people, and it will be felt what elements of fascination are ever before the eyes of the traveler in Japan. So little apparent friction in the crowded daily intercourse, such looks of childlike amiability on the faces of the young women! Call these, if you will, only skin-deep, still the skin is about all we see of the great majority of our fellow creatures, and how far pleasanter is it to look at when rippling with smiles than when fretted with careworn or angry lines! In Japan one perforce chimes in with Goethe's line, —

"Am farbigen Abglanz haben wir das Leben."

So, a loving good-by to the Flowery Kingdom, the Land of the Rising Sun, and good-by to all these lucubrations on her past, present, and future! She has broken away from the sleep and stagnation of Asia, has quit the quiet security of her land-locked Inland Sea, and tempted the open main. Welcome to the richer and deeper, the far more awful, far more sublime inheritance of the best in the western world! May she breathe around the sterner elements of this inheritance something of her own ineffable charm!

CHINA

L

I. AFTER being subjected for two months, as in Japan, to an unintermitting stream of novel impressions, what a wonderfully restful experience to feel one's self again at sea! It is like putting a tired child into the cradle, and gently rocking him to sleep, — at least when kindly Nurse Pacific refrains from setting too thumping a Hibernian foot on the rocker and rolling the baby from side to side to the croon of a typhoon. No loving mother, however, could have been more gentle with treadle and lullaby than the Pacific with us, all the way from Nagasaki, Japan, to Shanghai, China, and all the way from Shanghai to Hong Kong. Oh, the boon, each day, of the quiet monotony of the sea, unbroken by the intrusion of a whale or a porpoise! How it sponges up all nervously irritating brain impressions, and holds them in neutral solution! Indeed, a sea voyage round the world, all the way by land, would result in chronic insomnia. So blessings on the man who first invented for the globetrotter's sanity the sleep of the China Sea after Japan!

II. In Shanghai we stopped but twenty-four hours. This was long enough, however, to furnish a few first-hand impressions of the more salient points of difference between the Chinese and the Japanese. In Japan one is perpetually interested in observing the ways in which the race has worked up into its own shapes the ideas, manners, arts, manufactures, the architecture, philosophy, and religion, originally derived from China through Corea. Now at last the chance to see a little of the rock from which these Japanese people were intellectually and religiously hewn! A rock, in fact, it is in comparison with the sinuous, sparkling, restlessly mobile waters that have ebbed and flowed round it for centuries in the Land of the Rising Sun. Indeed, striking as is the contrast one feels the first time he crosses the Channel from France to England, between the lithe, vivacious, socially charming characteristics of the one people and the more heavily moulded and undemonstrative nature of the other, far greater is the contrast experienced on first setting foot on the soil of China, after a run of thirty hours from Japan.

In our own country we see but one variety of the Chinaman, — the laundry variety, taken from the lowest class of the indoor coolies, and cowed, too, at that, by the democratic exuberance of our hoodlums. He is no more like the breed at home than if he had been boiled along with the shirts in one of his own laundry-vats, and lifted out on a stick shrunk and dripping. In his own land John Chinaman is a big, portly fellow, who walks as though he owned the earth. He could swallow an average Japanese without looking larger. Vanity and conceit are no part of him, as they are of the Japanese. Indeed, vanity and conceit imply a measure of dependence on the estimate of others. For four thousand years the Chinaman has lived above this weakness, in an indomitable fortress of pride. Realities are simply realities. Ages before the European emerged from the lowest barbarism, if, indeed, he has yet emerged from it, the China-man knew everything and possessed everything worth having. He has simply to repeat the past, as the planets their revolutions. As for Confucius, he had looked into the whole matter of railroads, telegraph lines, and the spinning-jenny, forty cen-turies back, and dismissed them as beneath con-tempt.

Now, in this light-minded world of ours, it is very instructive to fall in with something thorough-bred, to see a fundamental principle, like that of the " wisdom of our ancestors," stoutly mounted, and then ridden, spite of wall or ditch, straight across country to its last break-neck logical conse-quences. At home in America, we pride ourselves on having evolved certain very creditably ossified types of the conservative, — now in a sporadic pro-fessor, now in a high and dry divine, here in an Anglomaniac member of an exclusive club. In China, the most obstinately-rooted of these, from Boston or New York, would be set up on steeples for weathercocks, the only function such variable creatures would be thought fit for.

Never the doggedest aider and abettor of the past with us, but inconsistently he will abandon the whole principle by giving in to lucifer matches superseding the flint and tinder box, to gas invading the sacred realm of whale oil, or, finally to the electric light advancing on the more ancient reign of gas.   Dignify such thistledown mobility with the august title of conservatism! No! there is but one portrait of an Occidental conservative that would awaken in the breast of a Chinaman an emotion of respect.   It was a caricature that was drawn fifty years ago in Vienna, in which, on the Day of Creation, Prince Metternich was depicted wringing his hands in agony and supplicating Deity, "O God, let us preserve the Chaos!"   The Chinese would have taken this caricature in perfect seriousness, and have set it up in a temple for the edification of the young.

Custom, then, in China, the thing that has been, is the one immutable law of the universe, to be respected as one respects summer and winter, night and day.   Do you foreigners cavil that our streets are filthy and pestilential?   It is not our custom to clean and deodorize them.   Do you insinuate that our frightful famines and inundations might be stopped? It is not our custom to stop famines and inundations.   Far rather would we die of hunger or be drowned out like rats than insult the wisdom of our ancestors by such reflections on their time-honored ways. Budge, then, the Chinaman will not, more than a granite boulder, unless pried out with fulcrum and crowbar.   Here at last, thank Heaven! the philosophic tourist, weary of such pitiful will-o'-the-wisps as we have at home, contemplates something as stable in comparison as a fixed star to a flighty comet, a wood-tick to a devil's darning-needle.

III. For fifty miles before reaching the northerly coast of China, one feels himself already developing a fairly "continental consciousness." It is stirred up from the depths of one's being in sympathy with the mud of the Yang-tse-Kiang River, poured out on so stupendous a scale as to lay down, in vast realms of oozy flats, the prophetic foundations of a future rice-paradise for millions, and still further to spread its turbid flood over countless square miles of otherwise bright blue sea. The eye looks on with awe at so enormous a process of world-building. Nothing, one feels, but a vast continent, with far-away ranges of colossal mountain chains, mighty river systems thousands of miles in length, can furnish the material for such work as this. Bread enough to feed four hundred millions of mouths, and all this fertilizing mud to spare ! surely this must be China !

Sailing up one of the streams of the immense delta, stretching along the coast a hundred miles, our steamship anchored off Wusung to take in cargo, while her passengers in a little steam-launch ran up the river fourteen miles farther to Shang-hai.

IV. Europe and China hobnobbing ! such is the scene Shanghai presents ; only that the hobnobbing is done arms-length, centuries-length, race-length apart. Here, on the one hand, a beautiful European city; open to breeze and sunshine; with stately buildings and lovely gardens; its broad, park-like quay, shaded with rows of trees, running along the river, and everything breathing sweet and healthful air! There, on the other hand, a Chinese walled town of 200,000 inhabitants, its streets narrow and filthy, its people pigging in together in tenements which are perpetual breeding-places of disease! Cheek by jowl, for fifty years have stood these two cities; the one steadily aspiring after growing beauty, comfort, healthfulness, the other serenely satisfied with its aboriginal perfection. Shakespeare and the Chinese are at one in the feeling that —

> "To gild refined gold, to paint the lily,
> To throw a perfume on the violet, . . .
> Is wastefuf and ridiculous excess."

As over against two such authorities, far be it from me to express a personal judgment. I am a simple reporter of impressions, a disinterested observer of the ways of my fellow-creatures, as they have been subjected to their varying planetary development. All I see is the reason why these two cities have not exerted a whit of perceptible influence on one another. The English, French, and Germans still follow their own ever-changing methods. If there is a new and promising-anti-cholera mixture, they take doses of it, to decide which is the better man, cholera or mixture; a new germ-killing disinfectant, they set on a free fight between it and microbes; a new astronomical or metaphysical theory of the universe, they import the book describing it, and here and there one of them, perhaps, reads it. Of all this freakiness of the innovating temperament, scarcely a trace in China town! Foul smells, cholera, bacteria, have their prescriptive rights to be treated in accordance with the wisdom of our ancestors, and are so treated, to the mutual satisfaction, apparently, of germ and human germinator, as they develop amicably together. So long, then, as the two have mastered the art of thus living in happy concord, why inaugurate between them the internecine warfare set on by the Englishman?

Now, to one just arrived from Japan, here is a vastly instructive sight in the way of comparative historical study. Through the force of a precisely similar object lesson, the same fifty years in which all this has been going on in Shanghai have revolutionized the other country. The moment the Japanese got a chance to see a better thing in the way of disinfectant, Herbert Spencer Scott's Emulsion of Cod Liver Oil, astronomical observatory for studying the real motions of the celestial bodies, they adopted it. Peremptorily, on the other hand, the Chinese despised and rejected it, on the absolute ground that no good thing could come out of the Nazareth of " outside barbarians " and " foreign devils." Their logic was perfect, though their premise may have been an instance of too hasty induction.

Contempt is a dangerous, though no doubt a soothing quality. Not that the Europeans do not

entertain it liberally toward the Chinese.   But the
return contempt of the Chinese in their pig-sty city
for the dwellers in the clean, beautiful European
city is, in comparison, colossally vaster.   It is a
contempt Atlas in height, continental in breadth,
oceanic in depth,— a contempt in sæcula sæculo-
rum.   One is awed by it.   One yearns for a mas-
siveness of nature capable of so Mt. Blanc a solidity of contempt-sensation.   I repeat it, something
sublime is there in beholding for once the virtue of
conservatism developed to Himalayan proportions.
If Confucius really did this, all of himself, then I
rank him next to the law of gravitation.

V.   Kind, though no doubt nationally preju-
diced friends in Shanghai had strongly
advised my friend and me not to attempt an exploration of the Chinese city.   They said it was sometimes perilous to life and limb, and at all times an
exposure to infectious disease, and that for twenty
years they had not thrust their own noses inside
the walls.   None the less we went, and went
alone, — with reprehensible traces in our breasts,
I fear, of that physical contempt for Chinese
prowess engendered in the American mind by home
contact with none but the bleached-out laundry
species.   For hours we strayed at our own sweet
will, penetrating all quarters, and frequently getting hopelessly lost, only at last to find ourselves
again.   The tastelessness and ugliness of the scene
to one fresh from Japan was the main impression
the sordid materialism of aspect everything wore.

No doubt there were plenty of good, patient, excellent people there. No doubt there was many a learned pundit ruminating the Chinese classics in many a house we passed, and, let us hope, thanking Heaven he was not as either of those two " foreign-devils " going by. Still, no use is there in attempting to account for Chinese Shanghai on the score of its being a seaport town, corrupted by the imitation of foreign manners and vices. The trouble with it is that it has imitated nothing, has kept itself so simon pure in its ancestral nastiness.

None the less, how strong and cheerful the people looked! What an effective system here on hand for killing off the sickly and feeble, and leaving none but the cholera and small-pox-proof! The survival of the fittest for standing such conditions of foul air, crowded quarters, barbaric medical treatment, such was the principle of natural selection palpably at work. Still, one man's meat is another man's poison; as equally experiments in natural selection require successive generations to work in. So at last my friend and I began to doubt our personal fitness to survive much longer. The one predominant feeling with us both, as we emerged from the gate, was a longing to be hung out for a month on a clothes-line, in a gale of wind. Carbolic acid and chloride of lime seemed perfumes of a rarer fragrance than heliotrope or tea roses.

VI. However, a drive of several hours out into the country now effected an aeration quite as brisk as hanging out on a clothes-line, along

with wider advantages for enjoying scenery. Very
depressing the aspect, it must be admitted, that is
imparted to the immediate surroundings of this
especial Chinese city by the enormous stretches
given up to burial-places for the dead. Here, if
anywhere in China, — especially when it is recalled that ancestor worship is the devoutest form
of religion that prevails, — one would look for some
imaginative expression of sentiment, some touch of
beauty or ideality, as in all the cemeteries of Japan,
where a like ancestral faith is rife. No suggestion
is there of any craving akin to this. Few or no
trees, no charm of greensward and constant floral
offerings, no venerable moss-grown monuments,
nothing but low mounds of naked or weed-grown
soil, and these by the million! Perforce, one calls
up the endless stretches of prairie-dog burrows on
the Colorado and Montana plains, only to be filled
with the same dazed wonder there evoked as to
how each several prairie-dog household ever contrives to feel sure of its own domestic hole. With
such back-lying successions of departed ancestors
to keep in ever green remembrance, it must be a
liberal education in itself to know just where to
find them.

Once, however, out beyond these dreary wastes,
there opens up a sight that cannot but inspire deep
reverence for China. The marvelous cultivation,
the patient, untiring industry that wrings the bread
of millions out of the soil of these vast river bot-
toms, the cheerfulness and solid, practical good
sense of the farming people here is something to

call out deep-rooted respect for millions of human beings under such stern stress of the law, "In the sweat of thy face shalt thou eat bread, till thou return unto the ground."

No wonder these people are averse to change! They have reached a state of stable equilibrium. They have got adjusted like the patient ox to the yoke, know just where it presses and how best to ease it, and do not want to be readjusted to a new-fangled one. Century-old products of these monotonous levels, these sluggish rivers and canals, these uniform methods of cultivation, their muscles have become solidly set to a plodding gait and their brains to a gait equally plodding. Expatiate, if you will, to a heavily moulded plough horse on the exhilaration felt by the fast trotter, and invite him on to the track to share it! The plough horse might be misguided enough to make a spurt for twenty rods. Far more settled in his solid muscular convictions, the plodding Chinese countryman!

No! to do over again the same old thing in the same old way, to think over again the same old maxim in the same old way, this is to "possess the earth." Nerves have they none. Of the heights of ecstasy, the abysses of despair, these modern physiological inventions entail on other unfortunate people, they are stolidly oblivious. They can sleep under a lullaby of gongs, and with wide-open mouths full of meandering flies. What big bodies and big bowling-alley-ball heads of real lignum-vitæ texture! While European nations are exhausting in excitement their nervous energies, these fellows are storing theirs up ; lying fallow a few thousand years, as did our vast western prairies against the grain crops that should one day be demanded of them. True, their existence now is commonplace and matter of fact, largely devoid of ideality, devoid of imagination. Of anything like the life of chivalrous love for woman, of consecration to an ideal of a great future for humanity, they know little and care less. Still, one cannot but feel there is latent in them the stuff of a giant future, after once the mighty throes of revolution that are at hand shall have steeped them in scalding tears and chilled them in icy waters and forged them under the trip-hammer blows of sure-coming destiny.

VII. Out there, far down the river, as we are driving back, we see looming up a huge ironclad. It is Chinese. On the river-bank, farther yet below, stretch the long lines of a powerful modern fort. It is Chinese. What do these mean ? They mean that a power mightier even than century-old Chinese conservatism is on the field, that Europe has already invaded and partially conquered China with the ideas of a new age. True, these ideas had to be driven home by the thunderbolt of war. They were never accepted of free choice, as in Japan. When England and France destroyed China's fleets of junks, took Canton, took Pekin, then China had to begin to think on new lines, had to submit to the crowbar prying out some of the sullen, dogmatic boulders deep sunk in the tenacious soil of her mind. Hauling down the imperial flag from the Pekin palace was as nothing to hauling down the flag of the century-old monomania of ancestral pride. But down it had to come; and perforce China sent to Europe for military engineers, ship-builders, drill-masters for her troops. Forts were constructed, arsenals and ship-yards founded, schools of instruction established, — only of course to be suffered to fall into gradual decay. None the less the iron wedge of destiny had entered, and begun to split rifts in the tough old gnarled log. And now to all this is added the terrible gadfly of Japan anchored just off her coasts; the gadfly become a hornet on a mission, with all the modern scientific apparatus at its tail's end for stinging home the inflammation of the new ideas. One stands hushed in awe to reflect on what all this inevitably involves in the future of four hundred million people.

I. IT was a charming run of three days from Shanghai, and never before in life did I chant more rapturously the rarely quoted line of Gray, " Where ignorance is bliss," than on sailing at sunrise through the strait that winds its picturesque way into Hong Kong harbor. About the island of Hong Kong, whether it was flat or perpendicular, prosaic or picturesque, I knew absolutely nothing. Suddenly, however, on stepping out on deck, what should be the revelation but a magnificent archipelago of islands like Mt. Deserts, though on a hundredfold grander scale! One could have weeded out a dozen Mt. Deserts without leaving the marine paradise before the eyes a whit less attractive. Then came the sail through the strait, a mile to two miles in width, and shut in on either hand by mountains. The coloring was indescribably beautiful. Largely naked of vegetation, their tops covered with dry bamboo grass, and their flanks a mingling of red granite and of red, yellow, and whitish clays and gravels, they fairly palpitated in the glow of the semi-tropical sun. Indeed, as I later found, this vivid glow characterizes the aspect of the mountains all day long. Look out over the harbor, even at noon, and you would think the ranges, completely environing it, were steeped in warm sunset light. At home we find fault with our sunsets, beautiful as they are while they last, because just as we are fairly yielding ourselves to the rapture of them, the curtain is rung down and they are gone. Here in Hong Kong this little æsthetic objection is removed by keeping them flushed and aglow all day long. Perhaps, in China, even sunsets have grown conservative, and dislike to change.

Once through the strait and into the harbor, the city itself is another delightful surprise. With only a narrow selvage of level ground along the water, its houses, many of them spacious and noble mansions, with beautiful gardens, rise, terrace on terrace, up the flank of an abrupt mountain, eighteen hundred feet high, it topmost summit crowned with villas and hotels in which Europeans seek refuge from the overpowering heat of the summer. One would think himself in Genoa, so strikingly similar is the architectural effect.

Only forty years ago this beautiful island was a nest of Chinese pirates. Even at a far later date, a European took his life in his hand if he ventured alone a mile out of the settlement, or embarked at night in a *sampan* for his ship. To-day, in charming contrast, the most blind-drunk sailor, with just consciousness enough left to know he wants to be rowed out and put aboard at midnight, has the ægis of his country lovingly extended over him in the shape of a gilt-buttoned official taking the number of the *sampan*, giving it just fifteen minutes to get back, and, in event of an instant's over-stay, firing a signal that forthwith sets the harbor swarming with armed launches. Thus by one electric flash of the higher civilization is murder discouraged in the Chinaman, and the mind of the European seafaring man relieved from the cor-rosion of anxiety as to just how much it may be wisest to drink ashore. Why the superiority of such a system is not immediately apparent to the Celestial mind is a standing marvel. And yet the sampan-scullers still insist that the older way was the better.

Very curious does it seem, indeed quite inter-national, to find that the policemen in Hong Kong are big red-turbaned Sikhs from India. It gives one a fresh conception of the resources England has to draw on. Equally curious is it to inspect the immense Chinese quarter of the city, with nearly a quarter of a million of inhabitants, and to see how much in the way of wider streets, sweeter sanitation, and the subjection of small-pox to the quill is possible. Not that it will do to make too hasty an induction that this is one proof more that the "quill is mightier than the sword," for here the two divide the honors. The quill has a hilt and a strong arm behind it to drive it in. "*Hinc illæ lachrymæ*" when the British doctors go round; along with some savage fights for "the wisdom of our ancestors." But Hong Kong be-longs to England, and here the "foreign devil" has his own "outside barbarian" will.

II. Canton lies ninety-five miles away from Hong Kong, up an enormous river, which — for fear of misspelling it, should I attempt the Chinese name — I will call, as the English do, the Canton River. We embarked at five P. M. on a fair-sized steamboat, the lower deck of which was littered with a swarm of third-class Chinese, pigging in together ; while the upper deck was set apart, forward for respectable Chinese, and aft for Europeans. The respectable Chinese furnished their own bedding and opium, and lay, cheek by jowl, beside one another ; while the Europeans had state-rooms to themselves, with soap, towels, and other foreign prejudices.

Scarcely had we started when an American lady came up to me in anxiety, and asked, " What's the reason there is a sword in my room ? " Indeed, pistols and rifles were everywhere lying around handy ; but the lady in question, who had never at home observed on the Fall River boats this especial kind of life-saving apparatus, seemed greatly nonplussed. So, to relieve her feelings, I was forced to tell her that the sword was for her to defend herself with to the last gasp, if the Chinese should attempt to seize the boat, murder the passengers, and loot their trunks : further calling her attention to certain strong iron gratings that had been let down and clamped over the gangways from the lower to the upper deck. She at once became composed, as the New England woman always is when she learns the reason why.

These little preliminaries were not indications of

a purely sportive fancy on the part of our captain.
Many the steamboat that has been served this turn
by pirates in the guise of passengers, the last instance occurring but two years ago. Our own trip,
however, proved entirely uneventful; and we could
only hope that the swarm on the lower deck had
not had their feelings unduly hurt by the seeming
distrust implied in the iron gratings. Still, it was
to be set down as another agreeable and romantic
surprise to find piracy still so rife in these waters,
and to learn how many desperate encounters,
involving the destruction of whole fleets of pirati-
cal junks, it had taken to bring matters even to
so comparative a state of safety as the present.
Indeed, in Canton itself I found the native river
passenger-boats — stern-wheelers, worked not by
steam power, but by the leg power of coolies on
a treadmill — were armed to the teeth with cannon
and smaller arms in the way of cutlasses and guns.
It seemed odd to think of such a state of things
existing on the interior water-ways of a vast empire, until I began to ask myself how long ago
it was since Dick Turpin was distinguishing himself in the immediate neighborhood of London by
overhauling reverend bishop on Hounslow Heath.
Furthermore, one of our party made disagreeable
allusions to holding up trains and looting their
passengers on some of our own American railways.
But these last are only infrequent interludes, when
the cowboys are feeling a little playful. Here they
are the chronic thing.

III. Never to be forgotten is the scene presented by the Canton River population. Here in their *sampans* and larger boats are born, live, and die a quarter of a million of people. They have no dwelling-place ashore. A diminutive section of the stern of the boat, covered with a matting, and often not over seven feet by four, is parlor, kitchen, bedroom, birth-chamber, death-chamber, of the whole family. With her baby tied on her back, the mother sweeps the heavy scull, while the older children take as naturally to the oar as ducks to their web-feet. Indeed, the women, as a general rule, command the boat, steer it, and make the bargains. As the phrase runs, "She bosses the boat, and her husband bosses her." But boss the boat she does, and a delectable sight it is to watch her skill. A ripple of indication that there is a fare of any kind, and fifty *sampans* dash for the spot like a flight of Florida turkey-buzzards suddenly cognizant of a dead dog. The mêlée that ensues is simply indescribable. Babies' heads, on the backs of their mothers, rolls round like a planetary system of bowling-alley balls, the centripetal force, however, so exactly balancing the centrifugal as to prevent their flying off into space. *Sampans* clash, thrust, and lever one another. The smaller children sit, or are jounced, in patient, impassive, Oriental imperturbability, while the father and the older ones poke with bamboo poles or fling themselves on their backs and skillfully kick at critical stages of the maternal tactics. Each family is a coöperative unit, for success means rice or no rice. Thus for miles the surface of the great river seems one successive human ant-heap, wriggling, with bamboo poles for antennæ and oars for nimble legs.

IV. Arriving as we did in Canton at the break of day, we had the best of chances to witness the religious devotions of the countless river swarm, consisting in the discharge of fire-crackers from each separate boat, to scare away the devils. Never before had we seen on so impressive a scale the practical application of the maxim, " Fight the devil with fire ! " and the spectacle inevitably led to certain profound speculations on the relation between business and religion. To supply the needful missals and breviaries for the morning devotions of such millions, the manufacture of fire-crackers in China must be on an absolutely colossal scale. Imagination refuses to grasp the numbers of powder and paper mills thus literally " rooted and grounded in the faith." Should foreign missionaries convert the millions of their customers to a creed prescribing a less noisy and more inward form of morning worship, total financial ruin would at once stare no end of manufacturers and workmen in the face. Forthwith would they band together to a man to destroy in blood the " execrable superstition." New and vivid light thus broke on Saint Paul's rough experience in Ephesus with the makers of images of Diana, till, just as the streets of that city rang with the cry, " Great is Diana of the Ephesians ! " so one seemed to hear all over China a mob of ferocious voices shouting, "Great is the Fire-cracker as a Devil Fighter!"

To see a familiar Scripture passage — worn so threadbare by repetition in the common pulpit — thus suddenly lighted up with such a blaze of fire and bang of emphasis, acts as a powerful imaginative stimulant to the traditional mind. Besides, it enlarges charity. If as sympathetic a tear as Laurence Sterne could shed comes stealing down the cheek for the ruined paper and powder manufacturers of China, why should it be thought unchristian to indulge in another as genuine over Alexander the coppersmith, and his poor fellow-craftsmen in Ephesus? Nay, were it venturing on a yet more reprehensible latitudinarianism of stricture to aver that even the little tots of the Chinese children on the *sampans* evinced a liveliness of interest in the morning devotions, not always manifest in those of the same immature age at family worship at home? Yet, we are forever insisting on the supreme importance of making religion attractive to the young.

V. In Canton, we were to be the guests of old and dear American friends, living in the large and beautiful park, the Shamien, the concession ceded by the Chinese government for the residence quarter of foreigners. This park, a mile and a quarter in circumference and surrounded on all sides by the river and by wide canals, makes a little bit of heaven in contrast with the crowding and squalor of the city within the walls. To it we were rowed down through the hurly-burly of the river, and oh! the blessed change of getting extricated from the mob of boats, mounting the steps of the high stone wall, and finding ourselves greeted under the banyan-trees, and again in the big, wide-verandahed, hospitable house, by such true-hearted friends.   Breakfast announced, how eagerly we fall to work discussing a tender beefsteak and still tenderer memories of loved ones at home!   Beautiful as the lotus flowering out of the mud, such, and more than such, the sight, out of the mud of the relation between man and woman in China, of a loving American husband and wife, and a bevy of sweet children to kiss.

No doubt the grace of charity is a beautiful thing, but ever with the proviso that a line is somewhere drawn between it and self-stultification.   It does not, then, seem to me invidious to say that the man who has ever had a mother, sisters, a wife, daughters, and lived with them in the richer, deeper relations habitual among ourselves, who does not start back as before an abyss of spiritual brutality at the contemplation of what, in comparison, even the ideal of these relations stands for in China, is simply to be ruled out of court as incompetent to express any comparative social judgment.   Not that there need be one whit of praise or blame, one ascription of personal merit or demerit in such judgments, more than in comparing a rose with a cabbage.   None the less there breathes an atmosphere of sentiment around the one that is wanting in the other; and just this prosaic lack of any atmosphere of sentiment is what makes China the cabbage of the nations.

VI. Breakfast over, we found that ample provision had been made by our host for our exploration of Canton. Four chairs on long bamboo poles, with three coolies apiece to bear them on their shoulders, stood ready, — one for the guide, one for our host, and one each for my friend and myself. Soon we were mounted aloft, and away trotted our coolies out through the leafy Eden of Shamien into the Inferno of Canton. On entering the walls of the city I took it for granted that the inscription over the gateway must read, "All hope abandon, ye who enter here!"

It is useless to try to describe an experience of seven hours within the walls of Canton. The thing must be seen, heard, felt, and smelt. I desire to do absolute justice to this mighty city of a million inhabitants, the Paris of China, as it has been called, and so freely admit at the outset that Shanghai seemed to me to bear off the honors in the variety and differentiation of nauseous smells engendered. In Canton the effect produced is, if I may use the term, more composite, — a blending of all the varieties in one heavy, fetid odor, akin, I take it, in an inverse way, to what is aimed at by French chemists in the perfume called "Mille Fleurs." But analysis is useless in such cases. I can only say that the smell of Canton is more massive, more metropolitan.

Even in our sparsely settled country, it is often

said that there are too many people in the world. Ah! to what nightmare dimensions the sense of this grows in Canton! The streets are from five to eight feet wide, the houses on either side are high, the slit of sky above is shut out by mattings, and the throngs pouring along are ceaseless, repulsive-looking, offensive to the touch. Of course, we, lifted on high on the shoulders of our coolies, escaped the push and elbowing, and, like the gods on Olympus, could look down serenely on the steaming, struggling humànity beneath us. Now and then we would meet the chair of some other Olympian mandarin like ourselves, coming the other way; and then the question of squeezing by threatened to become international.

Such, in outward aspects, was for hours our passage through the enormous city. There were few open squares, no park oases of trees, flowers, and water, no fine architectural effects, no ample and beautiful temple grounds. The largest open area embraced the dwelling and gardens of the former Manchu governor, which the English, on taking Canton, had insisted should be ceded, in token of submission, as the site of their own consulate. Perhaps the next area in size surrounded the Temple of Horrors, full of life-sized figures undergoing the tortures of the Buddhist hell, an area so crowded with hucksters, fortune-tellers, gamblers, beggars, and thieves as to elicit from my friend the remark that the " hell outside was as striking as the hell within." But we had made up our minds to do Canton, declining no invitation to go anywhere but

to the execution grounds to see some heads chopped
off. To the vermin-ridden prisons we did go, in
which among other wretched beings in heavy chains,
we saw one poor woman enduring a ten years' sentence. On my asking a high civil official what had
been her offense, he answered that it was because
her son had committed murder. Whereat, to my
further query as to why *she* was thus punished for
his crime, he replied, " Because she did not give
him better advice." This seemed to me the patri-
archal system of China with a vengeance. I may
have drawn a wrong inference from the words, but
do not think I did, as the law-officer spoke admirable English, and seemed to think the reason ought to
satisfy any rational mind, as it failed to mine, for
lack, no doubt, of a due sense of my own mother's
responsibility for all the scurvy things I have done
in life.

And yet, in contrast with all this outward ugliness, what a different world was opened upon visiting one after another a series of the little manufac-
tory shops. Oh, the exquisite silks and satins that
were unrolled, the fairy-like ivory carvings that
were brought out, the delicate filigree work in gold
and silver, the beautiful embroideries we saw growing under deft fingers before our eyes! The bronzes,
the porcelains, so marvelously finished, so harmonious in tints and dyes! And to reflect that all
this had been going on centuries ago as to-day, going on when we as peoples were sunk in barbarism!
What a beehive of industry the mighty city! What
legions of patient, cunning, tasteful craftsmen,

working their twelve and fifteen hours a day!
What temperamental phlegm of calm in every fibre
of body and mind, along with such quiet cheerfulness !

True, there is no indication of any high spiritual ideals of the beautiful or of the sublime in
the models they so deftly imitate. Again, as in
Japan, comes the thought " Great in little things,
little in great."   While in Greece and in Grecized
Italy, hosts of just as clever workmen reproduced
in endless number the statues of Phidias and
Praxiteles, the paintings of Apelles, till the poorest
households possessed them in niches and on their
painted walls, here nothing is reproduced but nests
of carved ivory balls delicate as gossamer, graceful designs in lacquer, grotesque dragon shapes
in bronze, wavy sheens in silk.   The contrast is not
raised for censure, but for clearness of impression.
China never evolved anything in the shape of an
artist sublimely inspired in thought or imagination.
Prosaic in the presence of this higher world, what
poetry she has works itself off in pretty and grotesque fancies.   The great models of a nation, not
its skillful imitators, is it that determine its standing in the realms of art, literature, philosophy, and
religion.

VII. No sight in all Canton is so full of interest
and so explains the genius, or rather lack of
original genius, of this mighty nation, as what, for
want of a better expression, might be called the
Examination Halls of the countless candidates for

positions in the civil service, the one opening to a career in China, from the grade of the most ordinary functionary to that of prime minister. China has no hereditary nobility. The highest place is free to the lowest man, and all through education. An ideal programme truly ! — if carried out in the spirit as well as in the flesh.

To call up before the untraveled American a vivid picture of the Examination Halls of Canton, the most practical thing would be to refer him point blank to the cattle-yards of Chicago, covering with their acres on acres of pens such vast areas of space. Then, should he mentally subtract from each several pen its ox, and substitute for him a Chinaman with ink and hair-pencil and paper, he will realize the whole scene as distinctly as if he were on the spot in China. In Canton, there are 12,000 of these pens, one for each of the 12,000 candidates. In this he is shut up by himself for three days and three nights, then let out for three, then returned for three more, at the end of which time he is supposed to have written out all the answers to the examination papers. Not infrequently a candidate is found to have died in his pen of anxiety and exhaustion; but there are plenty to take his place. Indeed, fairly appalling is the stress of competition. Sometimes, out of the 12,000, not over one or two hundred pass the ordeal which enrolls them among the literati, and renders them eligible to place in the public service. Still, the contest is renewed, till it is no very uncommon thing to find men of over eighty, and at times of over ninety, once again volunteering in the forlorn hope. The mind is awed at an illustration of the struggle for life on a scale as stupendous in the world of letters as that of the codfish and herring for survival in the sea.

What, however, is the nature of this terrible ordeal .through which the successful candidate must pass? In what classes of studies is he examined, and with what probable results on intellect, character, imagination, and ideal of life? The Chinese classics, the work of national sages who lived thousands of years ago — these, with the enormous commentaries on them, are the fountain-heads of knowledge from which the candidate is supposed to derive all his light. Great men were these sages, who digested many a pregnant thought, but who along with this elaborated a system of ceremonialism in manners so vast and intricate, a labyrinth of artificial formalism so confusing, that it is the study of a lifetime to know just what to do and what not to do on each public or private occasion, while yet it is civil and moral death to fail to know it. Fifty French dancing-masters condensed into one would remain a composite untutored barbarian in etiquette, in comparison with what is demanded of an average Chinese candidate. Memory is, then, the one intellectual faculty that counts most. The slightest departure from prescription, worse than a crime, is a ceremonial blunder, and a ceremonial blunder outweighs in deep-dyed guilt a whole catalogue of crimes.

Here, then, is a principle of natural selection

that weeds out from the start all variations from the permanent specific type. Variations are the black sheep of the flock, to be killed off outright, lest they should affect the uniform color of the intellectual wool. Should, by any freak of nature, a single pen be found infected by the presence of a sporadic youthful Harvey haunted with a new idea of the circulation of the blood, by a sporadic youthful Jenner mentally poisoned with the virus of vaccination, his career would end on the spot. As for a youthful Goethe, venturing in his examination paper on the wild suggestion that the human skull might be shown to consist of modified vertebræ, measures so stringent would at once be taken with his own vertebræ, that, in his case at least, no further demonstration of the truth or falsity of the theory would be available. No! every trace of innovation, every hint of a new idea, is the worse than worthless girl baby to be incontinently drowned. Thus is the Chinese man's head subjected to the same kind of aborting clamp as the Chinese woman's foot, with the like result of a life-long intellectual toddle.

Discouraging, then, to anything akin to originality of mind as this stupendous system must be admitted to be, bread and butter, career, wealth, dignities, all turn absolutely on never deviating into originality. The very name of originality is but the synonym not for mere lack of veneration, but for positive delirious desire to trample on the sacred images of Confucius and Mencius. None the less for the attainment of the great practical object it has in view, namely the grand anti-Darwinian demonstration of the permanence of species, at least in China, this vast educational system belongs among the most impressive spectacles in human history; achieving its end more perfectly and on a vaster scale than have any of the most potent educational systems — the Spartan, the Venetian, even that of the Catholic Church with its priesthood — the world has ever seen. While it weeds out originality, — the one bane of the immutable conservatism it would maintain, — it none the less unerringly selects the class of minds most effective for the end it has in view: men of strong health capable of enduring the severest strain; men of powerful memory of endless details; men of horse logic never troubled about premises; men in whom automatic repetition of the most intricate system of ceremonialism has replaced every impulse to spontaneity; men, in fine, who can decorously introduce more in the way of unimpeachable moral maxims into the preamble of the worst government " squeeze " than elsewhere can be paralleled. Thus has been fashioned the chilled steel die with the irresistible weight of pressure to force it home, through which one authorized image and superscription has been stamped on the mental coin of the empire.

VIII. Plato's dream, in his Republic, of a government administered solely by philosophers has in China been brought down from the sky of fanciful speculation into the solid world of beef and

pudding. Concrete in every atom, as soou would
the Chinaman think of separating a boulder from
the force of gravitation inherent in it, as theory
from practical every-day embodiment. No need,
therefore, for him to go with Plato to Syracuse to
hunt up an amiable, progressive tyrant to serve for
a *pou sto* from which to work his philosophic
lever. He takes his stand just where he is, and
begins to pry away.

Now this ideal of a government by philosophers,
or saints, or the two combined, is one that throughout human history has exerted a spell of fascination
over the higher order of minds. To them it has
stood for the legitimate reign of reason over chaos,
of virtue over vice, — the only reign worthy the
allegiance of a noble nature. Stupendous the scale
on which the Brahmins strove to carry out this
ideal in India; the Egyptian priesthood, in the
valley of the Nile; the mediæval Catholic Church,
in Europe; although in each of these great instances
philosophy was inseparably bound up with theology.
Here, in China, on the contrary, the colossal experiment has been on a purely mundane foundation.
" Respect the gods, but keep them at a distance! "
Heaven is their realm, China ours. Let them hoe
their row, while we hoe our own!

Sooner or later, every great race gets a lawgiver
or prophet made in its own image, while reacting
in turn on the race itself through the mass and
momentum of his own greater personality. Mohammed was, tooth and nail, the fiercest Bedouin
in all Arabia, though a highly sublimated Bedouin.

Gautama Buddha was the most absolute type of pessimist in all India, though carrying the habitual cheerfulness that is so unfailing a characteristic of pessimists to greater lengths than is possible with men in whom traces of optimism still survive. Look now at Confucius, the colossal man in whom first embodied itself the vast Mongolian race, only to be reacted on by the weight of his enormous return pressure! China, always traditional, made him, and then he re-made China. Impossible is it to speak of the man but in terms of wonder, reverence, and love ; as equally impossible is it to escape a half humorous smile at the prosaic, matter-of-fact, dead-level respectability of certain sides of his intelligence and character, — the measure, no doubt, of traditional Mongolian alloy requisite to fit his fine gold for a circulating medium tough enough to withstand the wear and tear of China.

Confucius said of himself — too much reverence for the wisdom of his ancestors had he not to say it! — that he was " not an originator but only a transmitter." Of the sin of originality — literally the " original sin " of China — he sought to shake his skirts clear from the start. Yao and Shun, certain impossible paragons of perfection in the way of mythical Chinese kings of the past, were held responsible for all his ideas, — kings apart from whose august sanction he would never have ventured on the impiety of entertaining ideas at all. Very much with the same solemnity of conviction might Newton have averred, of his own relation to the law of gravitation, that he was simply a transmitter of the long-established goings-on of the ancestral planetary system, indeed, had never gone a hair's breadth beyond a literal statement of what had been its venerated custom from the beginning. Well, if Confucius was not an original mind, an original character, an original forecaster of human destiny, then the doctrine of evolution should be allowed its own sweet will in resolving back all human personalities into the aboriginal pregnancy of the nebular mist !

The grand, wise, humane man, so benevolent and compassionate, so sagacious, so sweet and humorous, so consecrated to his mission, so devout, too, in his deep, though unimpassioned way! Moreover, such a sincere believer in Yao and Shun, and in the doctrine that manners make the man and that the two are one and inseparable ; in fine, in the immutable truth that there are at least three thousand external postures which, being reverentially assumed, become so many channels for the inflow into the soul of corresponding interior graces of genuine courtesy ! So exceptionally rich, too, in the man was his native soil of goodness that no doubt he could live up to every one of the three thousand external postures and inform them all with the spirit, whatever may be said of the dry rot of formalism and insincerity they have set on in the hearts of his countrymen.

Such a literal and matter-of-fact believer in the kingdom of heaven on earth as Confucius, the world never saw. Heaven meant to him an omnipotent, ever-embodied, tangible presence in the world now and here of a grand, orderly, beneficent law that need only be recognized and obeyed, and lo! its kingdom, the kingdom of heaven, was on hand. Here was the sublime side of the great sage. Profound was his insight into the laws of nature which alone can establish the well-founded state and family, and for all this China owes him an immeasurable debt. But now comes in the racial and personal limitation of the man, namely, his overpowering faith in the method of working from outside to inside. People at large, to use his own favorite expression, are like so much water, which always assumes the exact shape of whatever dish it is poured into. If only, then, he could fabricate the right kind of morally-shaped dish out of a few rules, all the rest desired would follow of itself. In all this, in his own lofty way, he believed as profoundly as the most commonplace pie-maker in his own power to make all his pies come out alike, if only he can subject their common dough to one and the same fluted tin-cutter.

Unhappily, on just this fatal inheritance from its mighty sage is founded the vast Chinese system of education for a government by philosophers. Of course it requires an immense supply of philosophers to fill all the offices of so immense an empire, while alas! by definition, a philosopher is a man who thinks, and yet most men do not think except in a sadly lopsided way. Not for a moment, however, does the practical Chinese mind suffer itself to be balked by any such purely theoretical difficulty. First-hand thinking enough, it says in substance, has already been done, and done supremely well. The moral-sage dish has been shaped to absolute perfection. Now squeeze into the mould, like so much clay, all candidates aspiring for place, and they will be turned out so many regulation-sized philosophic bricks, each one of them an exact copy of Confucius, repeating the same thoughts, never deviating from the same methods, and all able to imitate to a hair the same endless posturings. Thus, the most careless mind can hardly fail to be struck with certain salient points of difference between this brick-yard system pursued at Canton and the freer system adopted, say, at Harvard. Truly, a serious comparison of the Canton examination papers with those in use at any American or European college furnishes one of the most comically interesting and instructive historical studies that can be indulged in; and, if entered on soberly and discreetly, — a state of mind not so easy to maintain, — will throw a flood of light on China not to be gained from reading a dozen portly volumes. Let me modestly commend it to teachers of history in Harvard, Yale, or Columbia. Specimens of Chinese examination papers are easy to get at; for example, " The China Review," vol. viii. No. 6.

That such a system, carried out on so stupendous a scale, should prove a potent cause of national arrest of development is of course inevitable. Not that among the literati of China there have not been in every generation acute thinkers, and men of profound feeling and lofty character. No system can utterly destroy in powerful natures the germs of intellectual curiosity and native love of virtue, that, spite of every obstacle, will assert themselves. European scholars long resident in the country assert that from time to time books appear — secretly circulated indeed and hard to get hold of — that are characterized by strong, independent thinking. Indeed, such scholars further insist that, just as when great, overshadowing forests are cut down, an immediate regrowth of trees of a different species sets in, trees already on hand as plantlets and only awaiting a chance at sun and air, so would it prove in China with the upspringing of a new and vigorous mental growth, could only the present great Mandarin forest have the axe laid at its roots. Meanwhile, however, this forest continues to spread the deadly mildew of its shade over every tiny nursling, and thus does the mind and heart of the average educated Chinaman become mere punk and powder, while outwardly he flourishes like the green bay tree, through the simple activity of his external bark.

Such, then, is the system of education that sets its stamp on the politico-literary officials of China, the men who impart the tone to the ideas and policy of the empire. Thence spreads to the people at large insincerity and deep-rooted distrust between man and man. From top to bottom, as is admitted on all hands, government is honeycombed with corruption. The one honest service in the empire is the collection of customs, and that is administered by Europeans and Americans, because there China cannot help herself. With no concern

with government, the people scarcely know the
meaning of patriotism ; indeed, when the English
and French were besieging Pekin, cities all round
made private terms for themselves, supplying in
return provisions, bullock-carts, and coolies, — the
same thing as if, were Boston besieged, Salem,
Lynn, and Worcester should agree to furnish all
the beef, hay, and horses the enemy needed, so only
that they themselves were let alone.   Thus so hol-
low a shell as the Chinese Empire nowhere else
exists ; while none the less bodily and in latent mental capacity the Chinese are one of the most powerful races on the globe, — far the superiors of the
Japanese in solidity of mind, in business capacity,
in potential depth of thought and persistence of
will, in almost everything but artistic sensibility.[1]

[1] And yet a conflict between China and Japan has turned out
like a fight between an ox and a hornet, in which the hornet, able
to get in everywhere and the ox nowhere, the big, helpless bovine
runs bellowing across the plain.   So much will stereotyped routine and too protracted addiction to Yao and Shnn do with a
mighty people.

I. FROM Hong Kong, on a radiant December morning, we set sail on the German steamship Oldenburg for Singapore; and as the bracing winter weather had depressed the mercury as near the freezing point as 80° Fahrenheit, we got away in a fine exhilaration of spirits for the veritable Tropics. That Kaiser Wilhelm II. had close at heart keeping warm tender memories of the Vaterland in the breasts of his subjects, even in the farthest East, was made clear, not alone by the lively fluttering of the national flag aloft, but by the stirring strains of the Wacht am Rhein from a German brass band, and, deeper yet, by the broaching on deck of a keg of ice-cold Bavarian beer; this last a bit of symbolism as enthusiastically repeated each morning and afternoon of the voyage as the sunrise and sunset salute of the colors enjoined on the army at every military post.

Not, however, that due courtesies were not equally shown to the deepest national sensibilities of China. From our bows hung suspended an immense festoon of at least two hundred and fifty packs of fire-crackers; and if ever the devils were duly warned off from any ship, they were from ours when these started their spitfire fusillade. As large numbers of Chinese emigrants were steerage passengers, it was comforting to a humane mind to feel that they no doubt were experiencing a quietude of peace commensurate with the scale of the noisy thaumaturgic manifesto. Thus West and East met and kissed one another, as Teuton and Chinaman were made happy, each in his chosen way.

II. Far back in early boyhood days, when assiduously neglecting his studies at school, one none the less may have received some single impression which all through life has remained indelible. It was wrought, perhaps, on the imagination by a little view in his " Pictorial Geography " of the island peak of Teneriffe, — a view in which a perpendicular, snow-crowned mountain pierced sheer through the clouds into the upper sky, while at its base lay a ravishing dream of naked Negro boys, cocoanut-palms, sugar-cane, and heavily-laden banana-trees, all basking in a languishing atmosphere of peace, in which it seemed impossible that school should ever keep. Many the cent, no doubt, he had invested in bits of cocoanut, and even in cocoanut-cakes. But here was a land in which an ingenuous boy needed only duly to aggravate a monkey to procure gratis in return a volley of the blessed nuts, and then retire to the grateful shade, punch holes in the welcome missiles, and drink their delicious milk. Cows, as lacteal fonts, seemed prosaic in comparison. From that date followed a veritable passion for the tropics that haunted him through life. Such, at any rate, was my own child experience.

. In Singapore I felt sure of the genuine thing, — no miserable compromise, like Florida, between winter and summer, frost and fever, where a tiger would be subject to pulmonary complaints or a python too sluggish from cold to embrace with due fervor a deer. The region I craved must lie close to the equator and under the vertical sun. Its inhabitants must be innocent of clothing, lest the beauty of their bronze or jet-black bodies should be impaired. Flaming red turbans and red loin-cloths they might wear, to be in keeping with the equally flaming flowers of the jungle, but beyond this, nothing. The huts must be thatched with palm-leaves, the bread must grow on trees, the coffee-berries must thrust themselves in through the windows and ask to be plucked, roasted, and decocted; cinnamon, nutmeg, and cloves must drop spontaneously into the bread-fruit pudding, duly to flavor it; while mangoes, mangosteens, and pine-apples should voice their bewildering rival claims to furnish the luscious dessert.

III. Such was the blissful dream, as day after day we floated over summer seas, without the change of a degree in the direction or an increase for an hour in the gentle pressure abeam of the northeast monsoon. It was the poetry of sailing, in which it seemed that captain, crew, ship, and engines might all be lapsed in a long sweet siesta and no harm could come on such charmed waves. How tender and considerate, too, the geological providence that, in thrusting out the

Malay Peninsula a thousand miles, till it nearly touched the equator, had made such kindly provision that no planetary pilgrim should be able to girdle the earth without this tropical experience!

Singapore, a possession of Great Britain, — what does she not possess! — lies at the extreme southern point of the Malay Peninsula, and is only two degrees from the equator. I begrudged the two degrees; but one cannot have everything in a world so imperfectly constituted. The actual settlement is on a little island, not, however, so far from the mainland that a tiger cannot swim over from the domain of the Sultan of Johore, to pick up an appetizing native whenever so disposed. Visited with constant showers, it combines in its blazing sunshine and abundant moisture the conditions of the most exuberant tropical luxuriance. A richer variety of nationalities, moreover, could hardly be coveted by the most exacting ethnologist. To specify a few, there are Achinese, Africans, Arabs, Armenians, Bengalis, Burmese, Chinese, Dyaks, Javanese, Malays, Manillamen, Parsees, Persians, Siamese, Tamils. Singapore, in fine, is the great central meeting-place for the trade of China, Japan, Java, the Malayan Archipelago, India, Arabia, Abyssinia, and Europe, and is full of residents from each.

It was just after sunset that our steamship glided into the harbor, and so late before we were finally tied up to the pier that we hardly cared to venture ashore for the night. Indeed, two young men, who started out in search of a hotel, returned by midnight in a sadly demoralized nervous condition. They had secured a sleeping-room, but found that its tenancy was of the nature of the Box and Cox arrangement, in the familiar farce. Box was in occupancy. He was a huge serpent. In vain the landlord offered another room. They precipitately retired to the ship. None the less, their report looked so promising in the tropical way that the rest of us waited impatiently for the dawn.

How beautiful the dawn, and what a story was told to the finite little tourist as to his real position on the planet by the great sidereal clock of the heavens! Close down to the horizon in the north hung the pole star; while at fifteen degrees of elevation in the south stood the constellation of the Southern Cross. Gradually, absorbed in the excess of light of the rising sun, they vanished from sight.

IV. With sunrise began the bustle of day; and, as I looked out on the side toward the town, the first grateful sight was a rude cart drawn by a veritable pair of the cream-colored, humped-back, reversed-horn cattle, so familiar to all frequenters of Barnum's Circus. They were driven by an almost coal-black Tamil, in a bright red turban and red loin-cloth, — a piece of such fine naked realism that the great moral showman would have had essentially to modify it before presenting it to the decorous American public. None the less, over the cattle I could not help exclaiming : " They look as natural as though under their native tent on the Back Bay, Boston ! " On the other side of the ship, however, was soon revealed a spectacle such as Barnum in his most inspired hour would never have ventured on. Immense barges, filled with sacks of coal, each swarming with fifty or more naked fellows, equal in anatomy to any of the gladiatorial saints in Michel Angelo's Last Judgment, and who would have driven the austere and self-contained master wild with enthusiasm, had come out to coal our ship. *Ex tempore* scaffoldings were erected, on the various stages of which the men stood in ranges, heaving from one to another the heavy sacks. No conceivable attitude of grace, strength, and agility but was struck ; and such pure, unmitigated enjoyment of superb legs, and loins, and backs, and sinewy shoulders, I never reveled in before. Ah! why do not our artists come out to the tropics to pursue their studies ? We talk of our life-schools in New York and Boston, where a few fatty, academically posing, half-asleep models are set up to be drawn from at so much an hour. Life-schools ! Schools of death, in comparison with what is here before the eyes! These fellows, lifting, tossing, catching, re-tossing the two-bushel sacks of coal, have never heard of the Greek Laocoön, or the Discus-thrower, or the Athlete with the Scraper. But they are spontaneously enacting them at every turn, as free and unconscious in doing it as the runners and wrestlers Phidias looked on and sketched at the Olympian games.

V. The first thing on leaving the pier was to hire a *gharry*, — a small carriage drawn by a wiry little pony, capable of eight miles an hour under a heat of ninety-five degrees. The *gharry* has a thick roof, and is open on all sides, with slat-screens to draw for protection against the sun. As for the driver, he is simple perfection in the way of the picturesque, whatever he may be in morals. Malay by race, with a large piece of highly variegated silk wound round his waist, and falling in folds as a petticoat, with a scrupulously white tunic over his shoulders, and a red turban of stupendous dimensions on his head, he looks an Oriental sovereign cabman, with whom one feels at first as chary of bargaining as with the Grand Sultan. So figurative is he, however, in the style of his first financial proposition that one soon sees it would be utterly prosaic and Occidental to take him literally. A reduction to one third of the original amount is finally agreed on ; and then his Magnificence mounts the seat, and starts off the little pony like a shot.

What a drive we took ! The road was excellent, as it always is where imperial England or imperial Rome rules the province. On we whirled past the spacious, beautiful bungalows of the Europeans, the porches wreathed with a wealth of purple bourgainvillia vines, and splendid with flaming poinsettias and hibiscus, and picturesque with palms ; past the villages of Malay houses, set up on piles in swampy districts ; past the clay huts of the country people, thatched with palm-leaves and buried in thickets of banana, bread-fruit, and jak-trees, lightened up with the infinitely varied colors of the crotons. The last native town we had seen was heart-sickening Canton, its depressing memories and smells still clinging to the skirts of mind and coat. Now everything was sunny, happy, open-air life. Poverty is nothing in such a climate. What need of care where one can bring up a daughter to marriageable age for about three dollars! The more children, the merrier. At every step my friend and I were pulling one another right and left to say: " Did you see this? Did you see that? " Now it was a young mother, with such a glory of a little naked bronze child astride her hips; now an interior of Adamic innocence around the common dish, into which all dipped their five-pronged natural forks; now a fruit-seller, with such a strange variety of luscious specimens unknown by very name to us.

Then, too, the superb flora was all so novel. It was a universal Kew Gardens with the glass roof off. Jak-trees and calabash-trees bearing fruit so heavy that it would brain Og, Gog, and Magog, if it fell on their skulls! Clumps of bamboo ninety feet high and a hundred yards in circumference! Magnificent bread-fruit-trees, each separate leaf a miracle of size, lustre, and beauty of form! Banyan-trees, striding across country each like a hundred-armed vegetable Briareus, making after the Titans, not on all-fours, but on all eager hundreds at once! Enormous rubber-trees, their whole gigantic root system lying exposed above ground, coiling and recoiling on themselves like an acre of huge boa-constrictors! Who but has wished at times in life that some Titan might deracinate for him a giant oak, and hold it up that he could see at once the whole aerial superstructure, and the whole terrestrial substructure, and marvel at such a creation? Well, the grand, century-old rubber-tree gives one just this sight. One would think a Titan had torn it out of the ground, and then set it up, balanced and supported on its roots. The effect is that of Tennyson's " Flower in the Crannied Wall " raised to the ten-thousandth power, and with proportionate increase in the volume of the religious awe inspired. Yes, the school-boy's dream of Teneriffe had all come true; and the heart chimed in with Wordsworth's lyric burst : —

> " So was it when my life began; . . .
> So be it when I shall grow old,
> Or let me die ! "

VI.   Among the most interesting sights in Singapore is the Botanical Garden, in which are brought together the greatest possible varieties of tropical trees, shrubs, vines, and flowers. A great botanical garden ranks as a sort of vegetable anthology of the poetry of the natural creation, in which, within comparatively narrow bounds, all the choicest extracts from the genius of the Amazon, the Indus, the Ganges, the Irrawaddy, and the islands of the sea are brought together. Unassisted nature tends to run all to nutmegs, or cinnamon, or royal palms, or bread-fruit, or bamboo; and so art must step in to insist that every one of, say, two hundred and fifty varieties of palms shall have a chance to reveal its glories, and that perambulating banyans shall not be permitted to stride at will over the whole country. Permanent aboreal settlers there have their rights, as well as irresponsible vegetable tramps. The Botanical Garden, moreover, possesses another immense advantage in the way of mental peace. There, while the pleasure-seeker is inspecting the trees, he is freed from the necessity of standing up to his waist in a Borneo swamp, or keeping one eye out for an emulous boa-constrictor, or mistaking the stripes down a tiger's back for the sheen of a clump of small golden bamboos, and thus falling one more unwary victim to that dishonest "imitative principle in nature" so fitted to deceive the very elect. The æsthetic gain is immense.

VII. All the voyage south from Hong Kong, my traveling companion and I had been reading with keen delight Wallace's "Malay Archipelago."

How infinitely more vivid in interest every page now that we were actually entering on the vast island regions of Borneo, Celebes, Sumatra, Java, — that veritable El Dorado of the East which the Portuguese fought for from 1500 to 1600, the Dutch from 1600 to 1700, and the English throughout the present century! In none of the chapters of Wallace's book had we found greater pleasure than in the descriptions of his hunts in Borneo after the orang-utan, and his studies of the ways of that Caliban of the forests. What, then, was our delight at finding in the grounds of the Singapore garden a full-grown specimen of the brute!

The especial Borneo gentleman in question stands four feet two inches in height, while his fore arms more than touch the ground as he walks erect, after the most monstrous biped-quadruped fashion one could dream out in a nightmare. Covered with long, black, matted hair, and adorned with a red beard, he is further dowered with protruding jaws powerful enough to chew up whole cocoanuts and spit out the shells as easily as ours crush grapes and get rid of the skins. This, however, is but the Caliban side of the creature, the lower, elemental, evolutionary force that is now in travail with a higher spiritual force. Immense, then, was our surprise, on studying him more closely, to find that above his brute jaws arched a noble, philosophic brow, and under it lay a pair of profound, meditative eyes that irresistibly reminded one of Immanuel Kant. The contrast was fairly startling. Here, then, in epitome, was the whole creation groaning and travailing in pain until now, waiting for the adoption, to wit, the redemption of the brute body!

Our Borneo philosopher occupied an apartment twenty feet each way, with a bare tree in the middle, and shut in on the four sides and at the top by heavy iron gratings. In his periods of contemplative abstraction, the attitude assumed for his meditations differed from that I have read of as characteristic of any of the great German metaphysicians. Clinging to the centre of the iron grating at the top by one fore hand and one hind hand, the other fore arm was swung clear round the back of his head to support its cerebral weight, while the still remaining hind arm grasped the fore arm employed in actual suspension, the whole resulting in a perfection of pendent equilibrium which one felt must most essentially conduce to the harmonious balance of his intellectual faculties. Irresistibly he suggested the famous picture, in the Clouds of Aristophanes, of Socrates suspended in the basket and lost in aerial contemplation. From time to time a mischievous little monkey would run across the top of the grating and twitch the hair of the brooding philosopher, who then would slowly turn his head and look at him with an abstract gaze that saw and yet saw not.

Absolutely convinced were my friend and I that the great book on the true philosophy of evolution was then and there being brooded out. Thousands of years may elapse before it shall be permitted to issue from the press; but then will it assert itself as the work of one subjectively and objectively authorized to expound the vast theme, of one having all the slime and the lotus flower, all the brute and the angel, in his own compound organization. For now, in an instant, a revelation of the two contradictory elements in our arboreal Immanuel Kant! In the levity of our own minds growing weary of such protracted meditation, we would ask the keeper to bring a lot of paw-paws, when, lo! in a flash, the Caliban would dominate the philosopher; and down the gratings would he climb, working across the floor with an inconceivable monstrosity of brute awkwardness, and cramming the paw-paws into his terrible jaws. The brute in his nature laid to rest, again would the profound thinker resort to his aerial suspension, and resume the thread of broken contemplation. Oh, that Robert Browning, with his deep psychical insight, could have seen him! There was material there for a profounder poem than " Caliban on Setebos." Browning's Caliban had no outreaching, prophetic element in him. In this Caliban it was impossible not to feel it working, — an elemental, slowly differentiating, secular force !

CEYLON

I. Therе is a Mohammedan legend that, after their expulsion from the Garden of Eden, Adam and Eve were penally transported to Ceylon. How inconceivably beautiful must Eden have been if Ceylon was looked on in comparison as a sort of Botany Bay! Personally, I would brave the consequences of barrels of forbidden fruit for one day of exile there. As to the truth of the legend I cannot vouch, further than to attest that the shallow strait dividing Ceylon from India is called Adam's Strait, and one of the highest of the mountains Adam's Peak. Readers of the Indian epic, the Ramayana, will further recall that this was the strait bridged by the king of the monkeys, to enable heroic Rama to rescue his stolen wife, Sita.

On our voyage from Singapore, all the way through the Straits of Malacca and across the great southern ocean, we carried with us the same beautiful weather and smooth seas that had favored us the entire course from Japan. December 21 we sighted Ceylon in the late evening, and before ten o'clock the next morning had skirted the whole southern coast of the island, then turned northward, and rounded the great breakwater into the harbor of Colombo. Very beautiful was the sight from our steamship's deck. The handsome Renaissance architecture of the great hotels and government buildings along the quay, the immense, sweeping curves of the rose-tinted beaches, backed by forests of cocoanut-palms, and behind them the lofty peaks of the mountains of the interior, combined in a charming picture.

How one envies England the possession of so superb an island as Ceylon, two thirds as large as all Ireland! And how one must praise the magnificent way in which she administers its affairs! She is the legitimate successor of imperial Rome. Ruthlessly may she conquer, but in the train of conquest follows the broadest, the wisest, the most humane and tolerant statesmanship the world has ever witnessed. To be humbled by her is to be exalted by her. For back of the greedy, unscrupulous, mercantile adventurers and half pirates that are the first aggressors, lies the great truth-speaking, justice-loving, Christian civilization of the home nation, ever with its Edmund Burke, or kindred moral genius, to voice the deeper sentiment of the people for righteousness and mercy. What a noble breed of men the proconsuls she has sent out to rule a realm like India, — men heroic in courage, supremely loyal to duty, enlightened in intellect, devout in feeling, an honor to humanity, their biographies a more than modern Plutarch! Blessed the nation that has such constellations of worthies with which to fire the soul of its more generous and aspiring youth!

II.   The first drive on the island, one unbroken succession of fascinating tropical pictures, alike in the luxuriance of the vegetation and the grace and color of the Singhalese and Tamil men, women, and children, brought home to my friend and myself one exulting feeling, to which both gave hearty expression. " Heaven be praised! we are once more among an Aryan people! Blood is thicker than water!" Here were our own features, our own caste of thought and feeling, our own image cut in bronze or ebony. What if we did set out from our common home countless centuries ago, one branch of the family wandering to the farthest confines of India, and the other bringing up at last in San Francisco! Across the vast abyss had we ever, consciously or unconsciously, yearned in thought and aspiration, and when at length our great literatures came together, we found we had the same fond words for father and mother and hearth and home. I felt like hugging and kissing the whole Aryan race. For, be it confessed, the dreary weight of the vast Mongol-Malay race had for months been oppressing my soul with nightmare. Wherever I had struck it and whatever I had read of it, whether in Thibet, Tartary, China, Mongolia, Corea, Japan, or the fairly continental Malay Archipelago, it had seemed to me one and the same thing, devoid of deep inwardness of feeling, an exterior mask of manner, incapable of any of the achievements that are dearest to us, — the epic and drama of Homer and Kalidasa, of Dante and Shakespeare, the music of Beethoven and Mozart, the sculpture and architecture of Asia Minor, Persia, and Greece, the chivalrous worship of woman, the philosophy of Germany and India, the religion that has dowered Syria, India, and Europe with its hierarchy of saints. All in vain is it to say that the majority of Aryans know nothing of all this. They do: it is in their blood, in their literature, in their common speech, in their whole spiritual education, and ever ready to flower out afresh. But in the vast Mongol-Malay stock so wanting is it that, whether any given American, German, or Italian traveler is capable of analyzing the matter or not, or can only express his sentiments by profanity; he feels the ethnological fact by instinct, recoils from it, and is oppressed by it.

III. However brief his stay in Ceylon, the traveler generally spends a few days in Kandy, some eighteen hundred feet above the sea, among the mountains of the interior. Kandy is now reached by a railway, — a marvel of engineering skill, hardly to be surpassed by anything the world shows! Indescribable the view, as one skirts the flanks of the mountains, and looks down into an enormous gorge, its sides clad with the most varied and luxuriant foliage, and its streams winding among the trees and level bottom lands below, transformed into cascades and lakes of the exquisitely delicate green of the young rice! Indeed, in Ceylon the glory of the tropics fairly culminates. One would not believe it possible that such a sense of indescribable happiness could be set welling and gushing from the worn and weary heart by the mere presence of this luxuriant exuberance of nature. The influence is irresistible. Life's pain and grief seem absorbed into it, swallowed up by it, mantled all over, as it so quickly mantles its ruins with gorgeous flowering vines and stupendous trees.

Arrived in Kandy, one finds himself by the shore of a charming little lake, its banks embowered in wide-branching tamarind-trees and royal palms, and, above, diversified by the vine-clad bungalows of the European tea-planters. Close at hand is the picturesque little Malagawa Buddhist temple, the most sacred shrine on earth of Buddhism; for there is preserved for veneration an actual tooth of Buddha, which, though once sacrilegiously stolen by the Portuguese, and carried to Goa in India, and there solemnly burned to lime in the presence of a great concourse of ecclesiastics, still offers its merits for the edification of the faithful. As the tooth is two inches and a half long and one inch and a quarter broad, skeptics have doubted its human authenticity. Their cavils left me unmoved. Already had I seen, in two widely separate places, footprints of Buddha in granite, six feet, at least, in length. So far, then, from finding anything disproportionate in the size of the tooth, it served as a confirmation of my wavering faith in the footprints. Of far greater importance, however, is the fact that in this temple are preserved the ancient Pali texts, which bring the student of to-day into the nearest contact with original Buddhism that can now be had.

IV.　It was on Christmas Eve that we arrived in Kandy, and by sunrise the next morning I was out to greet in the tropics the blessed day. Child of the wintry North, where was I? No sound of sleigh-bells jingled on the frozen air. No frost-nipped imagination suggested overcoat or mittens. The charming little lake close at hand breathed, indeed, its invitation — not, however, to skim with skates its icy surface, but to jump into its bosom for a delicious swim. In circuit a mile or more, it was overhung with royal palms, — the the most beautiful of all the palms, — and with century-old tamarind-trees, dipping the feathery tips of their branches into the water. A wealth of flowering vines — scarlet, purple, gold — climbed every tree-trunk and festooned every cliff. Close at hand was the Buddhist monastery, and on its steps the yellow-robed monks and acolytes chanting their hymns and prayers. Men, women, and children on the road greeted me with a winning charm unknown to our angular race, their beautiful eyes suffused with a Nirvana-like peace, which, though their lips uttered no Merry Christmas, yet breathed its loving spirit on the air. Thus gently sauntering along, I completed the circuit of the lake to where its waters overflow in a plunge thirty feet down into a lovely pool. Then what a picture!

Men, women, and children were reveling in their early morning bath, — the men and boys rioting in splendid somersaults from the cliffs; the women huddled together more apart, but laughing and chattering in the merriest way. And now the genuine Christmas-gift spirit revived in my heart. No pent-up Utica of presents, as at home, of fur gloves and knit hug-me-tights longer contracted my powers. My soul expanded in tropical exuberance. I yearned to be an Indian prince with ample means to create crystal-clear Diana baths like this for happy people in Massachusetts to leap into on every early morning of December 25, — the blessed season of the year, when, as all New Englanders so well know, the air is so deliciously warm, the water so seductive in its invitation, and the pleasure so exquisite of lying out in the golden sunshine to dry.

On Christmas Day, if ever in the year, a principle of pure disinterested sympathy with the joys of others should be the dominant note of the soul. Yet, how much easier is it to be thus unselfish under certain conditions than under others! Nowhere, for example, the man who shares a more absolute faith than I in the tonic virtue of a zero winter climate, — especially shares it when lying out in luxurious ease in the tropics. That day, then, I felt so disinterestedly glad for all the dear ones in America, so thankful that they were experiencing the fine exhilaration of the snow and ice tingling in their blood, and that their cheeks were so ruddy and their appetites so whetted as with a scythe-stone. No trace of envy breathed a stain on the smooth mirror of my soul. Their superabundant energy, their freedom from any desire for a moment's rest, their magical power of extracting sunbeams from anthracite, their capacity to get pleasure out of one little evergreen bush, in alleviation of the bare, wind-lashed oaks and maples around them — yes, it seemed so graciously delightful to lie stretched out under a tamarind-tree, and to contemplate all this as the happy lot of others. Whole groups of them could I see, in my mind's eye, holding on tight to their hats and bonnets as they staggered out from their front doors to face the blizzard, while congratulatingly I cried: " Ah! that is the making of a hardy, brave, virtuous, and much-enduring people. Long may you be subjected to it! "

In the tropics, the sense of the sweetness of rest carries with it a primal, elemental meaning it can rarely share in a far northern climate. In Massachusetts, for example, it is Tennyson's poem of "Ulysses," the gray-haired old mariner, who at eighty is too nervously restless to sit down in quiet for an hour by his fireside to reflect on past experience, but must be projecting some new seal or walrus voyage to Baffin's Bay or beyond; it is the " Ulysses " that carries the day in attraction over any poetry of dreamy rest like " The Lotos-Eaters." While " The Lotos-Eaters " is an exquisite rendering of the inmost essence of the Buddhistic ideal of Nirvana, the only ideal of Nirvana that appears to sanction repose to the average American housekeeper, haunted by seven dust devils that will not go out of her, or harried by her exacerbated conscience into an endless vortex of committee meetings, seems to be the final goal of fairly earned collapse in nervous prostration.

Then first is her moral being temporarily at peace. "I would if I could; but, if I cannot, how can I? But ache hard, O head, and pain wearily, O spine, that I may feel myself justified in the eye of heaven and earth in submitting to the mortification of trying to compass a little rest!" This is not the view entertained in Ceylon.

No, all day long I could not but feel I was in a Buddhist land, — a land in which the natural appeal of climate to dreamy repose had been lifted by a great spiritual genius into the realm of an especial religious faith. It was Christmas Day, but of this the people all around me knew nothing. Had they kept holiday, it would have been in commemoration of their own saviour, the Buddha. No end of angel songs over his coming into the world had they wherewith to celebrate his advent day. He was, moreover, the nearest akin to Jesus, in the spirit of merciful compassion, of all the founders of the great world religions. It was, indeed, no such ideal of rest as Jesus revealed, — rest in the everlasting arms of omnipotent Wisdom, Holiness, and Love; but it was a rest none the less unspeakably sweet and tranquillizing, — rest from the care and fret of the finite, deliverance from the power of the external to perturb the mind's serenity or to wound with heart-ache.

Ah! the Occident and the Orient! — how pathetically do they need one another! The Western mind roots so in the finite and manifold that life becomes to it a fitful fever; while the Eastern so absorbs itself in the invisible and immutable that finite life evaporates in dream and illusion. Each sense is needful to temper the stress of the other; each is indispensable for sanity and for inward peace.

V.   A pleasant drive's distance from Kandy lie the famous Peradeniya Botanical Gardens. They contain, as an instance, two hundred and fifty varieties of palms, with everything else on the same magnificent scale. Why make a futile attempt to detail at length the joy of wandering in them ? A description of a clump of bamboo, one hundred feet in height and one hundred and fifty feet in circumference, its clustered polished reed columns surmounted by a world of feathery ostrich plumes, is a piece of barren statistics. The sight of it is a marvel forever. Enough that the traveler from the far north is enraptured with the single sense, "Behold new heavens and a new earth ! " For all is new. Instead of the apple there comes up the mango-tree, and instead of the oak the rubber-tree. Poor, sad-hearted Lessing, weary of the monotony of the ever-recurring spring, one day broke out, " Oh, that for once, instead of in the same eternal green, it would come out attired in red or orange or purple ! " Had he but gone to Ceylon, he would have found the exhilarating sensation of change he craved. An absolutely new flora seems to imply an absolutely new life in man. The caterpillar in his nature changes into a silkworm, the homely robin into a bird of paradise. Adam and Eve combined, and in their first fresh honeymoon in

Eden, could not have felt more supremely happy than I in wandering round and pocketing poetic nutmegs and cloves instead of prosaic hickory-nuts and filberts, in chewing a twig of spicy cinnamon instead of a twig of ordinary sweet-birch, — ay, and in going up to a cinchona-tree and slicing off a bit of the bark, and taking my quinine *au naturel*, instead of seeking out a duly licensed apothecary shop and buying a dozen highly sublimated pills of the same extraction. The fall in Adam was condoned and blotted out. I was restored to Paradise. All controversy over the original site of Eden for me was ended. It was *there* that " the Lord God planted a garden, and out of the ground made to grow every tree that is pleasant to the sight and good for food."

VI. Before leaving Kandy, it seemed evidently the proper thing that a solemn international ecclesiastical interview should take place between the high priest of Buddhism, presiding over the most sacred shrine of the faith on earth, and the peripatetic representative of a body that thinks itself the most enlightened in the Athens of America. So, procuring an interpreter, — whose theological attainments, I am sorry to say, did not reach beyond the rule of three, and his linguistic not so high, — I went with my traveling companion to the monastery; and, sending in our cards, we united with them the petition that we might have the privilege of a conference. The favor was at once conceded. Very likely, as Mrs. Besant

had lately been in Ceylon, assuring the natives of
the immense superiority of Buddhism over Christianity, the high priest regarded us as equally
hopeful subjects.

Curious was the scene that followed. The monastery was very humble in its appointments, but
with a dreamy atmosphere of all-day siesta about it.
On a rather dilapidated sofa sat the high priest, en-
wrapped in the traditional yellow of the Buddhist
monk, his right arm and shoulder bare, and no
apparent underclothing beneath the single sheetlike
garment, — a style of apparel which, in the sweep
it afforded the bare arm over the whole surface of
the body, seemed, in a climate in which relief is
often sought from cutaneous irritations, eminently
conducive to tranquillity of mind. He was seventy
years old, his skull as close-shaven as a cannon-ball,
and was, moreover, one who had certainly attained
the goal of Nirvana as far as teeth have any further power to ache. Around were gathered six or
eight young monks, one or two of them alert and
eager to join in the fray, as the talk proceeded.
As my traveling companion is a veteran editor,
our party was fully equipped with a rapid-firing
Gatling gun for the discharge of volleys of questions.

The discussion of nice metaphysical distinctions
through the medium of an interpreter so flagrantly
ignorant as to be graveled even over such a bagatelle
as the points of difference between the homogeneous
and the heterogeneous, is not wont to be conducive
either to sweetness or light. So the interview

proved of attraction rather in the way of picture and atmosphere than of positive illumination.

We began, of course, with an inquiry as to the high priest's view of Nirvana, whether a conscious or unconscious state, present or a future. He answered that it was too deep a question to be discussed in a short interview. We then passed on to the subject of creation and Creator. He replied: " The world never was created. It was not made, it grew," — an answer that while unimpeachable evolutionary orthodoxy, sounded oddly, from the way it was enunciated, like Topsy's in " Uncle Tom's Cabin," — " I warn't made : I jist growed." Next we asked for a succinct statement of the essential principle of Buddhism. He gave it in five negative prohibitions against killing, lying, stealing, and unchastity. Then we passed on to Christianity, inquiring if he had ever read the Gospels. He said he had, and had found their teachings very contradictory, — not half so plain as Buddhism. I finally thought I would try him as to the extent to which he would follow his five principles. " Suppose a cobra should come into the room here," I said ; " would you kill him ? " " No," he replied. " What would you do ? " I asked. " Remove him." This was accompanied with a gentle motion, as though he had taken up a broom and was quietly sweeping out a bit of paper. After all, the tone of voice and the quiet attitude with which this was expressed were the one memorable thing in our conversation. Could we have really come to close quarters intellectually, no doubt the venerable man would have lost us in a labyrinth of metaphysical subtleties from which we could hardly have found our way out to the light of day. But here was something better. Here was the deepest thing in Buddhism, its sense of the one universal life, its feeling of compassion with the vast sentient struggle going on from the serpent on his belly to Buddha lapsed in Nirvana, its identification of self with the all in all. How I longed to see a cobra come gliding in, then coil himself and rear his terrible poison-fanged head for a stroke, while the yellow-robed old patriarch should quietly rise, and with a feather-duster in hand as gently " remove " him as that dear old English Buddhist, Uncle Toby, did the fly, when he opened the window for him with the loving word, " The world is wide enough for thee and for me."   Not for a moment did I doubt that in the spell of his religion the quietistic old man could tenderly have done it ; whereas if either of us two devout Christians had undertaken the removal, even with a street-sweeper's broom of birch twigs, such enmity would have been set on between serpent and " seed of the woman " that the issue of the conflict would have been problem-atical to the last degree.

INDIA

I.

I.　THE voyage of thirteen hundred miles from Ceylon to Calcutta is pleasantly broken by a short stay in Pondicherry and in Madras, — sometimes also, it is true, unpleasantly broken by frightful typhoons, cyclonic mast and funnel twisters that extract by their roots these mighty columns of wood or iron as easily as a prairie stump-puller the fangs of pines and oaks. But still we sailed over the same summer seas.

Truly, if anywhere that saddest of thoughts, "it might have been," strikes home with sharp historic pang, it must be to the Frenchman disembarking at Pondicherry and looking around him at about all that remains of his country's once magnificent dream of Indian empire. There first the splendid genius of Desaix divined India, and flashed out in every detail the amazing, but entirely feasible, programme carried into execution by the practical minds of Clive, Hastings, Wellington, and Napier. Not Alexander starting out from Macedonia with a handful of disciplined Greeks to fling them on the millions of Asia, and to swell his forces with fresh armies of sepoys as he marched along, ever had a more prophetic eye than Desaix. As late even as 1802, Napoleon, with his passion for the "barbaric pearls and gold" of the East and his fascination by the cyclonic careers of the Ghengis Khans and Tamerlanes of Asia, was still nursing the same imperial dream.

Yet to-day in all effete and decaying Pondicherry, the most attractive thing the traveler finds to do is to go outside the settlement at sunrise to the public fountains and watch the beautiful young Indian women drawing the day's supply of water. The lithe and graceful Caryatides, each with her gauzy sheet of sky blue or scarlet girt round her waist and falling in folds to her ankles, the other end thrown over one shoulder and down the back, leaving exposed her bronzed sides and arms to support the shapely vase of brass poised on her head, — here is a life-school for the artist that might tempt him to many a lingering month of stay. Ah! sighs the enraptured gazer, why cannot use and beauty, work and play, thus always be made to harmonize? Doubtless, with our own boasted advent of the scientific age of plumbing, enabling each gracious damsel to draw, for herself and by herself, her prosaic pail of water at the kitchen sink, there came a deal of saving in the way of time and strength. But alas! for the sunshine, laughter, and gossip that went out with it. Where, under such a disenchanting dispensation, would have been the romantic idyl of Isaac and Rebecca, with all the wealth of poetry that has shed its halo around Indian, Syrian, Arabian, Persian maidens gathered at the public fountains to draw their vessels of crystal water?

II. Our plan, on arriving in Calcutta, was to strike at once northward to visit the Himalayas, and then return to see the city. As fit preparation for a sight of these stupendous ranges, and to give the mind the requisite geologic stretch to take them in, commend me to a sail up the Hoogly, one of the mighty streams through which the hundred-mouthed Ganges pours out into the ocean its continental waste. " By their works ye shall know them." Here, then, before the eyes are the works of the Himalayas, of their vast storehouses of snow, of their enormous rainfall, of their stupendous supplies of disintegrating material. What a process of world-building ! — enormous islands of mud forming in a day, and forthwith under the generative force of the tropical heat breeding dense jungles of vegetation and spawning for them their broods of serpents and tigers. Yet, dangerous for poor little man to tempt his fate amid such colossal operations of nature. The terror of rivers is the Hoogly to the sailor. Nowhere else do pilots receive such pay. Even Cæsar there would be too subdued for braggadocia, and humbly admit that no matter whether they carried him or the obscurest tourist, each would prove an equally insignificant midget in the face of such overwhelming forces. And the bluff John Bull pilot, too, would take him at the same lowly estimate. Experience of but a month back, and the pilot for to-day's run is turned into a superannuated Methuselah, so perpetually are shoal and current shifting. Touch bottom anywhere for a moment and so afford a pivot in the keel, and over and over does the mighty tide shoulder and roll ship and freight, whirling them under to destruction. Yes, here are the works of the Himalayas! How one longs to stand in their overwhelming presence!

III.   Three hundred and fifty miles due north from Calcutta lies Darjeeling.   In the little mountain province of Sikkim, thrust in between Bhotan to the east and Nepal to the west, it affords a superb platform, some seven thousand feet in height, from which to survey the Himalayas. Dear, likewise, to the English mother's heart as a place of refuge for her fair-haired, blue-eyed little Saxon boys and girls from the slaughter of the innocents decreed by the feller than Herod fury of the sun of India!

For the first three hundred miles the railway runs across the vast dead level of northern India, — a plain which, on an enormously greater scale, bears the same relation to the Himalayas as Lombardy to the Alps.   Substitute for the Po the Ganges and its tributaries; for the vine and mulberry, rice and jute fields, palms and bananas; and for Monte Rosa, Mt. Blanc, and the Jungfrau, peaks like Mt. Everest and Kinchinjanga, whose actual snow-line only starts at an elevation higher than the summit of Mt. Blanc, — and some slight estimate may be formed of the comparative geologic scale on which nature has wrought in the two regions.

These first three hundred miles of the journey I pass over, till the station of Silliguri is reached.

From this point to Darjeeling, fifty miles away, the ascent of over seven thousand feet is made by a narrow gauge railway, in open observation cars. The road is a marvelous piece of engineering skill. Seven hours are occupied in the ascent, but nowhere else in the world can so much of tropical beauty and mountain glory be crowded into the same space of time. The track winds and rewinds upon itself, now in mile-long serpentine curves, and now in little loops; but everywhere it opens views down into ravishing valleys and gorges, clad with the most luxuriant and varied vegetation of palms, bananas, tree ferns, thirty feet high, banyans, laurels, rhododendra, magnolias, evergreen oaks. Thus from zone to zone of steadily changing flora, one rises hour by hour.

The exuberant jungle life of the lower half of the ascent beggars description. It is a struggle for life between vine and tree, plant and parasite, in which each is victor; for all seems to triumph, and nothing to die, or, if it does, at once to rise again in new arboreal resurrection and ascension. To the topmost crest of the giant trees climb the enormous vines, mantling the trunks with their huge leaves, flinging out like banners their spikes or sprays of flowers, leaping across to seize hold of and overrun new giants or sending down a multitudinous rain of aerial roots to seek the earth again and with centripetal force begin afresh the fight of the strangling python vines with the mighty forest Laocoön. The fable of Antæus, his strength born again each time he touched his mother earth — here is no more a stale literary illustration.   In the tropics vine and tree alike have learned this secret. Plants are there which begin their career fifty feet aloft as parasites.   Then down to the earth they drop their aerial roots, fill vein and artery with the fructifying sap that steads them for an upward growth of limbs and crest, till, surrounded on all sides, the parent tree dies, rots, vanishes away, and the parasite alone is left, scaffolded fifty feet high on roots from whose original starting-point aloft first begins the trunk and limbs of the now victorious heir.   Perforce one sees a sly vegetable innuendo at certain radicals at home, so bent on a display of roots as to dwarf any suggestion of foliage atop to correspond.

Higher up, in a zone from three to five thousand feet in elevation, succeed the great clearings of the tree plantations, terraced step on step in gigantic flights of stairs up the flanks of the mountains; though, far above them, begins again the forest growth, now largely consisting of evergreen oaks, rhododendra, and magnolias.   Thus, after nearly six hours of the highest wrought delight, we had reached the point at which was to open upon us, and be carried with us to the end of the ride, the full glories of the Himalayas.   So far the mountain we had been slowly climbing had lain between us and them, but now with a single curve all was to leap in sight.

Alas! if ever I was tempted to believe in the Prince of Evil and his merciless malignity, now was his hour of triumph.   Up along the flanks of

our mountain came stealthily climbing the ob-
scuring mists. Thicker and thicker they grew, till
we were immersed in them, and all was blotted
out. " I told you so! I told you so!" was now
the mocking voice that filled the air. In pessimistic love had a dozen kindly friends in Calcutta
prophesied to us before we left, " You will have a
fatiguing journey, bury your heads in the clouds,
and come back sadder, even if wiser men about the
Himalayas." That such people should live and be
justified in the end seemed the insoluble enigma
of mortal life!

IV. Well, we had reached Darjeeling, and had
some hours of daylight to spare. Why care
for snow peaks! The proper study of mankind is
man! Were there not Nepalese, Bhoteans, Thibetans, in crowds to study? Were we not on the confines of mysterious Thibet, the unriddled country
which, though it will let no man in — unless he can
contrive to sew up his eyelids and to accumulate on
his person solid stratifications of dirt so as to pass
for a plausible native — still lets many of its people
out? We had struck Mongolians again. In vain
had we fled from the presence of the mighty yellow race, — fled from it in Japan, China, the Malay Archipelago. There were once more before us
the flattened face, the broad cheek-bones, the narrow, oblique eyes, the black stiff hair, the peculiar
tallowy hue of this vast Asian people. Wonder
ceases at the careers of the Attilas, the Ghengis
Khans, the Tamerlanes, with such countless hordes

to draw on. So swift for the bazaar we steered, to see, while daylight lasted, our yellow fellow-creatures and their baffling alloys, with all the coin of humanity that passes current among these Himalayan hill tribes.

In the vast migrations to and fro of the human race, a certain strain of Tartar blood seems to have been poured into the veins of all these hill tribe peoples. Nepalese, Bhoteans, dwellers in Sikkim, though they have had beauty enough to drown out much of the Tartar ugliness, still — great numbers of them — suggest the suspicion that somewhere back there was a Tartar in the wood-pile. Crowds of the people, however, were pure, unadulterated Thibetans, ugly enough to satisfy the claims of the portrait the Romans drew of Attila. Tartarus! no trouble longer about the origin of the word. No question, either, that this same great race had a hand in fashioning our Esquimaux and North American Indians. There was a railroad once across Behring Straits, in some earlier geologic epoch.

V. From a religious point of view, these Thibetans offer a field of study, if not spiritually elevating, still intensely interesting. Historically, their own land furnishes the most extraordinary example of a pure theocracy — minus a God, but with no end of devils — existing in the world. King, priest, magistrate, tax-gatherer, doctor, executioner, every function is exercised by a lama, the generic name of priest or monk.

Strange to say, the people are all Buddhists; and among them the great Indian Buddha had a second incarnation. Most certainly he needed it, to get rid of his previous conceptions; for in his second incarnation he had abandoned every trace of inwardness, and surrendered himself, root and branch, to sheer externalism. Of all the heels-over-head travesties of the whirligig of time, surely Thibetan Buddhism is the oddest. Now first I came in contact with literal, unadulterated machine-praying. Long before, I had thought to encounter this strange phenomenon in certain clergymen at home; but always, with them, the machine was the man himself. Here, however, the machine was wholly extra-human, — a small copper cylinder, internally filled with yards of rolled-up prayers, revolving on an upright handle. It goes with the speed of a top. Indeed, the devout Oxford clergyman whose standing bet it was that he could give any other man in England to Pontius Pilate and then beat him through the service, here would have found Othello's occupation gone. Every revolution is the whole service, liturgy and Athanasian creed included; and the revolutions are two hundred a minute. And yet these little cylinders, plentiful as rattles in babies' hands, were for private devotions only. In the temples we saw them three feet high and eighteen inches in diameter, capable of holding miles of prayers, and run by the hour by man-power. Water-power is often substituted where a fall can be secured, and is just as efficacious. In fact, the very winds are subsidized for devotions, as in Holland for windmills to grind the corn. From thousands of poles flutter long streamers on which the prayers are written, and every flutter says them all. In our own boasted land, we have but begun to grasp the higher applications of machinery.

In previous chapters I may have seemed somewhat unjust in my strictures on the lack of inwardness and the tendency to ceremonialism of the whole Mongol-Malay race, from Japan in the north to the Malay Archipelago in the south. I felt it by instinct three days after I was in Japan. I was utterly oppressed by it in China, where government, manners, education, literature, are one great outward web of ceremony divorced from inward organic life. And now, in my next encounter with this self-same Mongol race, I had found the whole thing gone to seed, — dry hay for succulent grass; not so much as lip-service, only machine service, for the devout overflow of the heart. By ceremonialism I mean simply the divorce between expression and impression, the parrot-like repetition of conventional formulæ substituted for the living man. Symbolism, on the contrary — symbolism raised to the pitch of delirium — is the root religious vice of India; and soon in Benares on the sacred Ganges shall we see it displayed in its most luxuriant jungle growth. But, of the two, the emaciated, trance-struck fakir is more attractive than the machine-twirling Buddhist of Thibet.

Fain would I describe an introduction we were
favored with to a lama and his wife. Such a
jolly personality, she, and such a living illustration
of the line, " Religion never was designed to make
our pleasures less " ! On her head she wore a
crown of red coral set with big unpolished turquoises, while her cheeks were smeared with pig's
blood, — a rouge which certainly effects its purpose. The face loomed round as a full moon rising red in a smoky autumn horizon ; and as her
religion entitled her spouse and herself to one
tenth of the income of the flock, she evidently felt
it a fitting outcome of the second incarnation of the
Buddha in Thibet. Not yet had she experienced
the depressing effect of what in New England is
called the " decrease in reverence for the clergy."
Should her husband die, a fierce contest would
ensue among his devout followers for a hair of his
head, a paring of his fingernails, to wear as a
charm in an amulet, or for one or the other of his
thigh bones to make a horn of, through which to
blow the praises of the faith. Alas! as I thought
in contrast of many a sweet, patient minister's
wife in Massachusetts, nagged by cross-grained
parishioners I could not but exclaim, " How
blessed thy lot, O woman! " Not a female in her
parish advanced enough to begrudge her her coral
crown set with turquoises, or even so much as to
raise the question whether she were not a trifle
too extravagant in the use of pig's blood on her
cheeks !

VI. The clouds and mist that had prevailed on our arrival in Darjeeling continued on through the afternoon and evening, and we went to bed sadly impressed with the fickle and moody temper of mountain ranges. Orders were left, however, that should the sky be clear we should be called half an hour before sunrise. Half an hour before sunrise there came a tap at our door on the ground floor of the hotel, and we knew the day was saved. Swift was our response; for it was the Himalayas calling us, and not Ameer, our servant. So, jumping at once into warm clothing and each swallowing a hot cup of tea (always in India brought to one's bedside on awakening), we stepped out on the broad terrace in front of the hotel.

The terrace stood on the steep flank of a mountain higher than the top of Mt. Washington, the mountain itself dipping down into a profound valley beneath, but one abyss in a billowy ocean of like mountains. All below was in impenetrable darkness, through which no distinct object could be made out; but over across the abyss, and seemingly floating on the upper sky, stood — hung rather — the snow-white peaks of Kinchinjanga (next to Everest the highest mountain in the world), dominating the colossal group of five called The Treasuries of the Snow. The white at first was of an almost spectral sheen, lucent, yet etherealized; and the elevation at which, perfectly defined, it hung above the vast lower darkness filled the mind with a sense of awe as before a spectacle wholly detached from the earth. Then the summit of Kinchinjanga began to flush with rosy light, the flush gradually descending till it touched the tops of all five sister peaks. And now ensued the beatific vision of God's glory. To right and left, over a circle of nearly ninety degrees, peak after peak began to flame, the lowest at an altitude of over twenty thousand feet, while still the darkness lingered on in the whole nether world. Often as the comparison has been made between the great discoverers, poets, and prophets of the ages — the Newtons, Dantes, Isaiahs — and the supreme mountain peaks heralding the advent of the sun while yet the rest of the world is wrapped in darkness, never before did I so feel its solemnity. How long, how long, did these mighty monarchs keep solely to themselves their light and glow, or but sympathetically share it with one another's kindred spirits, before the broadening illumination spread over the foothills and penetrated down into the valleys! But at last it reached them, dyeing in rich maroon the vast rolling sea of the inferior intervening mountains. When it is recalled that Kinchinjanga is over twenty-eight thousand feet high, and the group it dominates twenty-five thousand, it readily can be conceived that nowhere else on the globe can this sublime phenomenon so impress the imagination. In the presence of so grand a spectacle, time loses its petty finite measures; minutes assume the character of slow-moving secular durations. One holds his breath in awe at the sense of how long before the earth beneath has broken its sleep of night, these glorious heralds of the day have seen and greeted with their jubilees the far-away rising of the sun.

VII. We could not linger, however, too long on the terrace, for, to profit to the fullest by the early hours of the morning, we were to ascend fifteen hundred feet higher to the top of Tiger Hill, from which Mt. Everest would be opened up. Chairs were waiting for us, each with six Thibetan coolies, four for conſtant service and two for reliefs. Soon we were on their shoulders, moving at a swift and steady pace. Admirable mountaineers, accustomed to carry heavy burdens over the Himalayan passes, the lowest of them at an elevation of fifteen thousand feet, they made light work of us. Of all the luxurious methods of steadily surmounting heights and at the same time drinking in the prospect, commend me to the chair on the shoulders of four sure-footed carriers. The mind is disengaged and free. No more alternation between longing to abandon one's self to the glory of the transcendent scenery and the fear of spraining an ankle or breaking one's neck.

The path wound along the flank of Tiger Hill, through woods of magnolias, laurels, rhododendra, and evergreen oaks, with constant vistas of the whole Himalayan range. Arrived at Senchal, the abandoned site of an old military cantonment, Mt. Everest had already loomed up in the far distance, while at the summit of Tiger Hill we enjoyed the delight of distinctly making out all three peaks of this highest mountain on the globe. Twenty-nine thousand and two feet! For round numbers the two might have been spared, but who would belittle such an altitude by subtracting an inch? The three clustered peaks were over a hundred miles away, though so clear was the atmosphere that they stood out in perfect distinctness. Anyhow, we had seen Mt. Everest, and so in all after life could use it as an all-round-the-world club to beat down the pride of any who should presume to boast of Mt. Blanc in our majestic presence.

None the less, the real glory of the scene lay in the stupendous Kinchinjanga group. It, too, was forty-five miles away, though it seemed but ten. Indeed, on first getting into the presence of the Himalayas, one has to go through a fairly revolutionary mental process in grasping the proportions of things. A mountain, in the foreground, twice the height of Mt. Washington, is only an insignificant foothill. It has still three thousand feet to grow before reaching the level of the snow-line, and then, to become a peer of the great ones, would have to add from nine to thirteen thousand feet of snow. Mountains, in sight, over twenty-two thousand feet in height are thick as trees in the woods. Thus, for an ordinary mortal, it is no small feat to evolve a mind to match the mountains. Notwithstanding the educational advantages we started with, it took my friend and me fully twenty-four hours to do it.

VIII.   Comparisons, it is said, are odious. That depends. If the object of the comparison be light, and not heat, it is often a very helpful thing. Therefore, in comparing, for example, the Alps with the Himalayas, one would have to admit freely that the Alps, with their emerald green upland pastures contrasted with their snow-crowned domes and peaks, are far more beautiful. This grows partly from the fact that they are so much more easily manageable by mind and imagination, and do not so tensely stretch the mental tether. The Himalayas, so to speak, make an immense demand on the intellectual as well as the æsthetic imagination.

To grasp any adequate idea of their magnitude, the mind must expand to the conception that they are in reality two colossal ranges, the one fifty miles behind the other, and that in the continental abysses of the valleys between them are gathered the waters of the mighty Indus and the Brahmapootra, the first flowing round by their western flanks and the second by their eastern, to enter India, while all along down their southern slopes stream the thousand affluents of the Ganges. Then, to complete the picture, imagination must evoke the limitless expanse of the vast South Pacific Ocean, the feeder of the ever-renewed treasuries of their snows. For the six months of summer, the steadily blowing southeast monsoon conveys the enormous evaporation of such an ocean under the full blaze of a tropical sun, — an evaporation pouring down in deluges of rain on the plains, and falling in perpetual snow as it strikes the frozen elevations of the mountains. Easily, then, will it be seen in contrast that, to form an adequate conception of the Alps, alike of their beauty and their structure, no such immense demand is made on the powers. Further, among the Alps the eye takes in at a single glance an infinity of beautiful detail. It revels in the emerald sheen of the velvety upland pastures, and is transported with the amethystine blue of the glacial ice. It follows with charm the exquisite outlines of the snow-crowned Jungfrau and Silberhorn, or commands, far below, the poetic beauty of the Lauterbrunnen valley. No such thing as this is possible among the Himalayas. It would demand a telescopic eye.

Further back, I spoke of the necessity of evolving a mind to match the mountains. This holds true whether the mountains be Alps or Himalayas. And yet, to achieve a consummation so devoutly to be wished, I know of no so feasible way as to supply a Raphael or Mozart to voice the gracious beauty of the Alps, a Michelangelo or Beethoven to interpret the overpowering sublimity of the Himalayas. And yet, as the whole day long the same crystal purity of the atmosphere continued to prevail, and as on the following morning the same miracle of a sunrise was repeated, we could not but feel that two humble mortals at least had added many a cubit to their æsthetic and geologic stature. A stupendous sensation, constituting a veritable epoch in our lives, had we enjoyed.

II.

I. CALCUTTA, the English part of it, is a brilliant European capital, with immensely picturesque Asiatic adjuncts. Its enormous parks and stately avenues for riding and driving at once call to mind London, yet suggest a striking tropical contrast. Instead of elms and oaks, the trees are palms, banyans, bho-trees, tamarinds; and instead of red-faced, plush-clad John Bull coachmen and footmen, the drivers of the handsome private carriages are dark-skinned Hindus, in dress a splendid conflagration of scarlet and gold, before which even the flaming poinsettias and bourgainvillia vines pale their ineffectual fires. How infinitely becoming a scarlet and gold turban to a finely chiseled, well-nigh black face! Indeed, the English ladies and gentlemen within the carriages would hardly subject themselves to such a contrast if they knew it to be so æsthetically damaging. How anæmic and bleached out they look, as though they had grown in cellars! And yet how assuredly they look the real lords and masters! At a glance is read their superior force of body and mind, their courage, imperial might of will. A lion among a herd of timid deer could not more emphasize the fact. Clive's victory at Plassey,—it is here explained in a flash. Then look out to the right or left across the park. Here a game of cricket is going on, here one of golf, here one of polo. The Englishman is keeping up his muscle. Inevitably, comes to mind Wellington's saying that Waterloo was won on the foot-ball field at Eton.

Yes, one is in Bengal. The streets swarm with the motley colored population. Ten men dart to pick up your handkerchief, should you chance to drop it; a dozen to open the carriage door, should you chance to stop. Meanwhile, fifty are elbowing one another to sell you something. Five are sure you want a barber; ten, you want a pen-knife; all the rest, that you want photographs, flowers, a hand-mirror, a pair of embroidered slippers, a model of a temple, a scarf-pin. From the swarms that unite their frantic efforts to heave up the steps of the hotel your traveling bag, — in weight, perhaps, six pounds, — and then individually apply for a money recognition of their exhausting toil, you would think yourself present at the transportation of a colossal Egyptian sphinx from the quarries of the Lower Cataract to far-away Memphis. Up to your very bedroom they stream, each salaaming as before a Mogul emperor. What exuberant tropical imaginations, in the glamour of which the naked fact that they actually got within six feet of the handbag is glorified into an eternal obligation of reward! You wax angry, and order them out of the room. Still more profound the obeisances. At last the Tamerlane begins to rise within you, as you snatch a trunk-strap and feel like lashing the "pampered jades of Asia." Finally, you effect a deliverance, and slam the door in their faces. With what beautiful Oriental patience do they wait outside! Time is an illusion of the senses which has no objective existence to the Indian mind. Are we not ever sunk in the immutable and eternal? You emerge from the apartment, and there they are! Now, for the first time, you get to the bottom of the Parable of the Unjust Judge, who feared not God, neither regarded man, but had to give in none the less to the persistent clamor of the widow. Had he been the whole Supreme Court of the United States, Chief Justice Marshal included, you would not have the heart to blame him.

II.   I dwell on incidents like these because from the outset they are needful for any vivid interpretation of India. Human life here is ant-cheap, if not dirt-cheap. Go into the dining-room of the hotel — each guest has his private servant behind his chair. Walk through the passage-ways of the hotel after bedtime — a servant is sleeping on a mat before each door. A clap of the hands inside, and in a second he is on his feet. Self-help soon ceases to be so much as a reminiscence. Here am I, a man who, in democratic America, has been wont to tend his own furnace, and in all grave domestic crises to stand ready to act as second girl; but in India it is a struggle to be allowed to tie my own shoestrings or brush my own teeth. A knock at the door in the morning, and tea and toast are brought to my bedside, the bath is pronounced ready, and with difficulty, after falling back upon

the Declaration of Independence and proclaiming
that all men are born free and equal to handling a
towel, am I then permitted to dry my own skin.
I am getting demoralized. India is steadily under-
mining my manhood, emasculating my will, as she
did with the early Aryans, the Moguls, the Afghans.
Soon I shall not so much as know the meaning of
a shoe-brush, a furnace, a second girl. Sunk in ef-
feminacy, I shall hand over all the affairs of state
to my slaves and eunuchs. Then a fresh irruption
will break in from the barbarous, hardy north; and
a new Afghan or Mogul dynasty will be founded
on my ruins. Thus, in the disintegrating effect
wrought on one's own personality does a man soon
get all the needful historical data for the interpretation of the century-long story of India. A week's
experience of such demoralization is more edifying
than reading whole volumes of history. One becomes history. *De te fabula narratur.*

III. With such a teeming population as that of
Bengal, millions of families of six living on
a wage of fifty cents a week, utter subserviency of
body and mind, evincing itself in abject prostration
before man and the gods, is what must be looked
for. The way to favor with the strong has always
been groveling in the dust before them, and the
strong on earth and the strong in heaven are one and
the same to the Hindu mind. Hence the rankest
jungle growth of superstitions; hence religious rites
among the lower orders so hideously obscene that
one could hardly fathom how they could have origi-

nated but by recalling how hideously obscene were the lives of the earthly rulers these poor grovelers worshiped as their sole ideals of might and glory. The painted brothels of Pompeii are shrines of purity alongside the orgies of lust portrayed in the carvings of many a Hindu temple. The apotheosis of a beast, animal or human, — of a cobra, a jackal, a foul and bloodthirsty tyrant, — one perfectly comprehends it now. And yet among the higher classes of the Indians are encountered men of the loftiest and purest theistic faith, men at once of the rarest munificence of charitable action and of the devoutest spirit of contemplation. And the range of such characters is constantly growing, as familiarity with Western thought and organized charity spreads more widely, and supplements the overpowering tendency of the Indian mind to abstraction from all terrestrial interests.

How overpowering this tendency still remains is even to-day attested in acts that strike the Occidental mind with wonder. In Calcutta, in any of the great cities of India, it is no unusual incident to see a man who has made himself a millionaire becoming by the age of fifty so utterly world-weary, so tired with all the fret of the finite, as to throw up business, make over his property to his children, and himself wander forth naked but for a loincloth, a staff in his hand, and a beggar's bowl at his girdle, to spend the rest of his days in the forest in the contemplation of the infinite. Think, in contrast, of the consternation on Wall Street, had it suddenly been announced in the "Herald" or

"Tribune" that Jay Gould, weary of the long fret of the finite involved in wrecking railroads, had thrown up his millions and started out, a naked mendicant, to devote what remained of his life to absorption in the Absolute. Bloomingdale Asylum! would have been the exclamation on every lip. And yet, in any higher sense of the word, which of the two were the saner seems hardly open to question, — certainly it would not be in India.

I. Our first objective point on leaving Calcutta was Benares, on the banks of the sacred Ganges. It lies some four hundred and fifty miles away, in a northwesterly direction, the holiest city in India to the Hindus, as formerly to the Buddhists. Hither, five centuries and more before the Christian era, came Sakya Muni, after receiving his illumination under the bho-tree in Gaya, to preach the new faith in the very Jerusalem of Brahmanism. Buddhism passed away long centuries ago, and not a shrine remains in the city as a relic of its former power. But still Benares keeps on the Mecca of the Hindus. In vain the Moslems destroyed it in 1194, razing to the ground one thousand temples and building mosques in their place. The faith or superstition of the people proved too strong. For Benares was the city of the sacred Ganges, the threefold divine river that runs through heaven, hell, and earth. To die on its banks, to have one's ashes cast upon its waters, was the highway to the realms of peace. A thousand miles, barefoot, hungry, and sleeping by the roadside, will the poorest peasants travel to bathe in its flood and drink its water. Troops of them — men, women, and children — one constantly meets, journeying toward the holy city, or returning home with vessels filled at its sacred stream. To it are the feeble and dying carried, that they may pass away on its banks; and even, if too far inland for the journey, a portion of the body is sent to be burned to ashes and thrown on its swelling flood.

As a result of this faith, innumerable temples stretch for miles along the river side. From the elevation on which they stand descend superb flights of stone steps, called ghats, hundreds of feet broad and fifty feet in length, to the river brink. Along with the temples are solid palaces, constructed by princes of the different provinces, in which they or the members of their households may await the hour of death, while multitudes of poorer people lie tossing under the blazing sun till their lingering diseases quit their hold and the supreme hour of life's privilege arrives.

II. Strange, indeed, is the spectacle, as one elbows and squeezes his way through the narrow, crowded streets among the temples. The countless pilgrims, arrayed in their holiday attire, light up the scene with the tropical splendor of a flower garden. As each temple is an infallible cure for some specific disease, or of atonement for some form of ceremonial sin, a regular round of visitation is prescribed ; and, besides, the greedy Brahman priests in each must get their share of the spoils. What a sight to watch the crowds around the holy well, gulping down great draughts of the nasty, sacred liquid! As immense masses of flowers are thrown in as votive offerings, to ferment and rot there, the water has the consistency and smell of a thick, fetid vegetable soup. Chemically analyzed, the formula would be one third dysentery, one third diphtheria, and one third cholera, with a trace of water. Indeed, could certain holy wells like this and the one at Mecca be put in charge of a duly qualified Sanitary Deity, in the opinion of physicians the scourge of cholera might be stamped out. And yet, to the entranced devotees, the nectar of the gods could not furnish a more delicious draught. Such a triumph of faith over eye and nose could hardly be credited till seen in practical operation.

Meanwhile the gay-colored crowds are swarming through the narrow streets. Slow is one's progress at best, but the struggle is rendered tenfold harder by the large number of sacred cows that are meandering round at their own sweet will. Like all unduly privileged religious beings, — whether popes, grand lamas, fakirs, or venerated monkeys, — these cows take on insufferable airs of prescriptive sanctity. Ordinary human piety and humility are as nothing in their supernal sight. Now, undulating sideways and on the full trot, comes one of them, straight down the narrow, densely packed street. Right and left fall back the pilgrims, pressing into open doorways, jammed against walls, or knocked down and run over, as may be. Anyhow, the cow gets through, which is all she cares for. Then, a second sacred cow is seized, this time with a contemplative fit. Evidently, she is mastered by an impulse to meditate the Absolute, as straight across the narrow street, seven feet wide, she plants herself, — a sacred dam, heaping up the great human current. How the profane mind yearns to twist her holy tail! But to do so would mean to get one's own neck incontinently twisted. There is but one course, — patiently to wait till her mood of contemplative abstraction is over, — unless, perhaps, some devotee can divert her mind to earthly considerations by tempting her with a sacred cake from a temple, and so luring her round lengthwise to the street.

III. An hour or two at a time of this seething caldron of humanity is as much as any ordinary mortal, however interested in his species, can endure. So, working his way out of the press, he at last reaches the river-bank, and hires a boat. Ah! the relief to enjoy free elbow room and drink in a fresh breath of dehumanized air! It is a marvelous spectacle now before the eyes, as one rows along the ghats. For miles stretch the profusely carved towers of the temples and the lines of solid structures in which the richer pilgrims await the glad summons of death. Here and there are massive piles of ruins, attesting the power of the Ganges floods to undermine and topple down the heaviest masonry. Though marvelously picturesque from a distance, seen close to all wears a dilapidated look, with the exception of the superb stairways of the ghats themselves. On these are gathered thousands on thousands of devotees in holiday attire, — a splendor of color in the brilliant sunshine such as it is rarely given a mortal to see. Down to the river-bank they stream, throwing over themselves ample white, sheet-like coverings, from under which they slip off their gayer clothes. Then they wade into the heavenly polluted stream. How they plunge under the surface again and again! How they drink great double handfuls of the nauseous water, thick with the ashes of the funeral pyres! Too much of it outside and inside, they cannot absorb. Then, with what radiant faces do they emerge from the holy flood, — tottering old women, happy husbands and wives, laughing children! They will talk of this hour to their dying day, in villages a thousand miles away.

IV. Meanwhile, on great bare spaces between the ghats, is going on the perpetual burning of the dead, the real euthanasia of the favored of Krishna. At the sides stand enormous piles of wood, while into the open spaces between them are borne, on bamboo poles and wrapped in sheets, the bodies to be burned. For a while, for full baptism, the body is left immersed in the river, while the relatives are driving a cruel bargain with the sacerdotal wood-sellers and the especial sanctified wretch who has a monopoly of the sacred fire. Some have died rich enough to afford a cord of wood for the pyre, some a half-cord, some only a quarter. No matter. To all alike it means floating down the earthly river to where it joins the heavenly. The bargain struck, the wood is built up into a pyre, the body laid on it, more wood heaped on top, bits of sandal-wood thrown on for perfume, oil poured upon the whole, the sacred fire applied, and up leap the flames into the air. All around, like so many crows, perch on walls and pediments the troops of mourners; and, while their special pyre is burning, the ashes of a dozen extinct ones near it are being raked down by busy hands into the sacred flood. It is a ghastly sight. But all along the ghats below are thousands of ecstatic men, women, and children laving in the stream and drinking its divine waters. Here truly is witnessed India's tropical, jungle growth of religious imagination raised to its highest pitch.

On one pure outsider such was the impression left by the sights and scenes of holy Benares. But what can an outsider know of what was going on in the minds of these countless pilgrims? They did not see the filthy Ganges I saw. They saw a shining crystal stream flowing on to the land of Beulah. They did not shudder as I did at the cruel devouring flames. They sang, " Agni greets Agni ! " our " Fire ascending seeks the sun ! " Some inkling of this even I got. Not wholly ghastly, but partly solemnizing was the scene. As I floated along the current of the mighty symbolic river and looked off at the stupendous spectacle, in constant refrain came sounding through my mind the solemn imagery of the hymn, —

> " One army of the living God,
> To his command we bow.
> Part of the host have crossed the flood,
> And part are crossing now."

v.   One harrowing sight, however, we did not witness, nor does any man in these days, since it has been put down with an iron hand by the British government. I refer to Sati, or the self-immolation of the widow on the funeral pyre of her husband, an act of self-sacrifice so rooted in the admiration of the Hindu world that for a century government dared not face the wrath any attempt at its suppression would be sure to evoke. That there could have been any sublime and heroic side to such a ghastly superstition, few Occidental minds can conceive. So, as an illustration of the difference between the outside and the inside view of any venerated custom, I quote from the pages of a thoroughly emancipated Hindu writer a reminiscence of his own childhood days. Readers familiar with the Alcestis of Euripides will admit that the humble prose of the Hindu writer fairly matches, in the scene it calls up, the pathetic beauty of the Greek tragedian. It is, at any rate, a comfort to find a fresh illustration of the adage that there is a soul of goodness in things evil.

" When I was a little boy," says the Hindu writer, " my attention was one morning roused by hearing from my mother that my aunt was ' going on a Sati.' I pondered in my mind what the word ' Sati ' could mean. Being unable to solve the problem, I asked my mother for an explanation. She, with tears in her eyes, told me that my aunt was ' going to eat fire.' . . .

" I ran down to my aunt's room ; and what should I see there but a group of sombre-complexioned women, with my aunt in the middle. . . . She was evidently rapt in an ecstasy of devotion, earnest in all she did, quite calm and composed, as if nothing important was to happen. It appeared to me that all the women assembled were admiring the virtue and fortitude of my aunt, while not a few, falling at her feet, expressed a fond hope that they might possess a small particle of her virtue. Amidst all these surroundings, what surprised me most was my aunt's stretching out one of her hands and holding a finger right over the wick of the burning lamp for a few seconds, until it was scorched and forcibly withdrawn by the old lady who bade her do so, in order to test the firmness of her mind. The perfect composure with which she underwent this fiery ordeal convinced all that she was a real Sati, fit to abide with her husband in Boykinta, — paradise. . . .

"The body was laid on a *charpoy*. My aunt followed it, not in a closed, but in an open *palki.* She was unveiled; and regardless of the consequences of a public exposure, she was, in a manner, dead to the external world. In truth, she was evidently longing for the hour when her spirit and that of her husband should meet together and dwell in heaven.

"The dead body being placed on the pyre, my aunt was desired to walk seven times round it, which she did, while strewing flowers, cowries, and parched rice on the ground. . . . The Darogah stepped forward once more, and endeavored even at the last moment to deter her from her fatal determination.　But she, at the very threshold of ghastly death, the fatal torch of Yama before her, calmly ascended the funeral pile, and, lying down by the side of her husband, with one hand under his head and another on his breast, was heard to call in a half-suppressed voice, ' Hari ! Hari ! ' (Krishna ! Krishna !), — a sign of her firm belief in the reality of eternal beatitude. . . . A great shout of exultation then arose from the surrounding spectators, till both the dead and living bodies were converted into a handful of dust and ashes."

In submitting this heroic and pathetic story and simply leaving it to make its own impression, I can only humbly trust I shall not be subjected to the suspicion of being in secret a perfidious advocate of Sati, or Hindu widow-burning.

IV.

<table><tr><td>I.</td><td>

OUR first stopping-places after leaving Benares were Lucknow and Cawnpore, — Lucknow the scene of the heroic defense of the Regency under Lawrence and Havelock; Cawnpore that of the revolting brutalities exercised on the ill-fated men and women who, under General Wheeler, surrendered themselves to the tiger mercies of Nana Sahib. As the terrible ordeal of the Indian mutiny of 1857 brought out the indomitable qualities of British character even more signally than the original conquest, we naturally desired to see some of the memorable spots where these qualities had been illustrated at their highest pitch. In reality, the reconquest of India meant quite another thing from the conquest; for now it was a fight, not with cowardly and undisciplined natives, a host of whom would run in panic from a corporal's guard, but with Sepoys thoroughly trained in modern tactics, armed with the best weapons, inspired with fanatic, racial, and religious hate, and who had seized upon the great depositories of treasure, artillery, shot, and shell, and of cavalry and infantry equipment. No prairie fire, started at a hundred centres, and suddenly converging in a universal sheet of flame, could have surpassed in speed and fury this terrific outbreak.

</td></tr></table>

Lucknow, a city of over a quarter of a million inhabitants, was the luxurious capital of the kings of Oude till the last of them was deposed by the British and sent to Calcutta to linger out life on a pension of fifty thousand dollars a month and three hundred dancing-girls. Now, for the first time, one finds himself on strictly Mohammedan soil. The mosque with its slender minarets, onion-shaped domes, and severer Saracenic forms has mainly superseded the fantastic, nightmare delirium of the Hindu temple. Further, as the later kings of Oude were consumed by a regal passion for dancing that outdid Nero in his for acting and Commodus in his for gladiatorial fighting, highly interesting is it to inspect his palace, with its former endless zenana quarters for bewitching Nautch girls and mirrored halls for them to dance in, — the king himself ever graciously pleased to encourage their modest efforts with saltatory accompaniments of his own august heels; historically instructive, too, as showing how, just as the extreme of fondness for this graceful pastime kindled fires in the blood that enabled the daughter of Herodias to dance off John the Baptist's head, so, with their witcheries, these Nautch girls danced off the head of the last king of Oude, as grown too vertiginous with savagery and lust to be longer fit for affairs of state! Thus a lascivious art which, with us, has been reduced to a pale and bloodless abstraction is in the East so very concrete as to explain much history, political and religious.

II. It is one thing to read about the defense of the Regency of Lucknow, even under the inspiration of Tennyson's heroic poem; but it is quite another to be on the spot, and see the shattered ruins that testify to the literal hell-fire to which the short-handed garrison and crowd of helpless women were for five long months exposed. The Regency had formerly been an outlying palace of the king of Oude, with numerous groups of buildings for zenanas, barracks, festival halls, and the other appointments of an Indian court. Around all these, inclosing the great gardens, ran a ten-foot stone wall. But close up to this wall pressed on two sides the solidly built houses of the city, while on the other sides were eminences and fortress-like mosques, from which was completed the circle of flame. Night and day, without intermission, the roar and havoc went on.

Before being in Lucknow, I was familiar with the picture left by a town shattered by an earthquake; but it presented no such scene of destruction as this Regency. The buildings were simply riddled with shot and shell, and pitted as if with small-pox from the rain of rifle-balls. At any time the garrison of men could have cut their way out; but, alas, there were the women! Too well was understood the fate that awaited them should they fall into the hands of the Sepoys. And so for five long months, under the blaze of the summer sun of India, decimated with dysentery and cholera, devoured by swarms of flies, drinking hot and putrid water, their wounds refusing to heal, —

the women as heroic as the men, — the sublime defense went on. The way in which Tennyson weaves into his poem all these sickening details furnishes a striking illustration of the marvelous sense-perception of a poet's eye. A prosaic mind would no doubt have omitted the plague of flies as too undignified to allude to in company with bursting shells and exploding mines. In reality, this plague of flies was more terrible than shells and mines. They swarmed down upon the sick, the wounded, and the well, as though already carrion. The air and the ground were black with them, and it was a perpetual fight not to be eaten up alive.

And yet this scene of destruction, with its awful memories, was no mere tragic or pathetic sight. How could it be on such a resplendent day, when, as with the sun shining on the evil and on the good and the rain descending on the just and on the unjust, the exuberance of tropical nature was making haste to cover havoc and ruin in such robes of green and scarlet and gold that death seemed swallowed up in victory. Every memory, too, was bracing to the spirit. Had we met under ordinary circumstances the men and women who faced this stern ordeal, how tiresome and commonplace would the majority of them have seemed! What dreary garrison gossip should we have had to listen to, what reiteration of the grumblings that constitute the main wellspring of happiness to the British mind! what vulgar liberties taken with the letter "h"! But, when the crisis came, how magnificently all flamed out in valor, self-sacrifice, absolute devotion to one another, in the angelic care of the wounded and cholera-smitten, and in an heroic fortitude no stress of misery could break. Bracing, indeed, such witness that underneath our commonplace, of the earth earthy, humanity there lie such possibilities. It helps every one to hope of his own poor self, " Perhaps, after all, at the root of me I am not such a pitiful whipster as on the surface ! " Deeply one feels this as he stands in the great vaulted cellar in which the women were shut up for protection, and thinks of them, crowded in there, and, after high Roman fashion, searchingly debating whether, if the worst came to the worst, they would be justified in killing themselves to save their purity, or as Christians should endure to the end every horror permitted by the inscrutable will of God !

To be fair, brave, too, were the Sepoys, worthy of all praise for their desperate valor. But here was a fight of civilized reason with blind fanaticism, of stable order with weltering chaos ; above all a fight of chivalrous men for helpless women against a swarm of wretches, rather than fall into whose polluting hands they would have chosen the tender mercies of tigers. Cawnpore was soon to show the world from what fate these women were saved.

III. In Cawnpore, however, the scenes could call out no sentiments but those of pity or wrath. The flimsy, wretched intrenchment of earth which the " worst rider on the worst horse could have jumped over," into which were crowded

the soldiers, women, and children ; the imbecility
of their general, brave and devoted, but too old for
decisive action; the one well from which at night
— women and children continually shot down in
the service — they could draw their scant supply
of water in such torrid heat; the other well just beyond the intrenchment, into which after dark, and
equally under fire, they stealthily flung their mul-
tiplying dead, — all this presented the conditions
of a slaughter-pen too horrible to revive in imagination. Then, after twenty-three days, followed the
surrender, on the written pledge from Nana Sahib
of a safe passage down the Ganges to Allahabad.
It was written, not with a human hand, but with a
tiger's claw.

A couple of miles away on the river side lies the
ghat, or broad flight of stone steps descending to
the Ganges, to which the wretched victims were
marched. At first all seemed to show that Nana
Sahib was faithful to his pledge. The boats were
on hand, and into a number of them were loaded
the prisoners, and one after another started down
the river. Soon, however, it was noticed that only
the older women were allowed to embark, while the
younger were kept back. "We are betrayed!"
groaned General Wheeler; and his head sunk on
his breast. Forthwith, at a given signal, a blaze of
fire burst forth on the ghat, and from the trees on
the river-bank along which the boats were passing.
The native boatmen had already jumped into the
river, and were swimming ashore. In an instant
General Wheeler and his staff were shot dead;

while the merciless fire from the bank poured in
upon the poor men and women that had embarked,
and set the boats in flames.

To more than hint at the fate, for the next twenty
days, of the younger women, then marched back,
would be too revolting. Stories are told on the
spot which will never get into any of the public
histories. Even the avenger, in the shape of General Havelock and his little army, came too late for
them; for, on the first defeat of his forces, Nana
Sahib ordered in the town butchers with their
knives to slaughter the wretched women and their
children, who were then, dying and dead, thrown
into an adjoining well. Two hours later Havelock
and his army were on the spot. Ah, Christian
hero and so-called Christian soldiers, in the jungle
of your hearts lurks the bloodthirsty tiger as in the
Indian jungle! Vanished from sight the last faint
glimpse of the compassionate one on the cross with
his "Father forgive, they know not what they do!"
All hell broke loose in the hearts of the cursing,
hysterically weeping soldiers, and yet this hell
seeming a flame of sacred fire from heaven, the car-
nival of vengeance now set in. "General Neale,
you will see these prisoners properly executed,"
sternly commanded Havelock. Neale rolled up his
sleeves, and gave his order: "First drag these
devils through Christian blood!" It was obeyed,
and over the pools of the still warm blood of the
so lately butchered women the men were trailed.
Then, scores by scores, they were blown from the
mouths of cannon, or hung from the branches of a

neighboring tree till it could bear no further weight of its ghastly fruit.

Like looking down from the rim of a crater into the pit of fiery lava below, was it to stand on the very spot and listen to the tale of this volcanic outbreak of human passion from the lips of an old soldier who had come in with Havelock's force, and been an eye-witness of this scene.

Three ineffaceable memories will always linger in my mind as interpreters of these tragic scenes. The first, the Hindu temple which stands on the top of the ghat descending to the Ganges, and from the banks beside which the murderous fire was poured into the boats. The temple itself is carved and painted with obscenities so hideously revolting as to seem fit shrine to inspire such atrocities. The second will be that of the inscription over the gate of the cemetery, where beneath palms and feathery acacias sleep the majority of those who perished in the siege. The words were simply, "Tread softly." The third, the pathetic fitness of the Scripture passage chosen for the monument over the well into which were thrown the butchered women and children. It is from a verse of the Psalms, the startling realism of whose imagery of the wood-chopper and his chips had a thousand times impressed me, and which now seemed to revive its literal sense : "Our bones are scattered at the grave's mouth, as when one cutteth and cleaveth wood upon the earth."

Immense, however, as was the cost of the reconquest, and terrible as were the passions let loose, every day one spends in India convinces him more profoundly of the infinite boon it is to this vast population to be held in subjection by a power at once so strong, enlightened, and humane as that of Great Britain. To leave once again to themselves these peoples of such diverse races and fanaticisms would be like opening all the cages in a menagerie, and letting jaguar, leopard, lion, rhinoceros fight out the question of supremacy among themselves. The beast that would end off king would be the tiger ; and, as has significantly been added, the tiger would be the Mohammedan.

V.

I. As one travels by rail across the vast fertile plains of northern India, and every now and then comes out on a city, with its temples, mosques, and palaces of Maharajas, or of wealthy merchants, the whole social and political history of India is explained at a glance. As a rule, there is but one step from the hovel to the palace. Rude as the tepees of our North American Indians are the majority of the huts of the natives. Built, as a general rule, of dried mud, with no opening to the light and air but a door-frame minus a door, the roof a thatch of palm or bamboo grass, they literally swarm with children, and, no doubt, countless other tenants. Fifty or sixty of these huts are commonly huddled together, yet not so closely but that they are shaded with picturesque bananas, palms, and mangoes, the light and shade of which are glorified with the scarlet, green, and gold of the dresses of the women, and turned into an Eden of primeval innocence by the beautiful naked bodies, the animated bronze, of the children. Undue sympathy, however, for little boys and girls devoid of clothes is at once checked by the thought how vastly more comfortable they are without than with them. Besides, another happy reflection comes to the rescue. If too poor to wear clothes, there are none of them too poor to indulge in jewelry. Rarely a naked little tyke that has not silver bracelets on his wrists and silver anklets on his feet.

" I can get along without necessities, but I must have luxuries," is in India no mere witty Gallic paradox. It is hard, practical common sense. To sell a nose-ring for a dress would be to an Indian woman a far wilder freak of insanity than for an American woman to sell her dress for a nose-ring, and would draw down upon her graver censure from her sex. Accordingly, many the extremely poor Indian woman one meets, carrying on her head an unsightly load of dried cakes of cow-dung, the principal fuel, with both her arms six inches deep in bracelets, and both her ankles six deep in anklets, not to speak of stone-set rings in both flanges and the central cartilage of the nose, together with a miscellaneous collection hanging from the upper circles and the lobes of the ears.

In all conscience, this would seem jewelry enough for any reasonable woman in distressingly limited pecuniary circumstances to care to disport. Not at all. On the road one falls in with great troops of gypsies, who in addition wear on each toe a ring with a little tinkling bell attached, thus picturesquely illustrating the song, " She shall have music wherever she goes." Inevitably, is one carried back in imagination over two thousand years, as now in all its vividness is lighted up to him the stern denunciation of Isaiah : " Because the daughters of Zion are haughty, and walk with stretched forth necks and wanton eyes, walking and mincing as they go, and making a tinkling with their feet : . . . therefore the Lord will take away the bravery of their tinkling ornaments, . . . the bracelets, ear-rings, and nose jewels," together, in the sacred text, with a catalogue of other feminine adornments I have not had the good fortune to encounter even in India, but which most likely prevail in circles from which, on grounds of faith and practice, I am unhappily debarred.

But these poor, half-fed women I have been describing the sublime prophet could never have had the heart to denounce. The one and only savings-bank they have ever heard of is the nose, ears, wrists, ankles, and toes of a woman. There they store away their ancestral inheritance, their hard-earned savings, the future portion of their children. Scarcely would starvation induce them to break in upon the sacred hoard. And yet they, with a family of six, are living on two dollars and a half a month. Poor things, let them tinkle as they go! Not of them, but of their wanton Nautch-girl sisters in the zenanas, did Isaiah speak.

II. Continually, as we journeyed on, would the question arise, " Are these poor people at heart as miserable as their surroundings would seem to argue ? " It is a great relief to say that probably they are not. Theirs is a passive tem-

perament; their work is a quiet routine, no demon
of machinery goads them on to keep pace with its
whirling wheels. With plenty of leisure for talk
and laughter, they have no sons to put through
Harvard; their daughters are married at ten or
twelve; they enter on the Nirvana of grandfather
or grandmother at twenty-six; and finally their religion affords them, with its ceremonials and pilgrimages, a constant imaginative delight, broken,
it is true, by some frightful nightmares. Few,
indeed, the farmers, mechanics, or clerks who,
with us, could get off for such week-long holiday
tramps as they, to the temples of favorite deities
or saints, — tramps on which they take along with
them their wives and children and neighbors and
friends, all seeing the world together, and at the
same time washing away their sins. In fact, what
Saratoga, the White Sulphur Springs, Newport,
are to the well-off with us, that and more than
that are Benares, Jagannath, and a host of other
shrines, to millions of the poorest of the poor in
India.

Of course in the past history of India, wars,
harryings, and burnings must have wrought indescribable misery. And yet in a country like this,
and with such a people, devastations are rapidly
recovered from. Human nature adapts itself to
anything; and I am inclined to think that, in the
case of such a people, it is a good deal as with
the hawks and the sparrows. The hawk pounces
down, and there is a wild fluttering and screaming.
He secures his victim, and flies away. Soon all

is forgotten, and the little birds are twittering and singing on the branches as before.

In fine, what is so widely characterized as the deep-rooted melancholy and pessimism of India is a passive rather than an active, a soothing rather than an embittering, sentiment, at the last remove from the misanthropy of a Dean Swift rushing madly from a hateful world to "die of rage like a poisoned rat in his hole;" nearer akin, indeed, to Jaques in the Forest of Arden, with his, "I can suck melancholy out of a song, as a weasel sucks eggs. More, I prithee, more." Rather does it take the form of a vague and dreamy sense of the evanescence of human life and of tranquil indifference to what it has to offer. All this coil is not worth the price. Toil is pain, care is fever, dreamy rest alone is sweet. As opium to the nerves, such is religion to the spirit, the delicate haze that dissolves the hard outlines of reality, the sense of the serene universal life that quiets down all fret of the finite.

No wonder, then, that in India opium and religion are craved by the peasant as the two great tranquillizers. Thus among the causes of the final utter extinction of Buddhism in the land of its birth, and the rehabilitation in public favor of its rival, such scholars as Barth are disposed to rank chief the morbid monotony, in its later developments, of the Buddhistic insistence on an utterly pessimistic view of human existence along with a return to ascetic practices, all at the cost of the present realized peace so beautifully illustrated in the life of its founder. Indeed, in original Buddhism, pessimism served but as the negative to a positive, but as the vanishing point of the finite for entrance on non-finite blessedness. It was the Oriental solution of the paradox of losing the life to find it, of the paradox of St. Paul, " poor, yet making many rich, having nothing, and yet possessing all things." And so it became a gospel of present salvation from all consciousness of the ills of existence to millions, alike of the poor and ignorant who in such a climate crave mainly the feeling of sensuous — not sensual — repose, and to the wealthy and powerful who were wooed by it to turn away from the greeds and ambitions that heat the blood and fret the spirit toward the interior enjoyment of those gentle and kindly feelings in which alone tranquillity and peace abide.

III. Back in our own childhood days, many the moral drawn for our improvement from the bellicose propensities of cats and dogs in contrast with the loving spirit that should prevail in well-regulated households of little boys and girls. In India one often wonders whether the stupendous scale upon which this lesson is illustrated on the part of the whole animal creation has not had a vast deal to do with the depth of the national reaction in favor of mental peace. While the men, women, and children are vegetarians, all the other members of creation, from the Bengal tiger to the most invisible gnat, are not. Such apparatus of stings, claws, fangs, suction-tubes, incisors, all exquisitely contrived for the partition and assimilation of flesh and blood, hardly elsewhere can be paralleled. And yet nowhere else does such aversion prevail against taking life. When one sees great troops of stark-naked fakirs and mathematically calculates the area of surface they expose in invitation to mosquitoes, gnats, ants, ticks, and chigres, — not to speak of the graver temptations opened up to snakes, leopards, and lions, — one is lost in admiration of the positive refusal on the part of the fakir to retort in kind. In reality can he tranquilly "meditate the absolute and immutable" on an outdoor carpet of ants and under a canopy of gnats and feel "I am Brahma, and fiery skin and stinging pismire are but figments of a dream," while, with us, a single fly is enough to take all the tenderness out of a love-letter, the soundness out of a legal brief, nay, all the devoutness even out of a sermon? If he can, then what a joint miracle of interior absorption and exterior cuticular induration! The Occidental world needs such men as missionaries.

In view, then, of the richness and variety of the animal kingdom in India, and of its probable psychologic connection with certain of the most striking traits of the inhabitants, it would seem invidious on the part of the traveler to omit his meed of tribute to such divisions of it as especially have interested and instructed him. So personally I feel moved to devote a few words to snakes.

In Ceylon more people are killed by falls from

cocoa-nut palms than perish from snake-bites. Not that this is to be construed in mitigation of snakes, but it does seem to emphasize the moral responsibility of one portion of the globe for another in thus so clearly connecting every little cocoanut-eating boy at home in guilty complicity with the awful fate of widowhood in India. None the less, snakes abound everywhere, especially hooded cobras, so enshrined in religious veneration that not even the loss of a favorite child will induce any but the lowest caste Hindus to kill one of them.

From these low-caste Hindus is it that are recruited the ranks of the so-called snake-charmers, itinerant showmen whose main charm consists in cutting out the fangs and poison sacs of the brutes before disporting with them in public. Even then the hateful reptiles maintaiu a certain prestige of horror which sets fascinating cold chills running down the back as, spite of the loss of their venomous weapons, they still keep striking out in the most vicious manner. That the morality of every act lies solely in its intention is made plain to the obtusest ethical observers. Still, no intelligent traveler is willing to content himself with cobras with their fangs cut out, more than with tigers lapping gruel instead of blood. He wants to see the frightful reptile in all his terror and all his malignity, and this, if he will pay the price, the snake-charmers will give him a chance to witness in a fight between a full-fanged cobra and a mongoose.

IV. So imperfect are the sympathies of the average man with the cobra that from a purely spiritual point of view a fight between him and a mongoose has none of the drawbacks in the way of wounded sensibilities attendant on an encounter between two creatures of the higher rank of dogs. Spite of his adoption of the hood of a devout Carmelite, the cobra remains at heart a sinuous, slimy, pestiferous brute, whom hardly the Buddha could take home to his bosom and love. He glides into the arena, moreover, guilty of the blood of at least ten thousand men, women, and children a year in his native land. His adversary, on the other hand, is a lithe, mercurial, lightning-swift little lemur, of ferret or weasel build, — an electric flash of intelligence and aim irresistibly reminding one, in temperament and fibre, of the miraculous French scholastic champion Abélard, all on a quiver for an intellectual set-to with the most redoubtable swash-buckler of Nominalism or Realism, William of Champeaux or other. The very prince of subtle acumen, ready to let fly in an instant and with unerring aim at every joint in the armor of his antagonist, the mongoose sails into battle like the marvelous Frenchman, a derisive smile playing around his white teeth that prophesies victory from the start.

Plainly at the very outset the cobra is gravely disconcerted and would be glad to slink out of the controversy through any knot-hole. The convincing logical categories on which hitherto he has relied so confidently seem inconclusive in the presence of an intelligence so much more acute. But there is no escape. Every hair erect with metaphysical frenzy and eyes blood-shot with battle-flame, electric Abélard is circling round him. So out the cobra lashes with his terrible fangs in what is meant to be a mortal argument. Lightly the mongoose springs aside or leaps whole feet into the air, and the fangs strike idly into invulnerable space; while before the cobra can recover himself his quicksilver antagonist has got in on tail or body an irritating argumentative nip with his ferret teeth.

So far, all this on the mongoose's part is but a pleasant by-play of logical fence. His intuitive mind is simply preluding with the graver issue. Just where the force of his adversary's major premise lies is to him as plain as day, and that it lies not in his body or tail but in his brain. An unguarded movement, a promising opening, and with a lightning-swift spring through the air, the infallible logician has seized the cobra just back of the head where the turn is too short to bring the fangs to bear. Master of the situation, intellect and teeth are now concentrated on the single point at stake. All in vain the infuriated cobra writhes his coils round the mongoose's body, rolls him over and over along the arena, and thrashes him on the ground. Not for a moment is the clearness of his mental vision distracted by such specious sophistries. Steadily he hangs on to the major premise, gnawing his way ever higher and higher up till at last his keen-ground metaphysical teeth have pierced the brain. The quick of the controversy is reached and forever silenced. William of Champeaux lies stark and still, while without waste of further breath, victorious Abélard quietly withdraws from the university arena, leaving the assembled students lost in admiration at the brilliancy of his controversial tactics.

Surely, if fighting there must be, here is a kind in which the intellectual element so dominates the brutal as to render it distinctly educational. Wholly beyond, moreover, and realms above its mere dazzling brilliancy is felt its profound ethical and historical significance ; for, presumptuously as has been challenged for itself by another world-famous exhibition the title of the " Greatest Moral Show on Earth," this fairly may claim its right to the proud appellation. Frivolous, indeed, must be the nature on whose imagination the scene does not impress itself as a sublime piece of symbolism in which nothing less momentous is typified than the elemental struggle of light and darkness, good and evil. " Ah ! " soliloquizes the more reflective mind, — "ah ! that instead of poor, scatter-brained mother Eve our 'first parent' had been the mongoose. How different, then, the issue of the primal battles with the serpent, and how changed the subsequent event of human history ! "

VI.

I.   BEFORE going on to record the impressions left by Agra and Delhi, the two most splendid capitals of the Mogul dynasty, a brief historical sketch may not be out of place.

Several chapters back, a comparison was made between the Alps and the plain of Lombardy on the one hand and, on the other, the Himalayas and the enormous level stretches of northern India, the object being to show on how vastly more colossal a geological scale India was fashioned. Precisely the same overpowering impression on the imagination is made the moment one tries to form an adequate conception of the relation in which India has ever stood to the enormous races and nationalities environing her for thousands of miles to the west and the north, — in Arabia, Persia, Afghanistan, Turkestan, China, Tartary.

As one reads the story of the fall of the Roman Empire, he is awed at the thought of the hordes of Goths, Vandals, Lombards, Teutons, that stood ready to pour down on that narrow fringe of civilization around the Mediterranean; but how petty in numbers and range were these in comparison with the inconceivably vaster hordes — when once they should become unified under a conquering religion — to be drawn from the enormous expanses of western and northern Asia! One little swoop of their swarms in the far-back days of Attila came near destroying the Roman Empire; and yet this was but as a single wave of the ocean to the successive myriads of them breaking on and over the northern rock-barriers of India. Indeed, in thinking of Asia in comparison with Europe, one is perpetually reminded of a saying of Alexander the Great after he had embarked on his career of Oriental conquest: "When I get a dispatch from my little kingdom of Macedon, reporting to me the taking of some insignificant hill town or of a successful fight for the capture of a ford, I seem to be reading of the battles of the frogs and mice."

Through the birth and religion of Mohammed, who died in 632 A. D., came the flash that was to set aflame, not in one, but in century-successive, prairie fires, these vast inflammable areas of races and nationalities. Here was a religion which made paradise and plunder, loyalty and looting, one and indivisible, — an entrancing harmony of the ferocity of nature with the attractions of grace. "The possessions of the infidel are the inheritance of the faithful," had been the proclamation of the Prophet himself. What sanguinary Afghan, bloodthirsty Turcoman, ugly, squint-eyed Tartar, but would yearn to become a child of Allah when the news of such a gospel should reach him in his rugged mountain fastnesses, or on his wide, grass-waving steppes?

Well-nigh from the outset of the rise of the Mohammedan power, India was the Roman Empire of the south of Asia, on which the covetous eyes of the faithful were fixed. "Lieber Gott!" cried out rough-and-ready General Blücher, when he first saw London, "what a city to loot!" What might not have been said of India, with its mines of gold and jewels, its temples heaped with treasures, its cities teemiug with manufactories of silks and tissues of gold, its palaces of kings and princes? As early as 650 began the invasions from Arabia, while meantime conquests were pushed through Persia and clear up to the Hindu Kush. For centuries the struggle went on, ever increasing in fury and weight of numbers as the vast hordes of the north came under Mohammedan sway. Province after province was conquered and securely held, while at times devastating incursions like that of Timur, the Tartar, in 1398, swept everything helplessly before them. Not, however, till the invasion of Babar, sixth in descent from the terrible Timur, was anything like the foundation laid of a permanent Mohammedan dynasty ruling all India, — the famous Mogul dynasty, which continued on, in shadow at least, till, in the Sepoy rebellion, the last of its princes were dragged out from the subterranean chambers of their ancestors' tomb and shot dead by brutal Hodson of Hodson's Horse.

II. The term Mogul dynasty can easily become misleading, suggestive as it is of the stiff-haired, yellow-faced, squint-eyed Tartar. Long before the consolidation every trace of this kind of physical, mental, and moral strabismus had been drowned out of the royal family in overpowering mixtures of Afghan, Persian, Circassian, Saracen, Jewish, even Christian blood. Whatever the pros and cons as to polygamy, one thing is certain, — polygamy of the extra-racial kind is good for the Tartar. Cut off from, or æsthetically eschewing, Tartar wives, he is enabled steadily to efface himself for the benefit of his posterity. What with Aryan and Semitic wives at freest command, — the only two that, historically, are worthy of consideration, — he, in the course of generations, ultimately reduces to zero his horse-mane hair, squint eyes, and tallow face, and along with these their corresponding intellectual, æsthetic, and moral qualities. Then scratch his skin, and you will not find the Tartar. With the addition of the plural for the singular, the adage now proves true that a man owes all he is to — his mothers.

No, you will not find the Tartar in the emperors of the so-called Mogul dynasty. Swiftly they established a brilliant, cosmopolitan, and, in many ways, wise and scientific administration. In 1556, only sixty years after Babar's conquest, began the wonderful half-century reign of Akbar the Great, which inaugurated the renaissance age of India. Art, literature, philosophy, the spirit of cosmopolitan tolerance, all took a new start. Max Müller, indeed, pronounces Akbar the first founder of a "comparative study of the religions of the world" — even anticipating Chicago! Nothing so delighted him as to assemble learned Brahmans, Mussulmans, Zoroastrians, Jews, Jesuit padres, and skeptical philosophers, and to hear them argue with one another. " Gradually," says a bitter Mohammedan hater of his " spirit of inquiry, opposed to every Islamitic principle," —" gradually there grew, as the outline on a stone, the conviction in his heart that there were sensible men in all religions and abstemious thinkers." No mere intellectual critic, but a man profoundly devout in heart, Akbar finally built up a religion of his own, — a combination of all he thought wisest and best in Brahmanical teaching, Zoroastrian fire-worship, Mohammedan morality, and Christian dogma, even substituting for the usual formula, " Bismallah," etc., of Islam, the rather compound one of

"O thou whose names are Jesus 'and Christ,
We praise thee : there is no one beside thee, O God ! "

As one reads the story of Akbar's attitude toward the rival religions, impossible it is, spite of Max Müller's assertion, not to call to mind King Solomon, and to raise the historical query whether the title of first founder of the study of comparative religions does not more fitly belong to him. The cases are strikingly parallel. The old desert faith of the Hebrews had weakened; contact with Egypt and Assyria had brought rival religions into comparison; equally excellent wives from Tyre, Sidon, Babylon, Thebes, and Memphis, had softened the heart of the wisest of kings, and rendered him tender toward their respective creeds; and, besides all this, Solomon was himself a man of restless and subtle intellect. Akbar's was, no doubt, the devouter nature of the two;

yet still the renaissance in India and the renaissance in Judæa were such essentially similar phenomena, and so equally bound up with the individuality of two highly intellectual and widely married Oriental sovereigns, that it may not seem presumptuous to submit even to a Max Müller the propriety of a reconsideration of his statement. Certain it is that Akbar's Christian wife Mary exerted over his life an influence at once liberalizing and exalting, and so inclined his heart towards her creed. The subject at any rate opens up a novel chapter in the study of the part woman has played in the historical development of religion.

III. In Agra, Akbar the Great built for his glory and pleasure a gigantic fortress-palace a mile and a half in circuit, its massive crenelated walls seventy feet in height, entered on four sides by stupendous gateways, in themselves at once forts and sumptuous palaces. Within the vast inclosure there is room not merely for storehouses against a siege, barracks for the soldiery, dormitories for the retainers and troops of servants, grounds for horse-exercise, sports and elephant-fights, but immense areas for mosques, audience-halls, gardens, baths, zenanas. For air and freshness, along the top of the massive sandstone walls, are exquisitely wrought towers of pure white marble and ranges of apartments for noonday siestas; while on the marble surface of their level roofs above stretch wide spaces for gatherings in the cool of the evening or for lying out and sleeping under the stars. All command broad views over the richly cultivated country, the river Jumna winding in great sweeps through the landscape. It is, in fine, the Alhambra of India, the fortress for safety; the audience-halls for the administration of justice and the reception of ambassadors; the mosque for the worship of Allah; the zenanas for the beauties of Cashmere, Persia, Syria; the palaces for splendor, luxury, repose; the gardens, fountains, canals, and baths for coolness, perfume, murmuring sounds.

Apart from the mosques, the Saracenic Mohammedan architecture of India has one unfailing characteristic. It makes a rich, sensuous appeal to common human nature, and requires for its full appreciation no spiritual elevation of soul. Every man who, hot and thirsty, has felt the rapture of a plunge into a cool brook or of a long, delicious draught from a bubbling spring, has in himself the fundamental elements of sense and feeling to which this architecture and its surroundings are addressed. Every man, furthermore, who as he walks by the seashore delights to pluck a handful of bayberry leaves and eagerly inhale their aromatic perfume; every man who on a hot July afternoon feels the luxury of a dreamy siesta in his hammock, with a delicious breeze stealing over him; every man who finds it paradise to have his inamorata take her guitar and sing soothing songs to him while he reposes his weary Olympian brow on a sofa-cushion, — is, just in so far, perfectly capable of appreciating the æsthetic sense of an Akbar the Great or a Shah Jehan, when —

> " In Xanadu did Kubla Khan
> A stately pleasure-dome decree,
> Where Alph, the sacred river, ran
> Through caverns measureless to man
> Down to a sunless sea."

In India the climate is tropical. Air and shade are the primal requisites. There must be no staircases to climb. Apartment must succeed apartment on the same level. The roofs, too, must be utilized for ample spaces for the enjoyment of the starlight and the moonlight and the sweet sleep to be had on them. Still other airy buildings must be set a-top these roofs for wider outlook or yet more sequestered privacy. Screens of openwork marble, cut in exquisite patterns of vines and palms and lilies and pomegranates, shall be the sole walls of these buildings, that the jessamine-scented breezes may steal through them, and the brighter sunlight be transfigured into a golden twilight, and the moonlight into mysterious dreamlight.

Such, then, was the fairy-land, the midsummer-night's dream, that Akbar the Great undertook to make reality within the fort of Agra, and which his successors, Jehangir and Shah Jehan, carried to completeness. The yearning of Abt Vogler to arrest and make permanent the ravishment of his manifold music there found its genii to achieve the task. The fullness of time had come. Long before had the beauty-loving Saracenic genius, seizing upon the treasures of Greek and Roman architecture in the East, developed out of them bewitching architectural types suited to embody its own inborn cravings. Syria and Persia were full of master-builders; and from Italy, too, they could be drawn without stint. In India there were treasuries of gold and silver, and millions of subjects to toil for a pittance. Over all presided the undying genius of Greece in imperishable architectural forms that needed only modifications through the Saracenic arch, the extension of an inclined piazza roof for shade, and the freer use of graceful minarets and open cupolas, to evolve a new order, which for symmetry, grace, and appeal to the pleasure-craving, dreamy side of human nature is without rival in the world.

IV. Even in our own country, the relation borne by woman to architectural construction has been made a subject of grave comment by philosophic minds, — especially in its bearing on the multiplication of closets and corresponding shrinkage of size in the living and sleeping rooms, to leave space for the closets. In the Orient this influence becomes still more marked. A man with three hundred wives requires, of course, a domestic establishment differently arranged from that of a man with only one. Take, for example, the single instance of adequate provision for bathing. Were there but one little bath-room in so hot a climate, and did each several wife insist on lying in the tub half the day and the rest of the day on a Persian rug beside it, it will readily be seen that serious domestic complications might arise. Construct, on the other hand, immense marble halls, with swimming-pools of marble thirty feet long, and large areas of marble floors, on which could be laid a hundred rugs, whereon the beauties of India, Circassia, and Syria might stretch out and doze or gossip or eat sweetmeats, then what enhanced prospects of marital peace would at once ensue! Inlay the marble walls of these halls with exquisite designs in precious stones, and roof them with delicate mirror-work overrun with fairy-like marble traceries of vines and lilies, and why should not all be satisfied with bathing, dozing, telling stories, and doing nothing all day long?

Again, for an example of the influence of woman on architecture, take the so-called Jasmine Tower, erected by Shah Jehan for his favorite sultana. It overhangs the wall of the fortress, and is in-wrought with such indescribable beauty of open-work marble screens as to drive the fancy wild. Now Shah Jehan was extremely fond of playing chess with his prime vizier; but, like most Oriental sovereigns, he was also fond of mitigating the asperities of too protracted thought. So, on the floor of the court before the Jasmine Tower, needs must he have a chess-board constructed of marble flagging, each flag-stone large enough for a man or woman to stand on freely. Then, at a signal, the requisite numbers of his wives, gorgeously arrayed as kings and queens and bishops and knights and pawns, would file out of the zenana, while, luxuriously seated on their divans, Shah Jehan and the vizier would direct with finger or word the complicated movements of the game of living chess. In this way was taken off the perhaps too severe intellectual edge of an otherwise so exacting pastime.

Such little straws as these must serve to show which way the wind blows in the Mohammedan domestic architecture of India; and I must leave it to the imagination of my readers to carry these hints out into all the details of gardens and fountains and successive halls of splendor, and pools and marble canals mirroring and repeating in their transfigured reflections the dream‑world above. This Saracenic Mohammedan architecture, as I have said before, is the apotheosis of sensuous æstheticism. It has no lift to it, no ideal beyond what it sees already perfect. "If paradise be anywhere it is here, here, here!" wrote Shah Jehan over one of the portals. A man living under such conditions would, I should think, struggle fiercely never to die. What could there be to his sense-restricted imagination in the vision, "Eye hath not seen, nor ear heard, neither heart conceived the things God hath in store"? No. "If paradise be anywhere, it is here, it is here!"

V. In the fiery, sun-blistered deserts of Arabia, in which Mohammedanism took its rise, the physical basis of all imaginative visions of the paradise yearned after was the oasis. Paradise, indeed, was the oasis when the tongue‑parched wayfarer

struggled, faint and exhausted, out of the burning
sands, and flung himself down under the shade of
its palms and mimosas, and drank deep draughts
from its delicious springs. Allah had there done
his supremest creative feat, and revealed himself
in the highest to his creatures. What more divine
could he bring to pass in reward of the faithful
than to make just this kind of experience everlasting, — with the entrancing addition of the houris?
Such, then, was the vision of the celestial home ;
and the next step was to try to make it come on
earth, even as it lay awaiting in paradise.

This primitive idea of the oasis has dominated
the mind of Mohammedanism wherever the faith
has spread ; and Saracenic domestic and, I may
add, mortuary architecture is but its full and final
flower. In it are the original sense-impressions of
the blissful change from the glare of the desert to
the shade of the palms and the refreshment of the
springs, but raised to the seventh æsthetic heaven.
In his infinite mercy, had it not pleased Allah to
create for the faithful a substance called marble,
snowy white as his own purity; among stones, a
kind of precious stone enduring as granite and yet
capable of being made translucent as amber, and
wreathed all over with the most delicate traceries
of vines and flowers ? Then, further, to relieve its
perhaps too great monotony of white, had it not
equally pleased Allah to create the beryl, the onyx,
the jasper, the lapis lazuli, wherewith to inlay it,
and to assure delightful variety of hue and sheen ?
Still more, that all suggestion of glare might

utterly be removed, had not Allah caused to grow the palm, the tamarind, the cypress, the banyan, the orange, wherein to embower and relieve the shining white, and, along with these, made pure crystal waters to leap up in fountains, and fill the pools of courts, and reflect from the mirrored surface the porticoes and minarets and domes, and houris arrayed in robes of cashmere or unarrayed in aught but their own surpassing charms?

Now, it is in this ineffable unity of gardens, terraces, canals, fountains, minarets, snow-white domes, that lie the witchery and seduction of India's Saracenic architecture. All is dissolved into one melodious music, every object transfigured into element of one fairy-land. The eye is fed with gracious forms, the ear with murmuring sounds, the scent with delicious perfumes. Alternate sensations of languorous heat and refreshing coolness, of thirst and of oranges hanging down to slake it with, of invitation to rest with appeal to wander leisurely on, sensuously appeal to blended body and soul.

VI. There are two buildings in Agra which it is considered a mark of barbarism not to rave over, — the one, the Pearl Mosque within the walls of the fort; the other, the Taj Mahal, on the curving bank of the river Jumna, a mile or more away from the fort. The latter is the memorial tomb of Shah Jehan's favorite wife, Muntaz Mahal, "Chosen of the Palace." Taj is but the diminutive, the pet name of endearment for Muntaz, as we should say Nell for Ellen.

Now, in respect of the first of these two, the Pearl Mosque, no fear of æsthetic excommunication will prevent my saying that it suffers most severely from the lack of just that which is the crowning fascination of most Saracenic buildings. The glare of the desert, the fatal monotony of the unrelieved whiteness of marble, the absence anywhere of the oasis, with its springs and overshadowing trees, render it a place almost intolerable under the sun of India. Surpassingly beautiful are its outlines, with its pillared aisles, its three snowy domes, and its delicately carved cloisters surrounding the sides of the open court-yard; and in the rosy flush of early dawn, or under the dream-spell of moonlight, one might love to linger there, but not when the sun is riding high in the heavens. Then the direct smiting rays or their equally blinding reflections pierce everywhere; and one can conceive of none but a half-crazed fakir, making a merit of a crematory of the living flesh, ever seeking it as a place of prayer.

But of the Taj Mahal, in contrast, what shall I say? It is by thousands of judges pronounced the most beautiful building in the world; but never a one of them who has first drunk its intoxicating soma juice is ever again competent to pass a calmly reasoned verdict, whether it is or is not. Nor does it make any difference who beholds it. The most ideal young American girl, the driest student of comparative architecture, the most commonplace British Philistine, the emptiest-headed globe-trotter who has raked together money enough to go round the world and return home the same, only a bit more confused than he set out, — all are equally carried away, all lifted to the seventh heaven of their respective (short or long) celestial Jacob's ladders.

The Taj is not a building. It is an Arabian Night's dream, in which a building plays a queenly part. It is a tropical orchestra, in which earth, sky, grove, waters, flowers, precious stones, moon-orbed domes, snowy pinnacles, blend and flow into one Mozart symphony. All along on the way from Calcutta to Agra I had seen alabaster models of the Taj, and said to myself sadly, "Is that all?" The models left out only the golden clouds from around the sinking sun, the shining waters from beneath the rising moon, the lover's soul from the spell of his mistress's song, — only that, and no-thing more!

One enters the inclosure of the Taj by a superb gateway, through whose lofty arch he looks along the sky, grove, and dome reflecting surface of a marble-paved canal, bordered on either side by wide paths and beds of flowers and flanked by lines of dark, spiry cypress-trees, backed with groves on either hand. In vista at the end of this magic avenue, and repeated in transfiguration in the water, stands the Taj. How superb a setting! The marble platform on which it rests is a square three hundred and thirteen feet each way and eighteen feet in height. From each of the four corners mounts high aloft an indescribably graceful minaret, relieved in its ascent by three hanging galleries and surmounted by the beautiful Saracenic cupola. There in the middle of the grand platform rises the Taj, itself like the pinnacles, all of snowy, exquisitely carved marble, the finial of its marble dome two hundred and twenty feet aloft in the blue sky. Further, as one still looks out from the gateway, stretch to the right and left the great tropical gardens, beautiful with palms, mimosas, and tamarinds, lighted up by the splendor of the plumage of darting paroquets, and with a glory of scarlet, purple, and gold in the trailing vines.

I do not know whether the Taj is the most beautiful building in the world or not. I never want to know. If Euclid demonstrated to me in ten immutable axioms and ten immutable deductions from them that it was not, it would make no difference. I only know that in its combination with earth and sky it presents the most fairy-like scene on earth. Thought is not: in enjoyment it expires.

I saw the Taj by early morning light, by sunset light, and by moonlight, when every trace of materiality was so dissolved in ethereal spirit that it seemed as though all material barriers were melted away, and the living here and the living there must float together and feel neither out of sphere. And yet no glare, even of fiercest noonday, has power to break the poetic spell. Perennial oasis in life's so frequent waste, against it verdure, wellspring of delight, lotus land of dreams, no Libyan desert can prevail. And just as within its inmost shrine, illuminated not by windows, but only through the graceful openwork sprays of vines and flowers chiseled in marble screens, the blaze of the midday sunshine is transfigured into a soft, golden haze, so equally there the harshest sounds are transformed into melodious music. Let a strain be sung by the most discordant voice, even were it a snatch of a simple song, and forthwith is it taken up as by a choir of angels and sent circling and circling through the tremulously vibrating vault above, sweet and jubilant, as over Bethlehem the "Hymn of the Nativity." No word is repeated; only, as it were, the theme of the musician is taken up and revealed in its divine intent, revealed as he, too, shall later hear it, stored away and enriched in the sanctifying memory of God. All seems imbued as by an instinct of chaste purity that will be sullied by nothing discordant or profane, but which ignores it, and soars above it into a celestial realm. Even the sleeping woman there, the wife and mother who died in childbirth pangs, and in tender memory of whom all this miracle of beauty was evoked, suggests no thought of pain.

VII.

I.   WHAT more fitting preface to the little I shall have space to say about Delhi than the passionate cry of the French *savant*, James Darmesteter? " Delhi the royal! Delhi the imperial! Delhi the bleeding! I have had but four days to wander among thy ruins and thy tombs: it will be the eternal regret of my life. For two thousand years has the heart of India beaten there, whatever the color of the blood — Aryan, Turk, Afghan, Mogul — that the waves of invasion rolled thither. Whosoever would breathe with one breath the India of Brahma and the India of Allah, let him traverse, stone by stone, the forty-five square miles which Delhi in succession, along the banks of the Jumna, has peopled with ruins and phantoms."

Yes, the India of Brahma and the India of Allah, the awe-imposing phantoms of both are there. Thither Shah Jehan, sated with the magnificence of Agra, removed his court, and built a new Alhambra, rivaling in splendor and luxury the one he had left behind, while all about him in the area of forty square miles lay the ruins of the earlier perished cities of Afghan, Tartar, Persian conquerors, and of the far-back Hindu rulers. Ruined and deserted capitols, tenanted now but

by bats, owls, and fakirs, are the historical land-
marks of India, telling in monotony of repetition
the story of the ravages and insane caprices of
tyrannic and irresponsible power to which has been
subjected this veritable " Niobe of nations."   Next
to the passion of conquest, the passion of building
strikes the deepest root into the world's great
despots, — manifesting itself in all varieties of
ways, from rearing pyramids of skulls with Timur
to rearing pyramids of Gizeh with the Egyptian
Pharaohs. The world must hold in everlasting
remembrance the virtues of such benefactors ; and
to this end, in exquisite irony of logic, one after
the other they demolish the records of the virtues
of their predecessors, to rebuild with their material, only in turn to have their own demolished
that other phantoms may commemorate their
imperishable glory. Did Akbar the Great have
some premonition of this ironical smile in the
sleeve of Fate, when at Fatehpur-Sikri, after
building a magnificent city, — now deserted, — in
remembrance of a great victory of his grandfather
Babar, he inscribed over its stupendous gateway :
" Isa (Jesus), on whom be peace ! said, ' The
world is a bridge ; pass over it, but build no house
on it ' " ?

Delhi has been called the Rome of India. In
vastness and impressiveness of ruins it is a hundred Romes. When, in comparison, one recalls
the walls of Rome as they exist to-day, he credits
with entire historical faith the story of Romulus
killing his brother Remus for the little innuendo

implied in a hop, skip, and jump over them. Had Remus tried the like feat with the Cyclopean walls of Tughlakabad, one of the abandoned cities of Delhi, it would have been his own feelings that felt hurt and not those of Romulus. No: here is the work of giants. Hundred-armed Briareus, with gangs of Titans under him to quarry and heave, must have taken the contract for these stupendous towers and battlements. Deserted now for centuries, blackened with age, shaken with earthquakes, the city once within eaten out by the mordant tooth of Time, nothing left behind but a vast crater — how they overwhelm the mind, as, ant-like, one creeps along their awful base! Then the mausoleum of ferocious old Tughlak himself, " the bloody king," outside the south wall of the city, and once surrounded with a lake! It looks an impregnable fortress in itself. So terrible his record and so dire the estimate of the fate before him in the world to come, that his successor piously purchased at great expense written quittances of all he had cruelly outraged on earth and stored them in an iron chest at the head of the tomb, to be close at hand against the Day of Judgment. But, even with these authentic receipts in full, the sanguinary old tyrant seems to have looked forward with small relief to the call of the Mohammedan angel of the resurrection. How he barricaded himself in with gigantic walls and battlements, as though dynamite itself should never blow his dogged soul out of its fastness, and summon it before any tribunal short of its own ferocious will!

Four miles from there, under the shadow of the superb five-storied tower, the Kutb Minar, one comes upon another wilderness of Titanic ruins. Each fresh conqueror must found a new city to perpetuate his glory. Why should a taste for building have been implanted in the heart by Allah, and millions of cunning workmen put at one's disposal, but to create something with them that shall add an eighth wonder to the world? Besides, is not this the site of the original Hindu city of Dilli, where idolaters have spent centuries in making all magnificent with temples? Tear them down! Why go to the rude quarries for stone when Allah's blaspheming enemies have already hewn it for the faithful into walls and pillars? Only with divinest patience first mutilate every face of myriad carved god or goddess; for is it not written, "Thou shalt not make unto thyself any graven image"? Enough will then remain of Hindu, Buddhist, Jain glories of architecture — first piously smitten hard enough in the teeth to satisfy the sacred precept of the law — wherewith to rear magnificent cloisters. Then at the end of the vast court build a stupendous mosque, with five lofty Saracenic arches opening up its interior, all towering as high above the rest as Allah above the gods of the infidel. But, to make his divine supremacy sure, to proclaim it to sight for miles and miles around, rear on high the mighty Kutb Minar. Such a tower! Can the round world equal it? It and Giotto's in Florence are the two that utterly overpeer all others. Nearly fifty feet in its base diameter and rising to the height of two hundred and forty feet, broken at intervals by five beautiful corbeled balconies, the first three stories of red sandstone and the two upper ones of white marble, its superb shaft powerfully incised with alternate angular and rounded flutings and decorated with bands of inscriptions, it excites the mind with such positive invigoration as to call out literal shouts of admiration. To have built it seems greater than to have stormed Delhi.

Here are but passing glimpses of two of the ruined cities of these forty-five square miles of historic stones. Of Ferozabad and Indrapat I cannot stop to speak, vast and overwhelming as they are in their lonely and massive desolation. But the whole country around is strewn with ruins. Travelers speak of the profound impression left by the Appian Way of Rome! The tomb of Cecilia Metella would go unnoticed here. There are miles of three-domed, mosque-like tombs in which it could be hidden away as a toy. Then, too, the exquisite beauty of many of them, burial-shrines of poets, saints, daughters of kings, with such pathetic inscriptions as, for example, this : —

> "Save the green herb, place naught above my head :
> Such pall alone befits the lowly dead."

Often they are of purest white marble, inclosed by snowy openwork screens, wrought in infinitely graceful carvings of vines and tendrils.

All passes away, and naught remains. Pride and glory, they are dust and ashes. "A thousand years in thy sight are but as yesterday when it is past, and as a watch in the night." How often we prate this overpowering thought! But not in Delhi. No; here we feel it, know it, as everlasting yea and amen. The heart beats not in pulses of seconds, but in pulses of centuries. The mind is arrested not by the fleeting aspects of the hour, but is swayed by the flow and ebb of centuries. The very story of to-day, as we stand on the spot at Humayan's giant tomb, from which, in the Indian mutiny, brutal Hodson dragged out the last trembling descendants of Tamerlane, and shot them out of hand, — what was the thrice-repeated ring of that carbine but the thrice-repeated knell of the mighty Mogul dynasty? The mob of infuriated Mohammedans, with arms in their hands, that hung around the ruffian trooper and his hundred mounted men, and never dared to lift a hand while the last princes of their emperor's blood, piteously begging for their lives, were shot dead, — what a change from the days when their terrible ancestor had burst in like a cyclone from the north, sweeping everything before him! To-day in its place stands Great Britain's imperial dynasty. It needs but to lift a finger, and from the Himalayas of the north to Tuticorin in the south its will is law. But has this fleeting show of power and pomp any more abiding root? In Delhi one cannot believe it. Mournfully on every passing breeze sighs the strain, "Thou carriest them away as with a flood: they are as a sleep."

VIII.

I. FROM Delhi to Jeypore, the change was as great as from the solemn movement of Sir Thomas Browne's "Religio Medici" or of his chapters on Urn-Burial to a comic opera of Sullivan's. Stretched alongside a Jeypore street, Boston Public Garden in tulip-time would look gray and sombre. Such a feast of color in the red, orange, green, blue, white, gold dresses of the men, women, and children! It was a perpetually revolving human kaleidoscope. One did not so much as have to turn it; it turned itself. Even the elephants had caught the color infection. Entirely apart from their splendid trappings, their heads and trunks were painted in charming arabesques. Nor, considering the fact that an elephant is quite as much a colossal monument of architecture as he is a moving quadruped, did this decoration seem any more out of place than on the front of a temple.

Then, too, how kind the people of Jeypore! At least two splendid public wedding processions did they extemporize for our sole benefit. Oh, the contrast from crawling into a dozen black hacks, then closing the blinds, and driving to a roped-in church, as is the mournful marital custom

in America! No; marriage was never intended
for a selfish private affair between a sequestered
man and woman. It should be celebrated out-
doors in brilliant sunshine, and always with the
accompaniment of elephants! Without elephants
what union can ever hope to prove permanently
happy !

One of the processions we witnessed was of a
promising little boy of eleven and a bride presum-
ably of seven, though her we were not permitted
to see. But as the boy husband had most likely
scarcely set eyes on her himself, we could not, as
total strangers, feel seriously aggrieved. It was
a pleasant feature of the cortége that the invited
guests were for the most part lovely children, in
order, I take it, that the company might not be
too grown-up for the miniature bridegroom. First,
there came a huge scarlet-and-gold-caparisoned elephant, with a celestial troop of children high aloft
in the howdah. Next succeeded carriage after carriage filled with equally ravishing-looking children.
Then mamma and her older daughters, with nothing to detract from their Oriental beauty but the
jewels in their noses, — worse misplaced there than
jewels in the head of a toad, even though the Revised Version will insist that it was a nose-ring and
not an ear-ring that Isaac bestowed on Rebecca in
the effusion of his romantic love. Then a caval-
cade of led horses, resplendent with cloths thick-set
with gold or silver bosses, and on each horse the
perfect picture of a little Oriental prince or princess of from six to ten years old. What followed

next had some symbolical meaning which I did not understand. Two wiry, active men, in red from head to foot, kept leaping and slashing harmlessly at each other with long curved knives. Perhaps the occult idea was that evil would surely come should the happy couple ever draw on each other that sharpest of all edged knives — a railing tongue. But the boy husband himself! Horse and he were all of shining gold, while long gold tassels hung down over his face, to hide, I suppose, his too tumultuous feelings. The rear was brought up by a troop of singing, dancing girls, literally with "rings on their fingers and bells on their toes;" while, to impart due solemnity to the close, a final elephant, grave as a judge on the bench, rolled ponderously along.

Certainly, it was a bit sad to reflect that, should the pretty boy husband of eleven chance to die at the age of twelve, the poor little bride of eight could never remarry, but must end her days a despised, maltreated widow, at the mercy of a tyrant mother-in-law. While in America mothers-in-law are often found the tenderest and most self-sacrificing of women, in India there is to the young widow no such name of terror. In many a case in by-gone days even Sati, or widow-burning, was not a leap out of the frying-pan into the fire, but out of fifty years of frying-pan, held over the coals by a remorseless mother-in-law, into flames that involved but ten minutes of agony, and all was stilled forever.

II. The Maharajah of Jeypore has the reputation of being very polite to strangers. Certainly he was to my friend and me, fairly overwhelming our sensibilities by sending a gigantic elephant to take us to Amber, a ruined city several miles away on the mountain side. No vulgar omnibus elephant for Tom, Dick, and Harry, this! but the Oriental equivalent of a director's private Pullman car all to ourselves, — we monarchs of all we surveyed, which seemed a quarter of an acre when we got on the animal's back. Then the gracious condescension with which, on seeing how small we were, the lowly minded mammoth went down on all fours, and suffered a ladder to be placed against his side! Many the carved relief I had seen on Hindu temples of a midget of a man apparently worshiping an elephant, but this absolute reversal of the scene in the worship of the midget by the elephant was a lesson in humility time will never dislodge. True, when he got up it felt for a moment earthquaky; but can it rationally be expected that a two-story house, with a pillar at each corner for a leg, shall rise from its knees without somewhat discomposing the feelings of two quiet gentlemen in the second story?

It was a glorious ride the self-abnegating elephant gave us. Though he had been over the ground a hundred times himself, he knew it was all fresh to us, and never for a moment slighted the scenery by departure from the judicial dignity of his walk. Amber lies on a slope of the mountain side, its fortifications picturesquely rooted on a rocky base reflected in a lake below. There, from the days of Ptolemy, and how much farther back no man knows, had stood the capital of Jeypore, rich in multitudinous palaces and still more multitudinous temples and tombs, until in 1728 the site of the capital was removed six miles away to the level plain. The superb palaces of the Maharajah are still preserved in their former glory, while everything else has been suffered to fall into ruins. Any attempt to describe these palaces would be only to try to do again what was vainly tried for those in Agra. Enough that here again was the acme of the æsthetic Mohammedan paradise, a few short years of which one would think would suffice to reduce the Archangel Michael to a sensual imbecile. Cato himself, had he come to live here at eighty, would have become a warning to all young men before he had reached the age of eighty-four.

The most impressive sight of all, however, was to look off from the level marble roofs of the palaces over the ruined city. Fifty Pompeiis could not leave an equal impression of majestic desolation. Ruins become, as a rule, the haunts of bats and owls. In India they become also the haunts of fakirs, — naked, covered with dirt, mutilated with austerities, their matted hair hanging down to their loins. Extremes meet; and the natural reaction from the Mohammedan paradise is the brooding, self-torturing fakir, face to face with the emptiness, dust, and ashes of all earthly

glory.   Here in Amber is before his eyes a perpetual sermon from the text, *Sic transit,* which the
comment of the most eloquent preacher could only
serve to weaken.

Were I a fakir, I would live in Amber as surely
as, had I been a sculptor in the palmy days of
Greece, I would have gone to Athens.   No scenery of earth, luxurious landscape, arid waste, wreck
of by-gone glory, is ever deeply interpreted to the
feeling apart from living presences, animal or human.   What vultures are to the Parsee burial-
tower, or jackals to the ruined porticoes of Palmyra, such are fakirs to an abandoned Indian
city.   Already had I become acquainted with, seen,
handled, smelled, and explored with every sense
the genuine fakir, — whole troops of them at once.
In Cawnpore an intelligent missionary had given
me free introduction to large groups of them, and
furnished me in the flesh the most living commentary on the letters of St. Jerome I had ever read.
Naked but for an iron chain around their loins,
perpetually throwing dust over their grimy bodies,
their hair like strands of tarry rope-yarn, half
idiotic, stupefied with *bhang* to help on religious
vision, — so melancholy a spectacle of mental degradation I never saw outside an insane asylum.
And yet just such a spectacle as this — minus the
bhang, I doubt not — was for many years, before he
broke loose from asceticism, and before his interior
illumination, the world-saviour, Sakya Muni, the
Buddha of countless millions.   Singularly enough,
I saw at the same time a Christian convert, a man

of thirty, with wonderfully beautiful eyes and a radiant glow of love in his face, who had himself for many years been a fakir, and at last found his enlightenment under the sacred bho-tree of the religion of Jesus. In two so utterly different worlds had he lived, and so vivid was his analysis of the mental states of each, that a long talk with him gave me more insight into the soul experiences of Sakya Muni than all the books I have ever read.

The professional tramp in America and the professional tramp in India, the one secular, the other sacred, what a study in human nature to compare the two! So unlike and yet so like! Each, in sheer physical inertia, seeks Nirvana, the Nirvana of deliverance from the moil and strain of life; the one to invite it with vagabond society, lewd stories, whiskey, tobacco, and stolen freight-car rides to sunny climes in winter and cooler ones in summer; the other, in equal abnegation of every social duty, with opium-dreams, and vague reveries of a supernally quietistic infinite, lapsed in immutable siesta. Each testifies alike to his pessimistic creed — the one reasoned, the other unreasoned — that this world of trouble exists but to be renounced. Yet the American type is despised, brutally arrested, and set to breaking stone for the highways, while the Hindu is venerated as having chosen the better part. Nothing can more forcibly emphasize the contrast between an industrial civilization like ours and a reverie-bound, supernaturally overpowered civilization like that of India. Yet of the two

tramp types, give me the Hindu! From our own
we can hope no Buddha.

III. From Jeypore we journeyed on to Mt. Abu,
to visit there the famous Jain temples. The
ride of seventeen miles from the station is by jinrikisha, with six coolie power to propel the contemplative man inside. Not the "weeping philosopher" himself could have taken that ride
without all along making the rocks ring with
peals of laughter. Oh, the monkeys in the trees!
The blessing of Sancho Panza on him who first
invented them! A man of one language, said
Goethe, is a man of no language. Equally, the
man who has never seen the monkey but in a cage
has never seen the monkey. As the rose is naught
without its setting of green leaves and coruscat-
ing dewdrops, so is the monkey naught without
cliffs and trees to furnish him with spring-boards
and natural flying trapezes for his splendid evolutions.

The peculiar species that so kindly turned out
to beguile with their antics the tedium of our
ascent of the mountain were about three feet in
height, ashen-gray in color, with a three-foot tail,
white hair and beard, and a face as black as char-
coal. To come suddenly on a group of a dozen
or more of them, seated aloft on an acacia-tree
eagerly eating the pods, and then to raise a shout,
produces a scene that beggars all description. In
an instant the whole tree is all a-quiver with the
rattling pods, while one detachment of the mon-

keys scampers like mad to the tips of the branches and swings off in magnificent leaps of twenty or thirty feet to the branches of neighboring trees, and another makes headlong dives into the thickets below. The most diverting sight of all is to watch the mother monkeys, their little coal-black babies clinging by all four hands to the fur on the maternal stomach, thus leaving mamma free play of all her limbs for the execution of the most bewildering leaps. For an emergency — say a house a-fire and a natural desire on the maternal part to grab up as many silver spoons as possible before taking flight — monkey babies understand better how to keep out of the way than the most highly evolved of human babies.

I have introduced this monkey episode, and especially the latter part of it, not in a spirit of trifling, but for its serious architectural and, I may add, theological bearing on the immediate object we have in view. We are ascending Mt. Abu to see and interpret the famous Jain temples there. In their infinite elaboration of carvings of figures, animal and human, they present what I might fitly call an opium or hasheesh delirium of symbolism. Nothing stands for what it is, from the wing of a butterfly to the trunk of an elephant, but ever and always as suggestion of some underlying mystic meaning. Fortunately, it had so happened that only a few days before I had been reading the record of a controversy which took place ages ago between two rival Hindu sects. It was on the world-old subject of grace and free-will, so familiar to us all along from the days of St. Augustine. The Hindu champion of pure grace argued in a style that would have drawn applause from Jonathan Edwards. To man was allowed no single initiative in the work of his salvation: desire, will, act, all were outright work of God in him. What, however, was the crowning, triumphant illustration of the relation of the soul to Deity which the Hindu theologian employed? Precisely the one I had just been witnessing with my own eyes in the relation of the baby monkey to his mother. The baby monkey, he argued, simply clings by an instinctive act of faith to his mother, while she bears him safely over dizzy precipices, and rescues him from peril by flying leaps from tree to tree. But is not this clinging the individual act of a free agent? the caviler might ask. No, responds the profounder theologian, it is all free grace. The mother eats for him, drinks for him, assimilates for him, and through her milk pours into him instinct, desire, strength. Cut off from this fountain-head, he would at once be resolved into the nothingness of nothingness. The whole spectacle, went on the devout controversialist, is a piece of pure symbolism, enacted before man's eyes as he wanders in the woods, to reveal to him the interior relation of the soul to God. Would, then, the Occidental mind ever hope to penetrate into the inner shrine of Hindu mystic theology, at a glance it becomes clear how absolutely necessary it is to learn to take the monkey seriously!

To all this, the ordinary cut-and-dried, totally unimaginative Yankee tourist is as blind as a bat. On entering a Hindu temple, the first carving that arrests his eye is, perhaps, precisely that of a mother monkey leaping across an abyss with her baby monkey tight a-hold of the hair of her stomach; and forthwith he goes into fits of laughter. A precious lot these Hindus, he says, to let a graceless scamp of a stone-carver cut such monkey-shines as this in the house of God! Little he dreams that in this monkey-shine, as he calls it, the devout Hindu beside him is adoring a most touching symbol of the free grace of God safely bearing the soul of man across the abyss of sin. The Yankee might argue that the Hindu was lacking in sense of humor. The Hindu would retort that the Yankee lived but on the surface, and was devoid of all deeper insight into the symbolic meaning of the All.

Anyhow, I have used this long illustration simply to strike the keynote as to the only way in which the Western mind can ever learn to interpret sympathetically a Hindu temple or to see in it anything other than a kind of menagerie suddenly let loose by an earthquake. In their ornamentation the Mt. Abu temples are, as I have said, a veritable hasheesh delirium of symbolism. Beautifully situated in a vast mountain crater, four thousand feet high at its level, and surrounded by picturesque mountains, they seem literally out of the world. So they are, and so they always have been, only that for centuries on centuries countless thousands of pilgrims have visited them. Dating back, the older of them to 1032 A. D. and the newer to 1197, and constructed in their cloisters and shrines of white marble that now has the color of ivory, one marvels at their state of preservation. The older temples are simpler in their style, and so, to my eye, far more beautiful; but in the newer is witnessed the persistent tendency of the Hindu to lose all simplicity of form in rampant symbolism. Just as in the forests of India when a noble tree falls, a stately column in itself, it is forthwith buried out of recognition in ferns, cactuses, orchids, and pepel vines, so has it been with the history of Hindu architecture. The cloisters here are set three-aisle deep with pillars; and every pillar and every bay above and every doorway to the successive shrines are wrought with such a wilderness of figures that the world does not seem old enough to have allowed time to carve them. So with the pillars-set court-yard, so with the temple itself. The wildest hallucinations of fever dreams never take on such multitudinous and fantastic shapes.

Truly, nowhere so much as in its architecture does the inmost spirit of a people so incarnate, so materialize itself. Even more than in a Hindu epic does the mind of Hindu India reveal itself in the temple. There it stands all at once before the eye, the Ramayana, the Mahabharata, petrified — nay, rather, spiritually arrested — in stone.

Is all this beautiful? Fantastic certainly, historically impressive certainly, ushering, as it does, the mind into a realm thus arrested in stone, whose imagery never before coursed through a Western brain but in the delirium of fever.   How simple to us looks the world, its genera and species of trees, birds, reptiles, and beasts dominated by our scientific categories and reduced to an order so easily and yet so shallowly grasped! Not a little boy with us who cannot resolve it all into mineral, vegetable, and animal. But to the Hindu what a mystery, what a phantasmagoria, what a cloud dissolution of form into form, what an all and nothing, what a play of illusion where nothing is but what is not! Thence, what a world of symbols from serpent and tiger, from ant and elephant, from fly and hawk, from burrowing mole and cliff-scaling goat, to express its multitudinous infinity! Thence, what a bewilderment of deities to tell the story of the sources of all its terror and peace, its beauty and hideousness, its harvests and pestilences, its devastating passions and refuges of prayer!

Yet, it helps one to be plunged into the abysses of such a world. It awes and deepens him. It dissolves away the hard and fast outlines of the finite. Spite of the little of the symbolic enigma he can interpret, he feels in the presence of a universe freighted with occult meaning, in contrast with which how literal and prosaic the world in which too habitually he dwells! Still, here the whole process has been so deliriously overwrought! Plainly in such wanton abnegation of all law of limit has the line of sanity been passed. Imagination has grown monomaniac. The muse of inspiration has been nurtured, not on nectar and ambrosia, but on hasheesh. As with all Hindu literature and philosophy, — an epoch in the life of every man when first he drinks the soma juice of its intoxication and is made to feel how no one can be truly sane till first he has become insane, — so equally is it with the purely Hindu architecture. Structure is buried out of sight by accessory, unity sacrificed to lawless multiplicity, the Pantheon transformed into the pandemonium.

IV. A great deal, however, is to be seen in India of what may strictly be called Hindu architecture which is yet free from the reproach of the symbolic hallucination characteristic of the temples. But it is work done under the control of their earlier Mohammedan masters, men dominated by the severer and simpler taste of Semitic doctrine and ideals. Under the Sultans of Gujarat, in Ahmedabad, — a city visited by few Europeans, but which for wealth of architectural beauty ranks certainly next to Agra and Delhi, — legions of Hindu architects and armies of native workmen were set to work in the construction of one of the most magnificent capitals in the world. But the hand of the Arab prophet was laid sternly on their shoulders. "Look ye! no graven image or likeness of any thing that is in heaven above or on earth beneath or in the waters underneath. Flowers, yes, and trailing vines, arabesques, graceful as ye can make them! But idols none!"

Historically impressive is it to see the law of one great ethnical faith thus laid in stern restriction on the deepest-seated instinct of another, and to note the architectural result. Cut off at a stroke from all his pandemonium of gods and devils, from all his tangled overgrowth of symbolic bats and owls, the genius of the Hindu architect achieved creations of beauty that proved how his need of needs is the authoritative imposition of some sane law of reason and law of limit on the Saturnalia of imagination. The buildings he erected for his Mohammedan masters are mainly tombs, mosques, and marvelous underground structures for the storage of water, structures acres in extent and built gallery on gallery of pillared stories. But how noble in construction, how exquisite in ornamentation! As for the memorial tombs, such temples in themselves, it would be peace in dying to think of being laid to rest in a scene of such tranquil, cheerful beauty.

As one wanders around amidst all this architectural fascination in Ahmedabad, what a symbol is before the eyes both of the fate and of the deepest-rooted need of this Hindu people! It is the Hamlet of the nations, sicklied o'er with the pale cast of thought, yet so attractive, so profound, so pathetic in its incapacity for action. A thousand years before our era, the plummet of its thought had sounded the deepest abysses in the ocean of speculation, yet how impotent to-day to guide itself were it left alone! Its Mohammedan rulers taught it many a lesson of practical administration and regard for material realities, albeit they wrought such havoc with their rapacity and sensuality, and in degrading the former higher estate of woman laid the hand of pollution on the most sacred relation of society. Then, too, its Mohammedan fellow-subjects set the example at least of a simpler faith and of a more practical and self-regulated life. But the two races mixed no more than oil and water.

To-day England rules, and has brought to bear upon India the stupendous apparatus of Western thought and science. Railroads have been built and canals dug, manufactures established, famines largely stopped, population immensely increased. Hospitals have been founded, and schools and universities endowed, all based on recognition of human control of the unchanging laws of nature. Hundreds of thousands have been trained in the iron school of military discipline. The Hindu youth have flocked into the colleges, bringing their subtle intellectual acumen to deal with all the questions of European literature, jurisprudence, philosophy, and science. Thus, no such range and depth of influence has ever been exerted before. Will it serve as a make-weight to the unbridled imagination of India? Will it lead on to the most deep-seated of all the needed reforms of India, the education and elevation of woman? Ah! happy people, did they but know it, in being under the sway of the one nation of the world that can help them, an Aryan people like themselves, the first to recognize the depth and beauty of their highest achievement in literature, philosophy, theology, yet seeing with absolute clearness, and alone able to supply, just what as a nation they perish for the lack of.

EGYPT

I.

I. . As the ever-varying diorama of a journey around the world keeps unrolling itself before the eye, Goethe's saying, " Wouldst thou know the soul of a poet, visit the land of his birth," makes an increasingly vivid impression. So it proves with everything one had previously thought to get out of books alone. The first Oriental woman, prostrating herself and touching the ground before one with her forehead as in the presence of a superior being, teaches more history in a single sensation than can be learned from all John Stuart Mill's volume on the Subjection of Woman. The first experience of getting inextricably tied up in a network of trailing vines, with a general dank smell of orchids and a haunting suspicion of snakes and tigers, reveals more of the tropical jungle than all Wallace, Darwin, and Kipling have written. So with the feel of the swarming millions of Asia at one's first contact with Canton's river population or with the dense masses of pilgrims in Benares.

Equally true does all this hold of the Desert, the indispensable mental preparation for getting in touch with Egypt. To know it, you must wade knee-deep in its sand, be blinded with its glare, feel your cheeks tingle with the blowing silex grains, breathe sand, and grit it between your teeth. Then all at once you become intimately at home with the habitat of Abraham, Isaac, and Rebecca, of Moses and the Hebrews, of Mohammed and Ayesha, and last, but not least, of the camel, — all equally natural products of the desert, all as much indebted to it for their university training as are the patterns cut into our decanters and wineglasses to the fiercely flying atoms of the sand-blast tool. For ages has the desert, with its cyclone-driven sands, been, in the hand of the Almighty, an irresistible historical etching - needle, cutting deep and persistent ideals and passionate faiths into the very brain substance of whole races.

As far back as when he first sails into the savage jaws of the harbor of Aden on the southwestern extremity of Arabia, Egypt begins to stamp its first vital impression on the mind of the thoughtful traveler on his way by the Arabian Sea, the Red Sea, and the Suez Canal to that mysterious land. To the right and to the left of the entrance, divided only by a couple of miles of salt water, rise naked, fiercely rifted mountains, from one to two thousand feet in height. But every idea of verdure, seclusion, brook, and waterfall we are wont to associate with mountains is consumed in fire. Scorched, blasted, fairly writhing in the intolerable glare, they suggest the counterpart in nature of Dives in hell beseeching the poorest Lazarus of a beggar for a drop of water to cool his burning tongue. The very sands of the seashore, driven by the winds into the ravines, choking them up, and pursuing them aloft into their remotest windings, take on the mocking shape of descending glaciers, only glaciers of fiery sand. So literal is the resemblance that it is hard to dislodge the idea that the cruel deception was intended by malign Djins as a last refinement of torture.

For a hundred miles from Aden, as one skirts the western coast of Arabia, he carries with him the same series of sun-scorched, desiccated mountain ranges, and he knows what lies behind them. There are here and there gorges in which a little moisture is collected, and a struggle for life maintained by a few stunted shrubs. There are, besides, in part of the vast peninsula, comparatively fertile tracts, from which was derived the name Arabia Felix. But it takes very little in the way of verdure to make some people happy, particularly Arabians, habituated to a too monotonous strain of sun, sand, and calcareous hardpan. As is sometimes irreverentially said by rival religionists, "Your God is my devil," just in the same way might it be retorted by rival nationalities, "Your oasis is my desert."

II. But, after all, what a place in which to breed a Semitic prophet! All along I had felt Mohammed beginning to burn himself into my brain, as I imaged him hiding himself in these blasted mountains to have out the terrible wrestle from which he emerged aflame with the faith,

"There is one God; and I, Mohammed, am his prophet." Day by day had he had the awful monotheistic sun to help burn in the thought of unity and resistless sovereignty. That Allah, at least, endured no rival near the throne! A consuming fire, none could hide from his all-devouring eye. Terrible his wrath, as every withering grass-blade, every heat-riven rock attested. Nothing in all nature breathed a polytheistic word of nymph or triton. Submit, seek shelter under the shadow of a mighty rock, or meet annihilation!

All authorities in Oriental studies are now agreed that Mohammed derived his monotheistic idea from the Jews. But this was little. It was the consuming passion with which this son of the desert embraced it, — the irresistible iconoclastic will with which he made it one with the burning sands and flaming hearts of Arabia, in which lay the secret of his power. To what among such races would an abstract idea of unity amount? To no more than an inert bullet or bombshell, without a magazine of explosives behind it to give it annihilating momentum. Mohammed, besides being a great unitary intellect, as demonstrated in his power to grasp and hold unshaken the simplicity of a thought as sublime and all-pervading in the religious world as gravitation in the physical, was, more than all, a man of volcanic energy of passion.

Why is it, somewhere says Emerson, that the reasoned conclusions of a mind like Plato's can never carry with them the same sense of authority that pierces in the shriek of an Arab prophet? As well ask why a breeze gently wafting over the cornfields of Indiana can never work the effect of a cyclone whirling the disintegrated atoms of the desert into gigantic sand-spouts, before whose fury all goes down in prostrate suffocation or in literal entombment under the billows of a sea of desert fire. Every little circling vortex of sand one sees waltzing across the desert is more than a symbol, is a literal illustration of the career of Mohammedan religious conquest. The hot sirocco breath breathed into the Bedouin by Mohammed, at once of faith in Allah and his moral law, and of lust, rapine, and annihilation of the infidel, finds its perfect physical counterpart before the eye.

Mecca and Medina one does not see: first, because he cannot, as they lie far inland; and, second, because the ship now steers so far from shore that they would not be visible even if the sacred cities were thoughtful enough of tourists to stand directly on the coast. Still, it is a kind of historical comfort to feel them in the neighborhood. It helps imagination.

The first land sighted after quitting the more southerly coast of Arabia is, a day and a half later, the peninsula of Arabia Petræa, among whose sun-scorched peaks lies Mt. Sinai. It looks just as fit a place to bring the desert to bear on another and vastly earlier Semitic prophet, with his chosen people, as that already spoken of. Let it be clearly understood that the desert means two things, — here arid, desolate mountain ranges, and there arid and desolate levels of sand and hardpan. Their one point of amity is that, as far as possible, nothing shall grow on them. By this time the Red Sea is rapidly narrowing into the Gulf of Suez, and approximating the shores of Egypt and Arabia. To the east now stretch vast sand levels, while to the west runs the range of low mountains behind which lies the valley of the Nile. Then Suez is reached, and the ship enters the great canal shoveled out of the thirsty sands ever ready to drift into it again and pack it solid, as the snows into a cut through which a railway runs. Here and there a few lakes offered spells of relief to the terrible digging.

III. Before I had kept gazing eastward hour by hour, I could not have believed that mere stretches of sand could ever impart so indescribable an exhilaration; yet I perfectly shared the enthusiasm of the poor old countrywoman who, on first being taken to the seashore, cried out how glad she was to see for once in her life something there was enough of. The smallest oasis would have been an intrusion. The rim of the horizon was just such a perfect circle as embraces the ocean. All was straw-colored sand-sea, with a blue dome a-top. But what is a sea without ships? Ah! the desert has its ships. "Ships of the desert" are the camels called; and soon great convoys of them, heavily freighted to the sand-line, would heave into sight, never a clipper ship or fancy yacht built on more perfect lines for its especial work.

Camels in the desert are no intrusion. They simply enhance the sense of its loneliness and desolation. Gaunt, withered, silent-footed, a root out of the dry ground, with no form nor comeliness, they look as natural a product of its forces as Mohammed of old or a Mahdi of to-day. Simply blown together in a loose-jointed way by the winds creatively playing with the whirling sands, do they seem. You feel absolutely sure that they eat sand, drink sand; that currents of sand circulate through their veins; that, even when their baby camels suckle them, the queer, long-legged, knock-kneed little things only draw in a flow of sand, to them as nutritious as any other mother's milk.

Now for the first time the full sense of the meaning of the desert masters the imagination. From far away eastward in Arabia to the thousands-of-miles-distant Atlantic coast of Africa to the west, it reigns, almost unbroken but by the long narrow oasis of the valley of the Nile. You feel the desert — I repeat it — like a vast elemental Dives-thirst in hell for a drop of water to cool its burning tongue. Does it lie in the physical resources of the earth that any conceivable snow-crowned mountain ranges, any deluges of tropical rains, should suffice to feed a river thirty-three hundred miles long, and to force it, a vast, fructifying tide, through a thousand miles of these gaping sands and stones, and yet so brimming over, three months in the year, as to lay under water the whole long, narrow valley and the ninety-mile-wide expanse of the delta? This is the stupendous feat of the Nile, which every day at " High Nile " pours more than seven hundred thousand million cubic metres of water into the Mediterranean Sea, besides all that the parching soil has drunk to slake its thirst. To take all this in, it is infinitely more impressive to approach Egypt by the way of Aden in Arabia and the Red Sea than by the Mediterranean. First feel the desert, and then can you feel the Nile, — feel it physically, and feel it historically also. For, hot as is the thirst bred in its sands by the burning sun, hotter yet the passions of greed and envy to snatch from its lips the brimming cup that were bred in the sons of the desert, as they looked down from the bordering mountains of their scorpion fire-land on the luscious green of the wheat-fields and groves of date-palms of that miraculous oasis.

IV.	The landing-place for passengers from India, *via* the Suez Canal, is Ismailia, about sixty miles northward from Suez itself. It is a little town that grew up as a depot during the cutting of the great canal; and, as a small fresh-water canal was opened to the distant Nile to bring down a supply for the workmen, it furnishes to the novice an interesting exhibition, on a miniature scale, of the way of making the " desert blossom as the rose." Every tree makes one think of cattle driven to the river to drink, only that the trees do not budge and the river has to be driven to them. But drink they do, like trees " planted by the rivers of water, whose leaf also does not wither; " and they prosper fairly

well. But a man does not journey from the tropical
luxuriance of Boston Common to see little parks
kept from dying of thirst in Ismailia. The grand
attraction is the people, who are, perhaps, half
Arabs and half Fellahin, or native Egyptians, with
a small percentage of Turks.

Among the Arabs, one sees in little Ismailia
more magnificent-looking men in a day than he
would see in New York in a year, if ever. The
patriarch Abraham is met three times in every
hundred yards, perfectly capable of entertaining
the angels in his tent and then bowing them a gracious farewell with manners as celestial in dignity
as their own. Such noble heads and fine-cut,
bearded faces, such flowing robes, so superb a
gait! One wants to follow each one of them round
all day, simply to keep looking at him. Infinite
possibility of statesmen, warriors, or prophets does
there seem in them; and in comparison they make
Europeans look cheap, fussy, and contemptible.
To be able to maintain such manners on ten cents
a day is to a foreigner a standing miracle.

At the end of each street, however, shine the
glowing sands of the desert; and an irresistible
attraction leads one out to gaze over it again.
There are found the wandering Bedouins, driving
in their long trains of camels, forcing them to kneel
down, and unloading them of their heavy burdens.
How vividly are Old Testament and, later, Mohammedan scenes lighted up at every turn! Rebecca!
She was no such bedizened princess as painters
give us. She was just such a pretty camel-girl as

you see before you, drawing water out of a well. Ayesha, Mohammed's young virgin love, after Kadijah grew as old and wrinkled as the desert-aged women you see about you, — Ayesha, — why, there she stands by her camel! She will smile on you quite bewitchingly out of her lustrous eyes, as you communicate with her by signs and gestures, — the only dialect of Arabic at your command, — yes, and alas! will beg you for *bakshish*, whether an innovation introduced into her circle of ideas since Mohammed wooed her my erudition is too scant to say. The thousand, the three thousand years of interval vanish; and you are standing in the midst of identically similar scenery and personalities. Be sure, however, to keep a civil tongue in your head. Never lift a finger in menace against an Arab. He may be clad in rags, but a Chevalier Bayard is latent under them, who flashes fire like a flint struck by steel.

V. How different with the Fellahin, — the peasant-class descendants, however mixed in blood, of the old Egyptians! Significantly enough has Egypt been called the "Land of the Rod." "Spare the rod and spoil the child" nowhere else has received so stupendous an illustration. The rod, with backs to apply it to, built the Pyramids, dug the canals, collected the taxes, and to this day, though the English government is striving to abolish it, is taken as the natural and immutable order of things. To see a crowd of perhaps fifty natives surging down on a dozen or more tourists, each of the fifty yelling the merits of his donkey, and wild to have it taken, and then to watch the sight as two or three men leap from the boat and begin to belabor the poor devils with sticks, is certainly a novel and, to a free-born American, a painful sight. Right and left fall the resounding blows on heads and noses, and shoulders and loins, till your own skull and shoulders ache sympathetically. But not a particle of resistance is offered or the slightest sense of outrage manifested. A practical demonstration on such a scale of the results of the doctrine of non-resistance would excite every belligerent propensity in the most placid Quaker to the bull-dog pitch. Holding a hand to his half-cracked crown or battered jaw, each, as he falls back, keeps on yelling the praises of his beast: " Him bully donkey! Him General Grant donkey! Him Mark Twain donkey!" and, to emphasize the truth, a dozen of them are shoved pell-mell at you. To try to stretch your legs over one is to find two or three others thrust under you in a breath. Then another charge of the whackers, and a clearing is made sufficient to enable you to bestride not more than a couple of donkeys at once; and gradually you contrive so to contract your leg-compasses as to embrace but one.

Yes, you understand now how the Pyramids were built; and the whole atmosphere of Egypt in the past echoes with the reverberation of thwack! whack! on the muscles and bones of the poor wretches, whose works you, as an idle tourist, are going to see. It would be very interesting to read a statistical table, at the hands of some such competent Egyptologist as Mariette Pasha or Maspero, of how many thousands of cords of rods were used up on the bodies of the one hundred thousand workmen whom it took twenty years to build the one pyramid of Cheops. At the same time fresh light is thrown by the scene on the asperities of brick-making among the Bedouin Hebrews, who at last revolted and went out under Moses. Savory as were the leeks and onions of Egypt, one begins to understand how even the desert might present counterbalancing attractions. Broken heads and bones are bad, but a broken and abject manhood is worse. It was high time, if the world were to get any future Isaiahs out of the tribe, that the tonic of the desert should be brought to bear on it, where, disciplined by a predatory life of semi-starvation, it should be got in train to fall like famished wolves on the lands of the Canaanites.

Well, here is a long way round to get to Egypt; but often the longest way round is the shortest way home. I am but writing personal impressions; and this is the manner in which the actual experience impressed me. Just as one must be hot and thirsty before he can appreciate a delicious drink from a spring, so must he be hot and thirsty of the desert before he is sensitively ready for the brimming cup of Egypt. The desert and the Nile have been perpetually co-working factors in the evolution of civilization, religion, art, conquest, and commerce.

II.

I. From Ismailia by rail it is a four hours' ride to Cairo. The only peril besetting the first part of the way grows out of a possible stampede of camels across the track in the van along its line. To this we personally were treated. Of course, to encounter the like phenomenon with cows, one does not need to leave America. But cows are commonplace, while derailment by a camel stirs the romantic element within the breast. Certainly, for stretch of legs and speed, when once headed straight down track, the performance of a herd of camels makes that of a herd of cows seem tame. In appeal to imagination, there can be no comparison. Such close approximation of the camels of Abraham and the locomotive of Stephenson is significant; indeed, in its lively way, a symbolic parable on legs of the stampede of the Orient before the Occident.

A couple of hours and one is out of desert and semi-desert, plunged right into the heart of the land of Goshen. Oh, how green it looks! Such leeks, such onions, such a growth of alfalfa clover, such beauty of the graceful date-palms, such picturesque-looking clusters of square flat-roofed mud huts, overhung with palms, — buildings so fascinating to the artist, so Oriental to the tourist, and so fetid to live in! As the train would stop for a while before one of these villages, a curious spectacle was always at hand which might be of historic import. Indeed, what is the use of traveling if everything one sees does not take on historic dimensions ? Well, the Egyptians have been called the most patient of peoples in the world. This patience, does it root in their impassive nervous fibre, or is it the result of self-control? Certain it is that one sees no end of babies of six months, their faces thick with swarming flies, and each eye itself constantly run over by the legs of at least a dozen, who never so much as wink, much less lift a tiny hand to brush the pests away. Many the minister at home, a man of ascetic moral training and high spirituality, who is yet more carnally exercised, even in the full fervor of his discourse, by a single fly persistently disporting around the sensitive flanges of his nostrils, than are these little innocents by swarms of them. Under like aggravation, an American baby would make the welkin ring. The historic question, therefore, inevitably precipitated by such a nervous phenomenon is whether American babies, already so high-strung and rebellious at the age of six months, could ever develop into a race capable of building the Pyramids ?

No, all this infantile example means something of the gravest import. Here is a race in which in certain directions the ordinary reflex action of the nervous system has shrunk to practical atrophy. This child, in whom the legs of a fly coursing round his nostrils do not call out a reacting muscular twitch, is father of the man in whom a blow does not call out an answering blow, who will, without a finger lifted in resistance, suffer himself to be knocked down, kicked, and jumped on. Nothing perfectly analogous in the animal world is witnessed but in the conduct of the spaniel. Does this mean that if the odds are continuously and overwhelmingly against man or dog, the spirit at last succumbs, and even the physical instinct of nervous reaction dies of inanition? Rod enough and flies enough, will the very nerves at last throw up the sponge? Ah! here lies the pathetic heartbreak of so much one sees in Egypt.

II. I do not mean to say anything about Cairo now, but first to go up the Nile, and preliminarily to throw out a hint or two that may prove of use.

Until the accession of Thomas Cook & Son to the vacant throne of the Pharaohs of Egypt the old way of ascending the Nile was by small sail-vessels called "dahabiyehs." For fear of unguardedly misspelling them, I shall henceforth call them simply boats; but in this individual instance the spelling can be relied on as abreast with the latest scholarship in Arabic English. These boats required a party of eight or ten to share expenses, and, moreover, a whole winter at one's disposal to meet delays. It was undoubtedly the ideal way of seeing the Nile. Finally, however, Pharaoh Cook built a fleet of steamers; and by these almost all people travel to-day. The passengers on board

form what is called a "personally conducted party."
They have their own dragoman, who provides donkeys, routs donkey boys, and gives imperfect expla-
nations of hieroglyphical and mythological mysteries that might baffle the untutored mind.

The day was when the thought of ever becoming a member of a "personally conducted party"
would have made me shudder from sea to sea.
Had I not too often been startled in the Vatican by
the sudden, noisy irruption of the Cook barbarians,
heard the regulation hand-clap from the leader
for silence, and then listened to his inane routine
remarks as he personally conducted his victims
round from statue to statue? Had I not equally
reveled in the blessed stillness that followed when,
the short-lived tumult over, I was left alone once
more to the serene Olympian companionship of
Juno, Minerva, Apollo, and Zeus? And now
should I actually live to become a Cookite myself,
and that, too, in Egypt? No! by Isis and Osiris!
by jackal-headed Anubis and ram-skulled Kneph!
No! by sun-crowned Ra!

Well, I want to take a great deal of this frankly
back, — at least in so far as Egypt is concerned.
There are uninteresting reaches in the river which
the steamer carries one quickly by. Meanwhile
on board there are the satisfactions of excellent
fare, clean beds, attentive service, and perfect hon-
esty of treatment, while among so many passengers one makes sure of agreeable companionship.
Of course one sighs that he cannot have Egypt
more to himself. Still, driven to sufficient desper-

ation, man is rich in individual resources toward securing peace and quietness. On long excursions one may urge his donkey far ahead of the madding crowd, or imaginatively afflict him with such spavin as to serve as a pretext for mercifully keeping him in the rear. One may learn to spot and shun the various types of bores, as, in especial, the man whose sole interest in visiting Egyptian temples is to distinguish the cartouches, or seals, of the different kings, and who, for all the glorious architecture, would be quite as well off at home with a stick of sealing-wax, a candle, and a collection of authenticated scarabæi dies to stamp with.

Still, for the quietly ruminating man who yearns to have his temple to himself, the device of devices to study is how to keep out of sight and sound of the dragoman and his rabble Comus rout who want to have their minds improved. Providentially, the enormous size of the temples renders this quite feasible. The dragoman, as a general rule, is an Egyptian of very imperfect French or English articulation. He has scraped a purely business acquaintance with Isis, Anubis & Co., and thinks he knows them by their trade-marks. Old Egyptian mythology, however, is dreadfully confused. The numberless gods, goddesses, cults, and symbolic signs crossed, invaded, and annexed one another in a way that, in comparison, would make the genealogical tables of the Hohenstauffen and Hapsburg emperors easy reading. Indeed, often would it seem, on visiting a fresh temple, as though Amen-Ra, Horus, Kneph, Nit, Thoth,

and the rest had been startled out of a deep sleep
by the footsteps of the party, and, suddenly seizing
and putting on, higgledy-piggledy, one another's
crocodile's, cat's, ram's, or hawk's heads, had jumped
up and plastered themselves against the walls, so
as all to get into plausible shape to confound our
erudition. In the long, narrow passages, however,
of the underground tombs, these resources fail.
There is, then, nothing for it but to be as patient
under suffering as an Egyptian baby beset by a
swarm of buzzing flies. Calmer hours of reflection
will come later, in which memories of all you have
seen there will emerge beautiful as reborn dragon-
flies that have sloughed off and left behind their
rent and desiccated Cook strait-jackets.

III.   The departure from Cairo for one's voyage
up the Nile presents for the first two or three
hours a succession of fascinating pictures. The
city itself, crowned by the great citadel of Saladin, and at its summit by the five-domed mosque
of Mohammed-Ali, with its two slender, sky-pier-
cing minarets, smiles a gracious good-by and God
speed for a voyage of wonders. Into the very city
thrusts itself a great arm of the desert; and out
from stretches of straw-colored sand rise, like ex-
halations, the ruins of the beautiful tombs of the
Khalifs, to me the most charming of all the architectural glories of Cairo. In color the stone of
which their walls and domes are built differs little
from the unbroken sands around them, imparting,
as one sees them in the quivering glow of the sun-

shine, the sense, not to be reasoned with, that the desert genii have built them out of sand and graciously shaping winds, as with us the like semblance of temples is created of snowdrifts and winter storms. Further, from all quarters of the city rise at a hundred points the fanciful minarets of the Mohammedan mosques.

Past the palaces of the Khedive and past the long, narrow island of Roda, with its Nilometer and the traditional spot where Moses was found in the bulrushes, one follows the great curves of the river till the enormous pyramids of Gizeh rise up in naked distinctness from the desert.

Already had my friend and I visited these from Cairo and climbed Cheops. It is an instructive thing to do once; but I defy any one, even with the steadiest head against dizziness, to get any emotional pleasure, any sense of the lapse of the ages, anything but execration of the present, out of it. Each climber is obliged by law to take with him three Bedouins, — two to pull, and one to push. From start to finish it is one unintermitting yell for *bakshish*. With this they keep on tearing the ears of their victims. Personally, I had but two emotions, — the one that the old Egyptians were the most intolerable stair-builders in the world, the other that, were I on the jury, I would vote to acquit on the spot any tourist who had killed his Bedouins. Mine, strict justice forces me to admit, had one, perhaps exceptional, linguistic accomplishment. They had been taught by some misguided American (Allah reward him according to his works!) to sing the tune and words of "Yankee Doodle;" and, perforce, must I, two thirds up the pyramid of Cheops, join hands with these yelling Ishmaelites, and dance and sing this most trivial of all national anthems. Anything for peace! And so I did it, with a lingering sense of shame that "forty centuries were looking down" upon my caperings. Indeed, time which heals so many wounds, has never had the least effect in mitigating the exasperation of that climb of Cheops. It would have been such bliss to lie off half the day and muse. The blind, fierce pertinacity of flies settling on a festering sore was the only fit symbol of these human flies so fiercely preying on a festering spirit. If only I could come to look back humorously on the scene! But I cannot. Never does it revive in memory but I feel murder in my heart.

And yet, I repeat it, it is a good thing once and forever to have gone through this purgatory, — to use the milder word. A cairn of gigantic blocks of stone, covering at the base over thirteen acres, and rising to a height of nearly five hundred feet, built solid moreover, with the exception of a few narrow passages, from skin to core, is certainly the most stupendous feat of the wrestle of mind with brute matter the round world can show. Furthermore, as psychologists assure us, the rôle played by the muscular sense in all adequate appreciation of phenomena of weight is indispensable as a mental standard. Therefore, given a solid stone staircase, with risers averaging four to five feet, and a twenty-eight-inch stretch of legs·to surmount them with, and, before one is up three hundred and fifty feet, he has developed into a self-conscious derrick and apparatus of blocks and hawsers that will thenceforth enable him to weigh to a hair every colossal column or architrave he later on encounters in Egypt. The moment his eye lights on one, the consciousness will revive of just how many tons of matter and emotion it physically and mentally stands for, and the sense of awe will expand proportionally.

Seen, however, from the river, as one now sees the Gizeh pyramids in his voyage up the Nile, all one's old associations of reverence and mystery come back again. One is at rest and in peace. No Bedouin yell lacerates his ears, and the Hotspur in his blood is no longer " stung with pismires." Around these mighty cairns and behind them is the awful desert, and at their feet the Sphinx, time-worn and broken with her century-long brooding over the mystery of existence. Anywhere else but thus set in the naked simplicity of the desert they would lose their great effect. For they are not beautiful or sublime in the sense that a Greek or an Egyptian temple is beautiful or sublime. There is not range and variety enough of thought in their creation ; no thought, indeed, unless of enduring construction that shall defy war and earthquake and outdate time.

One does not, therefore, in the least wonder that so many scientific minds of a speculative cast have written elaborate books, such as " Our Inheritance in the Great Pyramid," to prove that these vast structures were built for purely geometrical and astronomical purposes, and stood for the indestructible standards of the old Egyptian metric system instead of being built as the Gibraltars of a single royal mummy. There to all ages they stand foursquare, a terrestrial apotheosis of the immutable axioms of geometry, colossal· memorial tributes reared as to the mind of Euclid. Reverentially, and not lightly, does it seem as though the hieroglyphic inscription on them ought to record that superb demonstration, "The square of the hypothenuse is equal to the sum of the squares of the other two sides." So enduring a feat of reason, was it not far worthier of embodiment in an everlasting pyramid than the memory of any battle?

In the mind of the non-mathematical tourist, however, such nineteenth-century heresy as this does not linger long. Rather, he broods over the long, deep sleep of King Khufu in his silent inmost chamber; over the drone of the priestly masses that for more than two thousand years were still kept up for the repose of his soul; over the impressive material-spiritual faith that incarnated itself in such enormous structures; over the hundred thousand slaves who for twenty years were under the lash, quarrying and upheaving these gigantic blocks to make sure that after life's fitful fever one fellow-mortal should sleep well; over the successive dynasties — Egyptian, Hyksos, Assyrian, Persian, Greek, Roman, Saracen, Turkish,

French, English — that have risen and perished like successive waves beneath a sea cliff at the base of these indestructible monuments. Yes, as one broods and broods, he gets back again the Pyramids of his early awe, — immutable standards, indeed, of measurement, — not, however, of the boundaries of farm lands nor of the bulk of granary stores of wheat, but of the epochs of human history. Up to their summits he gazes through the eyes of Khufu and Abraham, and Rameses, and Moses, and Cambyses, and Herodotus, and Alexander the Great, and Plato, and wanton Cleopatra, and Saladin, and Napoleon. The last trace of the discord of the yelling Bedouins lapses silently out of his mind; and he thanks God that in its place has succeeded the solemnizing pendulum-beat "Forever, Never!" of what seems the sidereal clock of the universe.

IV. An hour or two past the Gizeh Pyramids, and the boat stops at Sakkarah. "Now comes my fit again!" Of course, the bank is black as a crow-roost with braying donkeys and screaming donkey boys. *Sic itur ad astra* in Egypt, and as well might a dying dog hope to expostulate with the awaiting buzzards. So let this once for all suffice. You fight your way through the surging mob of arms, shoulders, hoofs, and tails, and, somehow or other, find yourself astride a beast. In the interim of waiting one frantic Egyptian is thrusting a scarabæus under your nose, another a mummy's foot, and so on and on till you are appealed to with the individual attractions of freshly manufactured antiques enough to set up a pseudo-Bulak museum.

At last you get away ; and, as on this special occasion there were about eighteen miles to ride, with stops for refreshment only at tombs, the pace adopted was severe. Still, it proved exciting till gradually it was brought home, by seeing friend after friend take a header, how little the Egyptian donkey has made of his " Inheritance in the Great Pyramid " in the way of standing foursquare on his base. Mine own especial donkey, Rameses II., while on the full tear, came down in a pile, with an abruptness that shot me over his head in a splendid parabolic curve that might have brained me but for the buffer of my inch-thick cork helmet.

As soon as possible, however, after getting away one must do his best — it is the only hope in Egypt — to retire into the depths of his inner consciousness, and there wall himself in as tight as old King Khufu in his Gizeh Pyramid. Much in the way of saving wear and tear of spirit can thus be achieved. Even as in a siege the mother with her babe can learn to sleep sound under a cannonade, and awaken only when the little one begins to fret for milk, so in Egypt itself can a well-disciplined mind learn to abandon itself to day-dreams under a fusillade of *bakshish*, and yet be all on the spot the moment an appeal is made to its tenderer historical or architectural emotions.

At first the way led along canal embankments

and through fields of the richest garden culture, while beyond lay the shining calcareous cliffs and hot shifting sands of the desert, — the contrast of never-failing interest to the traveler in Egypt.

An hour or more and we were now on the site of Memphis, on the site and on nothing else. Not a trace remains of this once splendid metropolis, founded, so runs tradition, by Menes, the first recorded Egyptian king, and, even so late as the day when Herodotus visited it, still the most magnificent city in the kingdom. Sovereign after sovereign enlarged and beautified it with temples, groves, lakes, colossal statues, and tombs; while within its vast necropolis, stretching over a region of forty-five miles, lay all the seventy pyramids of Egypt, from Abu Roash on the north to Medum on the south. But to-day, over the ground on which stood this luxurious capital, one rides through un-broken fields of wheat and barley and maize and onions to the edge of the desert, and finds as me-morials of all this glory of the past but two muti-lated colossal statues of Rameses II., now prone on their backs, but nearly fifty feet in height when they stood erect.

We had come, however, not to look at cornfields growing where once stood a mighty city, but to ride on into the desert to visit the scene of desola-tion presented by the ruins of the eleven pyramids of the Sakkarah plateau, among them the Step Pyramid, built not in triangular shape, but in three great stages. It is the oldest of all the pyramids, its present height from the base about one hundred and ninety-seven feet. What a wilderness of ruins! "The abomination of desolation," — here, of a truth, it is revealed! In many a land the fall to destruction of a great monument is but a signal to loving and bountiful nature for beautiful trees to root in its ruins and for birds to sing among their branches, for mosses and ferns to drape its flanks, for bluebells and columbines to nod their graceful flowers from its cornices. But in the desert to fall in ruins is the fate of the caravan dying of thirst in the burning sands. Bare, bleached bones are the only record. Around or on top of these gigantic ruins not a grass-blade grows, not a dry root out of the ground lifts a withered head; and the solemn burial service to read over all is, not "dust to dust, ashes to ashes," but "desert to desert, sand to sand."

It was the custom of the Egyptians to found the necropolis always in the desert behind the city, and never upon the fertile plain, as with our own beautiful cemeteries. Two main reasons determined this, — to get above the reach of the inundations of the Nile, and to secure in the cliffs the hard rock strata into which to cut chambers and galleries. Still another reason was security against body-snatchers, a form of robbery infinitely more tempting in a land where untold wealth of gold and jewels was often buried with the dead than in a land where no other use could be made of the mortal booty than to sell it to the doctors. Over thousands, however, of these rock-cut tombs have the winds of a hundred centuries swept the sands, till every trace of their site is lost. Thus what has been unveiled in Egypt is as nothing to what still lies buried. Beneath the sands over which one rides are endless cities of tombs forever hidden, — cities that, while Memphis itself hardly balanced deaths by births, doubled generation by generation their own ghostly population, still dreamily living on in mansions more spacious and costly than ever tenanted by those in the sunshine above. One sighs for the boon Harriet Martineau craved of some mighty god, to be made Boreas, with cyclones at command, to sweep away these sands. The boon was never granted. What was accorded was bestowed on a humbler, but more heroic, class of patient toilers.

V. To the patient digging of brave archæologists do we owe almost all our knowledge of the ancient glories of Egypt. They alone lifted the veil from the face of this mysterious Isis. Truly, of all the forms of modern heroism few are more worthy of applause than the patience, the courage in facing greedy ferocity and peril of life, the stern endurance of loneliness, privation, and the furnace of fiery heat displayed — no! hidden — summer and winter, year in, year out, by numbers of these devoted men. Foremost of all was the Frenchman, Mariette. Never knight of old more chivalrous and indomitable in rescuing from enchanted castle the imprisoned maiden there than he in delivering from the dungeon of the engulfing sands the pride and glory of the Egypt of old that

had been the torch-bearer of civilization to the be-
nighted nations of the world.

In the course of the ride over the toilsome sands
one comes to the lonely house where for so many
years this knight-errant of the desert had lived.
Close by it are his two great discoveries in this
region, — the Serapeum, or Apis Mausoleum, and
the Tomb of Thi. How he divined them hidden
beneath the sand is a story it would be pleasant to
tell did space permit. But divine where they were
he did, and then, with his army of laborers, painfully dug them out, the wind oftentimes undoing in
a night what it had taken a month to effect. To
our modern minds, in which the rooted tendency of
by-gone ages to identify symbol and reality as inseparably one no longer exists, it seems irreveren-
tial to have to translate so high-sounding a title
as "Apis Mausoleum" into "Memphian Westmin-
ster Abbey for Departed Bulls." Such, however,
not in plain prose, but in national veneration, it
really was! The bull, sacred to the god Apis, was
to the initiated priests a symbol of power; to the
ignorant multitude, a divine incarnation in horns,
hide, and hoofs. "He dwelt," says Rawlinson, "in
a temple of his own near the city, had his train of
attendant priests, his harem of cows, his meals of
the choicest food, his grooms and curry-combers,
his chamberlains who made his bed, his cup-bearers
who brought him water, and on fixed days was led
in a festive procession through the main streets of
the town, that the inhabitants might come forth to
make obeisance. When he died, he was carefully

embalmed and deposited, together with magnificent jewels, statuettes, and vases, in a polished granite sarcophagus cut out of a single block and weighing between sixty and seventy tons. The cost of an Apis funeral amounted sometimes, as we are told, to as much as £20,000 sterling."

While we of to-day may smile at all this, it would have been grim earnest had any one in the old Memphian times looked superiorly askance at this bovine divinity, this incarnation of the god on earth. Thirty centuries later a Roman soldier was torn in pieces by a mob for accidentally killing a cat sacred to some other deity. Indeed, the most sanguinary fights were always occurring between rival townships, the one of which deified the crocodile, and the other of which despised the crocodile and exalted the snake. Very curious was it — indeed involving a mental wrench in the attempt to get into sympathy with the feelings of one's fellow-creatures of five thousand years ago that put sore strain on the imagination — to thread the great underground passages in which, at wide intervals, had been deposited twenty-four sarcophagi containing the mummified bodies of these venerated animals. What magnificent monuments of stone-work they were ! — ten feet long, nine high, seven broad, and a foot thick, each made out of a single block of granite brought from five hundred miles away, covered by devout inscriptions, and all broken open by sacrilegious thieves. But the whole outside circuit of the Serapeum, dug out so painfully by Mariette, with its propylon, its crouching lions, its

avenue of sphinxes, is now, alas! sanded up once
more.　Poor Keats in his despair wrote for his
own epitaph, "Here lies one whose name was writ
in water!"　What a dry wit commentary on this,
these shifting sands effacing all record of the heroic toil of poor Mariette!

VI.　As devoted to the earthly and eternal interests of a human being, the Tomb of Thi,
next visited, naturally took stronger hold on sympathies rife in all hearts to-day than a tomb for
deified bulls.　Truly, the world offers few more
impressive experiences than to be riding over an
expanse of barren sand-hills, and then, suddenly, to
come upon a vast excavation, to descend its incline
to the portal once on a level with the whole city of
the dead, and then to find one's self ushered into the
pictured interior of an Egyptian mortuary home.
"The Egyptians," says Diodorus, "call their houses
hostelries, on account of the short period during
which they inhabit them; but they call their tombs
eternal dwelling-places."

Profoundly one feels this as he wanders through
the silent chambers, gazes on the infinitely varied
scenes depicted on the walls, and tries to get into
touch with a fellow-mortal, who, though he died
five thousand years ago, seems so on hand to welcome one to his abiding home.　Yes, the home feeling of the Egyptian tomb!　With us in America,
let a man become rich, his first desire is to build
himself a fine house above ground and straightway
make it a miscellaneous museum of Persian rugs,

Japanese bronzes, carved Indian furniture, and
Sèvres china. Not so with the Egyptian. He
spent his life in a plain house, and concentrated
all his wealth, taste, and feeling for domestic comfort on his tomb, experiencing as palpable zest in
fitting it up as in England or America a wealthy
young fellow in arranging to his mind his snug-
gery, with its store of embroidered slippers and
smoking-caps, of Turkish pipes and Havana cigars,
of vellum-bound books, crested writing-paper, and
Italian pictures. In just such spirit did the wealthy
Egyptian spend half his lifetime, with an army of
quarrymen, statuaries, and decorative artists under
his command, in getting his tomb exactly suited to
his taste. I use the word taste advisedly, for in
the disposition of this tomb provision was made
for every comfort, every idiosyncrasy even of body
and mind. Further, while with us the bitter pang
to the rich man is that no sooner may he have got
ensconced in his costly mansion than death will
tear him away, the Egyptian counted securely on
at least three thousand years of undisturbed tenancy.

As one wanders through the chambers of his
"eternal dwelling-place," and thinks of the keen
satisfaction the genial man must have taken in
watching, year by year, the progress of the work,
one fairly envies Thi. He had been poor, had
attained wealth and high rank, till finally he had
married into the royal family. But when riches
increased, he did not set his heart on them in any
but a supramundane sense. His, the solid, home-

spun Egyptian way of interpreting the text, "Lay
not up for yourself treasures upon earth, where
moth and rust do corrupt and thieves break through
and steal."   Such perennial dryness of desert situation he secured that no rust nor mould could in-
vade; and as for his treasures, were they not laid
up thick, and earthquake proof, in his tomb, where
his ghostly double and their ghostly double — the
real and enduring essence of them both — would live
on face to face.   How pleasant to contemplate the
pictures of these treasures on the walls, as Thi, his
wife, and sons are expatiating over their delights!
Here he is watching his servants bringing in on
their shoulders sacks of grain or fattening his
fowls by thrusting pellets of meal down their
throats.   Here he is inspecting his geese and
ducks swimming on a pond.   Here he is overlook-
ing his Nile boats laden with jars of wine and bales
of goods.   "Cows are crossing a ford, and cattle
browse in the meadows.   Oxen are ploughing, the
seed is sown, the corn is reaped.   Donkeys are
brought up with much fuss and use of the stick,
to carry away the sheaves to the farm-yard.   Some
of the scenes are drawn with inimitable humor."

Yes, Thi would have his laugh as well as his
solid comfort in his "eternal dwelling-place."   The
days had not yet come, as under the later empire,
when terrible pictures were portrayed on the walls
of tombs of the purgatories and hells of torment
through which the soul might have to pass.   All
was happy trust that the best of life but prefigured
the best of after life.   Alone or forgotten he would

not be. To his enduring mansion would come his children, and his children's children, to feast in the festival hall, and make him sympathetically enjoy along with them, though after his own disembodied fashion, the flavor and smell of the spiritual doubles of the roasts they were consuming in their ovine or bovine original.

In this naïve way of portraying the tangible satisfactions of the life to come there is, it must be confessed, something very winsome. It made me think of Rev. John W. Chadwick's poem, " Climbing the Mountain," where the weary footfarer, yearning for the vision of what shall be revealed on the other side, at last reaches the top, only to find the scene unrolled as homelike and sweet as that he had left behind. Far more of a prosaic photographer and less of a spiritual poet than Mr. Chadwick, the Egyptian, but each equally human in his faith. Ah! who but has felt a thousand times that here in the beauty and affections of earth are all the elements of the most beatific vision of heaven, and that, if we could but keep our dear ones tight-locked in our arms, with death at bay and God close by, — could but go on cheering, illuming, and crowning with blessings one another's days, — we could dream no fonder paradise?

III.

I. THE characteristics of the scenery of the Nile can be more easily realized from photographs than those of any other river in the world, so simple is the Nile in its outlines and so continuously the same from day to day. Beautiful the river cannot be called in the sense in which the Rhine and Hudson are beautiful. There are no forest-clad mountains, no rolling hills, no charm of variety afforded by pretty villages or spire-tipped cities. A comparatively narrow selvage of cultivation along the banks — a selvage sometimes a few yards and sometimes a few miles wide — is shut in on either hand by barren, sunscorched hills of limestone or by stretches of desert sand. The shapes of these denuded hills or semi-mountains are often very picturesque, and at times abut on the river's edge in noble cliffs, pitted all along their lines of harder stratification with entrances to cave tombs, just as with us similar cliffs are pitted with holes into swallows' nests. The flora is the most limited conceivable. It consists almost exclusively of mimosas, sycamore-figs, and date-palms. With the rising or setting sun behind their feathery tops, silhouetting them darkly against a rosy or opalescent sky, these palms are singularly beautiful. Indeed, everything in Egypt silhouettes marvelously. A train of camels, with their upward-curving necks, horizontal heads, and long, gaunt legs, reminds one irresistibly of the picture Coleridge draws in the "Ancient Mariner" of the sun raking through the ribs of the phantom ship. Ever on the air is the sound of the creaking levers of the shadufs by which, standing tier above tier, the natives lift from the falling river the irrigating water. And yet, spite of this constant monotony, a voyage on the Nile is singularly fascinating. The air is sweet and invigorating. The barren hills take on such varied colors under the morning and evening lights as to transfigure their arid reality into a fairy-land of aerial mirage.

It would prove only tedious to the reader to attempt to drag him round from tomb to tomb, from temple to temple. A glance at a map of the Nile will give the sites; and a brief study of any illustrated books on Egypt the pictures, carvings, and statues, as no pen can hope to reproduce them. All that the ordinary tourist can hope to do is to enliven the scene with some vividness of personal impression, and to throw here and there a ray of interpreting light on what looks so strange and grotesque in pictured illustrations of the monuments of Egypt. Indeed, the trouble with most callow travelers in Egypt, even with the objects before their eyes, is that they get lost in such a wilderness of details that they " cannot see the woods for the trees." So exhaustive a knowledge do they struggle after of just how many gums, spices, natron baths, amulets, sacred extracts, wrappings of linen, and canvas went to the embalming of a single mummy as to leave no brains for raising the preliminary question of why the mummy ever was embalmed at all. With a competent outfit, perhaps, for the position of an Egyptian undertaker, they yet lack the first requisites for that of a tentative historical or theological observer.

II. In the description given in the last chapter of Thi's tomb at Memphis allusion was made to the Egyptian doctrine of the double. Now just as surely as in Dr. Edward E. Hale's instructive story, "My Double and How He Undid Me," its unhappy writer was brought to grief by not fully taking in the exact nature of his own double, so equally will every embryo student of early Egyptian conceptions of spirit-life find himself "undone" if he does not take in the exact nature of the Egyptian's double. The double is fundamental, as much a part of the man and his belongings as are his own or their own shadows in the sunshine.

The religion of the earlier days of far-away Egypt was the most literally materialized system of pantheistic animism the world ever saw. Such a thing is there as a poetic system of pantheism that sees and feels Deity in high and beautiful things, — in sky, mountains, lakes, noble and beneficent human lives, — but which finds itself disinclined to indulge in the same devout emotions over chairs, tables, brooms, crocodiles, snakes, and cats, — rather is secretly disposed to the belief that, somehow or other, the devil had a hand in them. This higher poetic system of pantheism believes, indeed, in the body as the tabernacle of soul, especially when body takes the shape of the luminous eyes of a beautiful woman or of the broad, meditative brow of a sage, but feels little spiritual interest in such organs as the liver, spleen, and pancreas, — indeed, is inclined to think, very much as Emerson put it, that we could get on just as well without them. If it dreams of continued existence beyond the earthly life, this same poetic system of pantheism yearns for such existence in an etherealized shape, — in a state, indeed, in which there shall be no more vulgar buying and selling; no more marketing for fish, flesh, and vegetables; no more pew-rents for spiritual consolation; no more doctors nor apothecary shops. And yet, in the higher realm, it would retain Beulah mountains and lakes, music beyond that of Beethoven and Mozart, inspirers rapt in the visions of an Isaiah, or a St. John at Patmos; for these things seem all divine.

Not at all in this sublimated way, however, do the more ancient Egyptians appear to have felt. In the mass they were the most prosaically imaginative people conceivable, shut up to celestial yearnings for a sort of everlasting Dutch tulip garden and a pipe beside a canal. For the adequate enjoyment of this they wanted the body, and the whole of it, — hair, nails, skin, viscera; for each of these had its double who, if they did

not keep a sharp lookout, would be sure to undo
them. Therefore, no endearing little cherubs for
them, amputated just below the shoulders!

I must be permitted the use of very plain language or give up any attempt at being faithful to
fact. In truth, it is failure to resort to plain language and plain corresponding ideas that makes
so much that is written about this land of marvel
hazy and unreal. An Egyptian's tomb was indeed
his spirit house, but, as any one can see with half
an eye, a house in which his spirit needed his appetite, his bed, his three meals a day, his servants, his farm and kitchen-garden, his bath, his
cat and dog, even his doctor and his pills. All
these he could enjoy in a strange spiritual-material
way, for every one of these objects, even a carved
or painted figure of one of them, possessed or was
possessed by its corresponding double. Thus, a
chair that could be sat on by a living man weighing two hundred pounds had its phantasmal double
that could be sat on by a spirit weighing nothing,
each in his own especial way. Thus, a savory roast
of flesh, that could be inhaled with gusto by responsive material nostrils, could in its double be
inhaled by spiritual nostrils; indeed, the meat itself or its etherealized Liebig extract equally well
masticated and digested by material or by spiritual teeth and alimentary canals. But teeth and
alimentary canals of either kind there must be, or
a spirit would find himself as ill provided in his
tomb as a solid man in the flesh at his dinner-table.
Without realizing all this to our minds, after the

most literal and downright fashion, we shall make no step of headway in getting into touch with the vast tomb-world environing us. It is the old Egyptian we are talking about, not about ourselves. Where we smile, he was in dead earnest.

Now for the first time are we in position to understand why, in the Egypt of old, such enormous sums were lavished on the fitting up of tombs, such costly and elaborate processes of embalming resorted to, such endless galleries painted with wall pictures of all conceivable objects, the double of each one of which stood in immediate relation with the convenience or luxury of the double of the occupant himself, at last settled in his "eternal dwelling-place." Just as literally as any one of us would feel utterly nonplussed and miserable on returning to his home in New York or Boston to find there no chairs, no carpets, no cups and saucers, no meat in the larder, no family to greet him, no books to read, no Bridget in the kitchen, exactly in the same way did the old Egyptian spirit feel about his tomb. In wrath and exasperation would he haunt and make unendurable the lives of the son or daughter or wife who had subjected him to such intolerable privations. And while the minute and commonplace fidelity to details with which all this was believed in and carried out often strikes our minds in an irresistibly humorous light, to an Egyptian it was a matter of such serious import, that any neglect of it would have set his spirit as much beside itself as the temper of the average American householder, who, on returning of a cold night to his home, should find just such a carpet-less, bed-less, meat-less scene of distraction as was but now alluded to.

" A fellow-feeling makes us wondrous kind," and of what use is historic imagination unless it can be raised to a vivid enough pitch to enable one to " put himself in the place " of a justly aggrieved fellow-creature of five thousand years ago? But when all went well, and wife and son were tender and loyal, what comfort and satisfaction in the dear home-tomb! Truly life is sweet, and a pleasant thing is it to behold the sun. There the sun still shone, the harvests waved, the birds sailed through the skies, and the fishes leaped in the Nile. Alas! for the man who has not learned to live into the heart of, to join in the wealth of, the spiritual double in all things. Teach us, O Egyptians, teach us the profundity of thy love !

III. Very different is the impression made by the tombs of the later dynasties. The priesthood has become a gigantic hierarchical power; and the change in the pictorial emblems on the walls is as marked as in Europe between the earlier spiritual conceptions of the Gospels and the embodiment of all mediæval theology in the Hell, Purgatory, and Paradise of Dante. The body is still embalmed, the tomb is still the double's home, offerings are still made, and the old, familiar every-day scenes are on the walls. No outright break has been made with old ideas; and they live on in juxtaposition, no matter how incongruous with one another. But the whole scale of proportion is tipped the other way. The sense of personal accountability for the life on earth is now the preponderating feeling. The gods have assumed more definite attributes. The forty-two judges at the awful day demand each his categorical answer as to sins of lying, stealing, adultery, bearing false witness. In the presence of the gods the heart is weighed against a feather, emblem of truth and right, that under no gust of passion must swerve a hair. Thoth, the righteous judge, writes down the record and passes sentence; while Anubis watches the indicator of the balance, and behind him stands a devouring monster in waiting to seize upon the wicked. The judgment over, here a soul is changed into a hog for its sensuality, here is torn to pieces by the "Devourer," here is led into the blessed presence of Osiris.

Such, in million-fold forms, are the scenes now presented, as one threads the long passages and comes out into the pillared halls of tombs extending, perhaps, five hundred feet into the solid rock. The figures are carved or stamped in low relief, and colored. So incalculable their number, even in the few burial-places that have been opened, that one feels as though the entire population of Egypt must have been engrossed in this one work, with no time left for sowing or reaping. And yet the marvelous thing to think of is, that all this Dresden or Munich gallery, finally completed by its army of artists and artisans, was thenceforth never further to be beheld by any human eye. Perils to the dead have increased. Strength of masonry can no longer be trusted to, and concealment must be the hope. The mummy once deposited, the entrance was stoned up, the cliff broken down, and every possible trace of the whereabouts of the tomb destroyed. There were no more reception-rooms or festal halls. The days of the former pleasant, social intercourse between the dead and the living had gone, and the simple supramundane had passed over into the supernatural. Amenti, the heaven of the departed, now lay in remote regions in the west, across the Libyan Desert.

Now, in perfect sincerity, what is the inevitable impression made on a reflective mind of to-day by these pictorial representations of death, arraignment before the last tribunal, judgment, penalty, introduction to the blessed abode of Osiris? It is and it must be the strangest conceivable admixture of the pathetic and sublime with the grotesque and ludicrous. The first entrance is inevitably solemnizing. You pass in under the brow of the great cliff. You thread rock-hewn passages and halls, with the oppressive sense, so usual in caves, of the weight of the superincumbent mountain. It is pitch dark, and you light your way with a candle held up close to the pictures to examine them. Every now and then leaps out the flash of a bit of burning magnesium wire. Rembrandtesque effects of whitest light contrasted with blackest shadow reveal in sharp distinctness long stretches of pictured wall and ceiling. The great theme perpetually present with every one who, heir to the sense of moral accountability, yet trusts in a final beatific vision of God, is the theme before the eyes, as, thousands of years ago, it engrossed the minds and hearts of myriads of one's fellow-creatures. More solemnizing thoughts, in their spiritual import, than those that underlie these pictorial representations cannot be entertained by the human mind. They are, as I said but now, the recognition of an immutable moral law before which Pharaoh and peasant alike must bow, and which here is seen administered without fear or favor by divinities, each one of whom is an incarnation of some aspect of immutable law. He must be a brute, and not a man, who does not feel a sense of awe in such an Egyptian tomb. But now to turn to the other side of the appeal made to mind and feeling.

"Thou art weighed in the balance, and found wanting." How sublime and moving this judgment, as it falls from the lips of a Hebrew prophet over a once mighty king! We can understand how a Washington Allston burned his life to ashes in his vain struggle to give satisfying expression to it on his canvas. But how, in contrast, did the old Egyptian portray the scene of weighing the value of a human heart? He presented it in a picture of a horizontal balance, such as was daily used in the market for weighing grain or swine, with a vase with a heart in it on the one platform, and on the other an upright feather. The god Anubis, who is touching the indicator with the tip of his finger, — through what eyes is he reading the momentous record? Through the eyes of a jackal, set in the head of a long-eared jackal. Thoth, the righteous judge of the great cycle of the gods, who is writing down on a tablet the result of the judgment, — there he stands, peering over his tablet with the head and long bill of an ibis. Horus, a man-headed bird who conducts the soul to the awful bar of judgment, is himself a hawk-headed Mercury. Osiris, the beatific vision of whom is finally granted as the highest bliss of the soul, who would ever want to see him, — a swathed and bandaged mummy, with the crown of Upper Egypt a-top? Ah! what a remove from Shakespeare's " What a piece of work is a man! how noble in reason! how infinite in faculty! in form and moving how express and admirable! in action how like an angel! in apprehension how like a god! "

Such a motley masquerade of animal-headed divinities interferes sadly, it must be confessed, with the due seriousness of mind with which one would contemplate such awful subjects. Of course, one knows that these animal substitutes for the regal crown of the body in which reason is supposed to be enthroned are to be taken symbolically. But there are symbols and symbols. To the modern man who has lost all vital touch with these, the pictures so parody the solemn theme as to suggest the final judgment-day of jackals and hippopotami. The incongruity puts too severe a strain on the average mind to leave it duly impressed with such supernatural reasoners on " temperance, righteousness, and judgment to come," and so makes the interest largely archæological. And yet these hawk and jackal headed divinities go so seriously about their business, and seem so naïvely unconscious of how queer they look to us, that by degrees their earnestness communicates itself to the feelings, till the picture becomes, in a way, affecting. One's own mind grows Egyptianized. It helps, too, toward feeling with solemnity what these pictured scenes meant to those who of old looked on them, to read translations of the hieroglyphics written above and beside them. These contain most touching prayers, records of just and righteous judgments, summaries of the whole duty of man as bound up in the command to do justly, love mercy, and walk humbly with God. Still, in setting down honestly the strangely contrasting impressions sure to be made on the spectator, it must be clearly understood that one has first to accustom himself to seeing, for example, Amen-Ra, the highest divinity of Egypt, the one of whom, through whom, and to whom are all things, presented in the guise of a naked man, a necklace on his breast, bracelets on his arms, anklets on his legs, and a high feather in his cap, and, that done, to reconcile, as best he can, the picture with so sublime an invocation as that of the following hymn : —

> " Hail to thee, Lord God of law,
> Thee whose shrine none ever saw !
>
> .   .   .   .
>
> Forms to all the men that be,
> Color and variety,
> By his fiat are assigned.
> Unto him the poor men cry,
> And he helps them in distress.
> Kind of heart is he to all

> Who upon him called,
> God Almighty to deliver
> Him that is afraid and meek
> From the great ones who oppress,
> Judging ever
> 'Twixt the strong and weak."

Many superior people at home who have derived their whole idea of Egyptian religion and of Egyptian conceptions of the realms beyond from the most spiritual passages in the "Book of the Dead," or from the profoundest comments of Herodotus, Plato, and Plutarch, will perhaps be shocked at expressions one has to use in simply reporting what his own eyes see. After rising in an exalted frame of mind from reading Plutarch's "Isis and Osiris," such natures do not like to hear that among the mighty dead of the Del-el-Bahara cavern-tombs on the lonely Libyan hills, it was found, for example, that Queen Uast-em-Khebit was laid away to rest fully fitted out for the resurrection morn with a supply of curled and frizzled wigs. Not, indeed, that curled and frizzled wigs are much more incongruous with so triumphant an occasion than, religiously speaking, are analogous displays of head-gear that with us flower out on Easter Sunday, or that we are especially warranted in throwing stones at our poor mummy sisters for feeling the ruling passion strong in death! Only in Egypt, with such a background of the ages, and when one has seen the individual royal mummy that did it such æons since, the levity strikes home in a more solemnizing, perhaps a more pathetic way, bringing out in us the Hamlet feeling over poor Yorick's skull: "Now get you to my lady's chamber, and tell her, let her paint an inch thick, to this favor she must come; make her laugh at that!"

Yes, Egypt is the land of contrasts. Not for a moment can the thoughtful man forget that he stands on a soil where the initiated and elect could declare of absolute Deity, "He is not graven in marble. He is not beheld. His abode is not known. No shrine is found with painted figures of him. There is no building that can contain him. . . . His commencement is from the beginning. He doth not manifest his forms. Vain are all representations." Then, in contrast, as the visitor opens his eyes and looks about him, lo! this wilderness of representations largely in what are to us the most repulsive animal shapes; this nation of priestly undertakers reducing to a lucrative trade the whole business of supplying the departing spirits with circumstantial, extramundane Baedekers, in which every inch of the sorely beset way to the heaven of Osiris is mapped out, with specific directions as to just what amount of *bakshish* is enough for this or that obstructing fiend, and just what fulsome ceremonial titles will please the ear and secure the favor of this or that celestial protector.

Again and again has Robert Browning given eloquent expression to his conviction that if the glorious hope of immortality were degraded from a sublime trust of the higher instincts of the soul

into a dead-level sense-demonstration of external
fact, it would remove all that is most uplifting and
purifying. Too often, in Egypt, would he have felt
this conviction reinforced with the weary weight of
all the colossal stones piled on top of the materialized dogma. Excess of contact with its dusty prose
and dreary literalism would, I am sure, have broken
the wings of the spiritually soaring poet, till never
there could he have hailed his own arisen one in
the strain, —

"My lyric love, half angel and half bird!"

IV.　So far I have spoken but of pyramids and
tombs; while it is among the ruins of the
great temples of Abydos, Denderah, Edfu, Luxor,
Karnak, Philæ, that the mind is bowed under the
overpowering sense of the colossal and fairly super-
human genius of the Egypt of the past. Again
and again one shrinks at the thought of attempting to say anything about these temples, and goes
on to something else. Indeed, what can one say?
There are certain sensations we are wont to call
elemental, so massive are they, so overwhelming,
so submerged in the very substance of feeling
never to be defined or analyzed. The ocean, the
Himalayas, the Book of Job, the "Fifth Symphony," Rembrandt's "Night Watch," awaken in
us this elemental sense. Always in the effect produced there is involved the overpowering weight of
material mass; here, in a Beethoven as in a pressure as of seven atmospheres of sound; here, in
a Rembrandt as in the tangible presence of vast

realms through which is enacting the colossal struggle of light with darkness. It is the sense of thus dealing with the elemental that stirs up from the foundation the oceanic depths in genius, and furnishes shaping substance for its stupendous conceptions. For a more fitting expression, then, of what this meant to the Egyptian of the far past, I know not better where to turn than to the words of one who, thousands of years ago, thus recorded his own feeling on being led into the awful presence of the Pharaoh: " I was as one brought out of the dark. My tongue was dumb, my lips failed me, my heart was no longer in my body to know whether I was alive or dead."

" The fear of the Lord is the beginning of wisdom," said the deep heart of the Hebrew race. Without the sense of overwhelming awe, the sense of nothingness, how shall the poor conceit of man be humbled in the dust? Yet, there is the prostration of the cowering slave; and there is the prostration of the saint or prophet hushed in adoration, and with no words on his lips but " Not unto me ! " Never in any other temples reared by the hand of man do mind and heart so feel this sense of the finite overwhelmed by the infinite, in naked, dominating simplicity, as in the Egyptian. It is all there in the sublimest Gothic cathedrals ; but it is there blent with beauty, uplifted by triumphant soaring, and glorified with rainbow hues of vision. In Egypt it stands out alone.

What a tiny ant crawling along the base of a

mountain does a man feel himself as he enters a
temple like Luxor! Colossal statues forty feet in
height, seated in the immortal calm of ages, con-
front him with their awful silence till his own finite
griefs and petty ambitions dwindle to the insignificant trifles of an hour. He walks along avenues of columns so enormous in mass and height
that the overthrow of one of them would crush
an army of such insects as himself; and yet all
around him they lie, fallen, fallen, fallen. His
thought is dealing with dynasties so remote, embodied in royal shapes so colossal and in memorial temples so stupendous, as to seem the record
of a story that shall never perish. And yet, in the
presence of eternity, nay, of time itself, what are
they to be likened unto but the dust blown from
the balance. It is, then, this sense of prostration
beneath what at first seems utterly incommensura-
ble with the grasp of the human mind that consti-
tutes the " fear of the Lord which is the beginning
of wisdom " in the appreciation of an Egyptian
temple. Not that it continues a slavish fear.
No! "He that humbleth himself shall be exalted," and at last the exaltation comes. For is
it not witness of a spirit that has within itself the
keynote of vibration in harmony with all this
immensity, that man can finally so surmount the
sense of prostrate awe as to feel in all this mighty
Presence but a symbol of his own eternity? Luxor
and Karnak! in such a presence the most average
mind is lifted into a realm in which it seems native
to think and feel in the strain of a Pascal: " Man

is but a reed, the weakest in nature, but he is a thinking reed. It is not necessary that the entire universe arm itself to crush him. A breath of air, a drop of water, suffices to kill him. But were the universe to crush him, man would still be more noble than that which kills him, because he knows that he dies, while the universe knows nothing of the power it has over him."

The first great Egyptian temple visited on the way up the Nile is that of Denderah. In the approach to it one encounters what is the perpetual marvel of the Egypt now revealed to-day. Here is a vast structure that for ages was buried up from sight. The winds of the desert blew in the sands. Generation after generation of men built up their habitations of clay about it, till the walls were hidden; and then generation after generation plastered their mud huts, foul as crows' nests, over the gigantic blocks of the roofs. Now all is cleared away from within and without; and you thank God for the sands of the desert and the potsherds of the peasants, as the actual angels' wings that sheltered these priceless treasures against the vandalism of nature and man. Fresh cut as of yesterday come out the carvings.

This is not the place to describe the shape and arrangement of the Egyptian temple. Familiarity with these must be gained from engravings and photographs. One does not, as a general rule, enter their porticoes as he does the open porticoes of Greek temples. A screen is built up half-way high between the outer columns, all the way along the front, except between the two of them that open up the entrauce. They thus subserve the end of portico-halls rather than of porticoes, — a feature greatly enhancing their impressiveness through the stupendous effects of light and darkness. One enters. Physically and literally, the breathing is arrested and the heart almost stops its beating. Such a forest of gigantic columns, such a Druid grove in stone, such mysterious depths in the roofing overhead and in the vista of the halls opening out beyond! There are those who would call this the feeling of the barbarian. Then gloriously confess the barbarian's love of prostration beneath an overpowering sensation. Boldly say that in comparison with the effect wrought by such a portico-hall as that of Denderah, the effect of any such famous portico as that of the Pantheon in Rome is but as that of a pretty cluster of birch saplings to a California grove of giant redwoods. When in the forest a group of tree-trunks takes your breath away, when it awes you with the sense of thousands of years of growth, when you have to look up and up to cope with its majestic branching overhead, when you behold its mighty base in brilliant sunshine, and its dome overhead a vault of darkness and mystery, then first you get the sublime of what may fitly be called elemental arboreal sensation. This awful secret in stone the Egyptians knew as none that have ever lived before or since.

All through the course of human history man bears witness to the fact how keenly he suffers in presence of the overwhelming powers about him, through the sense of physical littleness and limitation. Against this he struggles with straining heart. His arm is puny; and, to supplement it, he invents levers and cranes. His eye is feeble; and, to give it range, he thinks out the telescope. His voice is weak and monotonous; and, to impart to it resonance and variety, he compasses the trumpet, the drum, the organ, the violin. Then he rises into freedom. Mind no longer dominated by brute matter, every force in matter becomes an attribute of mind. This freedom the Egyptians achieved through Titan power of handling enormous masses, and shaping them into a Titanic world. Their Pharaoh! A block of granite fifty feet in height, twenty to thirty in length and breadth, and weighing a thousand tons, alone could serve for the statue that should give adequate expression to the weight of his authority, the immovable foundation of his reign. For what did he stand to them? For a god upon earth. "Thou art like the sun in all that thou doest. Shouldst thou wish to make it day during the night, it is so forthwith. If thou sayest to the water, 'Come from the rock,' it will come in a torrent suddenly, at the word of thy mouth. The god Ra is like thee in his limbs, the god Khepra in creative force." Therefore, when, in the Book of Exodus, the God of the Hebrews hardens Pharaoh's heart, it is that He may "show his power," even over so awful a being, and "get glory of him." All this awe and prostration before the Pharaoh's might the Egyptian temple bodies forth. The Egyptians, too, hardened the heart of the rock, and made it brute, sullen, and rebellious, that they might show their power over it, and compel it to reveal their glory.

And how the rock does reveal their glory! This is the dominating feeling, as one wanders among the ruins of their temples, with at first a feeling of dazed, prostrate awe, and at last a feeling of exultation. The builders will touch no stone that would not leave other builders aghast at the bare thought of moving it. They roof with slabs thirty feet long, seven wide, and four thick, as we would roof with slates. Each column, each capital, each architrave, each ceiling, carries with it the sense of fear and trembling crowned with triumph. Our very ignorance of the means employed adds the feeling of supernatural mystery, till the giant colossi, seated immovable on their thrones, seem but images in their natural size of the sole beings who could rear such structures. And yet, withal, how is all tempered with beauty!

A few trivial figures sometimes help the mind as scales of relative proportion, though personally, I must confess, I have never felt profoundly indebted to the tape measure for more impressive estimates of the sublime. Still, to try the experiment on a single feature of one of the stupendous columns in the " Great Hall " of Karnak! It is computed that on top of one of the lotus-leaved capitals of these columns one hundred and fifty to two hundred men could stand. Well, in imagination set the dwarfed creatures up there like a swarm of flies, and stand off for a look at them. How maliciously would Dean Swift have reveled in the sight, delectable as anything he devised in Brobdingnag! With what a sardonic smile would he have doffed his shovel hat in deferential contempt to the little midgets! And yet in the very act of degrading he would but have exalted them. The midgets built the stupendous temple.

In this single hall there are twelve of these massive columns, each thirty-six feet in circumference and eighty feet in height, forming a central avenue, and, on either side, one hundred and twenty-two of only less gigantic dimensions distributed in aisles of seven, — one hundred and thirty-four columns in all. Atoms of the dust, did you rear this! Matter! it is the stuff of man's dreams as truly as of God's dreams, and mind a power compelling its brute mass as the winds the clouds. Orpheus singing into place the stones of the sacred city with the music of his lyre, it seems no idle fable.

Crowning marvel of all, these temples were never created for the multitude. They were but the meeting-place of the Pharaoh god with the god of the supernal realm. This temple of Karnak, from outermost pylon in front to sanctuary in the rear nearly a quarter of a mile in length, had no other significance but as audience chamber of consultation between the Divine Majesty on earth and the Divine Majesty in heaven. No wonder so supernal a conception demanded so supernal an embodiment! Yet once this overwhelming temple stood in direct connection by a broad sphinx-lined avenue of more than a mile with the vast Luxor temple, while equally over across the Nile, past the colossal Memnon statues, and on and on to the temple of Kurnah, the Ramesseum, and Medinet Habu, great sphinx-lined avenues brought it into like connection with these stupendous structures. Now first one begins to feel Thebes in its day of glory. All other ruins seem the ruins of little children at their child-play sport of building sand castles on the beach.

PALESTINE

I.   IT is from Port Said, at the Mediterranean end of the Suez Canal, that one embarks for Palestine. After dreamy weeks spent among the mysterious tombs and temples of the Upper Nile, the contrast is startling in coming out upon this congested highway of the traffic of the modern world. It is the Broadway, the Strand, along which, eastward-bound, westward-bound, unintermittingly stream the long files of steamships. What a cut-off of a whole vast continent by a hundred miles of digging, and what a concentration, as for a view on dress-parade, of the commercial fleets of the world!

As a witness, however, to the unity of creation and to the fact that no good is of merely private interpretation, it is gratifying to record how from the very start the fishes caught hold of the scope of De Lesseps' idea, leaping at the thought of the new epoch inaugurated by his enterprise for wider piscatory as well as human intercourse; those of the Red and Arabian seas at once rejoicingly plying tail and fin for closer acquaintanceship with their Mediterranean brothers, and those of the Mediterranean for wider ethnological relations with their congeners of the Orient. Who of enlarged benevolence but must rejoice over a millennial day in which the languid Red Sea mother-fish can now start out from those tepid waters with her small fry languid as herself, to brace their constitutions with the tonic coolness of more invigorating floods, while countless pulmonic sisters from the north, dreading for their own small fry a like inheritance, can thus secure a change, as beneficial, to the tropic waters of the south.

II. On the voyage from Port Said, one first touches Palestinian land at Jaffa. It has no harbor, and as a heavy sea is generally running the disembarkation into boats is more lively than agreeable. One jumps headlong from the ship's gangway into the arms of the boatmen, and reaches footing by faith and not by sight. No boatman, however, "muffs," and one cannot but admire the dexterity with which they catch "on the fly" very stout and hysterically shrieking elderly ladies.

Spite, however, of all this hurly-burly the well-regulated mind contrives to store away in vivid memory the picturesque promontory on which the town is perched, and the ragged reef off its southern end, over which the breakers leap in sheets of spray. Such mental photographs are of lasting value. Henceforth when one reads of the landing of the cedars of Lebanon for the temple of Jerusalem; of Jonah embarking for his eventful voyage; of Dorcas, standing reproof to most of us in that she "did what she could;" of St. Peter's vision of the sheet let down filled with clean and unclean beasts; of stout Judas Maccabeus assault-

ing the town; of the Crusaders again and again
landing there from the Venetian fleets; and finally
of Napoleon raising such a problem in humane
casuistry through his heroic practice in poisoning
the sick and wounded in the military hospitals, —
all will have in it an element of reality otherwise
not to be felt. Yes, even Perseus and Andromeda,
after one has seen the very rocks to which the sea-
monster bound the forlorn maiden, who can longer
doubt their story? Does not Pliny attest that
even in his day the chains were still rusting there!
And cannot we clinch his testimony by our own
attestation that the rocks are not yet gone!

III.   When Peter the Hermit and his fellow-pil-
grims went up to Jerusalem, it was under
volleys of curses and a hail of stones that tested
the metal of their faith. To-day one sneaks up by
rail. One cannot escape a haunting sense of hu-
miliation. Not that curses and stones would not
be plenty enough at this late date were the courage
equal to the will. One is on Mohammedan soil
and under the flag of the " unspeakable Turk,"
but respect for the Christian's 'cannon overpowers
hate of the Christian's creed. Fanaticism can only
" think damn," not act it out. Back in Armenia,
happily, it is otherwise. There the faithful can
slaughter Christian men, women, and children, even
the soldiers lending a helping hand, and the gov-
ernors diplomatically denying the facts when Europe begins to murmur. But here into the train
one mounts without so much as ground for a ro-

mantic hope that a sporadic little fanatic of an Islamite boy may throw a stone — not too large — through the window.

Immediately on quitting Jaffa, the train plunges into the great plain of Sharon, fertile, but, after the Nile valley, not very fertile; for, under the fiery sun of Syria and with no brimming river wherewith to slake its thirsty lips, its broad wheatfields and fig, orange, and mulberry plantations have no dependence but on the "earlier and later rains" of spring. They had already fallen, and all was beautiful as one now looked backward over the broad level of green relieved against the encroaching sea-sands, the snowy breakers, and the sky-blue expanse of the Mediterranean. Spots intimately associated with Scripture story were now pointed out on every hand; but the only one that struck home with any vivid sensation was the valley of Ajalon. There, at five o'clock in the afternoon, as we looked off over the valley, hung the moon directly above it. Such the haze of the atmosphere that the entire disk was distinctly visible. The leap to the lips was instantaneous: "Sun stand thou still upon Gibeon, and thou, moon, in the valley of Ajalon!"

After some twenty miles, the train begins to climb the monotonous, barren mountains. Blunted, rarely peaked in outline, the gray limestone rocks broken into narrow lines of cleavage, without trees except gnarled, century-old olives, there is little poetic charm in such scenery unless through aerial effects of light and shadow. One startling sen-

sation, however, the aspect does awaken. Everywhere are the shattered rocks so sprinkled with red
poppies and red anemones, or relieved against col-
lective masses of them, as to suggest the idea of
flecks and pools of blood. The blood besprinkled
Mount of Sacrifice! It is impossible to rid the
mind of the impression.

One leaves the train at a spot that could not
have been selected better by mediæval pilgrim or
modern artist for a first view of the Holy City.
On a level with Jerusalem itself three fourths of
a mile away, a deep abyss opening up between
the mountain on which it stands and the mountain from which one looks, there sits the sacred
city, its walls, its thirty towers, its wilderness of
domes, and dome-vaulted dwellings. How seemingly impregnable a situation for security, and yet
how irresistible an appeal to every heart that has
ever felt the aspiration and the tragedy, the degradation and the glory of its age-long human history!
Ah, the moans of despair, the yells of execration,
the anthems of triumph, with which these rocks
have echoed! Spite of its abrupt and isolated position, there is a profound sense in which the city
cannot "sit solitary." It is compassed about by
too great a cloud of witnesses ever to be beheld
apart from its environment in imagination. David
is storming the citadel of Mt. Zion. Solomon is
adorning it with palace and temple. Shishak, king
of Egypt, is besieging and plundering it. Nebu-
chadnezzar is haling away, lamenting sore, its sons
and daughters to captivity in Babylon. Jeremiah

is plaining its woes, and Isaiah prophesying the
coming glory. Ezra is restoring it. Jesus is weeping over it. Again Titus is razing it to the ground.
Constantine is re-adorning it. Khalif Omar is
breaking in from the desert to rear the mosque of
Allah on the site of the temple of Jehovah. Anon,
the ferocious Turks are clutching it by the throat,
and the Crusaders are wading in blood to their
saddle-girths through its courts, and Saladin is
once again planting the crescent on its battlements,
while to-day the Greek, Latin, Armenian, and Coptic churches of Christendom are vindictively fighting over its sacred relics as the Mohammedan looks
on in lofty scorn, and the Jewish remnant, a nest of
paupers, is supported by the pious alms of French
and German bankers.

Our quarters in Jerusalem lay just outside the
Jaffa Gate. Never to my dying day shall I cease
to be thankful for a quiet stroll of a couple of
hours that first evening around a portion of the
city walls. The fever of the day was over, and the
moon poured a flood of softest light over towers
and battlements and down into the valley of Je-
hoshaphat. Without and within all was a dream
of peace. The spiritual presence of Jesus, the
familiar paths his footsteps trod, the scenes on
which his eye daily rested, — all were blent in
one harmonious whole. Over yonder in distinct-
est outline across the abyss stood the Mount of
Olives, and low down to the right the Garden of
Gethsemane. Where in any religion is there a
symbol remotely to be compared with the story of

the passionate love, the mortal agony, the resurrection in spiritual triumph of the life of Jesus! Buddhism with its Nirvana of rest for him who in abandonment of despair has seen into the depths of the emptiness underlying the All, Brahmanism with its thought-less, desire-less, imagination-less, reabsorption into the Absolute, what are they beside Jesus' sublime trust in life eternal in the bosom of God for the lowliest. Ah, that after that hour dissolved in moonlight peace I had left Jerusalem and seen no more!

IV. With the morrow came the sense of disillusion. It had to be so. Sacred cities, call them Buddhist, Mohammedan, Christian, call them Benares, Mecca, Jerusalem, are one in essence. Deriving their repute from the inspiration of some prophet who thought to reveal higher spiritual conceptions to the world, they become in the end the gaping pilgrimage-resorts of millions of the ignorant and superstitious. Nor is this the worst. Whatever one's creed as to the spiritual worth of the " merits of the saints " held in fee by any church for eking out the demerits of the sinful, no doubt of their financial value can be entertained. As an investment in real estate, secure for a thousand years from fluctuation on the market, the tomb of a prophet eventually rises to a higher rate per foot than the most advantageous broker's site on Wall Street. It is idle to try to blink these ugly facts. " Where the carcass is, there will the vultures be gathered together."

Whether transacted in beef and pork, or in crosses and crescents, business is business, baptize it in whatever sacrilegious name one may.

Tens of thousands of pilgrims imply no end of greedy lodging-house keepers, imply the sharpest competition in driving a trade in candles, rosaries, and relics, in the sale of farm products from the country-people, and in the services of an army of rival priests and Levites. Thus, inevitably, the entire material prosperity of a holy city is as strictly based on the "merits of the saints" as Newcastle on coals or Manchester on calicoes; and as, in a great commercial city, each rival firm seeks to outdo its neighbor in display of attractions in its show-windows, so, in a great holy city, does each competing religious body vie with every other in the superior variety and marvel of its tinsel legends, authentic relics, and miraculous trumpery of every sort. In truth, the scourge of small cords works a jail-delivery only once. Soon the traders are back again, this time to realize a profit out of authentic strands of the very cords with which they were originally whipped.

V.   There are three frames of mind, each equally natural, in which a human being may wander round among the holy places of Jerusalem and Bethlehem. The first is that of the devout village pilgrims one encounters in shoals, largely unkempt, powerfully built Russian peasants, ignorant and superstitious beyond compare, and so hot-bloodedly emotional as to pass in a moment

from the most groveling prostration before a relic
to the most savage brutality in a fight with a Latin
or Coptic fellow-Christian of erroneous views.   The
second is that of the thorough-going disciple of
Mark Twain, without the genius of the master;
his only breviary the "Innocents Abroad."   He
journeys to Jerusalem in devoutest faith, that here
is sanctuary none other can rival for a chance
at cheap wit based on irreverence, and that once
there the dullest of men may cherish a rational
hope of manufacturing a really funny book out of
incongruities staring him in the face on every hand.
The third frame of mind is that of the at once
mediævally devout and mediævally scholastic man
of the Cardinal Newman type, one who, having
eyes, sees only through a haze of preconceptions,
but through this haze sees with a beauty vastly
edifying to all who, like himself, are staggered at
nothing.   What, then, shall the visitor do who has
neither the endowment of the Russian peasant, nor
of a pseudo-disciple of Mark Twain, nor of a fol-
lower of Cardinal Newman?   There seems but one
course for him.

He is going, say, to the Church of the Holy
Sepulchre.   What does he expect to find there?
The shrine of pilgrimage of millions of the human
race from the third or fourth century until to-day.
Does he suppose they have ever read Emerson
or Martineau?   Or is it his object to try conclusions between his own critical apparatus and
their purely uncritical imaginations?   The Empress Helena, wife of Constantine, with unlimited

means and a most obsequious bishop at command, —does he suppose that, when she went out to Palestine to settle the position of the holy places, she meant to be balked by idle archæological considerations? As an adjunct to her critical apparatus, had she not, for example, supernatural dreams to assure her just where under Golgotha the three crosses were buried? And, when a momentary doubt arose as to which one of the three was the cross of Jesus, did she not, by sending at once to the hospital for a moribund patient, furnish an opportunity to the true cross to work a miracle, and so settle the question beyond rational dispute?

No: there is but one way and one spirit in which the broadly educated man of to-day can intelligently and seriously view the Church of the Holy Sepulchre in Jerusalem. He is there neither to praise nor to blame, but to understand. He is in the presence of a growth of centuries differing totally from his own. The whole spectacle is to be taken as a unity, one and indivisible. The pillar marking the exact centre of the earth, as well as marking the spot from which was taken the dust out of which Adam was made, is as much a part of the whole imaginative creation as are the three authentic holes in the rock into which were thrust the three crosses of the crucifixion. The grave of Adam exactly underlying the cross of the Redeemer, so that the blood of the eternal sacrifice should trickle down and annul the original sin of him in whom fell the whole human race, rests on precisely the same foundation of authority as the spot where the Virgin Mother stood when Jesus commended her to the tender care of the beloved disciple.

On setting out, therefore, for the Church of the Holy Sepulchre, let one make a hard and fast vow to leave all cheap, rationalistic acumen at home. Rather, let him watch and try to enter into the feelings of the swarms of Russian pilgrims. See them as they break on entering under the high arch of the portal, and wildly precipitate themselves at the foot of the "Stone of Holy Unction." It is like seeing troops of horses just out of the desert break and precipitate themselves at the sight of pools of water. Here is the Gate of Heaven! Here is the Promised Land! Here can the blessed Saviour be seen, felt, handled, kissed, reveled in through every sense! The very stone on which his crucified body was laid for the anointing, the very spot on which Mary stood weeping, the very hole into which was thrust the foot of the cross, the very cave and sarcophagus in which rested the mangled body till the Angel of the Resurrection rent the rock asunder, — oh, to be thrice blessed of God in beholding all this, to be able to fling the arms passionately around each object, to kiss it over and over, to rub the forehead against it, to feel in outright contact with what his flesh and blood had been in contact with, — this is to see Christ, to become one with Christ, to find him tangible, palpable reality!

Now first one understands the true spirit of the

Crusades as he watches these pilgrims, men and women who had tramped their hundred or thousand miles to behold the kingdom of heaven radiant before their eyes in this vast, tawdry church; understands, too, in its massive material-spiritual significance, the great Middle Age dogma of transubstantiation, of bread made actual flesh of Christ, and wine made actual blood of Christ, till the believer *ate* and *drank* the real body and blood of his Lord, all else mere spiritual medium, empty and impalpable in comparison. No longer ask, then, what you think of all this marvelous spectacle. It matters not. Seek only to get at what these pilgrims think of it, what it actually is to them, what equally it has been to millions behind them and to the myriads of Crusaders who spilt their last drop of blood in rescuing these holy memorials from the hand of the infidel. Then opens to you, child of this nineteenth century, a new chapter in human history. What made this past so vital, so terrible, so glorious, is now before your eyes.

VI. From the Church of the Holy Sepulchre in Jerusalem it is a charming stroll of five or six miles to Bethlehem and the Church of the Nativity. After so many pilgrims and so much strain to live into ages that have gone by, it is very blissful to feel one's self once again in the living presence of nature and out under the old, unchanging sky. True, it is a barren and rugged nature about one. The very wheat-fields along the mountain crests — if fields they may be called — are so congested with sharply splintered stones that the partial clearing of one of them involves burying up a full half of the surface under piles of rock taken from the other half. Now strikes home new insight into the relation between man and his environment as one takes in at a glance why the prophets of Jerusalem so commonly met death by stoning. Murder in the heart of Saul, and St. Stephen there, the magazine of death-dealing missiles is right on hand. But this scene of cruel martyrdom, even though it bequeathed to the world so divine a prayer, one would now fain dismiss from the mind, and think rather of the sower who went forth to sow. No wonder so little seed fell upon the good ground. So little good ground was there. But the stony places, they were everywhere. All seemed like looking straight through the eyes of Jesus, the only way to look would one ever get in touch with his soul.

Ah! what a walk were this but for authentic sacred places. Every few hundred paces, and lo! another. Now, alas! one must pause duly to revere the slab of stone on which sublime Elijah sank when in collapse of despair he cried, " Lord, it is enough; now lettest thou thy servant die." Nothing more full of the heartbreak of a mighty spirit is there in all Hebrew literature. Does it gain by one's stopping to see, in physical attestation of the weight of the prophet's woe, the full-length impress of his body sunk as with a mortal die into the rock? O God! cries the soul in revolt, must the monkish awkward squad thus fire over each hallowed grave. From every side rings their ragged fusillade. Passing belief is the abject prose of literalism under which are degraded the most spontaneous outbursts of the soul. "If they should hold their peace, the stones would immediately cry out," Jesus passionately retorted to the Pharisées incensed with the multitude proclaiming, "Blessed the King that cometh in the name of the Lord!" Then think — by way of edifying comment on this metaphor of passion — of being shown in a shrine four or five authentic specimens of the very stones that would have cried out, only that the multitude did not hold their peace, and so there was no call for lithological rebuke.

VII.　The impression wrought by the Church of the Nativity is over again that of the Church of the Holy Sepulchre in Jerusalem. Once more is experienced the same dazed surprise at finding so many sacred places included within the walls of a single great building, the same incredulous wonder that each incident in the Gospel story should be located to the very inch. Here a star on the pavement marks the precise spot on which the Holy Child was born; here another star just where the Magi stood; here still another the position of the manger. On this hand a chapel shows the recess to which St. Joseph retired when he gave thanks at the moment of the Nativity; on this, where the angel descended to command the Flight into Egypt; on this, where the Innocents were gathered together and buried after Herod's massacre. Even the cave-stable, if here it is, is so bedizened with marble and tinsel as to be transformed into a tawdry doll-house.

A single inspired picture like Correggio's ecstatic " Nativity " in the Dresden Gallery, a single glorifying poem like Milton's " Christmas Hymn," and the soul is carried a thousand times nearer in actual time and space to the spirit that dictated the early Gospel narrative of cave, manger, shepherds. happy young mother, rejoicing of heaven with earth, than by all this Bethlehem child's-play. For the one is poetry and the other prose. Here, alas! is the whole devout story monopolized for vulgar sensation, and degraded to a sacred peep-show. Indeed, the very Turkish soldiers on guard to keep the Greek, Latin, and Armenian monks from tearing one another's hair, should the one venture to cross the staked-out " claim " of the other, are but fitting symbols of the worth of the whole ecclesiastical exhibition. Here, of a truth, one looks on at the real Gethsemane, the real Agony in the Garden, the crucifixion afresh of Jesus.

VIII. With the general aspects of nature, however, in and about Bethlehem and Jerusalem, and with the real gain in becoming familiar with them, the case is utterly different. Here, in truth, is the handiwork of God, — the material body in which the spirit once tabernacled, on which time has effected little change. The reputed site, say, for example, of the house of Martha and Mary in Bethany — one modern stone hovel amid a hundred as sordid would, one might think, awaken no trace of interest; but the view of earth and sky on which their eyes looked out, the stony hills, the terraces of vines and olives, the fertile spots of pasturage in the valley below, the paths trod by Jesus' feet to and from the Mount of Olives above, — these are more than historical : they are bound up with all the imagery of the parables and intimately associated with the one real home that was refuge and solace to him who so often had not " where to lay his head." So with a thousand objects in this whole region of spiritual story. One looks off over the barren hills among which David was a wanderer and an outcast.. The guide points out the site of the cave of Adullam, or, perhaps, the exact spot where the young hero, dying of thirst for a drink from the dear old well in Bethlehem, poured out the water on the ground, because, thus purchased, it was the " blood of his men." But there are countless such caves in the limestone of these mountains ; and what matters any idle fancy which exact one it was in which there gathered to the outlawed chief "every one that was in distress, and every one that was in debt, and every one that was discontented, and he became a captain over them." Enough that, with a single sweep of the eye, one thus takes in the scene of the bandit life, of the refuse material ripe for political revolution, of the Sir Philip Sidney chivalry of their heroic leader. A realistic setting is thus given to the

Bible story that is a distinct addition, and like instances might be multiplied without end.

Not, indeed, that one does not gladly welcome legends whenever there is any genuine human nature in them. In Bethlehem, to give an example, one visits a shrine built over the supposed spot to which Mary retired with the infant Jesus to prepare for the flight into Egypt. There one drop of her mother milk fell to the ground, ever after imparting to the dust of the place miraculous power to make the milk flow freely in the breasts of all mothers unable to nourish their own pining little ones. Crude as the legend is, it has at least something human in it, something in line with the loving tradition of the Gospels. For Jesus, once a babe, loved all babes, and knew how sweet was his mother Mary's milk. One can sympathize with the sad-eyed peasant woman he sees kneeling there, her emaciated baby in her arms. But asked to share the emotions of a troop of pilgrims hanging in idiotic simplicity of adoration over specimens of the stones that would have cried out, my own piety, I confess, fails.

IX. Of course, one goes to see and hear the wailing of the Jews over the sole remaining fragment of the foundation wall of their national temple, — probably one of the few genuine relics of the time of Solomon left in the city, unless the subterranean quarries. It is the hilarious custom with tourists to laugh at this spectacle as a sort of mock exhibition of grief akin to shedding tears over Adam's grave. To me the scene was affecting. Religion and patriotism are one and inseparable in the Jewish mind; and of all their former glories there remains to them, in their own ancestral city, but this stretch of ruined wall. If ever there was a " lost cause," the memory of which might remain locked up in the human heart generation on generation, surely this is one. Exiles in their own home; dominated by a hateful Mohammedan government; their temple site the seat, on which they dare not set foot, of the splendid Mosque of Omar; prohibited, at the risk of being torn to pieces by ferocious mobs, from so much as walking through the street of the Church of the Holy Sepulchre, — a real Via Dolorosa to them; with no future, but only a past, to fall back on for cheer and hope, — why should there not be pathetic sincerity in the litany they chant?

" Because of the palace which is deserted,
  We sit alone and weep.
   Because of the temple which is destroyed,
   Because of the walls which are broken down,
   Because of our greatness which is departed,
   Because of the precious stones of the temple ground to powder,
   Because of our priests who have erred and gone astray,
   Because of our kings who have contemned God, —
   We sit alone and weep."

In Jerusalem, its population three fourths Jewish and Mohammedan, its Christian temples maintained in safety solely through fear of European intervention, one feels as nowhere else the abiding spiritual characteristics of the Semitic race, and the greatness of the gulf that divides it from the

Aryan, — the outcome of whose distinct pantheistic and philosophical genius, superimposed on the simple story of the Gospel, is seen in the vast system of theological mythology here so crudely represented by the Greek and Latin churches. The Mosque of Omar and the Church of the Holy Sepulchre, the naked simplicity of the ritual of the one, the florid and grotesque symbolism of the other, — here are the two great races in salient contrast.

X. To us, in the saddle most of the time and under a blazing Syrian sun, great certainly was the fatigue, though greater far the interest, of the descent of nearly four thousand feet to Jericho, the Dead Sea, and the Jordan. That it is still possible on this memorable journey to "fall among thieves" — though the good Samaritan be more problematical — was evident in the fact that our little party of two tourists, a dragoman, and a servant, required the escort of a donkey-mounted scrap of a Bedouin, a highly decorated gun, six feet in length, strapped horizontally across his back. Once covenanting with this tawny son of Ishmael for a certain sum in shekels, metaphorically we were taken to have "eaten his salt," and so, under the protecting ægis of the laws of hospitality, to be exempt from further robbery at the hands of his tribe. As he would sway from side to side, the muzzle of his weapon described such areas of ninety or more degrees, that we who rode behind felt in him a veritable object of terror, and so possessed our souls in peace.

It was good to be out among the mountains, stern and forbidding as they looked, and to be storing away first-hand mental pictures. Every now and then we would come upon a gaunt, sun-blackened shepherd walking in front of his flock, the sheep "following him." "The Lord is my shepherd, I shall not want." Ay, but without a shepherd knowing where lies every nibble of grass and every trickling water-spring, how these thirsty, pining creatures must want. "Read with emphasis!" insisted in the school our early teachers. That one word *want*, — ah! with what emphasis did famine and thirst ejaculate it here. Yes, how deep-lying in sharp sensation is all poetic imagery! and how eternally true of facts, "They learn in suffering what they teach in song."

Then, farther on, we would come upon the ruins of an old Crusader castle, bleached, bare, and with no green ivy to mantle its wounds and scars. Oh, the cruel disillusioning that must have come over those fanatic warriors, their brains aflame with visions of the Promised Land, when, once they had stormed the sacred city and sated their lust of blood, they found themselves monotonously set down on these desolate mountains, amidst swarms more fanatic than themselves, to hold fast this Fata Morgana exhalation of desert sand. With what yearning must Europe have risen before the mind's eye, the castle on the Loire, the castle on the Rhine!

More impressive still, stand and gaze down into the savage gorge at the bottom of which courses the brook Cherith. For a picture of raven-fed

Elijah, what a background of solitary desolation!
Yes, God pity the prophet there whom the ravens
should not find out and succor! And yet to the
side of the gorge, like a limpet to a rock, clings
a monastery, where centuries on centuries successive bands of Carmelite monks have dwelt. Piteous
the irony of the fate of the poor Crusaders; but,
irony of ironies would you ponder and fathom it,
is it not witnessed in brotherhoods of ascetic monks,
self-exiled in this savage gorge to commune with
the mighty spirit of Elijah, and yet doomed to
seek their ravens in the profits of carving salad-
spoons for gadding tourists out of holy wood from
the Mount of Olives?

Striking views begin to open up over a wide
expanse as one nears the verge of the mountain
region. What a presence of ages of history and of
historical legend! In sight is the top of Pisgah
lifting from behind the mountains of Moab; in
sight, the river that rolled back for the passage of
Joshua's bands; in sight, the mound-heaps of old
Jericho, toppled down at the blast of the rams'
horns of the priests. These, and the Mount of
Temptation to which the Devil carried Jesus, the
grave of Moses set up in rivalry by the Mohammedans, the pool of bitter water Elisha made sweet
ever after by casting in a handful of salt, the whole
stretch of the Jordan valley, and, shining in the
distance, the glassy surface of the Dead Sea!

Unquestionably, over these Moab mountains descended Joshua and his desert-toughened, desert-
famished Bedouins. What the cry "The sea! the

sea!" of Xenophon's army, to their cry as their eyes feasted on the verdure of the Jordan valley as then it was!

Fresh from reading the Book of Joshua, fresh from the primitive chroniclers of the first Mohammedan campaigns, how realistically one saw and felt that it was one and the same historic story repeated at vast intervals of time. The same fiery and vindictive tribal God of the desert, — the supernatural Bedouin, with a few genuine tribal Bedouin virtues in his heart, ever ready to reward the faithful with the illimitable booty of idolatrous cities and idolatrous women, — such alike the Jahveh of Joshua and the Allah of Mohammed! One pays afresh his tribute of grateful reverence to devoutly brave old Christian Bishop Ulfilas, in that clear back in the fourth century he should have refused so stoutly to translate for his converted Goths the Book of Joshua. No, the Goths need no revelation from on high to incite to rapine and murder; enough of it have they by nature without the aid of grace! Such the ringing word of the stout old bishop. Yet out of these ferocious beginnings were to grow, at last, as consummate spiritual flower, the sublime strains of Isaiah and the parable of the Prodigal Son.

In contradiction of its name, forever will the Dead Sea hold in one mind, at least, a green and living memory. Not that its environing mountains are not desolate enough, but what sternness will not aerial light robe in a bridal veil of beauty! The air was breathless, and perfect the reflection of sky and range. Sodom and Gomorrah, Lot and his wicked daughters, fire and brimstone from on high, seemed all out of keeping with the radiant sunshine. For months nowhere had my friend and I found ourselves where it was possible to enjoy the luxury of a swim, and now red-hot with long hours in the saddle under such a blazing sun, rank ingratitude had it seemed not to answer the invitation of these crystal-clear waters.

Often as has been described the delight of floating on the buoyant surface of the Dead Sea, the experience is one only to be interpreted in terms of private consciousness. Under the spell of such sparkling levity, presto! vanishes the heavy and the weary weight of gravitation, in contemptuous refutation of every law of Newton. The elastic flood tosses one up in its arms as a proud and happy mother her crowing babe. Dainty Ariel, thistledown floating in the sunbeams, all other airy-fairy creatures, you are one with them in spirit now. The more you weigh, the less you weigh. Here is the real hydrostatic paradox!

From the shore of the Dead Sea to the ford of the Jordan, the traditional spot of the baptism of Jesus, the ride lies through an arid region whose chief foliage is a scrub growth of *Spina Christi*, the accredited plant of the crown of thorns. Only a narrow fringe of trees separates the stream from the alkali-eaten stretches on either side. Disappointing was the sight of the river as, swollen by the melting snows of Hermon far to the north, the swift and turbid current rolled and eddied along.

There, too, alas! was the noise and inane laughter of a swarm of lunching tourists. Ah! why are all tourists of another party so sacrilegiously commonplace? Temporarily one forgets good Bishop Ulfilas, and breathes a sigh that Joshua might descend once more from these Moab mountains to smite hip and thigh such Canaanitish idolaters. There is but one thing for it, to steal away to some quiet spot farther up or down the river and there to try to think one's own thought. "Thou, when thou prayest, enter thy closet and shut the door." How often in the Holy Land recur these words. Either find such inner sanctuary in the soul itself, or better be anywhere than in Palestine. And yet and yet! Every hour is the mind storing away imagery that in later days, when the dust has settled and the fever has cooled, will make a thousand incidents in the Gospel story so very, very real. And yet and yet!

> "O heart! weak follower of the weak,
>   That thou should'st compass land and sea
>   In this far place that God to seek,
>   Who long ago had come to thee."

BAALBEC AND DAMASCUS

I.

As on a sunny morning one steams into the harbor of Beyrout, in northern Syria, how entrancing a .picture! The Lebanon ranges are full in view, their higher peaks white with snow; while, embowered in plantations of fig, olive, mulberry, and orange trees, the white houses of the city peep through on the hillside. Along the sands below curve the fleecy wave-line and bright blue waters of the Mediterranean. For a week to come, we are to be driving over these mountains and down among the oasis valleys of Baalbec and Damascus.

Rather in Kansas or Montana than in Syria one would look for startling impressions of the march of modern improvement. It is a mistake. Go instead to Syria for a real sensation. The road on which one drives to-day equals any over the passes of Switzerland. What does this mean in the land of the " unspeakable Turk," under the blight of whose rule all mildews and goes to ruin? Only the iron hand of Europe laid in arrest on the shoulder of Asia, with its stern word, " So far and no farther!" The road, the work of French capital, is safeguarded against Moslem cupidity and kept in working order by French energy and science marshaling the labor of the native popu-

lation, and finding no more faithful labor anywhere, if fairly treated. Close beside this triumph
of modern engineering runs the old trail from
Damascus, torn and gullied almost out of recognition, over which are painfully laboring great caravans of heavily burdened asses and camels, the poor
brutes picking their way and bruising their knees
after the good old ancestral fashion. Further
still, already is a mountain railway from Beyrout
to Damascus in rapid advance before the eye, and
soon will be witnessed side by side the bewildering
medley of locomotives and trains shrieking their
fiery way along, of carriages and pack-wagons
rolling smoothly over a macadamized road, and
of long trains of camels, in alternate pathos of
patience and snarls of sullen wrath, floundering
their way among the rocks of the dilapidated old
trail. For thousands of years, from Damascus,
Palmyra, Aleppo, Bagdad, Jerusalem, Mecca, have
these vast caravans conveyed the trade between
India, Persia, Arabia, Syria, and the European
world. But lo! before the sight a new epoch in
history-building.

In the modern crusade of Europe against Asia,
Peter the Hermit has become a railway engineer,
no longer with the ragged rabble behind him he
first led out, but the science, literature, politics,
law, moral and religious ideas of a higher civilization. No farther back than 1860 had there been
a hideous massacre of the Christian population of
Damascus at the hand of Moslem fanaticism. This
led to French intervention, and thus did the blood

of the martyrs become the seed of the railway church.

In long circuitous curves to the top of the pass, at an altitude of over five thousand feet, the road winds its way, skirting mountain precipices and slopes treeless except for olives, but terraced up in dizziest heights for patches of wheat and vines. Where the grapes get the wit and patience to elaborate such rich juices out of so desiccated a soil is a moral lesson to all whose own mental soil belongs to a like arid geological formation. It fairly makes one tremble to think how inexorably he will be judged if, by hook or by crook, he does not contrive to grow and ferment bumpers of spiritual champagne.

Once at the top of the pass, however, the most poetic conception of the Pisgah outlook that has ever ravished the soul is faint before reality. Three thousand feet below, nestled down between the Lebanon and Anti-Lebanon ranges, stretches a level valley that shines like a lake of emerald. It is six or eight miles broad and thirty long, and the eye, turning to it from the sun-smitten mountains, fairly pastures on such greenness. Pre-existent states of soul emerge from long-forgotten æons of time when one was driven down with his fellow-kine from these arid heights to wander knee-deep in such lush exuberance, bruise out its streaming juices, and, fully sated, at length to lie down and ruminate in pastoral Nirvana. Yet, along with this elemental sense, the root in us of all higher sense, is blent the richer content of our dear human nature. While we still pasture below, we yet lift up our eyes on high. For yonder, over there, tower the snow-crowned ranges of Mt. Hermon, leading the mind on into Galilee.

II.   For a book to set a boy's mind on fire and awaken yearnings that some day will fulfill themselves in actual sight, commend me to William Ware's "Zenobia" and the visions it conjures up of Palmyra, — a dream of Greek architectural beauty set in a luxurious oasis and surrounded by thirsty desert, Bedouins and camels thrown in *ad libitum* to the top of a boy's enchanted imagination. Alas! we had not time to spare for Palmyra, but Baalbec is an example of the same type of city, and to Baalbec were we bound. The broad luxuriant valley but now described, and along which we were the next day driving, had been the feeder of its population, the great caravans had been the fleets that piled up its former wealth. A Græco-Roman city in Syria, — one of the host that once beautified this now for centuries devastated land, — a city, the foundation-walls of its Acropolis laid in gigantic blocks by old Assyrian Baal worshipers, then crowned with sumptuous Greek sun-temples by Roman emperors, then further surmounted with Mohammedan towers and forts, the ruins of all this were we to see, ruins to-day standing in loneliness of desolation, the city's former wealth, population, almost its very name, for ages gone.

Briskly rub Aladdin's lamp and the genie appears in a night to rear a stately city with its palaces and gardens. All through the East one learns to feel this imagery. The genii are water, labor at unlimited command and at infinitesimal price, caravans focusing in a given spot converging streams of wealth. Here are the magic powers by which the city rises like an exhalation, or, cut off from which, it sinks back into solitary ruin. Such a ruin is Baalbec to-day, a squalid, straggling village fringing an acropolis crowned by great temples and palaces that tell of by-gone glory.

That day, the first time for months, we were troubled by rain. What boy, however, brought up in childhood on William Ware but rises to the occasion! If the actual sun does not shine, he creates one and pours out its beams in golden glory over the superb colonnades. The fallen columns he sets up on end beside their still standing mates. The aqueducts he reconstructs and brims with creative water ; the naked hillsides he clothes with palaces and irrigated gardens ; the long gone commercial wealth he brings in again to the crowded bazaars on the backs of the gaunt camels. Out of the ruins rises before his mind's eye the once splendid and luxurious city, and into them he sees it sink again, ah, with what refrain of time and mortality sighing through his soul!

III. To reach Damascus one crosses the Anti-Lebanon range, setting out for an eight or nine hours' drive from Sthora. Ever more forbidding grow the scorched mountain defiles, till sud-

denly at their feet, a river from its birth, leaps out
at a bound the Abana. The magic wand is found.
" Give me water and a desert and I will create a
paradise!" lo! the Oriental version of Archimedes.

Truly with two forms of nature-worship, lifted
to devoutest and most grateful faith, the heart
lovingly sympathizes, — the worship of the sun
and the worship of water. "Are not Abana and
Pharphar, rivers of Damascus, better than all the
waters of Israel?" Yes, O Naaman, the Syrian,
recreant wert thou to the manifest divinities of thy
Damascus not thus to sound their praise!

Now at once springs forth a new creation.
Reeds and grass grow lush, flowers bloom scarlet
and gold, almond-trees fling out a wealth of white
blossoms, houses and embowering gardens line the
banks. In this magnificent water-supply, dispersed
over the immense plain through a thousand channels and leaping up into fountains in every court-
yard, one now reads the perennial story of Damascus: " While other cities of the East have risen
and decayed, it is still what it was. It was founded
long centuries before Baalbec and Palmyra, and it
has outlived them both. While Babylon is a heap
in the desert, and Tyre a ruin on the shore, it remains what it was called in the prophecies of Isaiah,
' the head of Syria.' "

Yet here, as in every region of Syria, the blight
of Mohammedanism and the slime of the Turk is
over all. Every element of the sensuous paradise
is at hand, — pools of water, the constant murmur
of rivulets, gardens of pomegranates, figs, plums,

apricots, marble-lined courts, shady and perfumed with fruit-laden orange-trees and cool with the spray of jetting fountains. Still, all wears a look of neglect and decay, of suspicion and fear. In the vast bazaars, shut in from the sun by overhead nettings, is displayed a bewildering variety of Oriental manufactures, — silks, weapons, saddles, embroideries, — and through them streams the strangest medley of tribes and garbs. But a scent of fanaticism, lust, and bloodthirstiness is on the very air. Uncaged tigers would not quicker leap to carnage than, dared they, would these tigers of Allah.

Visit such of the dwellings of the wealthy as strangers are admitted to, and what a story they tell of lack of any trace of the sanctity of the home, of any interest in thought; what a story of the mere sensuous existence of the bath, the harem, the siesta, coffee, and the pipe. On the outside these houses are blank walls, or, where they have windows, they are shut in with jealous screens of delicate openwork carving. But once within the courtyards, paved and on all sides faced with richly colored marbles, murmuring with the sound of water, and set with orange and myrtle, momentarily one feels the spell of the siren incantation. All this on earth, and paradise thrown in! Gracious is Allah to the faithful! Who would not renounce forever study, literature, society, art, philosophy, reform, to dream away life in such narcotic repose?

To such enticing questionings as these were we

men left in the courtyards, and to the improving
society of the coal-black eunuchs, brutes unskill-
fully carved in ebony, and ready at a sign to basti-
nado or bowstring the fairest of recalcitrant wives.
On the other hand, the ladies with us were admitted
into the inner sanctuary of the harem.

The only peoples, says Schopenhauer, who have
ever understood woman are the peoples of the
East. They lock her up, as unfit to go abroad.
Less grounded in philosophy, the ladies of our
party returned not duly impressed with the privilege of lounging all day on divans, eating sweetmeats, and smoking pipes, but rather with a look
in their eyes that seemed to presage a swift return
to America to preach a new crusade for the deliv-
ery of the Holy Sepulchre of their outraged sisterhood from the defiling hand of the infidel. In
vain we superiorly introduced them to the eunuchs
as the natural custodians of their unstable sex.
Ideals vary so! The most beatified conception
of the guardian angel of womanhood to which the
Mohammedan mind can rise assumes the guise of
the brute-jawed, coal-black eunuch.

Many the books on comparative religion we
read to-day, but an hour with one's own eyes is
worth them all. Mohammedanism is the only
great world-religion that originated with a semi-
barbarian, with a prophet who could neither read
nor write, a man of no knowledge outside the manners and traditions of a narrow desert tribe, a man
of such enormous sensual passion and bloodthirsty
ferocity as to be capable of slaughtering a husband

in the morning and forcing his wife to marriage the same night. From such a mind and character, a flame of native eloquence, impassioned in intensity of adoration of a deity who was a consuming fire against idolatry, a model, too, of equity, simplicity, and kindliness after the code of morals of a semi-nomad clan, — from such a prophet Islam derived its enduring ideal of the man after Allah's own heart, the infallible declarer of Allah's will, the exceptional favorite on whom Allah lavished, by special revelation of what he esteemed the choicest blessing at his command, a far larger multiplicity of wives than was accorded unto others. Into the minds and passions of millions Mohammed burned his own personal characteristics, and his followers have always borne his impress.

Utterly different was it with the ideal of the other great world-religions, the ideal of the Confucianist, of the Buddhist, of the Brahman, of the Zoroastrian, of the Christian. Confucius was a cultivated, reflective, benevolent sage; the Buddha was all tenderness and compassion; Zoroaster was a mind profoundly impressed with the stupendous conflict of Good with Evil; the thinkers of Brahmanism were deep speculative philosophers, recluses from the world of strife and passion; the central thought of Jesus was, "He that loveth dwelleth in God and God in him."

It is altogether idle to dream that such utterly contrasted ideals leave no mark on the peoples that embrace them. The moderation and equity of Confucius, the Buddha's tenderness of compassion, the piety and self-sacrifice of Jesus, survive in millions of hearts to-day, just as literally as the lust of Mohammed burns on in every harem in Delhi, Cairo, and Damascus, and in every slave-mart in the East; just as literally as the ferocity of Mohammed flames out afresh in every Bulgarian, Lebanon, or Armenian massacre.

Happy for Mohammedanism, by reason of its conquest of the Roman Empire of the East, of India, and of Græcized Persia, it shared at the outset the rare good fortune of entering on a splendid inheritance of culture, art, literature, and science.   But the revival that followed in architecture, philosophy, medicine, was never its original work.   It was the work of Greek scholars, artists, physicians in the pay of Islam; the work of Indian and Græco-Persian architects, poets, and thinkers, rebaptized with Mohammedan names.   So far as of its own spirit and essence it goes, in all places and in all times, — at least in the example of its rulers and privileged classes, — Mohammedanism has tended to kill out all higher life in the harem and to keep aflame tiger passions in the heart. While the rank and file of the humble — because too poor to indulge in its sensual paradise on earth — escape its worst blight, and are often models of industry, temperance, and fidelity to trust, they none the less share to the full its savage fanaticism, and postpone the harem only till they shall get to heaven.

Indeed, historically, has not the claim made in behalf of naked, numerical monotheism — unless as a protest against groveling idolatry — been utterly over-urged? The moral content, the genuine humanity of a deity, is there not here something of infinitely deeper import than his unity or his omnipotent sway? Why were not a hierarchy of such saints as Francis of Assisi, Philip Neri, and Vincent de Paul an unspeakable boon as spiritual rulers of the universe, and to be exalted over any sole and absolute divine monarch as yet imperfectly evolved out of the Bedouin stage? Surely to come home to the heart of woman and to help lift her out of a state of degradation into a realm of dignity, one Virgin Mary, enthroned on high by the worshiping heart as Queen of Heaven, is worth a thousand Allahs.

I. In delicious spring weather, the sail from Beyrout to Smyrna all around the southern and western coasts of Asia Minor, and among the islands of the archipelago, is one of the rich experiences of a lifetime. Even if the ever freshly unfolding scene spoke nothing historical, the mere sight of the snow-crowned Taurus ranges, the picturesque coasts and countless mountain-crested islands, would hold the mind in unbroken delight. But the whole atmosphere is as full of legend, history, and biography as the background of the Sistine Madonna of cherub heads. Almost from the start one meets Paul in Tarsus, Alexander the Great at Issus, Cicero in Cilicia. Iliad and Odyssey soon become realistic guidebooks. What a breeding-place these islands for the sea-rovers and pirates that at last stopped plundering one another, and joined their barks together for a general descent upon Troy! Then, too, the lazy, riotous fellows left behind, hating work, with endless capacity for meat and drink, and never taking no for an answer, even from the most distracted widow, — how easy to transform them into poor spinning Penelope's greedy suitors, needing to be thrust out neck and heels on the return home of the much wandering master. All the types are in unquick-

ened germ before the eye to-day, from Achilles to
Thersites, the hints in nature of what another
Homer might make of them. But, alas! the cities
of Ionia, the temples, the poets, the philosophers
are not, — only the sunny atmosphere that bred
their early splendid civilization.

Why is it, one cannot but exclaim, that our own
Atlantic coast is set up geologically after so nig-
gardly a fashion? It is a positive affront to the
American people, a stigma of commonplace stamped
on the brow of the great Republic! From Sandy
Hook to the end of Florida not an eminence rears
its head over seventy feet high, and then eminent
only for sand. Prosaic beyond description the
whole mortal stretch, while the Mediterranean
shores are one succession of scenic glories. Gratefully, perhaps, one may except the coast of Maine
as poetic enough for every-day prosaic republicans.
But even at Mt. Desert how sad the dearth of sirens
on Round Porcupine, of Cyclops on Burnt Porcupine, of Agamemnons, Nestors, and Ulysseses,
distributed as miniature kings, on the other little
Porcupines. Perhaps the Maine kings died without a Homer. Geologically speaking, nothing short
of a stupendous volcanic upheaval in the interest
of the picturesque from Sandy Hook to Key West
can ever give us the inspiration to poetry the Mediterranean furnishes at every turn.

II. Through its figs, every one cherishes with
Smyrna fond associations from his days of
earliest innocence, and to this tender tie a mature

one is added when he sails into its bay and harbor encircled with mountains, and beautiful as the Bay of Naples. The city fronts the water with a superb quay two miles in length, and backed by handsome residences. Of course, the French built it, — another outcome of the Damascus massacre, and as eyesore a reproof to the unspeakable Turk of how to do things as could be devised. Also due to the French is the paving of two or three of the streets behind the quay, an act perhaps even more offensive in its pointed reflection on the streets beyond.

For the life of me, in the first drive we took, I could not keep out of mind the image of a precise New England schoolmarm, passionately addicted to object-lessons, out for a drive with a class of little boys and girls, and bent on improving their minds with the contrast between French and Turkish methods of metropolitan administration. "Now, dear children," I seemed to hear her say, as the carriage rolled smoothly over the level pavement, "this is the French idea of how to pave a street. Here a vehicle would last for years, for, as you see, there is no strain nor wrench on wheel or axle." Then, suddenly, as, on turning a corner into another street, the carriage struck a nest of boulders that bounced the party a foot up into the air and knocked their heads together, on recovery did I seem to hear the faithful woman add gaspingly, "And this the Tur-tur-ki-ish!" But as the drive went on it was no more possible to hold the children's attention to the subject of compara-

tive metropolitan administration than were they so
many kernels of pop-corn on a fire. All was one
pathetic outcry over bruised knees, elbows, and
skulls. Still, so severe the intellectual impression
made, that the normally educated young woman returned — as I myself did — with deeper convictions than ever to her object-lessons. "History,
dear children, history, as you may recall my re-
marking more than once before, teaches by exam-
ples. How profound a truth! And now, while I
get out my bottle of chloroform liniment and my
box of Perry Davis's Pain Killer, and apply them
to you, remember that no knowledge not bought at
a price is of lasting value."

Smyrna has no churches, mosques, or ruins of
any historical interest, for which my friend and I
felt most devoutly grateful. Blessed, in certain
moods, the land that has no history! Four or five
days of delicious exemption from sensations of the
sublime or instructive in art or history! Days in
which we could lie in the lap of nature, smoothing
out the wrinkles on our thought-furrowed brows,
to resume sunny looks of youth for Athens. One
single feat of physical energy we did achieve, toiling up, by a gentle declivity, a height of fully
three hundred feet that overlooks the city, and is
crowned by the dilapidated ruins of an old Turkish
fort. What a view seaward over the bay and the
blue Mediterranean, landward over mountains and
fertile valleys, peaceful with a soft atmosphere as
of eternal childhood eating figs! Behind the mountains, charmingly hidden from sight, lay Ephesus.

Should we go there? No, the interest of Ephesus, we argued, is now wholly archæological. The temples are gone, and nothing but their sites remain. The same kind of site is here in the beauty of the surrounding scenery. Why not, then, lie here day-dreaming, and so reconstruct the temples! The argument proved unanswerable. In other words, we were on a tourist-strike.

III. The three most beautiful regions of the globe, said Alexander von Humboldt, are the Bay of Naples, the Bavarian Highlands, and Constantinople. It is a pleasure to quote so competent an authority, since to Constantinople my friend and I did not get. Cholera and quarantine, not desire or will, were the guilty cause. Great the temptation to hide the humiliating fact under a vivid eye-witness picture of the Bosphorus, constructed out of pure interior consciousness with hints from Murray. But, alas! this is a book of genuine personal impressions, and where there were none, wise or foolish, entertaining or stupid, they are conscientiously omitted.

IV. Our first introduction to Attica was finding ourselves at six in the morning off the promontory of Sunium, its abrupt precipice crowned with the columns of a ruined temple. Here was a classic greeting, for whose poetic fitness one could not but be devoutly grateful. For the morning itself, however, it was not easy to be so grateful. It was wet and chilly, and after nearly six

months of unbroken sunshine one becomes too
spoiled a child of warmth and color not to resent
the intrusion of a day of rain. Still, there, in
distinct outline before our eyes, were Ægina and
Salamis, and, later on, through the misty distance,
the Acropolis itself. Could we not, then, supply
sunshine enough out of Plato, Sophocles, and
Phidias to light up all with glory!

However widely one has traveled, it is a distinct
surprise on landing at a port like Piræus, where
the acquisition of Greek is attended with so little
pain, not to find the citizens sitting around on every
hand, enthusiastically reading the Crito or the Republic, or laughing hilariously over the humor of
the Clouds or the Birds. One fears the influence
even of classic literature is overrated, when, instead,
twenty men spring to supply a cab, and tooters
from rival hotels in Athens stuff whole stacks of
cards into his reluctant hands. Yet what but classic
literature has brought so many strangers here, or
thus furnished a mellow soil in which twenty cab-
men grow where before grew but one?

By noon we were in Athens, be it confessed
more eager to repair our own ruins with lunch
than to flee to others that we knew not of. That
done, the afternoon was all before us where to
choose. My friend elected to stay at home, to wait
for sunshine, and to knit up the raveled sleeve of
his emotions over Plato's Symposium or Murray's
Guide. So I sallied out alone, firm of intent to go
nowhere in especial, — a purpose that had been
carried out to the letter but that lo! a fresh illustra-

tion was suddenly called for of Cromwell's famous saying: "A man never goes so far as when he knows not whither he is going." Over a row of house-tops the Acropolis reared its head, and my fate was sealed.

V.   A sudden fear, as on opening a telegram, overcomes one when about to enter the august presence of an object he has for years read and dreamed about. What will the message evoke? Congratulations for a birth or the sense of blight at a death? The Parthenon, — how many happy hours had I enjoyed through life over its friezes and the superb figures from its pediments! How many books had I devoured, how many detail drawings studied, how many brilliant descriptions read of its first glories, till in imagination I could see in splendid pageant the procession climbing the steps of the Propylæa, and the temple stood forth the one matchless Pallas Athene, brain-birth of minds like Pericles and Phidias! And now in a moment I was to stand in its actual presence.

Hurrying up the steep flights of the Propylæa, and scarcely looking to the right or left till I reached the gateway through which the whole ruin of the Parthenon stands visible, what was the first sensation awaiting me? I must be sincere, though the æsthetic heavens fall, — a sensation of painful disappointment. Fresh from the presence of such overwhelming ruins as those of Denderah, Abydos, Luxor, and Karnak in Egypt, there was no sense of awe in what I saw before me, no suggestion of a Lear wrestle with the elements, in which the broken monarch stood out sublimer than all the rack of thunder, rain, and lightning. Ah, the pity of it, the pity of it! was the sharp cry of pain. There are buildings that can endure being ruined, and survive in triumph. A hall like Karnak, a mediæval castle like Conway, can be shattered by earthquake, blown up by gunpowder, battered and breached by cannon-balls, and still look more imperial than ever. But a perfect Grecian temple was never made for a ruin, any more than an orchestra to have its harp-strings cut and its viols shattered, any more than a lovely marble face to have an eye destroyed or its smile-wreathed lips dashed in. The harmony was all. In the spiritual contribution of each ' co-working feature lay the spell.

Of course, one knows beforehand that the Parthenon is in ruins. Who has not made his passionate Isis search for the mangled remnants of this beautiful Osiris, scattered through all the lands! It is those broken fragments, those floating strains of music, that have prophesied to us of the once perfect whole. Every section of its frieze, what a masterpiece of grace, dignity, action, fire! Every figure on its pediments, and the whole in combination, what a vision vouchsafed the sight of the gods on Olympus! Each column or architrave how it led on the mind to its harmonious relations with the rest! The material, too, costly as precious stones, was everywhere relieved with gilding and bronze, and with delicately shaded backgrounds, to set off the figures. To Phidias, what remains to-day would seem but the half-erected scaffolding. He who, compassed about with his glorious peers, had created this dream of beauty, could recreate it in his mind's eye. There it already preëxisted before a stone was laid. But who of us can reconstruct so much as a broken hand or dented brow or wind-tossed drapery? Here recasting imagination faints, and sinks moaning to the ground. The Orpheus lyre, whose harmonies should sing these scattered fragments into place, it is not ours to strike. There they lie, — the graciously wrought stones by the thousands of tons, as in a brute stone-cutter's yard. It is a sight to weep over. No, I repeat it, a perfected Greek temple was never made for a ruin. A group of detached columns, suggesting nothing beyond themselves, may make a beautiful picture. But there is at once too much and too little of the Parthenon left behind.

It was, I know, a dank, chilly afternoon, that of my first visit to the Acropolis ; and rain and ruins, mingling with constitutional tendencies to depression over the wrecks of time and fate, constitute an ill sort of personal equation that must be allowed for. Not so much as a light-minded tourist had ventured out to relieve my mind by jocular gayeties over the Venetian bombshell that had thus effectually hoisted with its petard so much good marble, or hilariously to demand if it would not have been fun to see things jump. For two whole hours, rain and chill and I had our comments all to ourselves over

Propylæa, Niké Apteros, Erectheion, Parthenon,
with frequent interpolations of texts from the fate-
burdened Lamentations of Jeremiah. Nothing
seemed wanting — but to behold somewhere, sitting
sunk in dejection, on a broken block, Michelangelo's tremendous figure of the prophet, and to
hear, sighing in the bleak wind: " How doth the
city sit solitary that was full of people! How is
she become even as a widow! She weepeth sore
in the night, and her tears are on her cheeks,
Among all her lovers she hath none to comfort
her."

Again and again did I afterwards climb the
Acropolis, and in warm, radiant sunshine. How
entrancing the view over the sea to Ægina and
Salamis, and landward over Hymettus and Pen-
telicus, and across the plain green with the young
wheat and gray with the olive orchards! Over
the wall one looks down into the amphitheatre of
Dionysus, where Æschylus purged with terror,
Sophocles with pity, and Aristophanes with peals
of laughter their responsive audiences; and yonder
across the blue sea lies the Strait of Salamis, so
easy to light up with the flash of the arms and
set resounding with the war-cries of the Athenian
and Persian fleets. All speaks, — valor, poetry,
eloquence, wisdom. But the flower that bloomed
full of the sap, purple and gold with the color,
redolent of the perfume of all this outburst of
human genius, — the Parthenon, — for all the pathetic search for the scattered petals of this consummate flower of creation, one poor, baffled,

heart-sore Isis must sadly confess that she cannot find and restore her slain Osiris. I look up through the columns at the blue sky. I see the sunshine flooding them; I feel the dignity and beauty of the wreck that remains; but the sense of bereavement swallows up the sense of joy.

VI. As the deepest seas lie at the base of the most towering mountains, and the profoundest abysses of human tragedy at the feet of the most radiant summits of prosperity, so has it been in Grecian history. Few countries does one visit where the wreck of former glory is so complete, till artistically the cry is on the lips, "The nearer to Rome, the farther from God!" A day in the Vatican or the museums of Naples and Florence, or in the villas surrounding Rome, and one lives, moves, and has his being in the atmosphere of Greek art as nowhere in the land of its birth. Still, to see that land is one more key wherewith to unlock its treasures and interpret the nature and life out of which they grew. One envies the happy fellows in the American school at Athens, with years at free disposal to study out the position of every lost site, living always in the hope of unearthing some new miracle of beauty. None the less, for all their labors, the interest of the ruins — the Acropolis, Theseion, and a few other monuments excepted — is mainly archæological.

One drives, for example, through the mountains and along the Sacred Way by the Strait of Salamis to Eleusis. The very landscape is sculpture as well as nature, so statuesquely outlined the mountain-shapes and so gracious the curves and recesses of the shores. The very severity of the scenery, the absence of all tropical luxuriance of foliage, is Doric Greek in impression.

Then, what a site had old Eleusis, elevated just enough to furnish a telling platform for its temples and to set them in relief against the broad wheat-sown plains and the simple environing mountains, with, on the other side, the blue waters of the strait. The Eleusinian Mysteries, too, once celebrated there, — the Ober-Ammergau Passion Play of Greece, — enacted, however, not by simple peasants, but by a priesthood steeped in the deepest mystic thought, poetry, art, and passion of Greece and of the Orient, — mysteries of the abysses of atonement, purification, redemption, in which, as perhaps nowhere else in Greece, the profoundest depths of the soul were sounded, — who has not had his dreams of these? But ah! as in our own far-western states, where once stood a forest of noble pines, their high interlacing branches a covert for the birds and the haunt of mysterious beauty, so often there stands to-day but a wilderness of scarred, unsightly stumps, and the forest-lover moans over the ruin; so, in Eleusis, of all that grove of stately temples, there remain but the stumps of a wilderness of columns three or four feet in height. So is it everywhere in Greece, go to Olympia or Delphi, go anywhere one will.

Yet, benedictions on the heads of the archæologists who have dug out these temple cemeteries and revealed what yet remains of the ribs, vertebræ, and skulls of the once glorified runners and leapers of the palmy days of Greece. Transfigured "Old Mortalities" they! in their piety keeping green the memories of worthies that should never die. In vain the callow tourist thinks to vent on them his private grief, with his despairing cry, "Son of man, can these dry bones live?" His eye lit with prophecy, each spade-shouldering Ezekiel among them proudly answers back, "Behold, I will cause breath to enter into them, and they shall live. And I will lay sinews upon them, and will bring up flesh upon them and cover them with skin. Come from the four winds, O breath, and breathe upon these slain, that they may live!"

VII. How much less genius is required to reconstruct a battlefield than a Parthenon! One feels this in all the elation of victory when he drives out to Marathon. Once on the spot, how easy to draw up in battle array the hundred thousand Persians, and then, as freeborn Greeks, to proceed to demolish them! Indeed, all these annihilating victories of a handful of hardy, disciplined troops over hordes of slaves without honor and without hearthstones to fight for are repetitions of the same story. Clive at Plassey, in India, and Miltiades in Greece are one.

In the East one learns to read the open secret. Not that one would pluck down Miltiades from his grand historical pedestal. But the excellency of the glory lies in being free men, in pride of civic character, in high intelligence, and obedience to reason's law. Given these, your hordes of slaves can no more stand up against them than the wheat stalks of the Dakota grainfields before the on-rolling steam-reapers.

Yet, it was a pleasure to visit the scene of this ever memorable feat in the history of civilization, — the bare, bleak mountains, the narrow valley against whose sides the Greeks protected their flanks, the broad, swampy plain in front, the blue waters of the Eubœan Strait in which lay the Persian fleet, — and there once more to ponder the deep-freighted lesson that the "heaviest battalion" does not always mean the one that will tip the scale in mere avoirdupois, but the one that to weight adds the momentum of liberty and sacrifice.

VIII. Our stay in Athens was crowned with a final night of peace and reconciliation that will ever linger in memory. The moon was nearly at its full, when, at nine o'clock, my friend and I climbed the Acropolis. A flood of softest light was pouring down among the broken columns of the Propylæa, while the little temple of Niké Ap-teros stood poised on its high pedestal, a fairy creation of moonbeams. All stains and scars of time were dissolved away till there was no more sorrow, nor crying, neither was there any more pain. Peaceful as a lovely cemetery in which the saintly ones are sleeping lay the vast area around the temple, strewn with its countless, softly gleaming blocks. Steeped in the full tide of moonlight hovering down upon its columns and nestling in their recesses, the whole eastern and southern sides of the Parthenon were transfigured into a still dream-world of light and sweetness. You cannot shatter dream-world. Here is a visionary realm whose material is of no substance that violence can smite and fracture. Its falling columns sink to the earth as gently as a drowsy child into its bed of down. The mind, too, is so at peace. No longer capable of suffering, it is translated into an ethereal sphere above the world of weight and wreck. The very yearning for perfection, which is the glory and the agony of human life, is laid to rest. One has reached Nirvana. Tears this night were no longer on the cheeks of disconsolate Pallas Athene. Her weeping was over, and she had lapsed into sweet, dreamless sleep.

INDEX

Abana, the, 340.
Abu, Mt., 245.
Aden, 257.
Adullam, cave of, 326.
Ægina, 352.
Agra, 220.
Ahmedabad, 251.
Ajalon, valley of, 314.
Akbar, the Great, 218.
Amber, 241.
Anti-Lebanon ranges, 339.
Apis Mausoleum, 282.
Arabia, 256.
Asia Minor, 347.
Atami, 42.
Athens, 354.

Baalbec, 338.
Benares, 186.
Bethlehem, 322.
Beyrout, 335.
Buddhism, in Japan, 48; in Thibet, 171.

Cairo, 272.
Calcutta, 165, 180.
Canton, 116.
Canton River, 113.
Cawnpore, 199.
Ceylon, 148.
Cheops, pyramid of, 273.
Cherith, Brook, 331.
China, 97.
China Sea, 97.
Chinese conservatism, 98.
Confucius, 128.

Daibutsu, the, 28.
Damascus, 166, 169.
Darjeeling, 339.
Dead Sea, 332.
Delhi, 232.
Denderah, 305.
Desaix, 163.
Desert, the, 255.

Egypt, 255.
Egyptian temples, 302.
Egyptian tombs, 284.
Eleusis, 358.
Enoshima, 35.
Everest, Mt., 166, 174.

Ferozabad, 236.
Forty-Seven Ronins, the, 68.
Fujisan, 10.

Ganges, the, 165, 186.
Gizeh, pyramids of, 273.

Hachiman, temple of, 28.
Hakone lake, 42.
Hermon, Mt., 338.
Himalayas, 166.
Hindu architecture, 251.
Holy Sepulchre, Church of, 321.
Hong Kong, 110.
Hoogly, the, 165.

Idzn, 42, 46.
India, 163.
Indrapat, 236.
Ismailia, 262.

Jaffa, 310.
Jain temples, 245.
Japan, 13.
Japanese architecture, 58.
    art, 72.
    bells, 60.
    characteristics of, 38.
    civilization, 58.
    crusading spirit, 89.
    manners, 63.
    missions, 82.
    moral standards, 68.
    smile, 20.
    temples, 56.
    women, 18.
Jasmine Tower, the, 224.
Jericho, 329.

Jerusalem, 313.
Jeypore, 238.
Jinrikishas, 36.
Jordan, the, 333.

Kamakura, 27.
Kamakura Buddha, the, 30.
Kandy, 152.
Karnak, temple of, 308.
Kinchinjanga, 166, 174.
Kurnah, temple of, 310.
Kuth Minar, the, 235.
Kyoto, Nijo Palace in, 75.

Lebanon ranges, 337.
Lucknow, 196.
Luxor, temple of, 304.

Madras, 163.
Malagawa Buddhist temple, 153,
　159.
Marathon, 359.
Mariette, 281.
Medinet Habu, 308.
Memnon, statues of, 308.
Memphis, 279.
Miyanoshita, 44, 46.
Moab, mountains of, 331.
Mogul dynasty, 217.
Mohammed, 257.
Mohammedanism, 340.

Nagasaki, 97.
Nijo Palace in Kyoto, 75.
Nikko, 48.
Nile, the, 269.

Olives, Mount of, 314.
Orang-utan, the, 144.

Palestine, 309.
Parthenon, the, 353.
Pearl Mosque, the, 227.
Peradeniya Botanical Gardens,
　158.

Piræus, the, 352.
Pisgah, 331.
Pondicherry, 163.
Port Said, 309.

Quannon, temple of, 28.

Ramesseum, the, 310.
Red Sea, 256.
Rocky Mountains, 4.

Sagami Bay, 28.
Sakkarah, 277.
Saracenic architecture in India,
　221.
Sati, 182.
Senchal, 176.
Serapeum, the, 282.
Shamien, the, 117.
Shanghai, 97, 101.
Shintoism, 87.
Sikkim, 166.
Silliguri, 166.
Singapore, 137.
Smyrna, 348.
St. Paul, Minnesota, 3.
Sthora, 339.
Suez, 260.
Sunium, 351.

Taj Mahal, the, 227.
Ten Province Pass, 42, 46.
Thi, Tomb of, 282.
Thibet, 168.
Tiger Hill, 176.
Tokyo, University of, 89.
Tropics, the, 135.
Tughlakabad, 234.

Wusung, 101.

Yang-tse-Kiang River, 101.
Yokohama, 15.
Yokohama bay, 10.
Yumoto, 42.

Books of Travel.

Louis and Elizabeth C. Agassiz.

A Journey in Brazil. Illustrated, and with new Map. Crown 8vo, gilt top, $2.50.

A most charming and instructive volume. — *Pall Mall Gazette.*

Thomas Bailey Aldrich.

From Ponkapog to Pesth. 16mo, $1.25.

Thoroughly fascinating, model travel-sketches. — *Hartford Courant.*

An Old Town by the Sea. 16mo, $1.00.

Delightful sketches of Portsmouth, N. H.

Alice M. Bacon.

Japanese Girls and Women. 16mo, $1.25.

A Japanese Interior. 16mo, $1.25.

Miss Bacon has had unusual opportunities to see and understand her Japanese sisters. — *Literary World* (Boston).

Ralph Waldo Emerson.

English Traits. 12mo, gilt top, $1.75.

A book of wonderful interest and charm, describing England and the English.

William Elliot Griffis, D. D.

Japan : In History, Folk-Lore, and Art. In Riverside Library for Young People. With Map. 16mo, 75 cents.

Brave Little Holland, and What She Taught Us. With Illustrations. 16mo, $1.25. In Riverside Library for Young People, small 16mo, 75 cents.

Two books of much value about two countries of great but very dissimilar interest.

Lafcadio Hearn.

Glimpses of Unfamiliar Japan. 2 vols. 8vo, gilt top, $4.00.

Mr. Hearn has succeeded in photographing, as it were, the Japanese soul. — *New York Evening Post.*

Out of the East. Reveries and Studies in New Japan. 16mo, $1.25.

The student will welcome this work not only as a cluster of literary gems, but also as a first-class contribution to the study of the Japanese mind. — *Literary World.*

George S. Hillard.

Six Months in Italy. 12mo, $2.00.

A charming book, which has become a sort of manual for travelers who visit Florence and Rome. — George Ticknor.

Oliver Wendell Holmes.

Our Hundred Days in Europe. New *Riverside Edition.* Crown 8vo, $1.50.

A delightful account of the places and people visited in his last triumphal journey to England and the Continent.

James M. Hoppin.

Old England ; Its Scenery, Art, and People. New Edition, enlarged. With Map. Crown 8vo, $1.75.

A most readable, valuable volume. — *The Independent* (New York).

Blanche Willis Howard.

One Year Abroad. Very bright Travel Sketches in Germany and Switzerland. 18mo, gilt top, $1.25.

William Dean Howells.

Italian Journeys. 12mo, $1.50.

The lifelike freshness and accuracy of his sketches. — *New York Tribune.*

Their Wedding Journey. Illustrated. New Edition, with additional chapter. 12mo, $1.50.

The Same. 18mo, $1.00.

A Chance Acquaintance. A Novel. Illustrated. 12mo, $1.50.

The Same. 18mo, $1.00.

These two books are a delightful combination of story and travel in New England, New York, and Canada.

Three Villages. (Shirley, Lexington, and Gnadenhütten.) 18mo, $1.25.

Tuscan Cities. Florence, Siena, Pisa, Lucca, Pistoja, Prato, Fiesole. 12mo, $1.50.

Venetian Life. 12mo, $1.50.

It gives a true and vivid and almost a complete picture of Venetian life. — *Pall Mall Gazette.*

Henry James, Jr.

Transatlantic Sketches. 12mo, $2.00.

A Little Tour in France. 12mo, $1.50.

Portraits of Places. 12mo, $1.50.

A more agreeable traveling companion it would be exceedingly difficult to meet. — *Chicago Inter-Ocean.*

Rodolfo Lanciani.

Pagan and Christian Rome. With numerous Illustrations. Square 8vo, gilt top, $6.00.

Ancient Rome in the Light of Recent Discoveries. With 36 full-page Plates (including several Heliotypes) and 64 Text Illustrations, Maps, and Plans. Square 8vo, gilt top, $6.00.

Books which will be especially welcomed by thorough classical students and by those who have passed months in Rome acquiring a real acquaintance with the Eternal City. — *Literary World* (Boston).

James Russell Lowell.

Fireside Travels. 12mo, gilt top, $1.50.

A Moosehead Journal. In Modern Classics, No. 31. 32mo, 75 cents. *School Edition,* 40 cents.

Andrew P. Peabody.

Reminiscences of European Travel. 16mo, $1.50.

Percival Lowell.

The Soul of the Far East. 16mo, gilt top, $1.25.

Chosön : The Land of the Morning Calm. A Sketch of Korea. Splendidly illustrated from Photographs by the Author. 4to, gilt top, $5.00; half calf, $9.00; tree calf, $12.00.

New *Library Edition.* With many of the above Illustrations. 8vo, gilt top, $3.00 ; half calf, $6.00.

Noto : An Unexplored Corner of Japan. 16mo, gilt top, $1.25.

Occult Japan : The Way of the Gods. Illustrated. Crown 8vo, gilt top, $1.75.

The book illuminates Japanese character and explains Japanese action. . . . The last chapters are devoted to an intensely interesting and subtle discussion of personality, Japanese and other. — *New York Times.*

Mr. Lowell is one of the best informed Americans [concerning Japan]. — *Congregationalist* (Boston).

Charles Eliot Norton.

Notes of Travel and Study in Italy. 16mo, $1.25.

He does not describe many places ; but what he does he brings fully before us, not merely their aspect but their inner life. — *Philadelphia Press.*

F. Hopkinson Smith.

A White Umbrella in Mexico. Illustrated by the Author. 16mo, gilt top, $1.50.

Well-Worn Roads of Spain, Holland, and Italy ; Traveled by a Painter in search of the Picturesque. Containing 16 full-page Phototype reproductions of water-color drawings, and many smaller pen-and-ink sketches, etc. With twelve chapters of incidents of travel and description by the Artist. Folio, gilt top, $15.00.

Popular Edition. The Text of tne above, including some of the Illustrations, reduced. 16mo, gilt top, $1.25.

William W. Story.

Roba di Roma. New Edition, from new plates. Revised, and with Notes. 2 vols. 16mo, gilt top, $2.50.

It would hardly be possible to know Rome better than Mr. Story knows her. — *Charleston News and Courier.*